THE
LAW PROFESSOR

WILFUL BLINDNESS

Lee Stuesser

D1739149

Tellwell Talent
www.tellwell.ca

ISBN
978-1-77370-921-5 (Hardcover)
978-1-77370-920-8 (Paperback)
978-1-77370-923-9 (eBook)

For Linda, my wife and partner in life.

ACKNOWLEDGMENTS

A book is never the work of an author alone. I was fortunate to receive advice, input and support from those who proofed and reviewed the manuscript in progress. My wife, Linda, and children, Kelly, Jenny and Brett, were subjected to early drafts and helped to make the book tighter and shorter. Jay Forder provided a professorial perspective and John Michaels a lawyer's perspective. Finally, Mrs. Joan Michaels did a detailed review of the manuscript for me and her assistance was greatly appreciated. I thank you all.

CHAPTER 1

Allison Klassen was a beautiful young woman. I could not help staring at the photograph of her, which was on the funeral order of service handed out as we entered the church. She was smiling and this highlighted her dimples. Her blond hair was cut short with a parted fringe waving past her light blue eyes. She wore little make-up, but she didn't need to as she was a natural beauty. I assumed that her background was Northern European. I could see Scandinavian Viking blood in her genes. She was quite tall with an athletic body. She was only 23 years old when she had taken her life.

My name is Andrew Sturgis, Professor of Law. In my long career of teaching law I had never been to a funeral for one of my students. Allison had just finished her first year at Flemington University School of Law in Flemington, Minnesota. I was her Criminal Law Professor, and my colleague, Professor Wilbur Flood, who taught Allison Contracts, drove together to the funeral. It was held in Allison's home town of Stanthorpe about an hour's drive due west from Flemington.

Stanthorpe, population 750, had by my quick count three churches. Allison's funeral was held in the largest and it was packed. A simple pine casket was already in the front sanctuary. A spray of yellow roses rested on the closed casket. The Minister arrived and took his place at the altar just to the side of the pulpit. A lone female singer then began to sing "Amazing Grace" as the family entered from a side door and took their seats.

I had met Allison's parents at a reception for new law students the year before. They were so very proud of their daughter. They told me that Allison was the first member of their family to go to university and now on to law school. They were also happy to have Allison closer to home because evidently she had gone to college on the West Coast. They were farm folk, strong, resilient, hardworking and now they were burying their eldest daughter. They must be heartbroken. I thought of my own children, all grown up; if one of them died I don't know if I could carry on. Yet the Klassens stoically took their place at their daughter's funeral. Seated beside them must be Allison's younger sister. She was a younger Allison to be sure.

"Amazing Grace" ended. I thought about how we could be singing in praise of God at a time like this when someone so young, so vibrant was taken away too soon. For those who believe in life ever after and a place in heaven I marvel at their faith. I am a non-believer and poorer for it. Many of my atheist friends are smug about religion. Because they have given up on believing, they cynically tend to look at those who believe as ignorant or naive. I admire people of faith. They have something to hope for and to work towards in this world. Those with no faith seemingly are, in many instances, lost souls who strive to maximize what they can take from this world with no consequences for their actions.

The Minister called us to prayer. He had a strong but gentle voice—a minister's voice. Following the prayer, he then spoke of Allison and her death. It was obvious that he knew her well. At times his voice belied the emotion that he too was struggling to keep under control. He mentioned her suicide, which I thought might be passed over. To his credit he addressed it head on and tied it to the pressures that young people now face in this ever more complex world. I could not help but wonder whether we at the law school were partly to blame. The thought haunted me. We were then invited to pray for the family.

A hymn brought us to our feet. I took the opportunity to look round the room at the congregated mourners. A large group of Allison's classmates were present. First year law is akin to military boot camp and the bonds it creates among the students are equally strong. Her classmates were here for their friend. Allison was well liked. She was a good person. I especially looked for Maria Dempster, who was my first year research assistant. She and Allison were inseparable. They sat together in each and every class. They were much alike, but not physically nor by way of background. Maria had black hair and a dark complexion and she was a city girl born and raised in Flemington. What they shared was a common personality. I do not accept the theory that opposites attract; rather, in my view, like people are more likely to find each other. Both were hardworking, enthusiastic students, well grounded and comfortable to be around. Maria was the smarter of the two in terms of the law. This is not to take anything away from Allison. She was a solid student, but she lacked Maria's life experience. Law is a practical discipline and students need to know how to apply the law to real people and real life problems. Those who have more life experience better understand the typical reactions of people. They better understand human nature. Maria was a few years older than Allison and it made a difference. Maria earned straight "A" grades in her first year and I was lucky to get her as my research assistant. There, I found her in the church. She was in the class cohort dressed in black and was drying her eyes. Law school would be a much lonelier place for Maria.

The hymn ended and we took our seats. The Minister read from the Bible. The verse that stuck with me was Psalm 23:4, "Yea, though I walk through the valley of the shadow of death, I will fear no evil: for thou art with me; thy rod and thy staff they comfort me."

Following the readings, the minister called on Megan Klassen to say a few words about her sister. Megan rose from her seat next to her parents and walked to the pulpit. There was stillness throughout

3

the church. What a brave thing to do. How difficult it must be. The congregation willed her to be strong and get through her words. We held our collective breath. Megan was so like her sister. She adjusted the microphone, unfolded her notes, looked up and began to speak. Her voice was soft but clear. She had a slow cadence and spoke in short sentences.

"Allison–Allie–was my big sister. She was three years older than I and she always led the way. Or should I say, I tagged along." Megan's voice grew stronger. She was gaining a rhythm. She continued, "At first I kind of resented Allie. She was always so good at everything she did. She was captain of the school volleyball team, star baseball player, and champion debater. And people would say to me, "Are you Allison's sister?" It was tough following in Allie's footsteps. But my resentment faded quickly. I became so proud of my older sister and what she accomplished."

"She was courageous. It took courage to leave the safety and love of Stanthorpe to go west to Trinity University. I know she was lonely. When she left she promised to write to me each and every week. She kept her promise and I cherished her weekly letters. She didn't need to write. We kept in regular contact online, but she always took the time to write. She was old fashioned in that way. She said writing a letter was more personal than the internet." Megan paused.

Her rhythm was slowing. The emotion of the moment was starting to take over. Megan collected herself, took a deep breath and said in a halting voice, "I do not know why God called for Allie, but I know that Allie is in a better place. And I know she is watching over me; her little sister. She has left us all memories of her good deeds."

Megan then looked down at the closed casket and spoke directly to her sister, "Allie I will miss you. You were my teacher, my guide and my best friend." She left the pulpit, touched the casket and returned to her seat.

My throat was tight, and my eyes misty. The love between the sisters filled the room. Megan's loss, the family's loss was so palpable, yet their faith remained so strong.

Everyone was emotionally drained. Another hymn, "How Great Thou Art", saved us all. The choir carried the singing. Most of the gathered merely mouthed the words whilst drying tears.

More prayer and more scripture readings followed and then the Minister called on Mr. Mark Labros to give the eulogy. I was surprised. Mark had been a student of mine some six or seven years ago. I wondered how it was that Mark was delivering the eulogy.

Mark took to the lectern and began to speak using no notes. "Our family lived beside the Klassen farm. I was six years older than Allie and I have to admit that I never had much to do with Allie until I started grade six. Sure we lived next to each other, but I was more interested in chasing a baseball or football with the guys. Little Megan and Allie were, quite honestly, a bit of a girl nuisance." He smiled at Megan and the Klassens.

"That all changed in grade six. You see Allie was now going to start school in grade one. Mrs. Klassen phoned my mother the night before the first day of school. I was in the kitchen so I caught my mother's side of the conversation. My mother said, "Sure Mark will look after Allie. See you at eight in the morning." My mother was looking right at me when she said that. When she hung-up the phone my mother gave me a mother's order–I was to take care of little Allie on her first day of school–or else. Great I thought; I'd have to watch over that little twerp." He was smiling again and a few in the audience laughed with him. He had us all enthralled. Like any good trial attorney, Mark was a story teller.

"The next day my mother and I walked to the highway to wait for the bus. I didn't want my mother to walk me to the highway. For crying out loud I was going into grade six. When I think back, and now being a parent myself, I know my mother wanted to come to the highway not for me, but to support Mrs. Klassen when she saw her little Allie get on that great big school bus." He looked at Mrs. Klassen, swallowed hard and continued.

"Mrs. Klassen and Allie were already at the highway waiting. Allie had on this pretty school outfit, a white blouse, plaid skirt and shiny black shoes. She didn't say much and didn't look at me, which was fine with me as I didn't want much to do with her either. I had my friends on the bus to see. The mothers chatted. My mother carried the conversation, I think in order to keep Mrs. Klassen's mind off of the momentous event to come. Soon the bus came into sight. Mrs. Swanson, the bus driver, ran a tight schedule. She stopped the bus, the door opened. Mrs. Klassen gave Allie a quick hug and Allie stepped on the bus landing. I followed. My mother's instructions were that I was to sit by Allie on this her first bus ride. Allie took the third seat behind Mrs. Swanson and I sat beside her. She had the window and I the aisle. I had planned to shift seats as soon as the bus got out of my mother's sight. But I thought better of it. My mother was friends with Mrs. Swanson. We were the second stop on the route. Only two other kids were on the bus. It takes 37 minutes to get to the Stanthorpe School from our place. As I said, Mrs. Swanson kept to a tight schedule. Allie and I didn't say a word to each other for the first ten minutes. More kids got on. Some were in high school. The volume in the bus rose and I could see that Allie was getting a little nervous. She glanced around with growing apprehension at all these new and big kids getting on the bus. I finally spoke to her and asked her about her teacher and if she knew her classroom. Allie was relieved and quietly told me that Mrs. Tolboom was her teacher. I assured her that Mrs. "T" was a great teacher. More high school kids got on board and they were getting a bit boisterous. Mrs. Swanson allowed the students on her bus to be noisy so long as there was no swearing, but the rising volume was a bit intimidating for a five year old. I remember the moment, like it was yesterday. We hit a bump in the road and a loud yelp went up through the bus. Allie grabbed my hand. I didn't know what to do, so I held her tiny hand and said "It's ok Allie. We'll be at school soon." She looked up at me and simply said, "Thanks." We arrived at school about five minutes later."

"At the end of the day, I found Allie to get her back on the right bus--mother's orders. As we got on to the bus, Allie took her window seat third behind Mrs. Swanson and she looked up at me with those big blue eyes. Folks what could I do?" Everyone laughed.

"I took my seat beside her. Ladies and gentlemen, for the next six years we sat together to and from school in the third seat behind Mrs. Swanson. During that time we came to talk about anything and everything. Allie became the sister I never had. On my last day of school, Allie gave me a small gift, which I still have with me. It is a silver key chain locket. In the locket is a compass with the engraving "For guiding me–AK." Being male I didn't think to get Allie anything."

"After high school I went to university and then on to law school. Allie and I remained in touch. I would always drop in when back on the farm to see Allie, Megan and Mr. and Mrs. Klassen. Allie and I would sit often on the porch talking. We talked about her going to Trinity University. She worried about leaving Megan and her parents. But the conversation I remember most was about two years ago in the fall. Allie was peppering me with questions about the law. She asked me how I could defend those who committed horrendous crimes and I gave her the standard lawyer answer, "We defend the guilty to see that innocent people will not be convicted." She was not convinced by that answer and then I said. "Allie most of my clients are guilty, but they need help and I like to help them if I can. That is what lawyers do, they help those in need." She seemed more comfortable with that answer, but didn't say anything until after a moment or two she asked me, "Mark can I be both a good Christian and a good lawyer?" She looked at me intently with those blue eyes. It was as though I was being subjected to a lie detector through her eyes. I looked at her and said that I believed she could and that she would make a wonderful lawyer because she wanted to help people. She continued to look at me as if to verify that I was being honest with her. Then she simply nodded and said, "Thanks." Just like she had said "thanks" many years before on that first bus ride. Later that year she applied to law school, was admitted and started her first year at Flemington School of Law." He paused.

"Allie would have made a great lawyer because she would have helped people. That is who she was. She has left us too soon. Her life was just beginning. I too will miss Allie the sister I never had. Megan, your sister was a wonderful person. Mr. and Mrs. Klassen you raised a beautiful, kind daughter. I ask that we all remember that beauty and kindness."

He then simply said, "Allie rest in peace," and walked from the pulpit.

The funeral ended with the Minister leading us in the Lord's Prayer. It had been years since I had said the Lord's Prayer, yet the words came back to me, fixed in the recesses of my memory.

The Minister then led the procession out of the church to the nearby cemetery for internment. We all filed out and gathered around the burial plot. As Allison Klassen was laid to rest, my one thought was why; why would such a beautiful young woman end her life? She had so much to live for.

Chapter 2

Usually I leave immediately after a funeral service; however, it just did not seem right to do so on this occasion. Wilbur felt the same.

The church ladies were busy with a luncheon in the church hall. Tables were chock full of sandwiches, dainties, and a wide assortment of cakes and pies. I bet all homemade—no store bought desserts here. I used self-restraint and gave the dessert table a pass; instead I got a glass of lemonade and went outside.

I was looking for Mark to compliment him on the eulogy. He had done a masterful job in difficult circumstances.

When I emerged from the church hall I saw a scrum of students standing on the grass just outside the church and went over. As I approached the group Maria caught sight of me, waved, and came to meet me. The closer she got the more I could see the pain on her face. The puffiness around the eyes told a tale. Without saying a word she gave me a hug. I put my arm around her and asked, "I know how close you and Allison were. How are you holding up?"

She replied, "I think I'm still in shock really, I've cried and cried some more."

I took my arm away. In this day and age any physical contact between students and professors is frowned upon and could be misconstrued, although given my age I figured I was exempt. I was more like a grandfather to the students.

In a hushed voice she murmured, "I just don't understand. We were finishing our research jobs and were looking forward to a week off before the start of school. Allison seemed just fine--happy."

"When did you last see her?"

"Thursday at the end of day. She was getting ready to go to Winnipeg for that conference with Professor Fraser. She was really looking forward to her first law conference."

I knew that Fraser went to this annual conference in Winnipeg, Canada, which is four or so hours north of Flemington. He presented a paper each year to build up his publication record. Allison was his research assistant, but I didn't know that she went along to the conference. I certainly had expected to see Fraser at the funeral. He was a no show.

"Did you talk to Allison after she got back?"

"No. She was going back home and I was staying in Flemington. I sent her a text. No reply. The next thing I get a phone call that she is dead." She bit her lip and took out a tissue, "I just don't know what to think. How could she? I'm angry, I'm mad, I'm sad, I'm confused all at the same time."

I commiserated and said, "You're not the only one."

We joined the other students. The guys were talking football probably to take their minds off the sadness of the day. This is Viking country and hope was high as it was the pre-season. I thought to myself that every fan of every team is optimistic before the season starts and then reality destroys the dream. I never mentioned to the students that I cheered for the Packers, which was not a popular position in this part of the country. Over the years I have found it more prudent to keep my allegiance to the Packers secret especially when the Vikings were suffering through losing seasons.

Behind me a voice called out my name.

I turned and immediately recognized a former student of mine, Richard Maurice. Richard was an interesting person. He was a police officer who was given a leave to study law. He felt that it would make him a better police officer and I think it did. A few years back the governor was in a tizzy because of a budget leak to a local journalist the day before the state budget was brought down. The governor and supporters demanded that the journalist be prosecuted. Richard was the officer in charge of the investigation. He refused to charge the journalist. In his view the journalist had committed no crime. And he was right in law. I know that his chief was not happy, nor were the political powers that be. Richard's decision was based on principle, and he was not prepared to sacrifice his principles to satisfy the mob. In short, Richard was a good cop. He had that self-assured, authoritarian, police demeanour as he walked towards me.

"Richard," I said and held out my hand to greet him, "good to see you."

"Please Professor, call me Ricky everyone does," he smiled.

"Well Richard, I will call you Ricky if you, in turn, call me Andrew."

Richard laughed, "Sorry no deal, you will always be Professor to me."

"Very well, Richard, are you a captain yet?" I inquired.

"No, I'm still a detective and you know I like it that way. Solving cases is far more fun than shuffling papers all day."

I thought to myself that Richard really had not changed at all. He still had that youthful, athletic build and easy going exterior. He would be great in the interrogation room. I bet he would coax confessions out of even the most savvy of criminals. Over the years I found that the most effective police interrogators were the laid back, soft spoken, non-aggressive types—forget the bellowing bullies. I asked him what department he was with these days.

"Homicide" was his reply.

I perked up. We had moved away from the students, and I asked him softly whether he was investigating Allison's death?

He explained, "Any time a person dies in unexpected circumstances homicide is required to investigate and I was assigned to this case, but Professor there was no homicide. I don't want any rumours to get started. This was a suicide."

"So what brings you to the funeral?" I asked.

"It's the family. They are quality people. I got to know them over the last couple of days as we tried to piece together Allison's movements and find any reason she would kill herself. I felt I needed to be here to pay my respects." He paused. Looked around and said, "Allison was quite a young woman. She had a lot going for her, loving family, good home, strong morals and it really makes no sense that she'd kill herself."

"You're sure it was suicide?" I added quickly, "Don't feel you have to answer."

"Nothing confidential Professor. It is public knowledge that Allison fell to her death from her apartment's tenth floor balcony. No one else was present as far as we know. The railing was high and solid. This was no accident. She jumped. People who accidentally fall or are pushed often cry out as they fall. Those who commit suicide by jumping often don't say a word as they fall. Allison was silent."

I too remained silent. Why? Why would she jump? I asked Richard, "Any reason found as to why she would commit suicide?"

Richard pondered the question. His response was slow and careful, "We probably will never know why. There was no history of mental illness. No history of trouble. No relationship that went sour. We checked her cell phone, emails and computer and found nothing. She didn't drink, and although the toxicology tests have not come back, I doubt very much she was doing drugs. And she was a devout Christian."

I commented, "How does being a devout Christian fit with suicide?"

"It doesn't," conceded Richard and went on, "some suicides are impulsive, completely unexpected, a response to an immediate pain, but we've found no such trigger with Allison."

We both stood without saying anything. I took another sip of my lemonade. Richard broke the silence, "I do know that the Klassens are really hurting. Losing Allison is a terrible tragedy for them and they blame themselves."

I looked at the receiving line where the Klassens were being comforted from those gathered. It had shortened. Now only a few people were standing in queue outside the open hall doors. "Well Richard, I must pay my respects to the Klassens."

"I already have." He put out his hand and said, "Good to see you again Professor. We must get together for a coffee sometime and I'll share some stories from my closed cases. They might provide grist for your criminal law class."

I shook his hand and replied, "I'd like that very much; I'll give you a call. Take care." I went back to the hall and took a place in the receiving line.

Ahead of me I saw the Dean of Law, John Clarke. We saw each other and gave silent greetings. Dean Clarke had taken up the deanship six years before, coming to Flemington from some elite East Coast law school. I forget which one. He was with the Associate Dean of Law, Gloria Wesley.

Inside the hall, Mr. and Mrs. Klassen were standing in the foyer greeting people. Megan stood beside her parents. As the line of mourners moved forward, Mrs. Klassen was the first to greet each guest. She knew everyone and thanked them for coming telling them that it meant a great deal to her and the family. I was next and was about to introduce myself when Mrs. Klassen looked at me, put out her hand and said, "Professor Sturgis thank you so much for coming."

I was caught off guard. I had never expected her to remember me. We had only met the once. Mrs. Klassen went on, "Allison spoke so well of you. She loved your class and believe me your cases caused a lot of debate around the supper table."

What to say in response? I had prepared to say the usual condolences, but that no longer seemed appropriate. I improvised with the truth, "Allison was a good student and a real pleasure to have in class. You can be very proud of her." Mrs. Klassen thanked me. She turned to Megan and introduced me to her. "Megan is in her second year studying sociology at Flemington."

I turned to Megan and said, "Your words today were a real tribute to your sister." She merely smiled and cast her eyes down. Mr. Klassen extended his hand. It was the tanned, calloused hand of a farmer. The grip was firm. I looked into his eyes. No words could properly convey my feelings. His little girl was gone. The sense I had was that Mrs. Klassen did the talking. I nodded in silence to him and he acknowledged my unspoken words with a similar nod.

They were good people in much pain.

My resolve dissolved and I headed to the dessert table. I took a piece of homemade apple pie. With my last mouthful done I looked for Mark. I found him leaning against a willow tree at the side of the church. He was having a smoke. I didn't know that he smoked. As I walked towards him he put out his cigarette and stood to greet me.

I always liked Mark. He was a good student diligent, thoughtful but quiet. He was not one to talk in class for the sake of hearing his own voice. Rather, his questions, comments or observations were always to the point and showed deep thought. Although quiet in class, when he entered a courtroom for a trial or appeal exercise there was a transformation. He was comfortable on his feet, never showing nerves, always in control and had a commanding presence. He graduated from Flemington and joined a small firm doing mostly criminal cases, where he honed his advocacy skills before juries. We had kept in contact over the years as periodically he called me for legal advice on some of his criminal cases. He was now starting to handle more civil cases. In fact, a year before, he had sued the university in a slip and fall case and won a substantial judgment.

Mark spoke first, "Professor, good to see you--nice of you to come."

We shook hands and I replied, "Mark, your eulogy was a wonderful tribute. I didn't know that you knew Allison, but you did a great job of capturing who she was. It must have been very difficult for you and I am so sorry for your loss."

"Thank you Professor," Mark went on, "when I heard about Allie I dropped everything and went to the Klassens. They were devastated and when Mrs. Klassen asked me to do the eulogy I couldn't refuse." He paused, gathered himself and continued, "I got to tell you, I struggled to find the right words. Allie was a very special person and friend."

I interjected to give him some breathing space, "Well you found the right words." I decided to change the subject. "You mentioned in the eulogy that you were a parent. When did that happen?"

He beamed, "Eleven months ago. Jane and I now have a little girl, Amy Amber. She is just starting to walk or should I say stagger."

"Congratulations. That is special. Enjoy her now. The world is a whole new place for one year olds and they soak up everything."

Mark was smiling, "You have that right. Amy gets into everything."

I continued on safe ground, "I haven't received any evening calls from you lately about your criminal trials. Does that mean you are no longer doing criminal work?"

He quickly replied, "No not at all. I'm still a criminal lawyer. I guess the trials haven't been too interesting of late for me to call you for advice or maybe I'm finally figuring out what I should have learned years ago in your class. I am doing more civil cases. They pay well, but the delays in getting cases to court are painful and as you know most civil cases settle."

I smiled and said, "The University certainly rues the day they took you to court last year. Seems to me that you got a healthy verdict and the publicity wasn't good for the University. I can tell you the administration was not happy."

Lawyers love to talk about their cases especially the winning ones. Mark was no exception. "In that case the University was very difficult to deal with. In particular, the in-house counsel was a real piece of work. I had a young woman who slipped on icy concrete steps and broke her leg and ankle in a number of places. The steps had not been cleared, sanded or salted since the snowfall the night before. She slipped going to class at ten the next morning. And do you know the University's defence?" he asked rhetorically. "Their defence was that it would cost overtime to have maintenance workers come in before 8:00 a.m. to clear the sidewalks and steps. Not much of a defence. Keep in mind this young woman was seriously hurt. Before the accident she ran track. Heck she had a university scholarship in track. Following the accident she couldn't run. She had three operations on her leg and ankle. And she would never be able to walk again without a limp. We were prepared to settle for a reasonable amount without going to court. The University refused. So we went to trial. I think Jeff Couster, who was brought in to try the case for the University, wasn't too pleased to take it to trial. Jeff's a good lawyer. But the University's in-house counsel was insistent. I forget his name, Sid something."

"Sid Ashter," I provided.

"Yeah, that's his name. We continued to trial and I could see the jury growing angrier and angrier towards the University. Poor Jeff could see it too and I know he was looking to settle. In the end, the $800,000 award was more than just. Is Sid Ashter still the University lawyer?"

I had had dealings with Sid Ashter—unfortunately. His specialty was obstruction and drafting incomprehensible university policies. I sighed, "Sid Ashter is still the University in-house counsel." Mark just shook his head.

It was time for us to leave. I could see Wilbur hanging out by the door of the hall. I thanked Mark, told him not to hesitate to call me should he get some interesting criminal cases. We shook hands and I gave him a pat on the back.

Wilbur and I drove back to Flemington. We didn't talk much. We were emotionally exhausted and preoccupied with our own thoughts.

CHAPTER 3

For almost four months over the summer the law school lay dormant. With the start of the school year came new life. Student voices once again echo throughout the sandstone halls. The first year class of a hundred new students has arrived. They arrive a day ahead of the upper year students. As I walked to my second floor office I saw them looking vulnerable seeking each other's support in the main floor foyer. Excitement and expectation filled the law school. The students were entering an uncertain domain and were unsure of exactly what awaited them. Each entry class is different and has unique personality. Some years are playful, some are far too serious and some are downright dour. Obviously we professors have a few favourite years and a few not so favourite.

The first year class was gathering to be welcomed to the law school by the Dean. I hope they don't expect a rousing speech; administrators are not good orators.

My class with the new students was at 10:00 a.m. The first class is important. To my mind, it sets the tone for the year. Some of my colleagues do a ten minute "greet and dismiss" for the first class. I find that approach wrong. I know we are not supposed to use the word "wrong", but it is wrong.

It is time for me to go to room 205. I like to arrive early. I use a "soft Socratic" teaching style, which means I question students about assigned cases and the student answers enliven the class. Ideas are raised, questioned, accepted or discarded. The reasoning of the judges is explored and challenged. The students soon learn that in order to get anything out of the class they need to have done the reading. The Socratic class invites student engagement and discussion. In my experience the less I talk the more students learn.

The clock showed 10:00 and I began.

I looked at the seated fresh, attentive faces. Students are creatures of habit. In my experience, they will in all likelihood return next day to the same seat. "Welcome to your first class at Flemington University School of Law. My name is Andrew Sturgis and it is my honour to be your professor of Criminal Law and Procedure."

My purpose in the first class is to give the students a taste of criminal law, show them what they can expect, and, above all, engage them. I continue, "One of my tasks is to hone your thinking. Often this is called getting you to think like a lawyer. Lawyers are problem solvers. I will present problems to you and call on you for a solution. Let's get started. Close your computers please." The students are in shock. You can see their angst; their security blanket has been taken away. "I want you to think and you will not find the answers I seek in your computers. Close them down please." The students reluctantly and hesitantly do so. Welcome to law school.

In the afternoon I had a meeting. Universities wallow in meetings and committees. The waste of time and productivity consumed by meetings is truly staggering. But I can't change the culture of inefficiency, and so I do my duty.

Our law school is small, with only twenty full time academic staff, and the result is that we bear a heavier burden of committee work. Over the years I have served on every committee imaginable. The meeting is of the Teaching and Learning Committee, of which I am the chair. The meeting will not be a pleasant one.

In the week before the start of classes the school administrator, Beth Jones, red flagged an issue with an upper year elective, Advanced Constitutional Law, taught by Assistant Professor Jerome Fraser. Instructors are required to provide an electronic copy of their course outline in advance of the term to be posted on the school's website. The administrator vets the outlines for any errors or problems. She noticed that Professor Fraser had indicated 50% for "class participation". The school has a policy that only 25% of any course assessment can be based on "class participation". She had communicated this to Fraser, who informed her in no uncertain terms that the 50% was to stay and to post it. Beth contacted me. It wasn't her battle to fight. She was also quite miffed by Fraser's dismissive attitude towards her.

I emailed Fraser to clarify and advised him of the policy. In a curt response he told me that Advanced Constitutional Law was his course and that he should be allowed to teach it as he willed. He cited "academic freedom", which is the academic cloak that hides many sins. I informed him that he would need to meet with the Teaching and Learning Committee in order to obtain an exemption from the policy and that this needed to be done before the upper year students returned for classes. In the interim his course outline would not be posted until the class participation assessment was clarified. The meeting was then scheduled.

I arrived at the meeting room a few minutes early, as is my habit. Professor Wilbur Flood was already there. Wilbur has taught at the law school for as long as I have. He is a genuinely nice man, soft spoken and is a committed teacher with a keen sense of fairness. The students love him. The third member of the Committee, Professor Gwen Mason-Hill, arrived. Gwen is an expat Australian. She left her native Australia when a teenager, but is still an Aussie at heart injecting wonderful and colourful Australian phrases into her everyday speech. She follows cricket, loves her Australia Rules Football, and barracks (we would say 'cheers') for the North Melbourne Kangaroos. Gwen joined the school about ten years ago. She is a real delight, direct, and to the point.

As we waited for Fraser to arrive, Gwen regaled us with tales from a conference in Athens, Greece that she had attended. She was not impressed with the Greeks. "You know they all were driving Mercedes and BMW's and bloody hell all I could afford was a three cylinder Renault, which was no bigger than a motorcycle with a top. Financial crisis? What financial crisis?"

I quipped, "Perhaps the European Union provided the cars, a gift from Germany?"

"You reckon," she laughed, using one of her favourite phrases. She soon changed topics. She had heard about Allison. Gwen had taught Allison Property Law. She asked whether we knew anything further about her suicide and we provided her with the limited information we had. She was sorry that she had missed the funeral, but was thankful that at least Wilbur and I had made it.

At seven minutes after the hour Fraser arrived. No apologies for his lateness. Obviously his time was more important than ours. I don't like him; it's as simple as that.

I started the meeting by distributing his proposed course outline and the law school's policy on assessment, and I pointed out that the issue today was whether an exemption to our policy should be made in this instance. I called on Fraser to address that issue.

Fraser is fairly tall, heavy set, late thirties. His hair is dense black impeccably combed. He has a small mouth; rarely does he smile. His dark brown eyes are intense and unfriendly. He is weasel like, but I'm biased. When he talks he rarely makes eye contact and has a sharp voice that becomes shrill when he is excited or agitated. He began his response by talking about legal education generally and how other schools are experimenting with various new methodologies. I guess he felt it necessary to educate us. He then talked about how students need to take responsibility for their learning. Gwen couldn't take it any longer; it had been two minutes of rambling nonsense. She interrupted him.

"Let's talk specifically about the 50% class participation grade. How are you going to mark that grade?"

Fraser was surprised that someone would interrupt his monologue and shot her a poisoned look. He replied in a slow pointed voice, "It is my intention to assess the students by what they contribute in the given class."

Gwen persisted, "Well, help me out here. What does that mean?"

"It means I will give the students a mark for their contributions or lack of contributions. I will do the assessing." He hadn't answered her question.

Wilbur asked, "How many students do you have in the class usually?"

"Up to thirty," he replied.

I knew he was inflating the numbers. Each seminar, such as Advanced Constitutional Law, is capped at thirty students. In the past it had been taught by a local federal prosecutor, who was a great teacher and knew his stuff. The class was always full. When Fraser arrived he persuaded Dean Clarke that full time staff should have priority and that if they wanted a course then they had dibs on it—part time adjunct instructors be damned no matter how good they may be. So it was that Fraser took over the course three years ago and the enrolment went down accordingly. He is not a well liked teacher and is lucky to get twenty students to sign up for the course. But I knew where Wilbur was going in his asking the question.

Wilbur followed up his inquiry, "I have taught thirty students in seminars Jerome, and assessing class participation is very difficult with that number. In fact, I found it difficult to do with any group above say ten students."

Fraser wasn't listening and was getting agitated, "I've taught now for almost ten years and I think that when an experienced instructor puts forth a particular assessment it should be accepted as a given that it will be done properly." His voice was getting shriller, "As I have already said, I intend to assess each student in each class."

Fraser inflated his teaching experience. He had been with us for five years and prior to that had taught for two more years. No point challenging him on his over statement.

Gwen zeroed in, "Alrighty— are you going to have the students give a presentation in each seminar? Are you going to conduct quizzes or tests? I'm still not sure how you are going to assess."

Fraser seemed to ignore Gwen. Instead he directed his answer at me and said, "I will, as I have said, use my experience to assess the student knowledge and preparation."

Gwen didn't like to be ignored, "If we accept your position, how would we be able to determine the appeal of a student's class participation grade?"

Fraser smiled at her and in a condescending way said, "Student's can't appeal class participation grades. You should know that. They can only appeal examinations and papers."

"I do know that," fired Gwen, "and I am troubled that 50% of the student's overall performance in a course cannot be appealed." Tensions were heightening.

Wilbur, ever the peacemaker, tried a different tack, "Jerome, the difficulty is that there is a need for transparency. Students need to know in concrete ways how they will be marked. What Professor Mason-Hill is outlining are more objective based assessments. The problem with class participation grades is that they can be very subjective and that is why the school's policy was brought in a number of years ago." Wilbur leaned forward to talk directly to Fraser, "I'm not suggesting that is the case with you at all. I fully expect that you will be rigorous; however, we have to look at it from the student perspective as well. If the class participation grade were broken down into component exercises then that would be more transparent."

Fraser wasn't in the mood to compromise and he failed to see Wilbur's olive branch. His response was short and strident, "You have my outline. I've told you I will properly assess and that should be enough for the Committee. If not, I'll go to the full Law School Council for a decision."

I finally spoke, "Jerome, you can't go to the Council for the current term. Under the law school regulations after the last meeting of the Law School Council in May, the Council delegates its authority to make exemptions on the assessment policy to the Teaching and Learning Committee for the upcoming fall term. You may bring the matter to the Council for consideration at its next meeting later this month, but any change or exemption would only be in place for future terms."

Fraser was caught off guard. He had not researched the law school's regulations, "Council can retroactively grant the exemption."

I calmly responded, "No, Council cannot. That would violate university policy, which requires that students be fully informed of their course evaluation before the start of the first class. That is why we are meeting today."

He was angry and said, "Do what you want. It seems to me that you've all made up your minds." He turned to leave with a parting comment, "I've got better things to do with my time."

As he opened the door to leave, I simply said, "Thank you for coming."

Nowhere else in any serious workplace setting would such behaviour be tolerated; however, in academia immature, downright rude behavior is all too prevalent. That is what happens when you give people job security. Under the cloak of "academic freedom" all sorts of misbehaviour is countenanced.

He left. We all looked at each other. Gwen started to laugh and said, "What a dag."

I asked her, "What the heck is a dag?"

"Not in polite company."

"Come on Gwen," I pleaded.

"Alrighty—you asked, dag is shit caught in the wool on a sheep's ass. Fits him perfectly."

I had to laugh. The Australians have such a rich vocabulary. I turned to the purpose of the meeting, "Dag or no, what about his request for an exemption?"

Gwen was quick to respond, "It seems to me that he has no clue as to what he will be assessing. He just came up with the idea and expects us to follow along. It smacks of teacher laziness. Wouldn't we all like to give out 50% for participation without much thought or scrutiny? I vote no." No mincing of words from Gwen.

"Wilbur?"

"It is troubling. He had no detailed outline for us. He wanted us to simply trust his judgment. The difficulty of course is that we would have to do the same for everyone and it sets a very dangerous precedent. Students would be left to the whims of the individual instructors, which is the reason we have the policy in the first place—to require transparency. Andrew, what are your thoughts?"

I knew that Wilbur would be more circumspect. I agreed with what both had already said. I called for a formal vote. We were unanimous; exemption denied. With our business done we sat around chatting.

"How did we ever hire Fraser in the first place?" Gwen asked.

With a twinkle in his eye, Wilbur said, "If I recall correctly Andrew was on the hiring committee, he will be able to tell us."

Wilbur and I liked to remind each other of our mistakes. Wilbur too had served on the hiring committee and had made a couple. The reality is that every faculty in every university has a core of good, dedicated, and competent people, but also has twenty to twenty-five percent of staff who should never have been hired in the first place and who should never have been granted tenure. Universities rarely admit their errors and the mistakes are allowed to fester; bringing pain to students and staff for decades to come. I replied to Wilbur's dig, "It was not an easy decision. We needed someone in Torts Law. Fraser fit the bill. He interviewed fairly well. His limited teaching evaluations were okay and the references from the university where he taught were glowing. We did the best we could in checking his background, but in this day and age getting any information from past employers is nearly impossible."

Gwen laughed, "His references were good. What do you expect? They wanted to get rid of him! Remember Jane, what's her name, I was just new when she was here."

"Jane Wilkerson," I helped.

"Yeah, that's her name. I remember you guys in the staff room were prepared to lie your heads off to get rid of her. She was applying for a deanship somewhere and you all wanted her gone." Gwen was on a roll.

Jane Wilkerson was a mistake. She had tenure but she hated teaching. Actually, she hated students. Instead of an open door policy with respect to students, she had a closed door policy. She would arrive at her office and immediately go into seclusion. I know, because I had the office next to her. Dean Alcock at the time tried to minimize the damage by having her teach a reduced load. Funny how it is that at universities incompetence is rewarded--the path of least administrative resistance is to have those academics who can't teach do nothing. After a few years of light loading there was a mutiny by a few of us with heavy teaching loads. I convinced the Dean that the only way to get rid of Professor Wilkerson was to have her teach a full load. She taught a full load for one year, hated it, and resigned to take up an inconsequential government post.

Wilbur took Gwen's bait, "Gwen, I am offended that you would suggest that I would lie about anyone in a reference." With mock indignation he said, "I always tell the truth, but truth can be interpreted in various ways. Regarding Jane Wilkerson I might have said, "She is an unusual Professor, which was true."

I offered, "The law school will not be the same without her."

Gwen joined in, "How about, "A person of uncommon brilliance," which can mean anything."

Wilbur added, "Or, she has an established reputation at Flemington School of Law."

"Isn't Fraser up for tenure this year?" Gwen turned serious.

"Yes he is," I replied and added, "We'll have our opportunity then to give feedback, but Gwen please don't call him a dag in your letter."

Gwen laughed, "No I'll be far more diplomatic, but the dag meaning will come through."

We adjourned. I had an email to send to Fraser telling him of our unanimous decision. He would not be pleased. So the new school year began.

CHAPTER 4

The next day the upper year students arrived. I heard that the class reps from the second year had gone to the Dean and requested that a memorial service be held for Allison. The Dean had said no. Evidently, he was sympathetic, but his hands were tied. University policy required prior approval for any such services and they were traditionally reserved for long serving members of the University community.

I saw things differently. The University's lawyer, Sid Ashter's fingerprints were all over this decision, and Dean Clarke would abide by central's dictate. Clarke was the new type of law dean–a bureaucrat. In the past, generally law deans assumed the position from the senior ranks of the professoriate and his or her primary concern was maintaining the quality of the law program. They were educators, still taught classes, and knew the students well. Their loyalty was to the law school first and they often fought the university central administration when necessary. The new deans are a creation of management. They are beholden to the central administration and their fundamental reason for being is to balance the budget and bring more money into the university. They are central administration minions. John Clarke was a perfect example. He was in his mid-forties, ambitious and striving to move up the university administrative ladder. He was hired by central and did their beckoning. The first rule of a bureaucrat is—do not make waves--and so it was that John Clarke flourished by doing nothing.

The University was paranoid about risk management and I could see that the University wanted to distance itself from the suicide of one of its students. They were fearful that people may start to link Allison's death with her studies at Flemington. Better to cut all ties. Sad but true.

I had an early morning class in Evidence with the second years. It was to be their first class for the fall term. The class is held in the main lecture hall, which seats over 100. Maria Dempster had contacted me late afternoon the day before. She asked whether I would be willing to allow the second year class to have an "unofficial" memorial service for Allison using the main lecture hall and my class time. I readily agreed; it was the right thing to do.

I arrived at the room early to see if the students needed any assistance. They didn't. A montage of photographs of Allison was projected on the hall's main screen. One of the students, who was an accomplished violin player, was playing background music. The hall was full. I took an assigned seat on the dais.

Marcia Driedger, who was the second year class rep, opened the memorial, "We are here today to remember Allison Klassen, a cherished classmate. We remember her, honour her, and celebrate the person she was." She called on Mark Isaacs to say a prayer. Before entering law school Mark studied theology and was a Deacon in his church. Mark's prayer was not only for Allison, but he spoke directly to his classmates, to their loss and to their pain. I was struck by the wonderful and diverse students we had.

Maria Dempster spoke next. She spoke from the heart and her heart was indeed breaking. "I have lost my best friend in law school. Allison was my confidante. I'd call her at midnight about some law assignment, test or case and Allison would settle me down. She was always there for me and for many of you. She cared about us, which was her nature. Remember the chocolate chip cookies she baked for all of us before our first law exam? Remember the Christmas hamper that she organized for the family in need and got us all thinking about something other than our examinations? I will miss Allison terribly ... " Maria was having difficulty continuing and she ended quickly, "She was a friend to us all." The students understood her pain and started applauding.

Two women from the class took to the podium and told of Allison the designated driver. They promised not to name names so all could rest easy. Allison did not drink so she was perfect to act as the driver on numerous girls' nights out. It seems that there were many nights out and that Allison not only was the driver, but acted as nurse to her partying passengers and caretaker in cleaning up after them. They told of one hilarious night out when an unnamed classmate fell asleep in a night club. The girls couldn't wake her and couldn't get her up, she was dead weight. Allison convinced two big bouncers that it was in their establishment's best interest to remove sleeping patrons and they carried the classmate to the car. A voice from the back called out, "Elizabeth do you remember?" Laughter followed by applause.

Marcia introduced a special tribute. We were invited to watch a video stream of photographs showing Allison with her classmates. How they managed to put this together on such short notice was impressive. Beethoven's "Ode to Joy" played in the background. I think every second year student was included. This was a closely knit group.

Marcia then asked whether other students would like to share some memories. Often this call at memorials or wakes is met with awkward silence. Not on this occasion. Three students took to the podium. Janet Peabody told of the time that she found that she had a flat tire in the parking lot. It was late at night, in the middle of January and it was cold. She was at a loss as to what to do. As she said in a mock *Gone With The Wind* moment, "I don't know nothin' bout changing tires." She also was a student, which meant she was poor; no Automobile Association membership for her. She was about to catch a bus when Allison turned up. When told about the problem, Allison asked for her keys so that she could get the car manual. Allison returned, studied the manual for a moment, went back out to the car and changed the tire. Janet ended by saying, "I was so impressed. She just did it." More applause.

Fred Ganz was next. Frederick is a gregarious soul, well liked and easy going. He is tall and lanky. He told the story of playing on the co-ed intramural volleyball team with Allison: "We were playing Medicine I think. It was our first game of the season and we didn't know each other too well. This guy on the other side had a wicked serve. And you could see that he was aiming at the girls."

"You mean women, Fred," a feminine voice was heard.

Without missing a beat Fred carried on, "As I was saying, he was aiming at the ladies on our team. His first serve went right at one of our ladies and she couldn't return it. So being the athlete I am I decided to lend a hand. The next serve was aimed at Allison. I was beside her and moved in front of her to take the serve. Of course, I missed it. Allison gave me an intense look and whispered, "You come into my space again I'll knock your block off," smiled and got ready for the next serve. Sure enough the guy hits another serve right at her, she sets it perfectly and we get the point. She was one heck of a volleyball player and believe me I wasn't going to get into her space again; I'm sure she would have belted me." More laughter and applause.

The final student was Evan Bergstresser. I was surprised to see him speak. He was a shy, introverted student, who rarely spoke in class or out. "I live in Helena, Montana, where my family owns a ranch. Allison and I got to know each other perhaps because of our farm backgrounds. Remember last winter, just before break, the weather was nasty. Allison knew I was going home. So before I left she prepared a care box for me. It was the size of a shoe box wrapped in a ribbon. Inside were some of her chocolate chip cookies, and two coupons for coffee at Denny's. There was also a note that said, "Stop and rest. Be safe. Return safe. Allison". She worried about me. She was like family to us all. And I don't know about you, but I sure feel like I've lost family. Thank you." The room erupted. The students all stood. Evan's words had captured the feeling of the entire class.

Marcia concluded by thanking all for coming. She indicated that a scholarship fund was going to be created in Allison's name to aid women entering the law school and that in the foyer there was coffee and chocolate chip cookies made by some of the students using Allison's recipe. She then turned to me, "Professor Sturgis, thank you for allowing us to use your class time."

As we were leaving, Maria asked, "Can I see you this afternoon?"

"Sure, what time works for you?"

"My last class ends at three."

"Works for me," I said, "See you then."

The first week of law school is filled with lunch time barbecues and various student events. I made my token appearances. This lunch hour I had a burnt hamburger and soda. A number of the second year students came up to thank me for the "unofficial memorial". You could see that they had wanted an opportunity to share their grief. Funerals and memorials are valuable to that end; they allow people closure, respects are paid, grieving is over and people can move on.

Wilbur sauntered by, munching on a hot dog, "I heard you had a good class this morning," and winked.

News of the unofficial memorial would eventually find its way to the Dean. Not to worry. So goes the saying, 'better to ask forgiveness than permission.'

Later that afternoon Maria knocked at my door. I beckoned her in and she closed the door behind her. This she normally did not do unless something confidential was at play. We exchanged mutual condolences and agreed that the memorial was an emotional release for all concerned. I then asked her, "Maria what's on your mind?"

She hesitated, "I don't know really where to begin." I let her take her time. "You heard the tributes today; does that sound like a person who would kill herself? It just makes no sense."

"Maria, there is no evidence of foul play. Everything points to Allison killing herself."

"I know," Maria replied in a deflated tone, "but she had so much to live for. I've been wracking my brain asking myself why. Why would she kill herself?"

"I've been asking myself that same question."

Maria then got to her point, "I think something happened in Winnipeg when she was at that law conference. I mean what else can explain this? Allison seemed happy before going. Then when she came back she contacted no one. She cut herself off. No texts saying what a great conference it was. Nothing. Nothing for two days and then she killed herself on the second day back. Something had to have happened in Winnipeg."

"What do you think happened?"

"I don't know. She doesn't drink, doesn't do drugs, and is very religious. She is a bloody saint."

"Some people kill themselves on impulse, with little reason and we often have no answer as to why."

Maria had been holding back, she took a deep breath and got to the point, "You know she never liked working for Professor Fraser. I think she was flattered by the job. Getting a research position is quite a plum but she felt uncomfortable around him."

"What do you mean, uncomfortable?"

"That is just it; it is hard to explain, but I felt the same about Professor Fraser. Did you know that I interviewed with him about the research position before taking up your offer?"

I admitted ignorance of that fact. I didn't interview students for the summer positions. By the end of term I knew the students well. No need to interview them.

"The interview was strange. The questions he asked made me uncomfortable. He told me about the work demands and then asked if I was dating anyone. I told him I had a boyfriend and he pursued that. Where was my boyfriend living? Was he in town over the summer? How long had we been going out? He was prying into my personal background. It looked like he wanted a student without any ties. That would be Allison—not me. He never offered me the job even though my marks were much better than Allison's."

"Did you see anything untoward between them over the summer?"

"No."

"Did Allison say to you anything about Professor Fraser?"

"No, other than he made her uncomfortable. I remember her saying that when she went to his office she always kept the door open. And she was glad the work was over."

"Maria, if something had been going on. If he had been bothering her, do you think she would have told you?"

"Yes, yes I do."

"Then the fact that she never said anything to you says much, doesn't it?"

"Yes, unless it was too personal, too bad to talk about."

"Except, Maria look at who Allison was. She was a strong, self-reliant person. Surely if something was going on that she didn't like she'd say something to you or someone else." I was playing devil's advocate, "You know that the police checked her phone and computer for any clues and came up empty?"

Maria seemed surprised by this information, but was not convinced, "I just don't know. It's a feeling. I do know that a number of the female students feel uncomfortable with Professor Fraser. Check to see the students who sign up for his elective."

"Look Maria I am not going to dismiss your concerns, but without proof of wrongdoing there's nothing I or anyone can do. Have you gone to the Dean?"

Maria in a mocking way answered, "No, Dean Clarke will do nothing and I have nothing."

I decided to offer her a way forward, "Let's treat this as a cold case, not a closed case. We can each keep our eyes open and quietly see if any evidence comes forward. I promise that I'll look into things from my end. But remember this, rumour and innuendo are dangerous, so we need to tread carefully. You promise to come to me if you find out anything. How does that sound?"

"Agreed and thank you. I needed to get this out there and talk to somebody."

She left.

I was left to ponder what she had told me. I too was very perplexed by Allison's suicide.

CHAPTER 5

I ride my bicycle to and from work; it fits the profile of a somewhat eccentric professor. Unfortunately, over the years I have become more of a fair weather rider. In earlier times I rode daily and year round. On the cold winter days the axle grease would thicken making each pedal all the harder. I only crashed once and that was because the ice patch was hidden by freshly fallen snow. If you see the ice you can ride accordingly. Using one of Gwen's Aussie sayings, "It's not the snakes you see that get you; it's the ones you don't see."

Our house is a little over three miles from the law school and it takes on average twenty minutes. I wind my way through the residential streets and back lanes of Flemington Heights. The streets are lined with oak, maple and elm trees interspersed with conical spruce of all kinds.

Cycling provides serenity, which allows the rider to take in the surroundings. You just do not see as much when driving. Over the years I have observed the subtle changes. Houses repainted. Roofs repaired. New decks built. Flowers planted and blossoming. Lawns cut or not.

I ride because I'm not disciplined enough to go to a gym and too cheap to hire a personal trainer. I've always believed in natural exercise. I ride to get to work and I get exercise at the same time. My bicycle, a Raleigh three speed, is almost as old as the rider. It has reached a point where I'm having trouble getting the right size tires and inner tubes. My bike is beautifully inefficient. Modern sophisticated bicycles allow riders to go faster with less effort. I want effort.

As I was riding this day, Maria's suspicions were weighing on my mind. I arrived home. Our house is a small postwar red brick one and a half storey. There is a porch that goes lengthwise in the front. For many years it was cluttered with children's toys, sporting equipment and whatever else they decided to leave. With our children grown up and gone the porch is tidier with two wicker lounges and a wicker coffee table. Without children life certainly is quieter, but less interesting. The rear of the house has a deck leading to a paved stone patio and a chain link fenced yard. The house is Middle America. When I first started out at Flemington a restless colleague complained that if he stayed teaching he'd end up with a house in the suburbs, two kids and two cars. He wanted more and chased the money. Last I heard he joined a large Wall Street firm. I wonder if he's happy.

I put my bike by the porch and heard barking from the back yard. That would be Bruce my middle daughter's golden retriever. My daughter, Leigh, is off traveling in Europe. Bruce is staying with us, which is no problem, but we would never admit that to our daughter. Bruce is a family bred golden, with a darker than normal rust coat. We had a golden when the kids were growing up. The dog was definitely part of the family and tolerated the children. Bruce is a female. My daughter was fixed on the name when we went to look at the litter of pups. One never goes simply to look at pups; one will inevitably buy a pup–can't be helped. Sure enough when we arrived at the dog owner's home the litter of eight week old pups were playing in the garage. But there was one problem, the last male had just been sold and there was only one pup left. This pup we found stuck behind a shovel. We decided that she had an adventurous spirit and bought her. Or as my daughter would say, "we adopted her". And my daughter insisted that she be named Bruce. She reasoned that dogs do not know about the gender of names, which is quite true. So Bruce the female golden retriever joined the family.

I went to the back yard. Bruce was whining and her tail was working in concentric circles. No matter how bad the day, the love and companionship of a dog makes the world a better place. I gave Bruce a pat, scratched her behind the ears and asked how her day had been. Bruce was responsible for keeping the squirrels away from the property. I threw her a stick and went inside to change and get into my dog walking gear--more natural exercise–walking a dog. I also went into my den and took out from my humidor a Romeo & Julieta number 3 Cuban cigar. I only have one or two cigars a month; they are my thinking cigars. The Romeo & Julieta number 3 is an ideal dog walking cigar as it lasts perfectly for twenty minutes.

I was ready and took Bruce with me through the back gate. We are fortunate to have a flood plain and river forest behind our house. Flemington is situated on the banks of the Kocheta River, which for most of the year is timid and tranquil; however, every once in a while should there be heavy winter snow fall and spring rain it gets angry and floods. Flemington tried to tame the river by building dikes and retaining walls. That didn't work. They then allowed the river more freedom to expand. Dikes were moved back, flood plains were created and more parks and walking paths were built. This seems to work much better. Now the Kocheta gets angry, but doesn't flood the city.

I lighted my cigar and we began our walk. Bruce is well trained; big dogs need to be. I laugh when I see dogs pulling their owners on strained leashes. They are examples of dogs walking owners. Bruce heels well and I do keep her on a leash until we get to the forest. My primary reason for this is to keep Bruce out of the foxtail grasses and nearby patch of cockleburs; otherwise I will spend an hour combing burrs out of her coat. The forest is a much friendlier place for Bruce and for me.

We entered the forest and I let Bruce off the leash. Bruce is a responsible dog. She keeps an eye on me as she explores. Bruce roams the forest paths sniffing, investigating and peeing. This is what dogs do. I think as I walk.

Maria is right; it makes no sense that Allison would kill herself. Did something happen in Winnipeg? And did Fraser have an eye for young, beautiful students. He wouldn't be the first young professor to dip into the student pool. He may not be handsome or overly personable, but he did have that professorial aura with which young students might become enamoured. How do I investigate? Should I even investigate? It isn't my job to do so. Am I being a busybody?

Where to start? Is Maria right? I can't go around conducting a student survey on Fraser's proclivities. I need to be careful. Wrongful allegations can be so unfair, even for a jerk like Fraser. I also know that the administration won't be of any assistance.

I'll start by talking to my wife, Julie. She is my sounding board and voice of calm reflection. She studied psychology at university and whilst raising the kids worked part time as an inner city youth counsellor. She now works full time at the university in student counselling. Julie has a strong understanding of human nature. She will be arriving home from work shortly. I take a last puff on my cigar and call Bruce to come. Bruce is content, quickly runs up and sits in front of me. She knows that a treat awaits and I don't disappoint her. We walk back to the house.

Julie is in the kitchen unloading groceries. I go up and give her a quick hello kiss.

"You've been smoking," she comments in a disapproving tone.

"I've been thinking. Would you like a drink?"

A drink on the porch before supper is a tradition. It allows us to catch up on the day's events and to relax from the ongoing angst of work. I pour the glasses of wine. Bruce lies at the top of the porch stairs watching the street. Julie plops into her wicker lounge. She has changed into beige shorts and a light pale green blouse. She is fit looking–not slim, not overweight–just right. Her skin is healthy and rosy. Minimal make-up. Her dark brown hair is cut stylishly short–easy to keep; no hair colouring. Flecks of gray are appearing, which give her more elegance. Her face is friendly, and she is ready to smile and laugh. She is a person content with who she is.

We have already discussed Allison's suicide. Julie knows suicide all too well. Her work in the inner city introduced her to a dysfunctional world filled with alcohol abuse, drug abuse, physical abuse and sexual abuse. She dealt with too many families where the parents should never have had children. Most of her clients were victims of poverty and had much pain and many scars. A number of them died, some by their own hand, and others mostly in gang violence.

I told Julie about my meeting with Maria and her suspicions. She listened intently. Counsellors are good listeners. She finally asked, "What do you make of what Maria told you?"

"I don't know. She told me that she didn't see anything between Fraser and Allison. All that she had was basically a feeling, a suspicion."

"Don't dismiss Maria's suspicions. A woman's intuition is often proven right. She is uncomfortable with Fraser and that says something."

"The problem is that we need proof and not suspicion. We can't act on suspicion."

"I'll share with you something. Remember the law school Christmas Party last year held at the University Club?"

"I remember, but what am I supposed to remember?"

"You must remember the two young women servers going around with the drinks and finger food?"

"Sorry, don't remember them."

"You are getting old. They were strikingly beautiful and both had figures to die for. Professor Fraser certainly noticed them. He ogled them throughout the evening. I watched him as he watched them. He was literally stalking them with his eyes and these girls were half his age. My danger antennae were raised. I thought to myself–pervert."

"You never mentioned this to me then."

"No, I kept it to myself; it was for my own reference. But it made me uncomfortable with him."

"I can't say I noticed anything."

"Well you missed a lot. What can I say?" She laughed then turned more serious, "My point is that women may detect danger signs that men may miss. We live in a more dangerous world than men. I'll give you an example: Where did you walk Bruce today?"

"In the bush."

"Right, do you know where I usually walk Bruce?" It was a rhetorical question, "I walk him on the street. Why? Because it is safer. The street is lit, there are people around, houses I can run to if threatened. I don't walk Bruce in the bush because it is isolated and frankly I don't feel safe. Did you even think about your safety for a moment this afternoon? I bet not."

Julie was right, I hadn't.

"We are, and I freely admit this, physically the weaker sex and that is why we need to be more careful, more aware of our surroundings and ever watchful of people. So please don't discount Maria's suspicions."

"I do appreciate what you are saying, but I don't even know if I should get involved. It is not my job. I have no authority to go around investigating."

"You don't really believe that do you? If so, it's a typical academic copout. All talk and no action. Think about it. A law student is dead. A staff member might be involved and nobody else is going to do anything. You owe it to Allison, to her family, to all the students at Flemington Law and you owe it to the law school where you have worked these past twenty-five years. Most importantly, you need to do this for yourself. Allison's death has been troubling you. I see that. You need to know why she killed herself. To do nothing leaves too much unanswered. You know how to investigate and what to investigate. You used to be a criminal defence attorney and you worked as a prosecutor. You know what to do. At the end of the day if you find no answers so be it. You at least tried. But doing nothing is not an option."

She was right.

Chapter 6

Friday came and I finally had some time to myself. I admit I had been very preoccupied with Allison's death. I needed some answers one way or the other. It was time to delve into her life at Flemington. I started by looking at her student file.

I dropped in to see Beth Jones–keeper of the student records. I knew that Beth would be deluged with students wanting course changes at this the end of week one. Beth's office was on the second floor. There is an ante room where Beth and her assistant Annet hold the fort and there is a back, dingy, windowless room where all the student records and past examinations are kept. University regulations require that we retain all student examinations both final and mid-term for two years.

Sure enough Beth and Annet were meeting with students and another half dozen were waiting in the hallway. I walked in and made eye contact with Beth, "Mrs. Jones, sorry I know you are busy." In front of the students Beth appreciates the formality, "I just have to check on the course enrolments and on a student's results. Is that fine? I can do it myself in the record room."

"Certainly Professor Sturgis, it is unlocked, and you know where the master summary sheets are kept. The class enrolments are still changing as final date for course changes is Wednesday of next week." She turned back to her student.

"I'll keep that in mind. I just want to get a feel for the enrolments." I went into the record room and closed the door. A filing cabinet stored the official student record for each student filed by year and then by last name. I pulled Allison's file. It was thin and typical for a normal student. Problem students have thick files. Allison's file included her Law Admission Test score; it was a solid 160 – 80th percentile. Her undergraduate GPA was also solid, 3.84. Her letter of acceptance was on file and her first year results. She obtained four "B" grades, a "B+" in Legal Methods, and then the "A" in Torts. That was it. I put the file back.

Next I looked at the master sheet for her year. It contained the grades of all the students and ranked them. We don't give out the student ranking. The most that we say in reference letters is "a top quartile student", or "on the Dean's Honour List", or perhaps "finished top in my class". If a student in the lower quartile wants me to write a reference letter, unless they did incredibly well in my course, I defer. I suggest that they talk to a professor in whose class they did well–makes for a much better letter of reference.

Allison finished her first year ranked 32nd out of the hundred students. Maria was ranked first and she had the highest grade in Torts; Allison had the third highest in her section. Without the "A" in Torts, say another "B" grade, I quickly eye-balled the ranking, Allison would have finished 45th – slightly above the class average, which frankly is good. The "A" stood out. Sometimes a student is good in one subject, but not that often.

Next I took out the master sheet outlining student enrolment in elective courses. Fraser's Advanced Constitutional Law class had nineteen students currently enrolled. As I expected he was far from the cap of thirty students. Of the nineteen students only four were women. Interestingly, Maria seemed to be right. I dug further by cross referencing the four women with their first year course instructors. I wanted to see if they had been taught by Fraser in first year. Often if a student likes a professor they take courses from him or her in subsequent years. A common piece of advice for students is, "Pick the professor and not the course." A great professor can make any subject interesting; a poor professor can and will destroy the most fascinating subject. I was surprised to find that all four women never took a class from Fraser. They were taking the course blind. It is interesting that no woman he taught in first year signed up for Advanced Constitutional Law. I wondered whether the women in Allison's year were sending a message through their course selections.

I then turned to the examinations meticulously arranged by year, course number and title, and the papers were all in alphabetical order. Each bundle of papers for a particular course was tied with a pink ribbon. Evidently Mrs. Jones, a great fan of the English television show "Rumpole of the Bailey", took the ribbon idea from English practice. 'Briefs' in England (we would say case files) are bundled by ribbons for the barristers. Mrs. Jones went so far as to order the bundling ribbon from an English office supply store.

I went to my course bundle first. A student wanted to review her final examination and I took it out along with another student's. Any student examination removed must be signed out in the record book and I duly did so. Next I looked at Fraser's Torts examinations. I found Allison's final and mid-term examinations, removed them, re-tied the bundle and placed it back on the shelf. I did not record the removal. I did not want to leave any trail. Was I being paranoid? Perhaps. But better not to be asked any questions; ask me no questions I'll tell you no lies. I intended to return Allison's examinations later that afternoon.

I sandwiched Allison's examinations between my two student final examinations. As I left, I told Mrs. Jones, "I signed out a couple examination papers. Thanks much." Beth nodded—deep in discussion with a student.

I go to my office, get a folder and put Allison's examinations in the folder. I then go to the library. There is a little used photocopier in the library for staff. I did not want to photocopy Allison's examinations in the main staff photocopy room because there are too many people around. The library is like a silent tomb. The students were all out on some student organized first week event and the teaching staff, well, this was a Friday. I finished the photocopying uninterrupted.

At 12:30 I return to the student record office. I had the one student's examination to return and Allison's. I went to the office deliberately over the lunch hour knowing that either Beth or Annet would be on break and there would be a good chance that the lone worker would be occupied with a student. Usually the record administrator would take the returning examination and re-shelve it. I wanted to do it myself. Annet was minding the office. She was with a student. I go in, "Hi Annet, just returning an examination. You're busy, I'll do it."

"Thanks Professor Sturgis. Don't forget to sign the ledger as returned."

"Will do," I returned the papers. Signed the ledger and felt very proud of my sleuthing.

There is a Friday afternoon tradition that Wilbur and I started years before, we have an end of the week 'seminar'. Of course the quality of any seminar, especially at such an unattractive hour during the week, is directly dependent upon the alcohol served. We meet in Wilbur's office. He has a grand old office in the northwest wing; it is set apart from the other faculty offices. His office was created before space managers took hold and mandated that each professor be allocated a 100 square foot office, a desk, one armless office chair, one bookshelf, two uncomfortable metal legged stacking chairs for students, a telephone and a computer. Wilbur's office is three times the mandated office size, lined with books. He has an enormous wooden walnut desk–not university approved–a rocking chair, two leather chairs and a leather sofa, all plush and comfortable. And, most importantly, there is a mini-fridge hidden away behind the desk. It is the perfect office for a 'seminar'.

Wilbur and I come from the old school. We enjoy being around the law school. Most of the newer colleagues escape to their home computers as fast as they can. Over the years certain regulars attended. Angela Crindle was a regular. Angela is a criminal defence attorney. She teaches the other section of first year criminal law from two to four in the afternoon on Fridays. She says she needs to unwind after the class. Angela won't be here today as her regular class hours don't start until next week. Gwen Mason-Hill was another regular, but she too couldn't make today's seminar; she had to attend a university committee meeting. I'm glad because I wanted to talk to Wilbur privately.

I arrived at 4:30 sharp. Wilbur is seated behind his desk. He is dishevelled as usual. Wilbur is a bachelor and his dress sense is sadly lacking. He usually looks like he slept in his clothes. In fact, I know that at times he has. When Wilbur is working on a project and on a roll he will not stop; he is consumed by the creative energy and the sofa becomes his temporary bed.

"Wine, beer or whiskey?" he demanded when he saw me.

"I need a whiskey today. How about you?"

He put his paper away, took his reading glasses off, and said, "No one should drink whiskey alone. Sounds serious, I'll bring out the good stuff. On the rocks?"

"Of course."

Wilbur took two glasses from a credenza, opened the fridge and brought out a small ice container. With practiced precision using an ice tong he placed three pieces of ice into a crystal whiskey glass. Wilbur insisted that whiskey be drunk using proper glasses. He never refrigerated the whiskey and he took his neat. He poured two fingers of Jack Daniel's Single Barrel Select into each glass. I watched without saying a word.

He offered me the whiskey on the rocks and raised his glass in toast, "To life and to another year at Flemington Law School."

"To life," I repeated and we took a sip of the burning, mellow whiskey to savour. This was sipping whiskey. Wilbur was now ready for discussion.

"Wilbur, I want to talk to you about something and it is in complete confidence." Wilbur watched me and said nothing. He waited. I told him about my conversation with Maria, her concerns, and that I had decided to do some investigating.

Wilbur finally spoke, "Allison's suicide has been on my mind too. Attending the funeral really brought it home to me. What Maria has told you is indeed worth following up. I can tell you that Jerome has made a few comments to me that I've been somewhat uncomfortable with. As you know, we both teach Torts and have to reconcile our grades. Often he will refer to his female students by way of their looks, in particular, their bust size. I put it down to immaturity. So tell me what are you going to investigate?"

"I've already started." I told him about what I found out today in the student records. I then got to the meat of what I wanted to say, "Wilbur, I also took out Allison's final and mid-term exams from the student records. I have copies with me in this folder. Allison got an "A" in Torts. Fraser then hired her to be his research assistant over the summer. I wonder if he wasn't grooming her, enticing her through bogus grades. I don't know. But it is suspicious. I liked Allison, but I think you would agree with me, she was a solid "B" student–not an "A" student. We both gave her "B" grades in our courses. I'd like you to read her examinations and verify that the papers are worthy of an "A". It's a big ask."

Wilbur took a sip of his whiskey, swished it around his mouth and took a slow swallow. "I'll do it. Not a big ask at all. As you know under our school policy we re-read the top paper from each other's section to ensure a measure of uniformity in grading. If something is going on we need to put a stop to it. I have a copy of Jerome's examination on line, his marking guide– such as it is--and a copy of the highest paper, which happened to be Maria's. I'll re-read Allison's paper, but can't get to it until early next week. I have a conference paper that has to be finished by Monday morning."

It was my turn to sip the whiskey and savour its warmth and the fact that Wilbur was on side. I mused, "You know it is scary isn't it that there are so few controls over our grading. We rely on the integrity of the professor. Yet, I know as a student, I sure wondered how certain professors came to the marks they did."

"Never mind as a student, I wonder as a professor." Wilbur continued, "Jerome would know that an "A" grade, so long as it is not the highest mark in the section would never be re-read or challenged by anyone. The student would never appeal an unexpected "A" grade and no one would be the wiser. Clever—devious if the case—but clever. Instead of roses to woo the damsel our suitor uses grades."

"Of course if the grade is legitimate I am back to square one."

"True," said Wilbur, "but I think we should hope that the grade is correct. Otherwise, we know not where the path will take us. We also must be careful; no one must know what we are up to."

We finished our drinks. I gave Wilbur the copies of Allison's examinations and left for home; Wilbur remained in his office to work.

Chapter 7

I received an email from Wilbur, which was a typical Wilbur email short and to the point, "Come and see me after Law School Council. W" I assumed that he had read Allison's paper.

Law School Council is the academic decision making body for the law school. All twenty of the full time academic staff are members and in addition there is a Bar Association representative and two student representatives. The Council is part of university governance. Over the years I have observed its dysfunctional work. The problem is that many of the academics invariably act in their own self-serving self-interest couched, of course, in platitudes to principle and precedent. Perhaps academics have too much time on their hands. And then there are a few of my colleagues who actually are incapable of making a decision. The result is that they stay on the sideline waiting to see what the majority decides and then they jump aboard. It is quite funny, if it were not so sad, they will hesitate on any vote to see where the majority falls. A vote is called, hands go up and then you see the hands of the indecisive crew. God forbid if the vote is close, then they are in a quandary and often abstain, which satisfies no one. The Council is an academic zoo; rarely does it rise above vested interests and pettiness. Fortunately, it only meets twice a teaching semester in weeks two and ten always on a Monday at 3:00 p.m.

I looked over the agenda for the day's Council meeting and saw nothing of any real importance. As Chair of the Teaching and

Learning Committee I was presenting a motion on teaching allocation, which I didn't see as too controversial. The Dean had asked the T&L Committee to draft a policy for guidance in allocating the teaching of courses. Traditionally this was a matter within the power and discretion of the Dean and our deans had wielded that power for decades with little complaint. I can only assume that the Dean wanted some added 'Council clout' to push back difficult colleagues. Dean Clarke was a weak dean and I guess he needed the support. I noted that Fraser had not put on the agenda the issue of class participation that we had knocked back the week before. It wasn't like Fraser to roll over; perhaps he was going to ask that it be added as a matter of new business. We shall see.

The Council gathered in the law school boardroom. We were surrounded by photographs of past deans and of United States Supreme Court Chief Justices. I thought to myself, it was an all male preserve. I was in my usual seat, opposite the Dean. Staff members, like students, are territorial and gravitate to the same seats. The Dean chaired the Council and called the meeting to order. Fifteen staff and one student were in attendance. The call for new business was met by silence. Fraser must have given up on class participation. We then went through a litany of committee reports. Universities do love committees. Each committee chair felt compelled to summarize the important work of their committee. Woe betide for a chair to rise and say, "No report. Did not meet." Most committees under their terms of reference had to meet at least once or twice a year, whether there was any point in doing so or not.

We finally got to matters on the agenda set for vote. The T&L Committee proposal on teaching allocation was now before the Council. I was asked by the Dean to open the discussion. I began, "Our recommendation is that as a guideline each full time faculty member teaches at least 50% of their course load from our core, mandatory subjects." In a presentation I believe in point first argument; I tell my audience what my conclusion or point is right off the top. I continued, "You have our report. We asked for your input last fall. The committee then contacted over one hundred law schools for any guidelines that they may have on teaching allocation. The result of our survey and recommendations are contained in our report. We recommend the 50% threshold first because in a small law school it falls on the full time staff to see that the core is covered. It is important that these core subjects be taught by our best instructors, who are at the law school and available for the students. Second it represents the current situation. All of the full time staff now teach 50% or more of their subjects from the core. I also emphasize that this is but a guideline. The ultimate discretion in terms of teaching rests with the Dean. I now formally put the motion before Council."

The Dean called for discussion. A number of hands immediately go up—Fraser was first. I now realized that this motion was more contentious than anticipated.

"I thank the committee for its work," Fraser started somewhat sarcastically, "but I question their result and I even question the need for such guidelines. What the motion represents is a stifling of innovation. Why shouldn't we have a measure of specialization? If we were to hire a human rights expert on to staff, why shouldn't that person teach two or three human rights subjects? The premise of the committee is that only full time staff can teach the core adequately. Yet we know that is not the case and that we have some very able part time staff teaching core subjects now. I also fear that this proposal will unduly fetter the discretion of the Dean and that really this motion goes to law school operations and is not a proper academic question for this Council. Accordingly, I will vote against this motion."

Self-interest I thought. Fraser wanted out of Torts, which was a core subject. He wanted to teach pet upper year seminar courses.

The Dean called on me for a response. I decided to pull him into the debate, "I will deal with the fettering of discretion first. Dean Clarke, you in fact asked the committee to prepare the guidelines. Did you regard this as a fettering of your discretion? Perhaps you could enlighten the Council as to why you asked the committee to undertake the drafting of teaching allocation guidelines."

Dean Clarke had to support the guidelines. He asked for them. "The discretion in terms of teaching always rests with the Dean. What I thought would be helpful is more transparency, so that all staff could see how teaching allocations were being made."

A number of younger staff spoke in favour of more flexibility, which I thought was not surprising. No one likes to teach a large class in civil procedure if you could teach a seminar on international human rights or say a course on law and the movies. Self-interest was rearing its head.

Others asked about why a guideline was even necessary; our survey of other law schools showed that a good number of schools had no teaching guidelines. Wilbur responded, "If you look at the survey results on page three of the report you will find that almost 70% of smaller schools, such as ours, have teaching guidelines. They do so because there is a need in smaller schools to see that the core is adequately covered. Professor Fraser raised the example of specialist professors teaching in their niche area. That may be fine and good for large, national schools; however, that is not who we are."

Fraser responded with an unnecessary personal attack, "The committee is sticking with the status quo. The committee is out of touch with modern legal education. Specialization is needed and is welcomed by progressive law schools. It seems to me that we need a little more change in this law school."

Gwen could not be held back, "Bloody bull," her Aussie accent was raging, "we weren't asked to look at the entire law program at Flemington. We were asked to look at the narrow issue of teaching load given our current program of study. And I'd like to correct Assistant Professor Fraser, all—and I repeat all—studies on legal education in the last hundred years call for more skills education and core subjects better to prepare our students to bloody well practice law."

The discussion had reached a high point of acrimony. A few others spoke. The key question, which was gaining traction, was why do we need any guidelines in the first place? Leave it to the Dean.

The Dean asked me, "Professor Sturgis do you wish to withdraw the motion at this time so that your committee can further consider the concerns raised in today's discussion?"

The Dean, who was a non-decisive person, was looking for a no decision. I wasn't going to let him have that. If I withdrew the motion, it would be back in our lap to do what with it I do not know. It was better that the motion be voted on and if the motion was defeated our job was over--self-interest. I responded, "No, the motion is tabled. We have had a good discussion and I think those around the table are ready for the question. I call the question."

The vote was 9 – 6 against, with one abstaining. There would be no guidelines. Gwen whispered in my ear, "A fine bit of work for nothing." I nodded.

The meeting ended. Thank God it was eight weeks before the next Law School Council.

I dropped into Wilbur's office, closing the door behind me.

"An interesting meeting," I said.

Wilbur grunted, "Yes." He paused and spoke deliberately, "We were ambushed. It's obvious that Jerome orchestrated the attack. He is a devious character."

"Machiavellian," I agreed.

"What he has succeeded in doing is to neutralize input from Gwen, you and me on his promotion and tenure application. Should we provide a negative recommendation it will be dismissed as biased. He knew that we were not impressed with his proposal last week, or for that matter with him. He will cite our decision on class participation and now the debate today as examples of how we are out to get him. No matter how valid our opinions of him may be, they will be discounted."

Wilbur was right. We had been cut down at the knees. Very clever. It explained why Fraser didn't bother with the class participation issue, which was a loser. Instead he chose to challenge the committee through the guideline motion. Whether he defeated the motion was of no moment. Speaking out against it was enough to raise the spectre of bias. The fact the motion was defeated was a bonus for him; it adds to our alleged bias. To quote Gwen, "Bloody bull."

I flopped deflated into one of the leather chairs, "Did you mark Allison's papers?"

Wilbur nodded yes.

"And?"

"Neither paper is worthy of an "A". The mid-term was out of 30. She got a 24. I put her grade at 20.5 to 21. She missed a good part of one question yet still got 8 out of 10 on the question. The same was true of the final. It was a "B" paper–no more–no less. It was definitely not an "A" paper. At the end of the day, Allison should have received a low "B" grade for the course. Instead she got an "A"."

"So he inflated her grades."

"Yes, and he did so starting in January with the mid-term. In my view this was not an isolated mistake. Not when done on two different papers at two different times. He was favouring her no doubt about that."

"What do we do?" I asked, without expecting any response.

"I can tell you what we don't do and that is go to the Dean or to Jerome. He will just admit a marking error and we will come across as a couple of old guard academics out to get the poor lad. He is a slippery eel. We need more."

We thought in silence for a moment and I finally spoke, "Fraser is a nasty piece of work. I bet he has done this before. Julie told me that she thought he had a roving eye, as did Maria. He had a research assistant last year as well didn't he? A woman."

"Yes," said Wilbur, "I forget her name. A pretty thing though. I've got last year's yearbook."

Wilbur went to one of his shelves and pulled out a yearbook. He flipped to the 1st year class, "There she is, Victoria Palmer. Nice kid, young and attractive."

He handed the yearbook to me. I never taught Victoria, but I remember seeing her around. She had an energetic walk and very pretty face. I noted that below her picture it said she was from Dunkirk, a small town in North Dakota. "Was she a good student?" I asked.

Wilbur was already pulling out his grade records from two years before, "Not really. I gave her a "B"."

I shared what we both were thinking, "I wonder what she got in Torts?"

"The final course change day is on Wednesday. I'll go and get her Torts papers, just like I got Allison's. Good thing we have to keep the examinations for two years, and I'll check the master grade sheet for that year as well. Do you have Fraser's examination and marking guide from two years ago?"

Wilbur replied that he certainly did, all online. He could re-mark Victoria's paper.

Wilbur looked at me and said, "The path we are on is taking us deeper into the woods."

CHAPTER 8

Evidence is a subject that requires a fine tuned awareness of human nature and grounding in the realities of trials. In simple terms, evidence is information that is sought to be admitted in a trial.

I begin with relevancy, which is the foundation for all evidence. If evidence is not relevant, it is not admissible. Relevancy, in turn, means information that will alter the probabilities about a matter in the mind of the reasonable juror. I emphasize "reasonable". The law of evidence is not intended to cater to the whims of unreasonable people.

Character evidence is the first heading under relevancy. A person's character is relevant. We accept, as a general proposition, that people tend to act in accord with their character. Kind people are more apt to do kind acts than selfish people; bad people are more likely to do bad acts than good people. True, we all know that this is not a universal rule and that there are many instances of supposed good, upstanding, honest people in the public eye, who in private commit all matter of depravity.

Today's class introduced the students to similar fact evidence. The starting point is that the prosecution is not allowed to lead evidence as to other criminal acts or bad acts committed by an accused on trial. Not because this evidence is irrelevant, but because it is too hot to handle for the jury. In legal terms we say it has too much potential prejudice against an accused. For example, it is too damning to introduce evidence that an accused on trial for theft was convicted of numerous counts of child molestation. The jury is apt to damn him for being a child molester. Sometimes the similar fact evidence may overwhelm a trial or make the trial too complex; the jury is inundated with bad acts committed by the accused and this overwhelms the actual evidence on the charge before the court. It is also unfair to an accused, who comes to trial prepared to defend against the charge before the court and then has to defend himself against other bad acts, which may well have occurred years before. The state has unlimited resources; a criminal defendant usually does not.

The prosecution may be allowed to introduce other bad acts of the accused if the evidence falls within the similar fact exception. I assigned some of the leading cases. What the cases illustrate is that there needs to be a weighing of potential prejudice against the relevancy—referred to as the 'probative value' of the evidence sought to be admitted. 'Probative value' is just a legal phrase that points to how important or valuable a piece of evidence is in proving the guilt or innocence of an accused. The probative value of the evidence must outweigh any potential prejudice.

The first case is an oldie but goodie, the 1915 English case "The Brides in the Bath". George Joseph Smith preyed on women for their money. He wooed them, married them and then killed them. His modus operandi was to kill them in the bath; it appears that when his wives were in the bath he would pull their legs up forcing their heads under the water and the water would rush into their noses and mouths causing immediate shock and unconsciousness. They then drowned with little sign of violence and Smith recovered the life insurance or inheritance. He killed three of his wives in this manner. He was finally tracked down when the police connected him to the three bath deaths. One new bride dying in the bath is a tragic accident, two is very suspicious and three is no coincidence. He was prosecuted for the murder of his one wife, and the evidence of the other two bath deaths was admitted into evidence to prove the act of murder. Smith was convicted and hanged. This is a classic case of similar fact evidence.

★ ★ ★

Following the class I went back to the student records office. As I anticipated, Beth and Annet were inundated by students changing classes on this the last day to do so. It seems that students, like all of us, work to deadlines; my experience is that human beings are procrastinators by nature. I merely waved at Beth, who was busy with a student, and went into the back student records room.

I first looked at the mark master sheet from two years ago. Victoria Palmer had two "C+" grades, three "B" grades and a lone "A" in Torts. She was not even as strong a student as Allison. Her grade in Torts would place her 4th in the class and she would fly under the re-mark procedure.

I dug further by going back to check on Fraser's Torts grades from when he first arrived on staff five years ago. In his second year of teaching he had a sabbatical leave and did not teach Torts. I carefully recorded the grades for the top female students from three years ago and from five years ago. I was particularly interested in those students who did uncharacteristically well in Torts as compared to their other courses. In both years there was a student who fit the profile. My guess was that they ended up as Fraser's research assistants, but I was getting ahead of myself; I'd have to check.

After the master sheet, I looked at the updated course enrollment for Fraser in Advanced Constitutional Law; his enrollment was down to 15 and to my surprise—no women. I then went to the old examination papers and took out one from my Criminal Law class as camouflage and then took Victoria Palmer's Torts examinations. I signed out my Criminal Law paper and left, waving at Beth as I walked out of the student record's office. The line-up of students waiting to change courses had grown.

I dropped in to Wilbur's office just before heading home. Wilber was on the phone. He nodded at me and I dropped the untitled envelope containing copies of Victoria's examinations on his desk without saying a word and left.

As I road home that day I mulled over in my mind where we were in our investigation of Allison's death. We had a professor who fudged the grades for one of his students. In response he would argue an honest mistake in marking. Should Victoria Palmer's grades be similarly "mistaken" we will have moved from an oversight in marking to a suspicious, very suspicious, pattern of favouritism. Accepting that he deliberately fudged the grades, what was his intention? We could presume that he liked the young women and wanted a relationship. I said to myself "cut the bullshit"–he wanted sex with them. But where was the evidence of seduction? Maria said that she saw nothing between Allison and Fraser and the police checked Allison's cell phone and computer and came up with nothing. In fact, Allison told Maria that she was uncomfortable with Fraser; unless, of course, Allison was lying to cover up a relationship with him. But I doubted that. Fraser was a morose character and I didn't see him seducing anyone. My conclusion was that we had very little to show for our digging.

When I got home Bruce was waiting, tail wagging at top speed. We headed for a walk along the river. When we got back home Julie was already on the front porch with a glass of wine in hand. This was not a good sign. Usually Julie would wait for me so that we could drink and talk together. I went into the kitchen and got a glass of wine, pushed open the screen door and let Bruce lead the way. She got suitable loving and petting from Julie and I sat down in one of the wicker rockers beside her. "Tough day," I asked.

"Yes, I had to deal with a very distraught young woman--a freshman eighteen years old. First week at college, away from home, she drank too much and did things she shouldn't have done and thinks that others did things that they shouldn't have done to her." She took a sip of wine, "There is so much pressure on these kids. She would want to belong and there is pressure to conform. And at colleges across this country this week "to conform" means drinking to excess and then having sex. It takes courage and guts to go against the flow, and to do what's right. How did our three kids ever survive?"

"They were taught to be independent and to know what is right and wrong. I think most importantly is that they had the self-confidence to say no. Keep in mind we don't know what went on do we? Parents are the last to know."

Julie laughed, "Yah, do you remember finding Leigh's false ID when she went away to college that aged her by three years? We found that a few years after the fact."

"I have to admit it was a damn good forgery."

We sat for a time and watched the sunlight low in the sky fighting its way through the trees, and in the long shadows the squirrels were busy collecting nuts for the winter. They are cute critters as long as they don't decide to nest in our attic. Bruce the guard dog was alert should they come too close.

"How was your day?" Julie asked after a time.

I told her the latest on Allison's investigation and shared with her my concerns that we weren't getting anywhere. I repeated to her that there was no proof of seduction.

"Maybe there wasn't any." Julie replied, "You're looking at this situation all too rationally and you think seduction is about sex; it may not be at all. I know that many men want the conquest, the control, and the sex is secondary. Fraser would fit the profile, if he seduced the other student the year before he then dumped her for his next victim. You are also assuming that the sex–if there was any–was consensual. This may not be seduction, but rape."

Julie was making all too much sense. I told Julie about the "Brides in the Bath" case that we had discussed in class earlier in the day. George Joseph Smith was a psychopath. He didn't care for his victims. He was also, like most psychopaths, cunning and manipulative. The profile fit Jerome Fraser.

Julie piped in, "You may well have a "Girls in the Class" case."
With that we went in to prepare dinner together.

Chapter 9

After class Thursday morning I dropped in to see Beth in student records. Beth was working alone and all was quiet in her office.

"You survived course change," I chirped as I walked in.

Beth looked up, smiled and said, "Just barely. It was particularly hectic this year. Lots of changes. I gave Annet the day off. She's worked incredibly hard and put in a number of long days working through the lunch hour."

"You should take a day off as well."

"I've been working for over twenty-five years and I've never taken a day off. It's not in my nature." She pushed back from her desk, "What can I do for you?"

"I didn't want to bother you during course changes, but I was wondering whether you have a record of our student summer research assistants and their supervisors?"

Beth turned back to her computer, "Sure. How far back do you want to go?"

I knew she'd have the information. Beth was meticulous. "Going back five years would be great."

She typed on the keyboard and without looking up asked, "Do you want a printout or should I send an email to your mailbox?"

"Just print it out now and I'll get out of your hair." As the printer warmed up, I asked, "Any dramas in the course changes?"

Beth sighed, all she said was, "Professor Fraser."

"What's he done now?" I inquired. This was not the first time that Professor Fraser has made Beth's scheduling tasks all the more difficult. I, as Chair of the Teaching and Learning Committee, often provided her with much needed support.

"He complained about the scheduling of his Advanced Constitutional elective. He didn't like that it was in the same time slot as Labour Law and he blamed that conflict for his low enrolment."

"How many are in his class now?"

"Eleven."

"Wow that is low for that course. But isn't Labour Law typically a third year elective and Advanced Constitutional is usually taken as a second year elective?"

"Yes, although third year students can still take the course once the second year student selections are complete and if space is available." Her voice turned angry, "He said I should never have scheduled the two courses in the same time slot and that was why an academic should take control of scheduling. He said he'd be talking to the Dean. He then stomped out of my office. He has been nothing but trouble ever since he arrived. And he is so arrogant and demeaning to me and Annet. You know he has told us to address him as "Dr. Fraser" in the presence of students. I hate faculty who are full of themselves. He has this, 'I'm a Dr. and the staff are just servants; you're a nothing attitude'."

I tried to reassure her, "You know a colleague of mine once said the problem with law schools these days is that there are too many doctors and not enough lawyers. My own theory is that many, not all, of the law PhD professors suffer from an implicit inferiority. You know what Bernard Shaw said, 'He who can does. He who cannot, teaches.' To get their PhD they spent years researching some minutiae legal point instead of practicing law; yet law is a practical discipline. They are defensive and need their work acknowledged. Don't let him get to you. There are always going to be course conflicts for electives and in my view his low student interest has more to do with him than with conflicts."

"I know, but he is trouble; he is real trouble." Beth obviously felt better having vented and having a safe listener. She handed me the printout.

"Thanks Beth. Hang in there and thanks for all your work with course changes." I headed out and, as I walked to my office, I glanced at the printout. It wasn't long. I checked the lists from three years ago and five years ago and saw what I needed. Fraser had indeed hired the two students that I had flagged, based on their marks. A pattern was apparent.

CHAPTER 10

Thank God it's Friday. I dropped by Wilbur's office for our weekly seminar. I needed a drink. Wilbur was waiting. Without saying a word he took out the whiskey, poured two drinks–mine on the rocks. In silence we each took a sip.

I broke the silence, I was anxious to know the result. "Did you mark Victoria's examinations?"

"Yes. In her December examination she got 80%. It should have been 70%. In her final she also got 80%, the exam was only a high 60's–not even a "B". This is the same thing as with Allison. What did you find out? You were going to see about past summer research assistants that he had."

"I checked the master sheet and flagged two students, females with "A" grades that were out of character for them. I also wrote down the details of other students, but they would not have fit the profile. I then saw Beth and asked her for the names of the summer research assistants and their supervisors for the past five years. The two students I had flagged were indeed hired as his summer students."

"Who were they?"

"Three years ago it was Jennifer Cunnigham and five years ago it was Ingrid Hedberg. I taught both. Nice young ladies, hard working, diligent, but not brilliant."

Wilbur went to his bookshelf where he kept the student yearbooks. As he pulled the two years he commented, "I remember

Ingrid, capable student. I never taught Jennifer." He gave me the one yearbook with Ingrid Hedberg. There was her smiling face, very Scandinavian. Wilbur handed me the second yearbook, "Here is Jennifer Cunningham. Notice anything?"

As I looked at the two yearbook photographs, it was obvious, "Fraser likes pretty blondes."

"Yes," said Wilbur and returned to his seat and his whiskey.

Out loud I spoke my thoughts, "We need to talk to Victoria, Jennifer and Ingrid, but when I say "we"—you and I shouldn't. We are the wrong age and gender."

"I quite agree," said Wilbur, "but who then? What's your idea?"

Wilbur knew me too well; I had been thinking about how we approach these young women, "I think we should ask Angela if she would be willing to get involved. She is a well respected defence attorney; a role model for women lawyers in the community, is savvy and, unlike most academics, knows what confidentiality means. I think she would be ideal to meet Jennifer and Ingrid. I checked already, they are both practicing in Flemington. Ingrid is with McMann and Topper and Jennifer is working with Freda Helms doing divorce cases. What do you think?"

Wilbur in his careful manner replied, "I agree. I had been thinking of Angela as well. Do you propose that she also talk to Victoria?"

"No. I suggest that Maria, my student assistant, talk to Victoria just to see Victoria's attitude towards Fraser. Maria is mature, will keep it confidential, and, as we both know, is extremely smart. She also was very close to Allison."

Wilbur was cautious, "I'm not sure about involving a student. We certainly can't tell Maria what we have already found out."

"True, I would pose to Maria that I'd like to know how Fraser's other student assistants felt about him and that she should approach Victoria very carefully and tell her that she is thinking about applying for a research position and was wondering what Fraser was like to work for and would like Victoria's input. And we see what goes from there."

"That is a safe approach, without having to give Maria too much information."

At that moment there was a light triple tap on the door; it was Angela. "Am I interrupting anything?" She said as she opened the door.

"Not at all," said Wilbur, "have a seat."

Angela took the offered seat. She had a ready smile, round face, which looked so innocent for a defence attorney. Her white blonde hair was in marked contrast to her big brown eyes. She confessed to us that she was an "Italian blonde". Her maiden name was Garibaldi.

"A drink?" asked Wilbur.

"I thought you'd never ask." Angela laughed, "A beer would be great." Angela drank little and oddly enough she never had wine. Light beer was her drink of choice. Wilbur kept some in stock just for her and she would regularly replenish it throughout the year. She drank it out of the can.

With beer in hand she proposed a toast, "To the start of another school year. May we all survive. Salute." She then took a swallow and savoured the golden brew.

"How was your class?" I asked.

"Good. They seem like a good bunch, but is it me or them; they seem to be getting younger each year."

"If you think they look young, how do you think we feel?" I responded.

Angela dead panned, "You probably feel old." She was right.

We spent some time talking about the summer and catching up. Angela had gone camping for three weeks in Montana and to her delight had seen a grizzly bear on her hike.

"What would you have done if it had turned on you?" I asked.

"I'd bop the grizzly on the nose," she said feigning a right jab.

"No Angela," I said, "You've got the wrong bear. You do that for black bears--for grizzlies you run like hell."

"Then I'm toast," she laughed, "I'm not a runner."

There was a lull in the conversation and I turned to the subject of Allison, "Angela, you heard about Allison Klassen's death."

"The first year student who committed suicide?"

"Yes."

"I never taught her, but it is such a tragedy. Did you both teach her?" Wilbur and I nodded our heads.

"Angela I want to raise something with you," and I outlined our investigation in our search for a trigger for Allison's suicide. I finished with what we had found out about Ingrid and Jennifer. "Angela we'd like you to talk to them."

Angela did not say anything immediately. "You know I don't know Professor Fraser."

Wilbur responded, "That is one reason we'd like you to talk to the women. You know how to interview people. We trust you will be careful and you have no history with Professor Fraser."

"You'd simply like me to do some probing as to how they were treated by Professor Fraser?"

"That's about it. Please don't tell them why you are making these inquiries. Tell them that it's confidential, which it is. Will you do it? Angela, we think you'd be ideal."

"Andrew, no need to flatter, although it does help. I'd be happy to do it. In fact, there is a women and the law luncheon next week. I'm the local president and I'll check the guest list. If they attend I'll have a quiet word with them; if they haven't signed up I'll invite them. I never taught either woman. Do you have a photograph?"

Wilbur passed her the yearbooks. "He likes blondes doesn't he?" she said without hesitation.

After looking at the yearbooks she turned to us and asked, "What other leads are you following?" This was Angela, the lawyer, speaking.

"I was thinking that I should take Detective Maurice up on his offer of a coffee. He was the detective assigned to the case."

"Ricky?" Angela interjected, "He is a good cop. He was a couple of years behind me at law school." She continued, "When you meet with him ask him about any drug analysis and also any signs of sexual activity. If Allison and Professor Fraser were having a fling then there may well be signs given the weekend away. What about the gap–four years ago? You have no research assistant for that year."

Wilbur answered, "He was on sabbatical that year and had no summer student."

"Where did he do his sabbatical?"

"He taught at a new law school in the Caribbean. I don't know the name off hand."

Angela was now on top of things, "You know you are painting a picture of a serial seducer. He stalks his prey, grooms them, presumably conquers them, and then dumps them. People like that don't take sabbaticals. Might be worth making some inquiries about what he did in the Caribbean."

I volunteered, "I'll look into where he went and we'll go from there." All seemed agreeable.

"When did he join the law school?" she asked.

"Five years ago," I replied.

"Did he teach before he came here? If so–I'd check that out as well."

"I'll do the checking," said Wilbur. "He came from Eastern Law School. I know some of the folks from there. In fact we'll all be at the Association of American Law Schools hiring fair in a few weeks in D.C."

"Good to have you aboard," I said to Angela as we wound up the Friday seminar.

Angela looked at me with a twinkle in her eye, "Happy to help. If the good professor did do something to that young woman to cause her death my feminist side says get a knife and cut you know what off. On the other hand, if he's innocent then he should be cleared, which is my defence side."

"Which side are you on now?" I asked.

"Get me a knife," she laughed.

CHAPTER 11

The excitement of the start of term had waned and the classes had taken on a rhythm of their own. This week we were starting causation in Criminal Law and I began with a mini-lecture. I had already written various terms on the whiteboard, as a memory aid for me and a guide for the students: factual causation, the "but for" test, legal causation, the thin skull rule, reasonably foreseeable, *novus actus, de minimis non curat lex*:

Some crimes are based on conduct alone. A person, who commits the conduct, commits the crime. For example, a person who strikes another commits an assault and the crime is complete. Other crimes require a consequence flowing from the conduct. Assault causing bodily harm is a consequence crime and causation must be proved. The prosecution must prove that the assault caused the resulting bodily harm. So too for murder, which requires that the accused cause the death of a human being.

There is factual causation and there is legal causation. You need both.

Factual causation rests on the "but for" test; but for the actions of the accused, X would not have occurred. But for Tom shooting Harry, Harry would not have died. The problem with factual causation is that it has too long a reach. Consider: but for Fred selling Tom the gun used to kill Harry, Harry would not have died. We have factual causation. Consider further: but for Tom's mother giving birth to Tom, Harry would not have died. We still have factual causation.

Factual causation must be reined in. Limits must be set. We do not want to punish Tom's mother for the sins of her son. This is where legal causation comes into play. In law are we prepared to say that the accused caused the consequence? You will see certain principles applied. There is the "thin skull rule"; you take your victims as you find them. If you use violence on another and that person dies from loss of blood because he is a hemophiliac, do not blame the victim's death on his disease. Or, if you injure a person who is a Jehovah's Witness and the person refused a life saving blood transfusion, do not blame the victim's death on religion. The thin skull rule includes physical, religious and psychological uniqueness. The thin skull rule is essentially–don't blame the victim rule.

Reasonable foreseeability is looked to. How reasonable is it to have foreseen the act that caused death? It is reasonable to foresee that hitting a person over the head and leaving them unconscious in a wheat field in the middle of a cold winter night in Minnesota may well result in the person's death by exposure. Leaving that person in the field in the middle of summer and having them struck by lightning is far less foreseeable.

We also look for *novus actus,* an independent act, which cuts the chain of causation. Should you leave the unconscious person in the wheat field and the farmer comes along, sees the victim, and kills him as a trespasser there is a new independent act. The accused may be guilty of assault, but the farmer's independent act caused the death.

From the above it is apparent that there can be more than one cause of death. We need not look for the sole cause; it is sufficient that the cause is a contributing one. Tom shot Harry and Fred sold him the gun–both caused Harry's death. Causation has a low threshold. All that is required is a contributing cause beyond the *de minimis. De minimis non curat lex* is a common law principle translated: the law is not concerned with trifles. A contributing cause must, therefore, be more than a trifling one.

We then turned to the first case assigned, *Stephenson v. State*. In 1925 D.C. Stephenson was grand dragon of the KKK in Indiana. He was convicted of the murder of Madge Oberholtzer, to whom he was introduced. Subsequently, he invited her to dinner on a couple of occasions. He was interested in her. Miss Oberholtzer was well educated and worked in the library system. In the court decision it was commented by some of the judges that she was a "virtuous woman". Stephenson and two of his lackeys abducted her and she was taken to a compartment on a train bound for Chicago. There she was viciously raped by Stephenson. He didn't just rape her; there were bite marks all over her body and a particularly open wound on her breast. They left the train in Hammond, Indiana for a hotel. Miss Oberholtzer convinced her abductors to let her go to a drug store. There she purchased bichloride of mercury—a poison. When left alone she took the poison and became very ill. Stephenson kept her for two more days and then she was returned to her home and a doctor was called. Stephenson was confident nothing would happen to him. The KKK was powerful at the time in Indiana and, in fact, he said to Miss Oberholtzer that "he was the law in Indiana". A month after the abduction Miss Oberholtzer died. On her death bed she gave a dying declaration where she outlined how she had been abducted, raped and assaulted by Stephenson. The exact cause of death was in doubt; her bite wounds had festered and she was in a weakened condition both from the attack and from the poisoning. At trial Stephenson argued that she died by her own voluntary act; she committed suicide and that he was not responsible. Both the jury and the Supreme Court of Indiana saw otherwise; it was held that her taking of the poison was directly attributable to Stephenson's actions. Therefore, Stephenson was guilty; he had in law caused Miss Oberholtzer's death.

To start the discussion I ask the class whether they agreed with the majority's finding. The hands shoot up, "James, you agree, why?"

"Stephenson said that she died by her own hand. If we accept that I think the majority was right to look at why she took the poison. She did so at a time when she was under the control of the kidnappers and had been viciously raped. There is factual causation: but for the abduction and rape she would not have taken the poison and would not have died."

"What if, she had taken the poison two weeks after the attack when she was at home recovering?"

James hesitated but responded, "I don't think it would matter. So long as you can link the taking of the poison to the attack you would have causation."

"What if it was a year later?"

"I think then the causal link becomes more difficult to prove, but I think it is still there. There are cases where people are injured and never recover, become depressed and kill themselves. The link is still there to the original attack."

"Kayla, do you agree? Will causation still be found one year after the attack?"

"Yes it can. In this case the attack was horrendous. It would have left a lasting scar on anyone."

"What if the attack was not as serious, and believe me I am not minimizing sexual assault, but say the terrible biting did not occur and the repeated rapes did not occur?" More hands went up, "Bridgette."

I was pleased to see Bridgette put her hand up. Normally she was a non-contributor, "The thin skull rule applies. Rape and rape trauma affects people differently. There still is a serious violation of a person and the accused must take his victim as he finds her."

"There was talk in the decision of "a virtuous woman" and it appears that Miss Oberholtzer was a virtuous woman. Does that have any place in our assessment of causation? Brett."

"That was mentioned by the trial judge, but I don't think it would be relevant. Essentially the judge is saying that a virtuous woman would, I suppose, take her virtue more seriously and that the accused would know that. Therefore, it would be more reasonable that he could foresee the possibility that she would be affected more and be more likely to commit suicide."

"Do you agree with that perspective?"

"No I don't. I agree with Bridgette, you take your victims as you find them."

I shifted gears, "The dissenting justices focused on what? Suzy."

"They didn't find proximate cause."

"What does proximate cause mean to you?"

"As far as I see it means the last cause leading to death. They seemed to focus on the final cause and ignored all that went on before. I don't agree with proximate cause and one of our other cases I think overruled that notion."

"We'll be getting to that case shortly. But before we do, I'll give you a brief postscript. In 1925 the KKK was very powerful in Indiana and Stephenson was instrumental in getting the then governor, Ed Jackson, elected and Stephenson fully anticipated that he would receive a pardon. He didn't. The winds of the times were blowing against him and the KKK. Stephenson went on to spend 30 years in prison. His was a sorry case of a person who believed he was above the law. Actually, he had viciously sexually assaulted other women, but had not been brought to justice—so he continued. It took Madge Oberholtzer's death to stop him. Any questions before we move on? Yes Margaret."

"I really don't understand why the other two men involved in the abduction weren't also found guilty of murder. My understanding is that they were acquitted."

"Good question. We will be looking down the road at parties to an offence, but a quick answer is that they may not have known what Stephenson had in mind. It also might be a case of the jury taking aim at Stephenson and letting his lackeys off. Let's move to the next case."

★　★　★

I met with Maria later in the afternoon. She was continuing as my research assistant throughout the term and was doing some research for me on the law of duress. We regularly met for updates. I noticed that Maria was not her usual self. She was down, depressed; her easy smile and laugh were gone. She was taking Allison's death very hard.

"Maria how are you doing?"

Maria sighed, "I'm okay. I have trouble concentrating. I just don't have the drive to get things done."

"Why don't you get away for a few days to refresh and re-energize? The duress research can wait. I won't be able to get to it for a while and you can bank the ten hours per week."

"Thank you. I wish I could take a few days off, but you know what it's like. I'm swamped with reading."

"Maria there's a saying in law school that in first year we scare students to death, in second year we work students to death, and in third year we bore students to death."

Maria made a pained smile, "I'd take boredom right now."

"Okay, I understand that the Canadian law recognizes both common law duress and has a duress statute, which is unique, and there is a recent Supreme Court of Canada decision on duress. I'd like you to research the Canadian law; start with that Supreme Court of Canada decision. But there is no rush, as I've said, bank the hours."

Maria nodded without saying anything. She wasn't the type of person to take time off. I tried. I then decided to raise with Maria about contacting Victoria Palmer, "Do you know Victoria Palmer? She's a third year student."

"Yes, we played on the girl's intramural law soccer team."

"She was also Professor Fraser's research assistant the year before and I was wondering whether you would talk to her. I'd like to know how she found working for Professor Fraser. Is that something you'd be comfortable doing?"

Maria immediately perked up and replied, "Definitely."

I then cautioned Maria, "This must be done carefully and confidentially. As we have discussed before, rumours and innuendo can be devastating. I suggest that you simply tell her that you are interested in a research assistant position next summer and want to know what it was like to work with Professor Fraser."

"I understand completely. Is there anything specific I should ask?" Maria was already ahead of me.

"Yes, ask her if she went to the Winnipeg conference with him and what that was like. Other than that, just see where the conversation goes. Note her reactions. But you must not press her and you must not in any way link your questions to Allison's death. Okay."

"I'll be very careful."

"And this must be kept completely confidential."

"Understood. Have you found anything more about Allison's death?"

I could not tell her the truth; however, I wasn't going to lie, "Maria all I can say is that I'm looking into things, as I promised to you, and that is all I can say at this time."

Maria gave me a penetrating look, paused, and said, "I'll try to talk with Victoria sometime this week."

"I appreciate that, and I do hope that I'm not putting you in a difficult position."

Maria picked up her backpack, "I'll drop by after I've talked to Victoria." She left. She seemed to have more life in her step.

CHAPTER 12

Late in the day on Thursday, I finished my last class and turned to tackle my email inbox. There were seventeen new messages. We are flooded by mindless, time wasting email traffic. The ones I particularly hate are the faintly witty tidbits of worthless information that some colleagues deem to be so important that they send out via an "all staff" email. It took me five minutes to wade through the seventeen emails, all of which I deleted. Next I turned to my voicemail. There was a message from Angela Crindle; it was short and business like: "Andrew, I spoke with Ingrid, I'm meeting with a client shortly. I'll call you tonight. We need to talk. Give me a number where I can reach you. Angela."

Angela doesn't waste time or words. It must be important for her to want to call me. I phoned her back, got her voice message, told her I'd be home, and left my home phone number.

The phone rang shortly after 7:00 in the evening. On the call display, I saw it was Angela's number. I took the phone and headed to the den, "Hi Angela. Are you still at the office?"

"Yes, you've forgotten what it is like to practice law."

"What's up?" I inquired as I sat down in my reading chair.

"Are you sitting down? This might take a while."

"I'm seated in my favourite chair."

Angela continued, "Ingrid was at the luncheon today and we got together after it was over. She told me something very disturbing." She paused for a moment, "I began by asking whether she had heard about Allison Klassen's suicide. She told me that she had and she found it so sad. I then told her that Allison had been a summer research assistant for Professor Fraser. She hadn't known that and I can tell you her face went white and I could see the anger welling in her."

"I decided to be straight with her. I told her that you and Professor Flood were investigating whether there was any connection between Allison's death and a trip that she and Professor Fraser had taken to Winnipeg for a conference a few days before her death. When I told her that she gasped–literally gasped–and then said, and these were her exact words, "That animal. He did it again.""

"Did what?" I asked.

Angela's voice took on a quiet harder tone, "Andrew, Ingrid opened up to me. She told me that Professor Fraser raped her when they were at that same conference in Winnipeg. The same conference!"

"Raped!" I was shocked, "Did she report it?"

"She did and she didn't. She did not go to the Canadian police. You can't blame her; she didn't know who to talk to or their system. She also had been drinking and admitted that she was drunk the night of the rape. She drank too much at the conference hospitality room in the hotel. Professor Fraser then took her back to their hotel. Before going up to her room, they had separate but adjoining rooms, he said that she needed a coffee and they went to the hotel's cafe. She went to the washroom and returned to her coffee. After drinking the coffee she felt sick, light headed and found it difficult to walk and talk. She thinks she was drugged. Professor Fraser took her up to her room and that is where she was raped. Although drugged she still had a sense of what was happening. She couldn't move. It was fuzzy to her, but she was sure she was raped–repeatedly. The next morning, when she woke up, she was in her pyjamas. She didn't remember putting her pyjamas on. She also said she knew she had been raped."

"You said that she did or didn't report it, what does that mean?"

"This is where it gets interesting. She drove back to her home in Wishart, Minnesota on the Sunday. She didn't tell anyone. She thought about what she should do. Remember the conference is the week or two before law school starts. It wasn't until she got back to law school that she reported the rape. She saw Professor Fraser in the hallway and he walked by her as though she didn't exist. She went to Dean Clarke and reported the rape. He asked her to make a full statement, which she did. He also called in the university lawyer."

"That would be Sid Ashter," I interjected.

"Yes, Ashter. She repeated her story. Now get this, Ashter advised her that she was bound by the university policy on sexual assault, which meant that she was not to tell any other person about the allegations other than a university sex assault counsellor. He asked her if she wanted a counsellor and she declined. Andrew... they gagged her. She couldn't talk to anyone. They promised that they would investigate. She waited. A week went by and then, in her words, she was summoned to the Dean's office. Once again, present was the university lawyer, Dean Clarke and a secretary. She said that the meeting was frosty. She was told by Dean Clarke that they took her claim of rape very seriously, had investigated and had spoken to Professor Fraser, who denied any rape and felt aggrieved that she would suggest such a thing. He told them that he had helped her to her room, because she was indeed drunk. That was it. Nothing happened. She was then drilled as to why she hadn't reported the rape. Why she waited almost two weeks until back at law school. The university lawyer warned her about making false complaints and that to do so was defamation. He reminded her that under the policy she was not to say a word about the alleged rape other than to a counsellor. Dean Clarke warned her that a false complaint could lead to expulsion."

Angela paused. She collected her thoughts. "They were browbeating this young woman into withdrawing the complaint. Ingrid was smart enough to see what they were doing. She was told that a hearing would be required and was warned that the faculty association was going to defend Fraser to the hilt. Dean Clarke threw out a life line, perhaps she was mistaken because, after all, she admitted that she was intoxicated at the time. Sid Ashter told her that her claim would be very difficult to prove–speaking as a lawyer. There was no physical evidence, she delayed reporting, and she was intoxicated. The bottom line is that Ingrid withdrew her complaint. She told them that she might have been mistaken because of her state of intoxication. They even had her sign a statement to that effect, which she did."

I was completely blown away by what Angela was telling me. Angela was angry, "How could anyone in this day and age treat a rape victim like they did and then hide behind the university's own sexual assault policy to gag her, which is a policy supposedly there to protect the confidentiality of complainants."

I commiserated with her, "I bet their primary concern was preserving the school's reputation and they conveniently folded when faced by the faculty association pressure. The association terrorizes timid university administrators. Will Ingrid now go to the police?"

"The Canadian police, what's the point? You know as well as I that in the absence of new evidence her case is a tough one. And she sure in heck is not going to make a complaint to the university after how she was treated." Angela continued, "However, she did say that she would cooperate if and only if there is evidence that Allison was raped by Professor Fraser in similar circumstances. For the time being she agreed to let me tell both you and Professor Flood to assist you in your investigation, but that's it. She trusts you and Professor Flood, but she is not prepared to re-open her case or provide anything in writing–at this time."

My weak response was, "Wow, I don't know what to say. I had no idea we'd be finding something like this."

"Andrew, you've been teaching criminal law for a long time and I've been working with criminals for almost ten years now. We both have seen the cesspool of human behaviour. I guess we shouldn't be surprised. Bad people are everywhere."

"Yes, unfortunately they are."

Angela concluded the call, "I'll see you tomorrow. I'll try to meet with Jennifer, but that might have to wait until next week."

"Angela, thank you. Bye." When I hung up, I thought--that bastard. I remained in my chair thinking and in shock. Julie came in.

"That sounded serious," she said as she sat down in my desk chair. That was a cue to tell her about the call. When I was working as a lawyer we rarely talked about my cases, as she knew I was bound by solicitor-client privilege. However, there is no professor privilege. I told Julie what Angela had told me. She didn't say a word; just listened. Julie is a good listener.

When I had ended she asked, "What are you going to do?"

"I know what I'm not going to do; I'm not going to the Dean or the University. They will want to cover this up. If Allison was attacked by Fraser in the same way there is no way they would want this information made public."

"What about going to the police?"

"I do intend to meet with Richard Maurice, the detective assigned to the case, but I'm not sure what he can do. The problem is one of proof. I may think that Fraser did something to Allison, but I need the evidence to prove my case. We need more proof. Also all of this happened in Canada. It's outside his jurisdiction."

"You know as a counsellor at the university I've been involved in a half dozen sexual assault complaints. I don't even know what happened to these complaints. There is a veil of secrecy that descends, which is designed to protect the victims and encourage them to come forward. Instead it ends up protecting the rapists and the university."

She got up to leave, "The one thing is for sure you can't let this go. He'll do it again."

I was left to my thoughts. After a few minutes, I went to my computer and sent an email to Beth Jones in student records:

> Beth, I need to talk to you tomorrow about a very sensitive matter. Let me know when you are free to discuss confidentially. Andrew

Chapter 13

Beth got back to me and was free at noon. Annet would be on lunch at that time and the student records office was closed over the lunch hour. When I got to the student records office the door was already locked. I knocked on the door and Beth came from her desk to open the door.

"Let's go into the record's storage room that way no one will see us talking," she suggested and relocked the door. We went into the inner room in silence.

The sparseness of the room reminded me of the interrogation rooms that I was so familiar with as a prosecutor many years ago. We took chairs across from one another with the bare work table between us. I decided to put on my prosecutor hat. I wanted Beth to talk, but didn't know how comfortable or cooperative she would be to do so.

"Beth, we've known each other for a long time and I'm going to raise with you a very serious matter." She didn't say a word--just nodded.

"I've been looking into Allison Klassen's death. I've spoken to the investigating police officer, Richard Maurice. You remember him, he was a former student." She nodded again--not a word. I wanted her to know that I had spoken to the authorities. "The police investigation shows that Allison committed suicide. What bothered me was why? Why would she kill herself?"

I paused. My approach was to show that I knew a great deal and was simply looking for confirmation from her. "I received information that something may have happened between Professor Fraser and Allison when they were at the Winnipeg conference." I was watching Beth's reaction. There was a blink of uncertainty in her eyes and she was wringing her hands together. I didn't take my eyes off her and continued.

"I also have information that Ingrid Hedberg, Professor Fraser's summer research assistant five years ago made a complaint that she had been raped by Professor Fraser when they attended the same conference that Allison and Fraser attended a few days before she killed herself." Beth bit her lower lip. She again said nothing. She was nervous and flushed.

"My information is that Ingrid met in the Dean's office with the university lawyer, Sid Ashter. She met with them twice and in the second meeting you were present." There was no denial from her. I knew I was right. "Shirley, the Dean's executive secretary, always takes the first few weeks of term off on holidays. She was away and when she's away you fill in for her." No denial.

"In this second meeting the Dean and Sid Ashter convinced Ingrid to withdraw her complaint and a retraction letter was prepared for her to sign. Beth, you prepared that retraction letter." Still nothing from her, but I could see pain in her eyes. I had set the scene; I now needed her to talk.

"Beth, a few days ago you said something to me that stuck with me. We were talking about Professor Fraser and you said, "He's trouble--real trouble." You knew about the past complaint and I also know how much you care about this school and the students. You are like a mother to them. Beth, we need to protect the students. You tell me if I'm wrong. There was an earlier complaint of rape brought by Ingrid Hedberg wasn't there?"

Beth finally spoke. Her eyes were watery. Her voice was weak, "It was so wrong what they did. They didn't want to see Ingrid's complaint go any further. I saw the correspondence from the faculty association to the Dean. They threatened a multi-million dollar lawsuit for defamation. Yes, I prepared the retraction letter. I was told not to give Ingrid a copy. Andrew, I was told by both the Dean and Sid Ashter that all was confidential and under threat of losing my job I was not ever to mention this false complaint. They called it a false complaint. I've kept silent until now. I thought you were up to something when you asked for the past summer research assistants. I can't be drawn into this. I'm a single mother with two kids heading to college and I need the tuition waiver that Flemington provides to its employees. Andrew, I need my job."

I needed to console and re-assure her, "Beth I know I've put you in a difficult position. Believe me I have no intention of going to the university. I do intend to go to the authorities, when I have uncovered all that I need. You're not the whistle blower–I am. We've got to stop Fraser. If I'm right he has raped two of our students and I'm of the view there are more."

Beth looked relieved. I continued to re-assure her, "I want you to know that I'm not alone. Professor Flood and Angela Crindle are working with me. I also know that you will protect the confidentiality of what I've told you today. The university and Fraser must not know anything until the time is right."

"I won't say a word. You know that." She took a deep breath, "Just a moment." She then went to a locked filing cabinet, opened it, and took out a sealed brown letter sized envelope. She handed it to me. There was no marking on the envelope. "I was told by the Dean to put all the relevant papers relating to Ingrid's complaint in an envelope to seal it and return it to him for safe keeping. Dean Alcock would have done that himself, not Dean Clarke. I made a copy and have kept it here for five years. It's yours. I trust you to do something with it, but you can't tell anyone how you got it. I need your word on that."

Beth's hand was shaking when she handed the envelope to me. She continued to wring her hands. "Beth, I promise I won't reveal the source. You've done the right thing."

She wiped her eyes and nodded her head.

"One other thing, do you have the hotel details where Fraser and Allison stayed when they were in Winnipeg?"

"Yes, all expenses for student research assistants are funnelled through me for reimbursement. It will take just a moment." Beth went back into her main office and returned with a file.

"Here it is a receipt for the Artist Hotel in Winnipeg two nights. I'll make you a copy."

She handed me the original to look at: Artist Hotel, Rembrandt 1 & 2. "Do you know what the Rembrandt 1 & 2 mean?" I asked.

"No idea, but it is the Artist Hotel."

"I'll check it out online and see. Thanks Beth." She took the original back, made a copy and brought it back to me. I got up to leave.

Beth said, "You know I'm relieved. I've felt so helpless all these years. Andrew, get him." I gave Beth a quick squeeze of her shoulder and left with the file burning in my hand.

I tried not to run to my office. Instead I walked fast. Once at my office I closed the door and opened the envelope. It contained a detailed statement from Ingrid, a statement from Fraser, who had a faculty lawyer present. I thought how ironic in that the student complainant is unrepresented but the accused law professor has a lawyer. There was an email exchange in which the faculty association lawyer threatened a ten million dollar defamation action. There was a summary of the second meeting, prepared by Beth. And Dean Clarke wrote a self-serving memo painting Ingrid as evasive, confused, and referred repeatedly to her intoxication on the day of the "alleged rape"–his term. We'd gone from "rape" to "alleged rape". The Dean concluded the memo by saying that "after careful consideration" it was his view that Ingrid had made a false complaint. This was a cover your ass memo designed to be referred to years later, to justify his inaction. Finally there was the letter of retraction.

I then searched online the Artist Hotel in Winnipeg. It was a small boutique hotel that, true to its name, had theme rooms that included the artwork of famous artists: Rembrandt, van Gogh, Michelangelo, Dali, Monet and others. Evidently Fraser and Allison were in Rembrandt rooms. My interest was piqued because Ingrid in her statement had mentioned that she and Fraser were staying at the Artist Hotel as well.

The afternoon seminar in Wilbur's office was somber. No drinks. It was a strategy session. I filled Wilbur in on what Angela had told me and I showed him the documents given to me by Beth. Angela arrived and I told her about my meeting with Beth and passed the documents over to her. As she read them, her head was shaking "no—no—no" interspersed with whispered expletives. When finished she looked at the two of us and said, "I can't believe that they treated Ingrid like that. They victimized the victim. They bullied her into a retraction."

"The question is what we do now." I went on, "I still don't think we have the proof and without solid proof I am certain the university will want to bury Ingrid's complaint and bury us for making unfounded allegations in the case of Allison's death."

"Has Maria gotten back to you about Victoria Palmer?" Wilbur asked.

"Not yet."

"And what about Jennifer Cunningham?"

"We're playing voicemail tag," Angela said, "But rest assured I'll talk to her early next week. I do agree with Andy, we need more proof. Also we must keep everything absolutely confidential—no leaks. My suggestion is that it is time for Andy to talk to Richard Maurice off the record. I've dealt with Richard before. He is a straight shooter and will respect confidentiality."

I interjected, "I have a coffee meeting with Richard set for Tuesday late in the day. What do I tell him--suggestions?"

Angela responded, "You've got to give him something to get something in return. I suggest raising with him that you have done some digging and found that Professor Fraser may have been involved with other female students. No more at this stage. But we do need to know about any toxicology results. It would also be helpful to know if there were any signs of sexual activity. He might give you that without requiring us to give him more."

"Should we not ask him to re-open the investigation? He has the expertise and all the resources at his disposal." Wilbur was exploring options.

"I don't think we should," I responded, "we've uncovered disturbing information in our informal, amateur way. I'm really worried about tipping off Fraser. He is clever and manipulative. Surprise is our biggest advantage. I think it best just to feel Richard out. He has his plate full with the recent spate of murders in the city."

Angela agreed with me and Wilbur nodded his approval.

"What about Fraser's sabbatical?" She asked.

I volunteered, "I'll get the university. It was a new law school. I'll get the name."

"No need," Wilbur answered, "Professor Fraser has applied for tenure and promotion. The Dean circulated the notice today. Have you checked your emails this afternoon?"

"I try to avoid checking them," I confessed in a half serious way. "So it is official."

"Yes," Wilbur looked at his computer, "Included with the notice and request for input was Professor Fraser's C.V." Talking out loud he continued, "Let's see. He was on sabbatical at the Caribbean University of Law in Georgetown, Cayman Islands."

"Check out that law school Wilbur. I've never heard of it." said Angela.

Wilbur did some more searching. "Established just six years ago. It is private with an emphasis on preparing students for the practice of law." Wilbur searched a little more, "Nice looking campus, which is located just across the road from Seven Mile Beach. They also have job postings for more law professors. Tell me again, why are we teaching in Northern Minnesota?"

"I volunteer to travel to the Caymans and investigate," Angela chipped in quickly, "Dibs."

"Not so fast," Wilbur was still searching, "I'm checking the American Association of Law Schools website. It seems that the Caribbean University of Law is a member of the AALS and it just so happens that the school will be attending the Association's Faculty Recruiting Conference in two weeks time in D.C. and I will be there as Chair of our Hiring Committee. I can talk to the people from Caribbean at that time."

"Sounds like a plan," I said.

"I still volunteer to travel to the Caymans," pouted Angela.

"What are you going to do with the documents?" Angela was moving on.

"I thought I'd make one copy that is all and then I'll put one in my safety deposit box and secure the other in my den. Julie is the only other person who knows my hiding place."

"I've seen your den. No one could find anything in that room," laughed Wilbur.

I changed topic and showed them the receipt from the Artist Hotel, "This is the receipt for Fraser and Allison's stay in Winnipeg–the Artist Hotel. That's the same hotel that Ingrid mentioned in her statement. Fraser uses the same hotel. I think it worth a trip to Winnipeg to see what is what. It's not the Cayman Islands to be sure, but Julie and I have been looking for a short weekend trip and I've not been to Winnipeg for years. Your thoughts?"

"I think you should go," Angela was quick to agree, "It can't hurt. Besides you get Winnipeg and I get dibs on the Caymans." She laughed.

"When will you go?" asked Wilbur.

"I was thinking the same weekend you are in D.C."

"Check with the night staff in reception, in any restaurant and check to see about surveillance cameras." Angela was back in her defence attorney frame of mind.

"I've never been to Winnipeg," said Wilbur, "I've travelled the world, five continents, but never to our Northern neighbor. Strange isn't it? How long is the drive?"

"Four to five hours, about that," I replied and continued, "one other thing I've been pondering. Angela, do you know Mark Labros?"

"Oh yes, Mark and I have worked on a few criminal cases. He's good."

"He also is a very close friend of the Klassen's. He gave the eulogy at Allison's funeral. I'd like to bring Mark into the loop. We will need to get the Klassen's onside with what we are doing. Perhaps not right now, but maybe soon. Mark would be a perfect liaison. What I propose at this time is an off the record conversation. I think we can trust Mark, but want both of your input."

My suggestion was met by silence. Wilbur then spoke, "Mark sued the university last year didn't he?"

"Yes, and that is partly why I'd like to approach Mark. He knows the university administration. He knows the university. I also believe that he will keep everything we tell him confidential."

Angela helped me out, "Mark is a person of integrity. I trust him completely. We've had a couple of dealings where confidential information was exchanged and he was true to his word not to disclose. I can't say that about too many other prosecutors or defence attorneys in town. We also are going to need the family's support. I think we should fill him in. Get his view. He has a good trial lawyer's mind."

Angela paused and then continued, "I'm also concerned about confidentiality. Correct me if I'm wrong, but I don't think either of you are licensed to practice law. Right? Well there is no such thing as 'professor-client' or 'professor work product' privilege. A wise course would be to have Mark hire you as his unpaid investigative assistants. I only do criminal law so the courts would in all likelihood reject my claim of privilege through you, but Mark has sued the university. He does civil litigation."

Angela was right. We needed the protection of some form of privilege.

"You are quite correct," said Wilbur, "What about the information we have already uncovered? What about Beth's documentation? Is it protected? Andy you're the evidence Prof."

"I doubt that it would be protected," I conceded, "However, without a lawyer involved we would not have any hope of keeping it protected. If Mark does hire us as investigative assistants, then we have a good shot at least initially to keep the information and our sources privileged under the work product rule–information gathered by a lawyer or party in contemplation of litigation is protected. Since none of us would be a party to the litigation, we need a lawyer directing our gathering of evidence."

"You've convinced me," said Wilbur, "I've always liked Mark. When can you talk to him?"

"I'll try and set up a meeting in the next few weeks. Let me see how my meeting with Richard goes."

We adjourned. The Friday afternoon seminar had turned into a war council.

CHAPTER 14

Julie was up for a road trip. On the weekend, I went to the Artist Hotel's website. The hotel was listed at 3.5 stars touting its character, friendly staff and downtown Winnipeg location. I phoned the hotel directly because I wanted a Rembrandt room. The reservation receptionist was indeed friendly and accommodating. We booked into Rembrandt 1, which I was told was the nicer and larger of the Rembrandt rooms. Rembrandt 2 was an adjoining room.

On Monday I had a meeting with Maria. She looked perkier, more energized. First we discussed the duress research; she provided me with a summary of the recent Supreme Court of Canada case.

I then asked Maria about whether she had spoken to Victoria Palmer. She had.

Maria took a moment to collect her thoughts, "I arranged to meet her in one of the library work rooms and I told her that I was thinking of applying for a summer research assistant position with Professor Fraser, as we discussed. Since she had summered for him two years ago I asked her how he was to work for. She told me that his research wasn't that interesting and that he was ok. Would she recommend him as a supervisor? She didn't say anything, so I threw in that Allison had said that at times she was uncomfortable working for him. That struck a nerve. She said that uncomfortable was the right word. And I asked her to help me out, what did that mean."

Maria continued, "She said that he seemed too interested in her at times. He never did anything inappropriate; it was more of a feeling—a vibe—an uncomfortable vibe."

"Did you ask her about going to Winnipeg for the legal conference?"

"Yes, but she said that she really didn't remember much."

"That's odd. Why?"

"I asked her the same thing. She said that on the Saturday night she must have had too much to drink because she doesn't remember anything after the conference supper. She woke up in her hotel room Sunday morning. That's it. She did say that she has never blacked out before."

"Was her hotel at the conference sight?" I asked.

"No. She was staying at some artist hotel downtown and the conference was at a suburban hotel."

"Did she know how she got to her hotel room?"

"No."

"Did Professor Fraser take her back?"

"She doesn't remember."

Maria was somewhat downcast, "Sorry not much for you."

"Don't be sorry," I consoled, "she told you what she remembers."

"Is there anything else I can do?"

"Well, Professor Fraser is applying for tenure and promotion and student input is requested. You can pass the word along to the students that their views do matter."

"I'll do that; I'm on the law student council and will raise that with the executive."

"Thanks Maria for doing this. Let's meet again in two weeks to go over the duress research. Same time?"

"Sounds good."

After Maria left I prepared a memo outlining the conversation. Although there was nothing concrete. It was interesting that the same hotel was used by Fraser and that Victoria's story was consistent with being drugged—or yes drunk.

Later in the day I got a call from Angela. She had spoken with Jennifer Cunningham. "Andy, I finally met with Jennifer. I dropped in to see her at her office."

"And, anything?"

"Well I can tell you she doesn't like Professor Fraser at all. In her words, "he is bad news stay away from him.""

"Did she go to the Winnipeg conference?" I asked.

"Yes, but she wouldn't talk about it. She told me point blank that she wasn't going to talk about the conference. I told her that Allison had gone to Winnipeg with him."

"How did she react to that?"

"She sighed and simply said, "Poor girl—that pig". That's all she would say. Andy something happened to her in Winnipeg, but she is not able or not willing to talk about it."

"How did you leave the conversation?"

"I asked her to keep everything confidential and thanked her for her time. No doubt she's hiding something."

"That doesn't help us does it?" I said in exasperation.

"No. On the other hand she never said that all was rosy working with Professor Fraser did she?"

I filled her in on my conversation with Maria and what she had found out from Victoria Palmer.

"Well Andy, we are on the right track. Got to go."

I thanked Angela and returned to my thoughts. Jennifer was acting in exactly the same way as Victoria. I agreed with Angela, something happened to her. It was up to us to prove the something.

The next day after work I cycled my way south to Piccolini's Coffee Shop, where I was going to meet with Detective Maurice. A strong north wind pushed me along. Winter was in the air; it was a reminder of the colder weather to come.

Piccolini's was an old student haunt. It was a converted ice cream parlour—out with the ice cream and in with coffee. Everything about it had a student touch. The tables were old wooden bench tables. Carved into them were graffiti from generations past. The wooden floor creaked and protested each step. The shop wasn't dingy; it was homey.

I locked my bicycle in the stand out front and ordered a cappuccino mug. I was a few minutes early and I took a table by the window, which basked in the late afternoon sun. I absorbed its rays like a turtle on a rock. At precisely 4:00 Detective Maurice arrived. He entered did a quick glance around the room, saw me and went to the counter to order. He had a policeman's eye; I could tell that in his quick casing of the room he had observed all. With coffee in hand he walked over, a policeman's walk, confident and sure.

"Good to see you Richard. I knew you'd be on time so I already ordered."

"Good to see you Professor and you give me too much credit for being on time."

"This place has a lot of memories for me," he said as he took his seat, "I used to study here when I was going to law school. I sat over there in the corner." He pointed to the back corner. "I'd order an extra large coffee and study for three hours at a time. The owner, Luigi put up with me. He also knew I was a cop; it helped. Good memories."

"Well the coffee must have helped. You did pretty darn well at law school."

"Had to--the pride of the police force was on the line," he smiled.

"I've read about the murders in town. Must be keeping you busy."

"Yes. Most are gang turf killings. Not that it matters, but when we see the victims they aren't particularly innocent folks. We're trying to clamp down on the gangs, but once they get established it's hard to break their grip."

Richard then paused, took a sip of coffee, looked at me and asked, "And what can I do for you?"

He was getting right to the point. I decided to do the same, "Allison Klassen's suicide. When we last chatted at the funeral you said that you were waiting for toxicology results. Can you share with me, did the toxicology tests turn up anything?"

Richard took another sip of coffee, "No, Allison was clean, no drugs. No alcohol in her system when she died. Any reason you have this continued interest in Allison's death?"

Honesty was the best response. "It has been bothering me. Why would she kill herself? So I have been doing some digging." I decided to give him some more information. "You know that she killed herself two days after returning from a law conference in Winnipeg?"

Richard nodded.

I went on, "Before I continue, what I'm about to tell you is off the record and confidential. Is that alright with you?"

"Agreed," said Richard.

"I think something happened in Winnipeg. Strange that she never contacted anyone after returning from the conference. Allison went there with Professor Jerome Fraser. I've looked into it, over the last five years Professor Fraser has attended that conference four times. Each time he has taken his summer research assistant. Each was female. Each was blonde." Richard was listening intently.

"One of the students complained that she was drugged and raped by Professor Fraser when in Winnipeg." That caught his attention. "The university did nothing. One of the other women says that she blacked out, which is consistent with being drunk or drugged. And the third student simply will not talk about what happened in Winnipeg. Richard I think Allison was attacked by Professor Fraser in Winnipeg, but I can't prove it–yet."

"The student who says that she was raped, did she go to the police in Winnipeg?"

"No. Would you? Strange city. Strange country. She reported it to the university and they basically forced her to recant."

"You know that this is outside my jurisdiction?"

"Yes and no," I replied, "Yes the rapes may have occurred in Canada, but do you remember the Stephenson case from Criminal law; he was the Klu Klux Klan leader in Indiana."

"Yeah–the guy who abducted a woman, took her on a train, attacked her and bit her all over, and then she tried to kill herself. Your criminal cases are forever etched in my memory never to be forgotten."

"That's the one," I carried on, "In that case the attacks all occurred within Indiana, but what if the attack had not occurred until the train got to Chicago. Let me ask you this, she died in Indiana. Even if the attacks that led to her death occurred in Illinois, wouldn't you accept that Indiana had jurisdiction because of where she died?"

"So what you are saying to me is that if Allison was attacked in Canada and that led to her death here in Minnesota it is my homicide."

"That's what I'm saying."

Richard worked on his coffee. He was thinking, "Wow the link between Winnipeg and the suicide would be tough to prove. It would be so much easier proceeding with rape or sexual assault charges in Canada. I know some detectives in the City of Winnipeg Police Service and in the RCMP. The other student would have to make a complaint for sure."

"Not going to happen. She has been through too much. She also knows that it was five years ago, she didn't immediately report the rape, she had been drinking and then there is the subsequent recantation. She is not going to proceed, unless we find something more about what happened to Allison."

"Do you want me to interview Professor Fraser? He wasn't there when I was at the law school. I could, as part of Allison's suicide investigation, at least talk to him."

"I'd prefer that you didn't. Professor Fraser is smart. Right now what I am doing is under his and the university's radar and I want to keep it that way. I promise that once I have more proof I will come to you. But right now there is no case. I'm telling you that as a former prosecutor."

"What do you want from me then?" Richard knew that I called this meeting for a reason.

"Information," I said. "I'm looking for information that you are free to give and some indirect assistance, once again, that you are free to give."

"What information?"

"Well you already told me about the toxicology results. That is helpful. Would it be possible for me to talk to the medical examiner who did the autopsy?"

Richard thought for a moment, "Yes, but you'll need the parent's permission. You talk to the Klassens and if they want access to the medical examiner I'll see that you get it."

"Sounds fair. I'll contact them."

"Anything else?"

"Could you contact the Winnipeg police and ask them about The Artist Hotel on Portage Avenue in Winnipeg. That is where Professor Fraser always stays in Winnipeg." Richard wrote it down.

"Julie and I are traveling to Winnipeg next week. We're going to stay at the Artist Hotel and see what we see."

Richard responded, "I'll contact a detective I know well in Winnipeg and give him a heads up that you are coming. He might be able to help if needed. I'll check with him and get back to you." He went on, "I'll also run a check on Professor Fraser in our system. What was his first name again?"

"Jerome."

Richard closed his notebook, put his pen away, and finished his coffee, "I appreciate what you're doing professor, but you need to be careful and you need to respect the line when we need to take over. Please keep me in the loop."

"Thanks Richard. This is delicate. I promise to keep you in the loop. I'll get back to you after talking with the Klassens."

Richard gave me a long look, put out his hand, "Got to go. It has been an interesting conversation."

I agreed. He headed to his car and I headed to my bicycle.

CHAPTER 15

When I got home after meeting with Richard I emailed Mark Labros and asked for thirty minutes of his time. Mark replied within the hour. He was free the next day at 5:30. We'd meet at his firm's new office downtown.

As I drove to downtown I was going against the afternoon rush hour traffic. Flemington may not be that big, but rush hour it had. I didn't miss for a moment the commute downtown. I recall it provided an excuse to stay late in order to avoid the peak traffic. The result was that 11-12 hour days became the norm.

Mark's firm recently had taken a lease in one of Flemington's oldest office buildings. The Henderson Building was built in the glory days of the 1920's. Craftsmanship and quality adorned the facade. The intricacy of the masonry work could not be duplicated these days; functional pre-cast concrete would be used instead. The building had been saved from demolition a few years before and a local entrepreneur took up the challenge of restoring the building. It is said that he bought the building for one dollar and had an arrangement with the city that for every one million dollars he put into the building the city would provide tax forgiveness for one year. The rumour is that he put ten million into the building. Mark's firm was one of his first tenants.

I entered the grand foyer. An ornate tin ceiling reflected the afternoon sun through the high oval peep hole windows, which I was certain were designed precisely to capture those late day rays of light. The entire west wall had six large windows with half moon toppers. The floors were white and black marble—original but polished and finished to glisten. The foyer resonated strength and security. I stood in admiration. We in America live in a society that is too functional, too prepared to discard the past for efficiency. I thought of the great cities of Europe where the character, history and glory of the past is cherished and preserved.

Mark's office was on the sixth floor. The elevator actually still had the secondary gate to be pulled across. In days gone by a doorman would have been on duty. When I got to the sixth floor I followed the directional sign for Theopold, Stenson and Labros. Mark had made partner. The massive walnut door led to a comfortable reception area and seated behind a dark mahogany desk was a very young receptionist. She was smartly dressed, but in a casual, comfortable sort of way.

"Hello, I'm Andrew Sturgis to see Mark Labros."

She smiled, "I'll ring Mr. Labros and let him know that you are here."

After calling Mark, she asked if I'd like a coffee or water. I declined, "You're putting in a late day." I said.

"Oh, not really, I'm a student at Flemington College. I just work the end of day shift from four to six. It works out great, I have to bus downtown anyway after class and yet I still have evenings free."

I was the only person in the waiting room and commented on how quiet it seemed. In my experience in the law the work day rarely ended before the early evening hours.

She smiled again. I could see that smiling came easily to her, "This firm is different. Our staff generally finishes at 4:30 and some are on flex hours."

"Now that is refreshing to hear," I replied. At that moment a side door opened and Mark appeared.

"I trust that Margaret has taken good care of you. Sorry I had a phone call."

"She has taken good care of me indeed."

"Coffee, tea, water?"

"No thank you, Margaret already asked. Mark what a lovely building. When did you move in?"

"Just three months ago. We have yet to turn our minds to a grand opening. It is a beautiful building; do you have time for a quick tour?"

"Love to, but do you have time?"

"I certainly do."

Mark then took me through the office space. Each room was carefully decorated to reflect the history of the building. He first showed me a staff lounge. There was a big screen television hidden behind a wood panelled wall. The room had a fabulous view of the Kocheta River.

"This is our library," Mark said half laughing.

"Really, it looks like a lounge to me."

"No it is our library," he replied. "We decided that we didn't need a law firm library. In this day and age all primary reports are online and many secondary reports. Each lawyer can access them from his or her desk." He then went to the inner wall, pressed on the wood panels and two large doors opened out to reveal a wall of shelves that contained legal text books. "These are the texts that we cannot get on line. We only keep the most updated editions. One of the lawyers is in charge of purchasing, which isn't much of a burden, as we have standing orders with the main legal publishers. When a new edition comes in, a memo is circulated should one of the lawyers like to keep the outdated edition in their office. If we don't hear anything the outdated copy is shredded."

"Yes, the era of the book is under peril," I lamented, "but it certainly saves you space."

"The room is flexible--staff room, lounge, boardroom and library."

Mark then took me through the offices. The three partners had slightly larger offices, but nothing like the grandeur of days gone by. Mark's was at one end of the office hallway. There were ten offices in total. All had views of the city and river. Away from the exterior, the inner space had the reception area, some storage, the photocopier, and main computer terminal. There was also a board room and two other smaller meeting rooms. This allowed for smaller offices; meetings with four or more people could adjourn to the meeting rooms. There was an office work room for staff; although it was not on the outer wall there was a glass opening at the top of the wall which allowed for light to flow in from the "library". All was spacious and comfortable.

Throughout the tour we ran into only one other lawyer, a new associate, who had joined the firm a few months before. He was from Flemington, but had gone to the University of Minnesota for his law degree.

With the tour complete, we returned to Mark's office. He adorned his desk and walls with photos of Jane and daughter Amy; he was a proud husband and father. We sat down in leather wing back chairs separated by a round mahogany coffee table.

I had to ask, "Mark, where is everybody?"

He laughed, "We are a small firm and we look at things a little differently. Jeff, Mary and I, when we decided to move to this space had a good sit down. All of us are fairly young. We all have young families and we all make a good living. We decided that we can make a comfortable living working civilized hours. Life balance is the phrase. We have five associates. They all work on salary, and yes, bonuses are paid as incentives. We do not have fixed billable hour targets. In fact we often enter into fixed fee arrangements with clients. We are experienced enough to estimate the time and effort on files and we give the clients benchmarks in terms of our costs. We encourage all of our lawyers and staff to keep regular hours. I remember when I first started out I felt I couldn't go home until the last partner left. Those were long days. Here we rarely are around after six. Sure when in a trial late nights are the norm."

"I'm impressed. There are so many burnout and mental health issues within the profession these days."

"True, we decided on a different path and so far it has been working well. You know most lawyer partners are the product of their environment; ridiculous hours, billable hour pressure, and so they spend years in the legal sweatshop. When they reach partner they know no better and the cycle continues. Do they have a life? No. Do they have money? Yes. I'll take a little less money in order to have more of a life."

Mark changed the subject, "Now you wanted to pick my brain. Usually I want to pick yours."

I began, "Yes, first what I am about to tell you is confidential. In fact, can I retain you for a dollar to be my lawyer?" I took a dollar bill out of my wallet.

Mark laughed, "You have retained a lawyer. I'm cheap."

Over the next twenty minutes I carefully outlined what I had found about Allison Klassen's death. Mark listened. He took no notes and only occasionally asked questions for clarification. He knew I had command of the facts and would not ramble as many clients do.

"That's it," I ended.

Mark's face was grave. This was personal to him. "So you are looking to continue investigating?"

"Yes, Julie and I are going to Winnipeg next weekend. I've already booked in at the Artist Hotel."

"You know that there is a potential lawsuit against not only Professor Fraser but the university as well?"

"Yes, but I don't think there is enough evidence right now. We have suspicions, even strong suspicions, but no direct evidence of Fraser attacking Allison in Winnipeg."

"I agree with you. You mentioned talking to the medical examiner and that would require the Klassen's approval."

"Yes and that is one of the reasons I came to you. I'd like you to help me get the Klassen's approval. You know them. They trust you. You are their friend."

"Actually, Jane, Amy and I are traveling home to see the folks this weekend. We're giving Megan Klassen a ride home as well. I'm going over there Saturday afternoon around 2:00 for a visit. Can you make it? I think it would be important for you to be there."

I did a quick calculation. Julie and I were going to close up our summer cottage on the weekend, but that only took a day and could wait until Sunday. "I can make it," I said.

"Good, I think as well that we should only say that you have been looking into Allison's death, trying to find out if something happened in Winnipeg. Right now we don't have solid evidence and I wouldn't want the Klassens to be tormented by things that may never have occurred."

"I agree with you completely."

"I will get them to retain me to investigate Allison's death. My retainer will be at this stage one dollar."

"Sounds good. Now I'm also concerned about my role and protecting the information I uncover. I cannot be a party, nor can Wilbur and Angela; however, I was thinking that you could hire us as investigative assistants. That way any and all information could be protected by work product privilege. What are your thoughts?"

Mark tapped his finger on the arm of his chair. "It makes sense. To tell you the truth I'm a little concerned about having amateurs investigate. Don't take offence."

"None taken, it's true."

"But in your case, all of you are familiar with the law and have quite frankly found out a great deal of information. Secrecy, as you say, is critical." He was thinking aloud, "We do need to protect that information. Yes, hiring you all makes sense. I will prepare a short retainer letter advising that you are working on my behalf in support of my client, the Klassens, to investigate Allison Klassen's death. I could email that to you."

"Mark, I'd prefer there is no email trail. You mentioned a lawsuit against the university and we all work for the university. Could you prepare that document right now, make copies and I'll get Wilbur and Angela to sign?"

Mark didn't hesitate, "I'll do it right now."

"Also, we can't be paid. Any outside employment has to be reported to the university. Pro bono work is not covered."

He got up went to his computer and started typing. I sat taking in the view. The sun was very low in the sky; it was after 6:30. The water in the river sparkled reflecting the late day light. In a few minutes Mark had a draft done.

The "Hiring Agreement" was subject to approval by the Klassens. It was limited to the investigation of Allison Klassen's death, and it was on a pro bono basis pending completion of the investigation. I read it over, "That is perfect." Mark made four copies. I signed one and returned it to him. "I'll get Angela and Wilbur to sign on Friday."

Mark nodded, "You know I've been troubled by Allison's suicide. Depressed might be a better word. It hurt. I couldn't help but blame her for hurting all of us. Now I'm starting to think that there was far more to it. If Professor Fraser hurt Allison I promise I will get him. He will pay and the university will pay. I feel better that we are doing something. Thank you for coming to me."

"Mark I feel exactly the same. I'll see you on Saturday. What's the address?"

"Drop by my family's place. You'll see a sign post, Labros Ranch, on the west side of the road. It is eighteen miles north of Stanthorpe on Highway 37. I'll give you my cell number in case you get lost."

Mark walked me to the door. Margaret had left. We shook hands. It felt very good to have Mark Labros on board.

CHAPTER 16

Our Friday seminar was less somber than the week before. Angela brought a six pack of light beer and we toasted her munificence. I started by summarizing my meeting with Richard. He had sent me the contact details of the detective in Winnipeg. His name was Arno Semchuk, Detective Constable with the Winnipeg Police Service.

"Andy what exactly are you looking for in Winnipeg?" Wilbur asked.

"I honestly don't know. But it is always helpful to go to the scene."

Angela added, "Perhaps the most critical thing is video surveillance. You have the date and can zero in on the times. You might need detective Semchuk to help you."

"I've already arranged to meet with the manager of the hotel and coffee shop cafe at the hotel. He seems like an obliging type. When I told him that I was following up on a student who had died a few days after returning from staying at the Artist hotel I think he was afraid that we were looking to sue him for food poisoning or something. I had to reassure him that it was a suicide. He seemed relieved. I also intend to speak to the night shift workers. He told me that he has a small staff and the two on duty when we are there were on shift when Allison was at the hotel."

The conversation then turned to the three students who attended the conference with Fraser in past years. Angela was of the view that Ingrid was our key witness, "If we can show her that there is a case being built involving Allison I think Ingrid can then be persuaded to join the action. Once we get Ingrid then we go back to Jennifer and Victoria."

"What we need is proof of an assault upon Allison–that is crucial–and right now we don't have that." Wilbur reminded us.

"We'll get it. We are getting close. We just keep digging." I said encouragingly, Angela and Wilbur nodded in agreement. I continued, "Let me tell you about my meeting with Mark Labros." I brought out the hire agreements. "Mark has agreed to take the case. He and I are going to meet with the Klassens tomorrow. Mark is going to Stanthorpe to visit his folks and we are getting together with the Klassens. In advance of that meeting Mark prepared this hire agreement for you to sign." I handed them the agreement. "I've already signed."

After looking at the agreement Angela asked, "What's the extent of Mark's agreement with the Klassens?"

"He only wants them to agree to have him conduct an investigation. In fact, Mark doesn't want to tell the Klassens all the details of what we have found. He feels, and I think he's right about this, that we don't need to raise with the Klassens our suspicion that Fraser assaulted Allison. Rather, he'd like simply to limit the retainer to investigating whether something happened in Winnipeg."

"I'm glad to hear that. The Klassens have been through enough," said Wilbur, as he signed the agreement. "I won't give up my day job given my pay as an investigator," he quipped.

"I'm glad that Mark is supporting us. I feel much relieved to be working with a law firm. It gives us much more protection. Do you have some of Mark's cards?" Angela signed the agreement and returned it to me.

"Nope, I'll ask him for some on the weekend."

Silence descended upon the three of us. Just at that moment there was a knock on the door, Gwen had arrived. She opened the door without waiting for an invitation and called out, "G'day mates!"

We all welcomed Gwen. She was away for three weeks or more having travelled home to deliver a paper at an Australian university.

"When did you get back?" I inquired as I moved a chair for her to sit on.

"Two days ago. I needed a day to recover from the flight and this is my first day back." Gwen looked around, "I was thirsty so I figured I'd drop in here."

"Angela kindly brought us some beer. Would you like one?" Wilbur was ever the host.

"That would be grand indeed."

Wilbur got a beer from the fridge, "Anyone else? There is more. I've had a few chilling for a while."

"I'll have another Wilbur, but two is my limit," I said.

Wilbur shot back, "I'd cut you off at two. I don't want you falling off your bicycle."

Angela declined. She was nursing her one drink as she usually did.

"Have I missed any juicy gossip since being away?" asked Gwen.

"The Dean married a goat, but we're not sure that is legal in Minnesota." Wilbur deadpanned.

Without missing a beat Gwen replied, "I could see him going for a goat, although I'd a thought he'd be more interested in a donkey given that he's an ass."

"Fraser has formally applied for tenure and promotion," I threw in.

"Yes, I saw that. When is the deadline for sending in our comments?"

"I think the first week of October," I said.

"Will it make any difference?" asked Angela.

"I'm afraid that it probably won't. I was visited the other day by the Associate Dean. She was acting as a messenger ensuring that we all knew of Jerome's application and the October deadline." Wilbur took a sip of beer and continued, "But there was more to it. It was obvious that she was going around drumming up support for him."

"Do you think she was Dean Clarke's messenger?" I asked.

"The Associate Dean doesn't take a crap without the Dean's permission," Gwen gave her opinion.

Wilbur, being Wilbur, was more diplomatic, "I would think that she was acting on instructions from the Dean."

"Why would he support Fraser's application?" Gwen asked.

"I think he's afraid of Fraser," I said. "Remember Clarke is an administrator first and foremost and they look for the path of least resistance. If Fraser were to be denied tenure and promotion he will appeal and that will be very messy for the Dean. Hold your nose and pass him is the easier course of action and he wants to head off strong opposition from other faculty members."

"Hold your nose and pass, that should be our school's motto," Gwen said in a tone of disgust.

We were not going to solve the ills of legal education, but venting helped. We finished our beers and adjourned.

Chapter 17

The day was grey, drizzly rain interspersed with squalls blowing in from the west. It was a depressing day. I took solace, it could have been worse; it could be snowing. This was the type of day where you find a good book, snuggle up in a comfy arm chair by the fire and read trying to escape from the dreariness outside.

I was nearing Stanthorpe about to turn north on Highway 37 to the Labros Ranch. I set my trip odometer–eighteen miles to the destination. The fields had been harvested. The brown fields of barley and wheat and yellow fields of canola returned to black soil. The entire region seemed to be in waiting for the approaching winter.

I saw the Labros Ranch sign and turned on to the gravel road leading to the farm house. The house was a typical white clad two story with a veranda porch extending along the entire length of the front. Spruce trees combined with willows circled the yard as a wind break. A tool storage shed, red barn and a row of granaries were built on the perimeter. Farm equipment found places next to many of the buildings. There was order in the disorder; this was a working farm.

I parked the car next to a Ford 150 truck and Dodge Caravan. I assumed the Caravan was Mark's; anyone with a family needed a van. As I closed the door the ubiquitous farm dog emerged from the barn. Not much of a guard dog, a bit late off the mark. The dog was a mixed breed, probably part collie, retriever, and German shepherd all in one. He was an old dog. Telltale white fur marked his face and his gait was slow and deliberate; his back legs swayed a tell tale sign of hip problems. He made his way towards me barking as he approached. The wagging of his tail belied a gentle disposition–all bark and no bite. He came up to me and I asked him how he was doing. No answer, but he looked up and I scratched him behind his ears. We became close friends.

I heard the door open and Mark came out, "Ben is not much of a guard dog. He is more like the official greeter. Welcome to the Labros Ranch."

"Nice to be here," I said.

"Come on in and meet the family." I went up the wooden steps to the porch and inside. The house was warm with smells of baking. Mr. Labros was a bear of a man: big, bearded and well weathered. His handshake was as strong as was his voice. Mrs. Labros surprised me. I had expected a plump hausfrau wrapped in an apron. Instead Mrs. Labros was demure, slim and dressed in a track outfit.

She extended her hand and introduced herself, "Helen. Sorry for greeting you like this Professor," she said, "I just finished my aerobics class." She shook my hand; there were no false kisses on the cheek in this part of the world. I could see that although small in stature she had real strength.

"Please call me Andy; I'm so pleased to meet you."

"Mark has told us a great deal about you. You seem to have been Mark's favourite professor at Flemington."

"Kind of him to say, but I think he says that about all of us at Flemington."

She gave me a sideways look and with a sly smile replied, "Not all."

Jane came into the hallway. We had met before. She was holding Amy, who wanted down.

"Hello Jane. I see that you have a handful."

"Yes, this is Amy, aka our one year old terror."

"Hello Amy." She immediately hid her face in her mother's shoulder.

Helen asked, "Would you like to come in for a coffee or tea?"

Mark interjected, "Sorry mom I told the Klassens two o'clock and you know that Mrs. Klassen will have something prepared."

"You're right, perhaps when you get back."

Mark took charge, "Why don't we walk over now. It has stopped raining. We'll take the long way and chat." Mark put on his leather jacket and boots and guided me out the door.

"Nice to meet you all," I said as I turned round to leave.

We walked down the gravel road towards the highway. Ben joined us. We huddled against the wind.

"Sorry about rushing you out, but I didn't want you to be subjected to cross-examination by my mother. She'd be curious about why you came and believe me she can be tenacious. No mercy would be shown."

"No problem," I said. "How do you want to raise the topic of Allison? It won't be easy."

Mark was thoughtful in his response, "I'm going to be straight with them. They are honest, direct people and deserve that from me. We'll get comfortable and I'll raise Allie. As we discussed, I'll tell them that you have done some investigating and have some concerns. Focus on Allie's return from Winnipeg and your concern that something may have happened to her in Winnipeg. We'll go from there. They respect you and the fact that you came today will mean a great deal to them. They are still grieving and to be honest I really don't know if they will agree to us investigating. We'll see."

We turned south and walked along the highway for about one hundred yards. Ben abandoned us and returned home. We then turned down another gravel road. There was a wooden home-made bus shelter; it resembled an outhouse or, to be charitable, a guardhouse. There was a window looking north, which was the bus lookout window. The shelter could use a coat of paint and grass and weeds were taking over. It was obvious the shelter was no longer being used.

The gravel road had a barb wire fence along its north side hidden behind a row of poplar trees. To the south there was a row of spruce trees acting as sentinels. The road curved to the south to the farmhouse. It was a one story farm bungalow, had an enclosed porch, and vaulted roof. The house was finished by cedar siding. The siding was well preserved. If cedar is left to the elements it turns grey and you might as well have used spruce. This siding still had a rich golden texture.

Our boots crunched on the gravel. Mark was filling in the walk by talking about the farms. The Klassens were third generation farmers. They owned a full section and a half and rented at least another section. Half of the acreage was in wheat, another quarter was in canola, and the remainder was pasture. Mark thought they had fifty to seventy-five head of cattle. The farm was meticulous, far more ordered than the Labros Ranch. There was a large equipment storage building, a barn and row of granaries. The equipment must be in the storage building as it was nowhere to be seen. A flower garden rimmed the house. At this time of year the yellow, russet, and bronze mums provided a splash of colour to brighten an otherwise dreary day.

We walked up the porch steps. No dog to be seen. The front door opened. The Klassens were waiting and saw us coming. Mrs. Klassen filled the doorway, "Hello Mark. Hello Professor. Welcome. Welcome."

Mark gave Mrs. Klassen a hug, and I took Mrs. Klassen's hand in both of mine, "Mrs. Klassen, please call me Andy."

"And you must call me Doreen; Mrs. Klassen makes me feel too old."

"It's a deal."

Mr. Klassen arrived, "Nice to see you again, Professor – er Andy, Fred."

"Fred, my pleasure," we all shook hands. Mark had his arm around Fred's shoulder.

Megan arrived. "Megan, you remember Professor Sturgis," said Doreen.

"Nice to see you again Megan," we nodded at each other. Mark gave Megan a playful hug. He was a part of the Klassen family.

Doreen led us into the kitchen. She had indeed prepared something for us. "Have a seat, fresh coffee is brewed and I made a pumpkin pie this morning."

"Made with real pumpkin?" Mark asked mischievously.

"You know better than that Mark Labros. Of course, it is made with real pumpkin."

"Everyone want ice cream?" asked Megan.

It was unanimous. We all did.

Coffee was poured. Pie was eaten. Talk centred around the crops and the weather. Mark waited until we had all finished our pieces of pie. He then began, "Professor Sturgis and I have something to discuss with you all." He paused. He had their attention; they knew something serious was afoot. "Professor Sturgis has been doing some investigating at Flemington. He, like all of us, was shocked by Allie's death. And he, like all of us, wondered why. He came to see me this week. I think he has uncovered some concerning facts about Allie's trip to Winnipeg a few days before she died." There was silence. The Klassens were waiting.

I backed up Mark, "Maria Dempster, my research assistant and a close friend of Allison's, came to me. She felt it odd that Allison made no contact with her after returning from Winnipeg. Had she contacted you?" I wanted to get the Klassens talking.

After a moment Doreen replied, "No. I think Megan got a text message. We had expected Allie to come home on the Sunday. She didn't."

Mark followed up, "Megan, if you don't mind me asking, what did Allie say in the text?"

"She just said, 'Made it home safe. Love A.'"

"That is what concerned Maria," I continued, "Allison was so excited about going to the conference and then when she returned home—no contact--nothing. Something was bothering Allison. I can tell you that other students have also raised concerns and I have decided to travel to Winnipeg next weekend to make some inquiries."

"Yes, and I support Professor Sturgis in going." Mark was following my lead, "In fact, I have hired him as my investigative assistant."

"To investigate what?" asked Fred.

"Honestly, I'm not sure," I replied, "however, something traumatic may have happened in Winnipeg and if we don't investigate we'll never know. I also have the assistance of Detective Maurice. He investigated Allison's death and was a former student of mine. He has given me the name and contact of a police detective in Winnipeg."

"Right now we aren't sure of anything," said Mark, "but Professor Sturgis is so concerned that something might have happened he is taking the time to travel to Winnipeg and came here today to meet with you. That says a great deal. We also need your approval and assistance."

"What approval and assistance?" Doreen asked.

"I'd like you to authorize me to act on your behalf in investigating Allison's death. We need your authorization or no one will talk either to me or to Professor Sturgis. For instance, I'd like to talk to Allie's doctor to see if there were any health issues. We'd like to speak with him."

"It's a her, Dr. Susan Burnett. She is my doctor as well in Flemington." said Megan.

"Oh, do you know when Allie last had a visit?" asked Mark.

Doreen answered, "It was in early August I think. I'll check the calendar." Doreen went to her calendar pinned to a notice board. The calendar was well thumbed through. Obviously it kept track of all family business. "Yes, it was August 4th."

Fred finally spoke, "You want us to hire you?"

"No, not hire me. Yes, I'd like you to retain me for one dollar, to retain me only to investigate Allie's death. That is it. Professor

Sturgis is working for me for nothing. If we find out something we come and tell you. That is it."

"I'm afraid of a lawsuit. I don't want to go through a court trial. I can't." said Doreen in a tired voice. Fred with head bowed nodded in agreement. "Nothing will bring her back."

Megan countered, "Mom and Dad. We have to know. I have to know. I'm so angry and hurt by Allie's death. If something happened to her I need to know."

"Please think about all of this. I'd like you all to agree. It is your decision." Mark played the conciliator. "Do you want to talk it over? Professor Sturgis and I can give you some time alone."

"No lawsuit?" Doreen looked at Mark.

"No lawsuit. All that we want to do is investigate. If that uncovers something we come back to you. You are only authorizing us to investigate Allison's death."

"Professor, you mentioned concerns have been raised, what concerns are those?" Fred asked me directly.

I could not lie, but all I had were suspicions that would be painful for any family to hear. I looked at Mark, his look said, "You're on your own". "Mr. Klassen, Fred, my concerns are at this stage suspicions only. I'd like to dig further to either confirm or reject them. I'm a former prosecutor and I'm really concerned about giving you false news. So if you would bear with me and trust me, after I finish investigating I will come back to you and either confirm my concerns or tell you that those concerns were false leads. I know that's not a complete answer, but it's the best I can do at this time."

"We trust you both," said Doreen. She had made her decision. "I'll sign the authorization. I need to know as well." Fred nodded his head in agreement. Megan was already on side.

"Good. I was hoping you would. I have prepared the documentation," said Mark, "Please read it over." He handed each a copy. "I'd like you all to sign three copies, one for me, one for you, and one for Professor Sturgis." Each read the short authorization over and the copies were signed. After signing the documents Mark cautioned them, "It is important that you don't tell anyone about our investigation. Everything must be kept confidential--it is critical to our investigation." They all nodded.

With the signing over, Doreen asked us all to pray. We joined hands around the table. "Lord, please help us understand Allie's death. We miss her so much and grieve for her. We search for answers and may You guide us in that search. Our thanks and blessings go out to Professor Sturgis and Mark. We are honoured that they are helping us to find answers. Bless them dear Lord. Amen."

"Amen" was repeated by all.

Our business was concluded. We were tied together in the search for answers.

"Anyone like a second piece of pie?" asked Doreen.

I couldn't resist; nor could Mark.

We stayed for a little while longer and then said our goodbyes. Megan and Mark made arrangements for the trip back to Flemington the next day.

Mark and I walked back to the Labros Ranch. We didn't say much. Ben joined us just before the Labros farm yard. Mark said he'd make further copies of the authorization and drop it in my mailbox early in the week. He gave me a dozen of his cards. We also decided that it was best that he speak with Dr. Burnett himself. Doctors are wary of divulging patient confidences and it would be best that the lawyer hired by the family do the asking rather than an assistant, who might be taken as a nosy professor at that.

The weather was turning colder. The wind had shifted to the north. The rain started anew and was turning more into a cutting sleet. I decided to return to Flemington as soon as possible and gave my regrets to Mr. and Mrs. Labros. She insisted that I take some baked cookies with me for the drive back. There was no saying no.

As I drove back to Flemington my mind raced with all manner of thoughts. I had no idea what I'd find in Winnipeg.

CHAPTER 18

On Sunday Julie and I were up early; it was closing the cabin day. Julie had already prepared sandwiches and snacks for the trip. We were travelling light, in expectation of returning with a full load. Bruce took her seat in the Hyundai SUV—so much for travelling light. She loved the lake and we couldn't bring ourselves to deprive her of a last trip. We left the house before nine.

The lake is our little piece of serenity. The cabin is old, not fancy, but it makes for a comfortable refuge. It was built by Julie's father after the war. He bought the lot for a few hundred dollars and then over the next few summers built the cabin by hand. There was no electricity at the time. Every board was sawn by hand; every nail hammered—no air compressor nailers.

When Julie and I arrived we, as per custom, walked down to the lake to survey the surrounds. None of the neighbours were down, but we could see campfire smoke from across the lake. It was calm and quiet. Even Bruce stood still. After our moment of contemplation we started the close-up.

By mid-afternoon our tasks were complete. The cabin was locked. All was checked. The SUV was packed. Bruce was partly dried after spending an afternoon chasing a family of merganser ducks. We'd have the odor of wet dog to accompany us home. We said good bye to the cabin. Another lake season was over.

On the way home we listened to the news and sports. The Vikings had won. Life was good in Viking Land. Julie brought up Fraser.

"Have you written your letter to the tenure and promotion committee?" she asked.

"Not yet. I was thinking of working on a draft tonight," I replied.

"What are you going to say?"

"It won't be favourable that is for sure. I also believe in being short and to the point. I can't say anything about my suspicions, but have plenty of other things to raise especially about his teaching."

"Do you think it'll make a difference?"

"I doubt it. Fraser has done some writing, not in major peer reviewed journals, but probably enough to get by on the research end. The real problem is his teaching. I'll comment on that, but I'm sure he'll have some cronies say that he is a great teacher. The students may provide some written comments, but generally they don't." I sighed, "He'll probably get through."

"I just don't understand universities. Don't they want to get rid of poor teachers, poor colleagues."

"It takes real effort to get rid of someone. The Dean doesn't have it in him. The easier thing to do is to support the application. That is the path of least resistance; same thing with failing students. It is so much easier to fudge them through. If you fail a student there will be re-writes, the student may appeal; it will be turned around as your failure in teaching rather than the student's failure in learning."

Julie moved on, "You know I looked through my psychology textbooks a few days ago. If Fraser is doing what we think he's doing, he is a serial rapist. So I looked up the profile of serial criminals. According to studies there are four different categories of serial offenders. I can't remember them all, but I remember placing Fraser into the category of an 'organized non-social offender'."

"What are the characteristics of an 'organized non-social offender'?" I asked.

"Glad you asked. They are loners, very bright, not likely to be suspected, manipulative and take great care in planning their attacks. The victims are not random, but picked, often groomed. They also are power assertive and have an extreme sense of their own superiority. Sound like Fraser?"

I thought for a moment, "You have described Fraser to a T."

"That's what I thought."

"There is something else. Many serial killers or rapists collect trophies from their victims. Not all, but many do. In some of the more macabre cases serial killers collected body parts of their victims, heads even. The trophies are personal to their victims, perhaps shoes, underwear, clothing, jewelry, photographs or hair. In this way the attacker can re-live their crimes over and over again."

"Or videotapes. A Canadian serial killer and rapist, Paul Bernardo, videotaped his victims."

"Yes, or videotapes," Julie continued, "My point is that the first student, who made the rape complaint, should be asked about whether anything she had or worn was taken—anything."

"You're right. I'll check on that. "

Upon arriving home, we unloaded and I got the hair dryer out to dry Bruce, which was not an easy task given that she was a big dog with much hair. She did not enjoy having it done and I did not enjoy doing it. Both Julie and I were tired after the trip and opted for a quick frozen pizza.

I then adjourned to my den. I retrieved Ingrid Hedberg's file and re-read her statement. There was nothing about anything being taken or missing. I emailed Richard Maurice and attached the Klassen authorization asking if he'd mind paving the way for me to speak with the medical examiner.

Richard replied a few minutes later. He had contacted the medical examiner, Dr. Frederick Markes. It was fine for me to contact Dr. Markes and I was provided with the good doctor's cell number. Richard's email read:

> Dr. Markes is most willing to talk with you as a representative of the Klassen family. His cell phone number is provided below. Don't hesitate to contact Dr. Markes at any time; he works 24/7.

So I did. I phoned Dr. Markes and he answered his cell phone immediately.

"Hello Markes here."

"Dr. Markes, Andrew Sturgis calling."

"That's fast. Detective Maurice just called me. You'd like to see me about the Klassen girl's death?"

Dr. Markes wasted few words, "Yes, I'm helping Mark Labros, who is doing some investigating for the Klassens."

"When would you like to see me?" He was direct and to the point.

"I'm free any time after 4:00 pm everyday this week except Friday."

"How about 4:30 on Tuesday at the General Hospital. You know where the morgue is?"

"Yes, I used to be a prosecutor and visited the morgue a few times. I'll be there at 4:30. Thanks doctor."

"Not a problem. See you then." He hung up.

I also checked the website for the annual Winnipeg conference on the law attended by Fraser. I thought that since I was going to Winnipeg I might as well talk with the organizer; perhaps he knew something about Allison or Fraser. The organizer's name was Associate Professor William Burnside. So I contacted him by email, told him that I was travelling up to Winnipeg, and would like to talk with him in person about the annual conference and suggested a possible time of early Friday afternoon.

Finally, I started my letter to the tenure and promotion committee:

> Dear Tenure and Promotion Committee:
>
> RE: APPLICATION OF ASSISTANT PROFESSOR JEROME FRASER
>
> I cannot recommend Assistant Professor Fraser for tenure or promotion...

CHAPTER 19

The General Hospital was built in the 1960's and, as typical for that era, was functional but not aesthetically pleasing; it was a box with windows. The morgue was located in the basement and was a secured department. I buzzed, indicated who I was and that I had an appointment with Dr. Markes. I was let in to an ante-room, which was stark white with no wall adornments of any kind to add a splash of colour—or life. There were a number of chairs along the walls and two doors on either side of the room. No one was in the room and I sat down to wait. I didn't wait long. A door opened and a large man with thick grey hair, glasses perched on top of his head, wearing a doctor's lab coat came through the door and directly to me. His hand was outstretched, "I'm Dr. Frederick Markes, and you must be Professor Sturgis."

I decided to refer to him by title. He had a slight European accent and I thought that a measure of formality may be appropriate, "Dr. Markes thank you for meeting with me."

"No problem at all, I understand that you are here to assist the family. Part of the purpose of this office is to bring closure for the families of the deceased. Please come with me to my office." He turned and opened the locked door from whence he came by tapping his ID badge on the sensor. We walked down a hallway, which continued the stark white theme and had a medicinal smell. Dr. Markes' office was Spartan. He had his degrees framed on one wall and a picture of a woman and two children on his desk–nothing else other than files. Along one of the walls was a bookshelf, wall to wall and floor to ceiling, filled with books, reports and binders. He motioned for me to have a seat and sat down in an ancient office chair covered by well worn cracked leather. It was ancient but looked extremely comfortable.

"Before we begin Professor, do you have a copy of the authorization from the family? I need it for my records. We must keep the clerks happy."

I had brought a copy of the authority with me and took it out of my satchel. "Yes, here it is. I am acting for Mark Labros, who is representing the Klassens." Dr. Markes representing the Klassens." did a quick read and put the authorization aside.

"I have made a copy of the autopsy for you. I'd be happy to go through it with you."

He handed the autopsy report to me. It was prepared on a six page form with boxes to be ticked, columns and spaces to be filled in. On page five there were diagrams showing visible body injuries. As I was looking through the report Dr. Markes continued, "Ms Klassen died of massive internal injuries consistent with a fall from a significant height. My understanding is that she fell from her tenth floor apartment. Most of her key organs were torn by the impact or pierced by broken bones. Her spinal cord was severed; her aorta was lacerated. In my view death would have been instantaneous. But tell me, what is it you are looking for?"

I could see that Dr. Markes was passionate about his work. He spoke in a paced, matter of fact, but at the same time a sincere manner. He had a knack of explaining things in simple ways. He would be a superb expert witness precisely because he didn't sound like an expert. I answered his question, "We accept that Allison's death was a suicide. Doctor, what the family is looking for is why. Why would she commit suicide?"

He replied, "That is always a difficult question to answer. There was no note. You know we often never know why."

"True, but I have some specific questions. I believe that most of these relate to page six of the report, which contains the serology and toxicology findings." Dr. Markes turned to that page and I continued, "Were any drugs found in her system?"

Dr. Markes looked at the toxicology report. "If you refer to line 75, it documents the drugs in her system. We tested her blood, urine and hair for an array of drugs: common opiates, marijuana, and synthetic drugs such as ecstasy. All tests were negative. Ms Klassen had no drugs in her system. It also seems that she was taking no medication."

I was somewhat disappointed. I had hoped that a date rape drug may have been found. "What about a date rape drug? Would that have been included in the testing?"

"Professor, the problem with the so-called date rape drugs is that they all dissipate in the body very quickly. The most common drugs are rohypnol, GHB and ketamine and they all dissipate within approximately twelve hours. Much depends on the dose, the strength of the drug, the size of the person ingesting the drug and whether or not the person had also consumed alcohol. I know that there have been some studies that suggest hair follicles can be tested for these drugs well after the fact, but those tests are not reliable. Nothing showed up in our testing."

"These date rape drugs are perfect for any would be rapist," I commented. "What are the symptoms?"

"Yes, unfortunately they are. They are a rapist's best friend. The symptoms—well, the victim will become incapacitated very quickly. Each of the drugs is slightly different, but within fifteen to thirty minutes after ingesting the drug the victim will probably experience dizziness, nausea, have difficulty talking, loss of consciousness, loss of motor function and, most importantly, have difficulty remembering what happened. GHB is the most popular because its effects tend to last longer than the other drugs."

"How long would that be?"

"For GHB, depending on the dose, it could be between three and six hours."

"What do these drugs look like?"

"It varies. Rohypnol is usually in a pill, although the pill can be crushed. A dye has been injected into the rohypnol pills by the manufacturer and that will turn a clear liquid bright blue. Of course, a coffee or cola will mask the colour. GHB may be in liquid form and is odorless and colorless. It also is available as a white powder. GHB does leave a salty taste. Ketamine may come in liquid form or as a white powder." Dr. Markes paused and asked, "Why are you asking about a date rape drug? Do you suspect Ms Klassen was the victim of such a rape?"

I was honest with the doctor, "We have some suspicion that she may have been raped two days before her death. She died Monday night and we are concerned that she may have been raped on the Saturday night."

"48 hours before. The date rape drugs would have dissipated. I'm sorry to say," he said categorically.

I moved away from the drugs, "Did Ms Klassen have alcohol in her system?"

"No. See line 81. There was no alcohol in her system. You can see the columns indicating the blood, urine and hair tests all came back negative."

"Wouldn't the alcohol have dissipated just like the date rape drugs?"

"Yes to a certain extent; however, we use an ETG test. It tests for ethanol, which is the ingested alcohol, for up to 80 hours in the blood and urine and in the hair for up to 90 days. Ms Klassen obviously was a non-drinker as the ETG tests came back negative. She certainly had not been drinking two days before."

"It is our understanding that Ms Klassen was a non-drinker and the results are consistent with that. Did you examine her genital area?"

"You mean did I conduct a sexual assault examination? No. However, I did examine her pelvic area. As you can see on page five a number of injuries were noted. All are consistent with trauma from the fall. I did not observe any specific physical indicia of sexual injury or activity."

"Doctor, if Ms Klassen had been raped two nights before would you expect to see any physical injury to the vagina?"

"No I would not. Many sexual assaults leave no physical injuries. Much depends on the nature of the assault, its repetition and duration. The vagina area has strong blood supply, which results in speedy healing of any cuts, abrasions or bruising." He continued, "However, go to lines 86 and 88 and you will see the results from swabs taken internally from the vagina."

"You see on line 86 that no spermatozoa were observed, which is an indicator that no sex occurred. Under our protocols, spermatozoa can be detected up to 72 hours after ejaculation. Of course if a condom was used no spermatozoa would be present." He smiled and went on to say, "But there is more."

He was holding me in suspense. "Look at line 88. You see that PDMS was observed in trace amounts."

He waited for me to ask, "What is PDMS?"

"PDMS is a silicon based lubricant commonly used on condoms. PDMS is not absorbed into the condom, is colorless, odorless, provides good lubrication and is not absorbed in the body. The literature is not in agreement as to how long it can be detected in the body. The figure twenty hours is often bandied about as a threshold. In my view and experience PDMS can be detected for much longer, up to 72 hours after condom use. Studies have found that the death of the victim preserves the PDMS in the vagina cavity."

"And of course a rapist would use a condom so as not to leave any DNA."

"Exactly, but the presence of PDMS is consistent with sexual activity."

I ended our conversation by asking a question that I always ask an expert, "Doctor is there anything else that the report or your observations reveal that we should know?"

Dr. Markes took his time. He flipped through all of the report, "No I think not, but if I do think of something I will certainly contact you and should you require anything further of me please do not hesitate to get in touch. I do have a question for you Professor. Why are you involved?"

My throat tightened, "Allison was a student of mine. She was a beautiful person and I too need to know why she took her life. I'd like to do that for the Klassens. They are good people."

"I thought it was personal. I hope for your sake and for her parents and family you find the answer."

We shook hands and Dr. Markes escorted me out.

CHAPTER 20

The remainder of the week was a busy one. I had scheduled a mid-term test in my Criminal Law class. This was the students' first assessment in law school and they were antsy, needing hand holding. The test was worth only 10% of their grade. In my experience this would be their worst assessment. Being new to law, the students were still learning how to apply the law, which is what lawyers do. Most first year students are content merely to regurgitate the law, which is what they did in their undergraduate courses. They end up describing the law, with little or no application to the given facts. What they need to do is to become problem solvers; have the discipline to identify the critical issues, and then apply the correct law to the facts. I provide detailed feedback on their papers, which hopefully assists them when it comes to write the end of term examinations. Needless to say I had students at my door non-stop.

Maria also dropped in for a quick chat. She was frustrated. The law student executive continued to debate their response to Fraser's application for tenure and promotion. Some of the students were adamant that a strongly worded negative letter should be sent. Others, most of whom had not had Fraser as a teacher, weren't prepared to sign on, and a few thought that Fraser was 'okay'. Reaching a consensus would be difficult and would lead to a watered down letter of concern. Without a united front the students would have to write individual letters. Most would not. The reason is simple they fear retribution; students are well aware of the power dynamic in law schools. The professors through their marks control the futures of the students. I doubted many students would take it upon themselves to write negative letters. Fraser wins.

I never told Maria that I was going to Winnipeg.

I finally received a return email from Professor Burnside at the University of Manitoba. It was short and not overly friendly,

"I am in on Friday. What is it you want to discuss?"

I decided to take his email as a 'yes' and replied:

"Good to hear that you are available. I want to discuss with you the annual conference that you co-ordinate and I'd like some further information about it. Would 2:00 be fine? What is your office number? Looking forward to meeting you."

I received a curt reply shortly after:

"Room 200h. Second floor Faculty of Law Building. See you then. W."

Julie and I hit the road a little before 9:00 a.m. Friday morning. Bruce was left in the back yard well supplied with water and food. Our next door neighbor, Mrs. Hilderman, volunteered to care for Bruce. She had a terrier for years and the dog had died a few months before. She took the loss hard. I think she needed dog companionship and Bruce would oblige.

We headed west through the rolling hills of Northern Minnesota. The crops were harvested and the fields lay bare ready for next year's seeding. The day was bright and sunny. The drive gave us a chance to talk as partners do. We discussed our children, their lives, hopes and adventures; always worrying as parents are prone to do. We discussed our future: how long would we continue to work? What to do in our retirement? And we discussed what it was that we hoped to achieve in Winnipeg.

Julie had a travel brochure on Winnipeg. I had been there only once many years ago. I couldn't even remember why. There were a number of "must sees". We narrowed it down to two. First there was the polar bear exhibit at the zoo, which according to all accounts was spectacular. Second there was the Canadian Museum of Human Rights. We felt that there was only time to do one. Which one? Julie finally broke the impasse.

"Every day on the news I see man's inhumanity towards his fellow man. I'm not up to going to a museum that is built on that inhumanity. Call me callous, but I want uplifting. I want happy. Let's visit the bears." Julie had decided.

"Fine with me."

We turned north on I29–a dual lane freeway--next stop Canada. I29 follows the Red River Valley, which is the remnant of a great glacial lake and is dead flat prairie. Scenic it is not.

We arrived at the border ahead of schedule. The line-up at the border crossing was not long. The custom's officer was a young woman. She asked us for our passports. No smile. I think that they are trained that way, although after a few years on the job they tend to loosen up. She inputted our data into her computer and turned back to us.

"Where are you from?"

"Flemington, Minnesota."

"Where are you going?"

"To Winnipeg."

"What is the purpose of your trip?"

"Just a visit."

"What are you intending to see in Winnipeg?"

"The polar bears." I replied without a bit of hesitation.

A smile moved across her lips–a sign of personality. That crack in her façade revealed that under that uniform was a real person. "I know you'll enjoy them. Welcome to Canada." She waved us through.

The highway continued as a dual lane, but the surface was not as well maintained as south of the border. Signs reminded us that we were now in a metric country and not to assume that the speed of "100" was in miles per hour. More flatness, but it was dotted by raised farm yards and houses or they were enclosed by dikes protecting the property. This was a residue of the 1997 flood.

The signs for Winnipeg counted down. We were right on schedule; it was just before 1:30. The University of Manitoba is located in the south part of the city and our GPS guided us well. We stopped at the visitor centre and a young man gave us a campus map and showed us where to park. He warned us that we needed to plug the meter as the parking police were ever vigilant even on this a Friday afternoon before the long weekend. We followed his directions through the campus maze. The university was large and not overly personal. My impression was that it lacked character. Functionality prevailed over aesthetic considerations. The buildings lacked cohesion. There did not appear to be any grand architectural plan for the campus. The buildings were a mishmash of styles: red brick, sandstone, brutal concrete and even black metal.

We found the parking lot back of the law school. I plugged the meter. It was 1:55. We went in. All was quiet. The law school was typical. There were pillars in the front. Law schools like pillars, they exude strength and gravitas. The main level actually was somewhat dark. There was a large central foyer. Classrooms lined both sides and there was a student lounge. Julie and I agreed to meet back at the lounge in a half hour. The offices were on the second floor, I took the stairs and Julie said she was content to do some exploring around the campus.

On the second floor the offices lined both sides of the building. They were lined up like academic prison cells. None of the doors was open. I went down the one side. No one was to be seen. I moved to the other side and saw one door open halfway down the hall. There was life after all. I moved to the open door. The name plate read Associate Professor W. Burnside. I knocked and entered.

Associate Professor William Burnside was standing behind his desk taking a book from a bookshelf. The office was extremely ordered. His desk was clear—no debris. Photographs on the wall were arranged in military formation. The bookshelves had the books and reports in precise order. The room lacked any warmth or charm—perhaps reflecting its occupant. Burnside was tall and slim, early 40's, his hair was short in a harsh cut and he had a gaunt chiselled look. His mouth was small, prissy.

"Professor Burnside, Andy Sturgis." I held out my hand. He turned. Gave me a hurtful smile, took my hand. His grip was weak, wimpy.

"Pleased to meet you, Professor Sturgis. Have a seat."

"Quiet around here," I commented.

"Yes, it's Friday before a long weekend. A lot of the students and staff take off."

"You seem to be minding the mint. I hope you didn't stay here for me."

"No, no I'm working on an article and will probably spend the weekend finishing it."

"Been there, done that," I consoled.

"When did you get into Winnipeg?" There was no warmth in his inquiries. He was going through the motions.

"Just arrived a few minutes ago."

"So what can I do for you?" He wasn't wasting any time.

"Well, you coordinate the annual conference on developments in the law and I wanted to ask you some questions about that."

"Professor Fraser is at your law school. Have you spoken with him?"

"That's right, Jerome does go to this conference every year. No, I haven't spoken to him. I thought I'd come to you directly."

"He was appointed to our advisory board this year." I had read that in his curriculum vitae. Convenient I thought, it looks good on a C.V. no matter how small the conference; it would bolster his application for tenure and promotion.

Burnside seemed guarded. I was somewhat surprised because usually those who run a conference want to go on about how wonderful their particular conference is and how I must attend. Not Associate Professor Burnside, he was tight lipped.

"There are a few things I'd like to know about the conference if you don't mind. First, how are topics and papers chosen each year?"

"We have a panel: a local judge, a professor in sociology, and me. There is a call sent out for topics and papers and we meet and screen them."

"How many submissions do you usually receive?"

"It depends, but usually anywhere from twenty to thirty each year."

"How many do you accept?"

"That also depends on their quality. If all are good we'll go with them all and judge our time accordingly. One of the purposes of the conference is to provide a forum for new academics to present."

"Do you hold the conference on campus?"

"No, we prefer a local hotel. It gets us away from the law school and its distractions. The hotels actually give us a pretty good deal. You know how expensive food services can be on a university campus."

"Yes, I think it is a universal truth, all universities charge top dollar for mediocre food served without a smile. Where was the conference held this past year?"

"At the Ramada Hotel South, just down Pembina Highway. We were very happy with the price and service."

We spent a few minutes talking about trends in the law and compared the situation in Canadian and American law schools. I asked about his areas of research. I assumed that would get him talking. I was wrong. He remained taciturn; a man of few words and not at all engaging.

I decided to move on to Allison. "It is my understanding that Professor Fraser brought a student with him this past year. Do you remember Allison Klassen? Let me show you a photograph of her." I had enlarged the photograph from her funeral service and I handed it to him.

I could see recognition. I also saw beads of sweat on his forehead, "Yes, I do remember her. Nice young lady."

"Did you know that she died two days after returning home from your conference?"

"Oh no, how awful. I never knew that."

I didn't get a sense that he was being genuine. He never asked how she died! He knew already! It dawned on me; he must have contacted Fraser. Christ what an idiot I am. Fraser now knew that I was asking questions. Our element of surprise was lost. All of this flooded into my mind in a flash. I cursed my folly and regretted contacting Burnside. I should have known that he may have a close relationship with Fraser. The damage was already done. I might as well probe a little further. "She committed suicide. Do you remember seeing her on the Saturday evening of the conference?"

"This is terrible. Such a beautiful young woman. Give me a moment to think." He took a Kleenex out and feigned cleaning his glasses. He actually brushed the sweat off his brow. "I last saw her at the hospitality suite in the hotel. The Saturday session ended at about 4:30. It was followed by a reception and end of conference supper that went to about 8:00. Following that many of the participants went to the hospitality suite where everyone can have a drink and mingle. She was there. What I do remember is that she was having a good time and was with a number of the Manitoba students. They were all drinking, enjoying themselves. I think they went out partying. They left about 9:00 or so."

He was either very mistaken about the drinking or lying. The toxicology report told me so. I had to change topics otherwise the focus of my visit would become more obvious than it already was. Why had I shown him the photograph? What an idiot I am. I changed topics. "You may or may not know that Professor Fraser has applied for tenure this year."

"I didn't know that. What I can say is that his work over the last four or five years at and for the conference has been exceptional, just exceptional." Burnside was a Fraser fan, that was confirmed. I was watching Burnside closely. He was nervous; his eyes were darting all over. He didn't want to look me in the eye. He was another Fraser in this regard.

"So I take it that you would rate his work highly."

"Yes I certainly would."

It was time for me to leave. "I've taken enough of your time. You've given me something to think about with your conference. I promised my wife that I'd meet her in the student lounge that was five minutes ago and we've got a city to explore. Thank you so much for your time."

We shook hands and I left.

I continued kicking myself as I walked down the stairs. I bet Burnside would be phoning Fraser with a report on the visit at this very minute.

When I got to the student lounge Julie was seated in one of the tired armchairs reading the local university student newspaper. "Let's roll," I said as I approached.

She looked at me with a bit of a startled look, "What's the rush?"

"I'll tell you in the car." I just wanted to get out of the law school.

Once in the car I told her my conclusion, "Burnside has been in contact with Fraser. I know that and that means Fraser will know about my visit. He'll know that I'm snooping. Damn it!"

Julie tried to settle me down, "How do you know that he's been in contact with Fraser?"

"Julie when I told him that Allison had died two days after attending his conference what would you ask next?"

"I'd ask how she died."

"Exactly and he didn't."

Julie had no rejoinder.

As we drove towards the downtown and the Artist Hotel, Julie looked to assuage my mistake. She pointed out that I had not told Burnside that I was investigating Allison's death, had not mentioned working for Mark, and had not even raised any concerns about what may have happened to Allison in Winnipeg. All that Burnside could say is that I, on my own, was asking questions. I felt better, but not much.

We drove past the Ramada Inn South. The Artist Hotel was on Portage Avenue in the downtown. Traffic became heavy as we navigated through the maze of one way streets. Eventually we found the hotel and drove to the covered reception parking area. The hotel was a 1930's building, four stories high. Evidently it had been salvaged from demolition and had been refurbished about ten years before. The renovation was true to the 1930's era.

The foyer had a high ceiling and large crystal chandelier. The ceiling was ornate and countless paintings adorned the walls. Some were reproduced masters and others were by local artists, which were displayed for sale. I went to reception and was greeted by a young man, impeccably dressed in a red, black trimmed, hotel suit; Serge was his name.

"Good day, Bonjour." I knew I was in Canada. I had booked Rembrandt room 1, but Julie demurred. She couldn't bring herself to sleep in the same hotel room which may have been defiled by Fraser. She was right—as usual. I wasn't thinking. I asked Serge if we could change the room. Not a problem. He put us into the Monet room on the same floor. I asked him if by chance we could have a look at Rembrandt 1and 2. He was most obliging. He said it shouldn't be a problem as housekeeping was on that floor and the room was still being cleaned. He phoned housekeeping and confirmed that they were still on the floor. It was arranged that we would contact them when we went up to the floor. The hotel had underground parking, and after getting directions I parked the car.

Julie and I took the elevator to our room on the fourth floor. The Monet room overlooked Portage Avenue and was filled with impressionist landscape paintings. House-keeping was just finishing Rembrandt 2. The woman let us into the Rembrandt rooms for a peek, while she moved to a room down the hall. Rembrandt 1 was at the end of the hall. It overlooked a side street. The room was beautifully preserved. A wooden mahogany pedestal bed and accompanying dresser dominated the room. There was a matching desk and chair, with a small tea table. A dark brown leather armchair was placed by the window. Three of Rembrandt's paintings were strategically hung. The largest over the bed was that of Christ

Driving the Money-changers from the Temple. There was also a Self-portrait and The Anatomy Lesson of Dr. Tulp. Small plaques provided the names and year. The paintings were dark, as was Rembrandt's style. They fit the dark furnishings.

Rembrandt 2 had similar décor to Rembrandt 1. I quickly took pictures. There was an adjoining door. Like most adjoining doors there were two doors one from each room. To provide an opening between the rooms both doors had to be unlocked. The most compelling feature of the room was the painting, The Man with the Golden Helmet, which was placed above the bed and was not exactly a romantic backdrop. There was an asterisk—evidently the painting is no longer attributed to Rembrandt.

What did get my attention is that the Rembrandt rooms were down the hall from other rooms. They seemed isolated and the thick concrete walls and plush heavy carpets would make them very sound proof.

We thanked the house-keeping woman and returned to our Monet room, which felt so friendly and full of life in comparison to the Rembrandt rooms. I decided that I much preferred Monet's paintings of water lilies, irises, and gardens. The centre piece of our room was the painting, Garden at Giverny, which was a testament to nature's beauty.

We quickly unpacked our suitcases. It was just after 3:30 in the afternoon and we wanted to do some exploring. I also wanted to make contact with people before the weekend.

CHAPTER 21

I had already spoken to the manager of the hotel, who was very pleasant on the phone, and we had left it that I would contact him when I got into Winnipeg in the late afternoon. I changed into my "professorial garb" putting on my green tweed jacket–leather elbow patches of course–and brown slacks. I also took with me my satchel.

Julie and I went down to the lobby. The elevators were located in the center of the foyer and I noted that one would have to go past the reception desk to access them. A side hallway led to the "Precious Beans Coffee Shop and Cafe". The cafe was separated from the hotel foyer by a pair of glass doors. The cafe also had a separate street entrance on Portage Avenue. It was my understanding that the hotel owned the cafe.

Serge was still on duty and, as things were slow, I had a brief word with him. "Serge, is the Manager in?"

A look of alarm immediately clouded his face. "Is there something wrong? Perhaps I can help you?"

"Oh, no nothing wrong at all. The room is perfect. I do have something to discuss with the manager, Mr. Pangatan, I believe. He is expecting me."

Serge looked relieved, "I'll call and see. Just a moment, please." Serge then took the phone and in a quiet voice spoke into the receiver. "He'll be out in just a few minutes."

"Thank you Serge. Do you mind me asking; is someone at reception 24/7?"

"Yes, in the downtown you couldn't leave the front doors unattended."

"I understand completely."

At that moment a small, compact man, impeccably dressed in a black suit, red tie and matching breast pocket handkerchief --old fashioned and yet dapper, professional looking--came through the back reception door. He was, if I were to guess, Filipino by origin. He went up to Serge and looked past him at myself and Julie. "I'm Michel Pangatan, manager of the Artist Hotel. You must be Professor Sturgis?" He flashed a wide smile. He was used to dealing with people and disarming them with grace and courtesy.

I smiled back, "Mr. Pangatan, thank you for seeing us, this is my wife Julie."

"Mrs. Sturgis, a pleasure. Please come into my office." Mr. Pangatan opened the rear door and led us into the office area of the hotel. We walked by a couple of small offices occupied by two women busy on the phones. Mr. Pangatan had a lovely corner office that overlooked the side street. He offered a chair to Julie and motioned for me to sit in another chair; he took a seat behind his desk, which is the power position.

Once seated Mr. Pangatan opened the conversation, "Now Professor how can I help you?"

My plan was to be honest, sincere and reassuring, "First Mr. Pangatan, thank you for seeing us," I paused, "as I told you over the phone, I am a Professor of Law at Flemington University in Minnesota and I'm here about one of our students." I took out of the satchel a photograph of Allison and passed it to him. He looked at it. "This is Allison Klassen," I told him.

"A very attractive young woman."

"Yes," I agreed, "as I mentioned to you, she died almost two months ago. She committed suicide."

"That is tragic. So young. Such a waste."

"Yes," I agreed once more. "We are here investigating her death. More specifically, trying to find out why she would kill herself. I'm an investigative agent for the law firm of Theopold, Stenson and Labros in Flemington, Minnesota. Here is a copy of my authorization from them and also a copy of an authorization that Allison's parents signed agreeing to have us investigate." Mr. Pangatan looked at each in turn and seemed satisfied.

I continued, "Allison stayed here for two nights on August 14 and 15 of this year. She committed suicide on Monday the 17th of August. She was here for a law conference with a professor from our law school. Mr. Pangatan, I have been doing some investigating and I have reason to believe that something happened to Allison here in Winnipeg. Something terrible."

Mr. Pangatan looked concerned, "That could make us liable? Shouldn't I talk to our lawyers?"

I was worried about this. Lawyers would bugger things up good. "Mr. Pangatan, I appreciate your concern, but let me say this to you. Your hotel is not responsible for what the guests may do in their rooms. It is my belief that Allison was attacked in her room by a person she knew. There was nothing that the hotel would be liable for. Let me tell you what I'm looking for and you will see that it has nothing to do with the hotel."

Mr. Pangatan nodded.

"You have security surveillance cameras?"

"Yes we do."

"I'd like to look at the tapes for the evening of Saturday the 15th. That should give me some idea of who was with Allison and how she appeared."

"Let me stop you there," said Mr. Pangatan. "We have two surveillance systems. One is for the hotel public areas and the second is for the cafe. I have to tell you that the hotel system only saves data—we don't have tapes anymore—for a period of thirty days. The cost of storing the data is quite high and there are ten surveillance cameras in the hotel; we couldn't justify a greater storage capacity."

"So you don't have any surveillance going back to the 15th of August?" I was despondent.

"Not in the hotel; however, we have a newer and smaller system in the cafe. The cafe has had some incidents and I can tell you that the data in that surveillance system is saved for sixty days."

I was relieved, "So you still have the cafe surveillance?"

"Yes."

I went back to outlining what I was looking for, "We would like to review that surveillance for the evening of August 15. We'd also like to talk to your staff, who were working that evening to see if they remember anything about Allison. That is it. It is all about who was with Allison and how she appeared."

Mr. Pangatan didn't seem convinced. He was unsure. He fidgeted in his chair, not making eye contact with us. He was thinking.

Julie stepped in, "Mr. Pangatan do you have any daughters?"

He smiled, "Yes, two."

"We also have two daughters and if one of them killed herself I would be devastated. I'd be blaming myself. That is exactly what the Klassens are doing. They blame themselves. They grieve for what they did or didn't do. They are hurting. What we want to do is to tell them why. Why their beautiful daughter killed herself and we believe that she did so because of something that happened here in Winnipeg. We need to show them that it was not their fault. Mr. Pangatan, we need your help."

He looked long and hard at Julie. She had hit a chord. He smiled, "If anything happened to my daughters I would do anything to know why. Mrs. Sturgis you are right. What you ask is not too much. Thank you." He rose out of his chair, "Professor Sturgis, Mrs. Sturgis come with me."

He directed us into a small windowless room, which was filled with recording equipment. On one table there was a data recorder and a monitor showing ten separate split screens, one for each of the camera locations. On a separate table there was a smaller recorder and monitor with three split screens.

"These are our surveillance systems. We have ten surveillance cameras in the hotel. As I said, that system only keeps the data for thirty days. At this table is the system for the cafe. You can see that it is smaller and newer. We have three cameras. One is located above the doorway outside of the cafe; it shows the street view. The second is behind the counter and is aimed at the customers as they come to the counter; it provides a facial view of the customers at the cashier. The third is located above the entry to the hotel and shows the length of the cafe sitting area."

Mr. Pangatan was very familiar with the system. He asked us for the date and inputted that into the recorder. "What I suggest is that one of you watches screen two and the other screen three. What time do you want to start?"

I went back to what Burnside had told me, "Could we start at 9:00 p.m.?"

Mr. Pangatan nodded and inputted the time. "Here is the fast forward button. Here is the pause and reverse." He showed us each. "It shouldn't take you too long. I'll be in my office and check the employee records to see who was on that evening both in the hotel and in the cafe. Let me know if you find anything."

"Thank you so much," I was truly grateful, "what time does the cafe close?"

"11 p.m. You'll see that the screens go mostly dark. The cameras do keep rolling. Good luck." He left.

Julie and I were left to watch the screens.

"How did you know he had daughters?" I asked.

"Elementary my dear Watson," she laughed, "He was married. I could see that by his wedding ring. He was also Filipino, if I'm not mistaken by his looks and name, and the Philippines is primary Catholic. I simply took a chance that he would have children and he did."

"You are a great detective," I congratulated her.

We started to review the videos. Soon we were adept at fast-forwarding until customers entered the cafe. At 9:47 bingo–I identified Allison first. She was dressed in a white blouse and dark skirt. She entered with Fraser. He wore a sports jacket. I concentrated on the counter camera. Julia watched the cafe table camera. Allison took a seat at the window. Fraser came up to the counter. He spoke to the barista. The order was taken. Fraser then took a seat opposite Allison. All seemed in order, there was nothing untoward happening. Allison seemed to be fine. The video was quite good. She seemed steady and sober.

After a few minutes–2 minutes 35 seconds to be exact–Fraser got up and went to the counter. He picked up the two drink orders, which were in take away cups, and went over to the fixings table where the sugar, milk, creams and lids were located. At this point we could not see exactly what he did. But it looked like he put something into the drinks and stirred them. I thought that I saw him take something out of his right jacket pocket, but the camera angle was not good. His right side was hidden from the camera. He turned towards Allison, which shielded his right side and right jacket pocket. It is at that time I thought he took something out of his jacket pocket. He certainly stirred both drinks and then took them to their table. Allison sipped her drink and continued to drink. It seemed like Fraser proposed a toast. They touched cups and took a drink. She continued to drink from the cup. At 10:03 I noticed that Allison was shaking her head. She wiped her forehead with her hand. She seemed unsteady. Two minutes later her head almost fell to the table. At that Fraser got up. He took her cup and put it in the garbage. She tried to get up, but was unsteady on her feet. We watched as he helped her up. He had his hand around her waist. She leaned into him. He helped her walk out. We last saw them leave the cafe through the doors to the hotel. Allison could not walk without assistance. They left at 10:05 and 27 seconds.

Julie and I didn't say a word. It was obvious to us that Allison had been drugged. Julie broke the silence, "That bastard. That bloody bastard. He probably helped her up to her room and had access to her key. Then he'd open up the adjoining doors and have her to himself. That bastard."

"We'll need a copy of this video," I was shaken by what I had seen.

"Should I go get Mr. Pangatan?" Julie asked.

"Let's just review the rest of the surveillance to 11:00. Just to make sure."

We skipped things quickly. There were few customers. Then at 10:39 I saw him. A single man came into the cafe. He was tall and slim. It was Burnside. What the hell was Burnside doing there? He ordered a drink. Put a lid on it and walked into the hotel at 10:41. He walked into the hotel! Christ, was Burnside part of this? I told Julie. We fell silent. Julie went and got Mr. Pangatan. They arrived in the room a moment later.

"Mr. Pangatan we have something to show you. Would you please go to 9:47 pm?" He seated himself in front of the recorder and set the playback for 9:47. We watched again as Allison and Fraser entered the cafe.

"She seems fine doesn't she," I observed.

"Yes she does."

"Watch." We watched again as Fraser ordered the drinks and went to the cream and sugar table. We paused the playback, "I think it was here that he put something into Allison's drink." We watched in silence. Fraser did something with his right hand, but what?

We resumed playing the tape and watched again as Allison quickly lost coordination. There was silence as Allison was helped out of the cafe. Mr. Pangatan's face was white. He asked, "Do you know the man?"

"Yes, it is Professor Fraser. He booked the rooms."

"You suspect that he attacked Miss Allison?"

"Yes. We need copies of this surveillance."

"Of course," Mr. Pangatan said quietly. "We can download the surveillance data onto a USB. Do you have any?"

"No, where can we get any nearby?" I asked.

"There is the Hudson's Bay Store just down the street. It will be open until 9:00."

"What size USB's do you recommend?"

"At least 8 gigabytes."

I turned to Julie, "Do you mind going and getting three 8 gigabyte USB's? I need Mr. Pangatan to help me here."

"No, no," insisted Mr. Pangatan. "I will not have your wife walking down town with it getting dark at this time. I'll get one of my employees to go. They know where the store is. Just a moment." Mr. Pangatan left the room and came back a few minutes later.

"Mr. Pangatan, I need you to authentic the copies. That means that you do the copying and confirm that the copy is a true representation of the original. Do you mind?"

He thought for a moment. "I will do it." As we waited for his employee to return with the USBs, I prepared a short affidavit in hand. It identified Mr. Pangatan, his position, age, address and confirmed that he made threes copies from the original recording system.

There was a knock on the door. A slight youth had three USBs. They were $35.67. Mr. Pangatan wanted to pay, but I insisted. I told him that we needed to do everything above board. I paid for the USBs and received a receipt. I did give the young man a $10 tip.

Mr. Pangatan then recorded everything on the USBs from 9:30 to 11:00. That way we had a complete record including, of course, Burnside's appearance. Three copies were made.

When this was done Mr. Pangatan gave me the names of the employees working the evening and night of August 15. They were regular weekend employees and would be working the next day. Mr. Pangatan told us that he would contact each and ask them to make themselves available to talk to us.

"Is there anything else I can do?" he asked.

I hesitated, but I think Mr. Pangatan was incensed by what he had seen on the surveillance tape, so I asked, "Could you please confirm that Professor Fraser reserved rooms here over the last five years?"

"Would they be booked under his name?"

"That I don't know. It could be Flemington University School of Law."

"Our reservation supervisor is still here. I'll ask her to check. If we are finished here, let's adjourn to my office."

"Before leaving can you ensure that the original data will not be destroyed after sixty days?"

"I've already done that. The data for August 14-16 has been saved in the system." Mr. Pangatan replied. We got up and as we returned to his office, Mr. Pangatan dropped into an adjoining room and spoke to the woman there. She wrote notes on a pad, nodded and said, "Just give me a minute or two."

Once in his office, we all looked at each other. Mr. Pangatan broke the silence, "That poor girl was helpless, completely helpless."

"Yes," I replied, "we suspect that it was a fast acting date rape drug. She wouldn't have suspected anything." There was a soft knock on the door. The woman in the adjoining office opened the door and provided a data sheet to Mr. Pangatan. He looked at it and gave it to me. It provided the reservations for Professor Fraser and the room occupants for the past five years. There was Ingrid Hedberg, Jennifer Cunningham, Victoria Palmer, and Allison Klassen all named as occupying Rembrandt 2. Fraser always occupied Rembrandt 1. There was also a reservation for Professor Jerome Fraser and the Flemington School of Law for August 13 and 14 of next year. He was going to do it again! The summary was on the Artist Hotel letterhead. I asked Mr. Pangatan to sign it as "a true copy of data prepared during the course of business for the Artist Hotel". In my view this was sufficient to get it admitted as a business record in a court of law–if need be.

We were done. It was almost 6:00 p.m. Mr. Pangatan told us that it was time for him to go home. We all rose. "If there is anything else, my staff knows how to contact me." He put out his hand.

I took it, "Thank you. I will also be contacting the police so they may want the original data."

"I understand that."

"I also have a few favours to ask."

"If I can assist I will," Mr. Pangatan was ever the gracious hotelier.

"First, I'd like to keep everything that we've seen today confidential. Second, if anyone contacts you, other than the police, about your surveillance system could you let me know? Here is my card with my contact details."

"Of course, all is understood. I'm honoured to help that young lady and to help you both."

"Thank you Mr. Pangatan," Julie said, "Thank you so much." She gave him a quick hug, which I think he truly appreciated.

Chapter 22

That night we went to a steak house that Serge had recommended; it was only a ten minute walk. He suggested that we make a reservation for after 7:00 p.m. because there was a Winnipeg Jets pre-season home game in the downtown arena that started at 7:00. All eating establishments would be swarmed by Jets fans until game time. We left the hotel at a few minutes before 7:00 and immediately ran into tardy fans wearing their Jets regalia. Serge was right, the city was hockey mad. When we got to the restaurant the fan base was gone.

We were both mentally exhausted by the day's travel and events. We were gathering further and further pieces of evidence that pointed to Fraser assaulting Allison; however, the problem was simple, the case was all circumstantial and if there was a reasonable alternative explanation then Fraser would never be convicted in a criminal trial or found liable in a civil one. He could easily explain away the cafe surveillance: Allison became ill and he merely helped her to her room and that was it. We couldn't prove otherwise.

I decided to give Detective Semchuk a call the next day. At least he would be put on notice. We finished our meal and made our way back to the hotel. It was a very pleasant evening, calm, and although the air was fresh it was not cold. It was, in short, a crisp fall evening. We passed by the arena and the building pulsated with outbursts of cheering. The Winnipeg fans were not only dedicated, they were vocal.

We made it back to our Monet room and went to bed beneath lavender landscapes.

Next morning we were off to Assiniboine Park to see the bears. We were not disappointed. The Journey to Churchill was unique. There they were--truly magnificent animals hunting for their meaty meal. Their paws were gigantic. One swipe of those claws and that would be it. Game over. The exhibit allowed these apex giants of the Arctic room to roam; it did them justice. You could view them from many vantage points. There were dens for hiding and rest and, best of all, pools for a cooling swim. Viewing tunnels beneath the pools allowed us breath taking close ups of them. Visitors ran back and forth in the tunnels trying for that perfect picture. Underside views of belly and paws and their thick silky fur coat floating above us was amazing. A trip to Churchill, Manitoba to see the bears in their natural environment was now on the bucket list.

The rest of the zoo--well--was a zoo. I have mixed feelings about zoos. Not every animal is in a good exhibit. The big cats at this zoo have poor space, which needs changing. Zoos are great for education and research but not so good for most of the animals that live there and not in their natural homes.

We had coffee at the Tundra Grill overlooking the polar bear enclosure. A couple of young bears were playing. Too cute. I have to admit that for sick, orphaned or injured bears to find a home here would beat the alternative—death.

There was a pay phone in the restaurant and I phoned Detective Semchuk. He had a strong but welcoming voice, which surprised me; I had expected a gruff, authoritarian voice. He asked where we were and when I told him he said that he would be over in thirty minutes. We arranged to meet at the picnic area at the Duck Pond in Assiniboine Park. Evidently he lived nearby, and was going to jog over.

We arrived at the Duck Pond and it was packed with migrating geese and ducks. We found a picnic table free of bird droppings and took in the bird show; soon a tall, muscular man, light hair, cut short, wearing a dark blue jogging suit came up to us.

"You must be Mr. and Mrs. Sturgis", he stated.

"And you must be Detective Semchuk."

"Call me Arno, I'm off duty."

"Julie and Andrew," we exchanged greetings.

"Sorry to bother you on your day off," I felt badly.

"Don't sweat it. This is my morning jog." He had a big jovial voice that resonated power and confidence, "Ricky said that you were one of his law professors."

"Yes. It was great having Richard in my criminal law class. He'd give us all a dose of reality."

"Sounds like you are looking for Canadian crimes now," he laughed.

"Well we may have found one. Have a seat; we have something to show you." We had brought our Mac laptop with us. I filled him in on our investigation highlighting Ingrid's complaint of rape five years before.

"Did she go to the police? Did the university go to the police?"

"Unfortunately, no."

Detective Semchuk shook his head, "You know everyone complains about low conviction rates for sexual assaults, but if people aren't going to report a crime there won't be any convictions. I've been to some of the university sexual awareness sessions and I'd encourage the victims to come forward then the next bloody speaker would say—no, no—it is your choice, you need not go to the police. Sorry, it's frustrating. I interrupted you. Go on."

I ended with Allison's suicide and gave him a photograph. I also gave him a photograph of Fraser. I then set the scene to watch the surveillance tape.

"We think that Professor Fraser raped Allison, just as he had done before with Ingrid. Ingrid described being drugged and we think that is exactly what he did to Allison. I have spoken to the medical examiner. Keep this in mind; Allison had no alcohol in her system. She didn't drink. I'm going to show you a surveillance tape from the cafe of the hotel where she and Fraser stayed in adjoining rooms." We then played the tape. As it played I introduced Allison and Fraser. I stopped it after they left the cafe.

"She was drugged," said Detective Semchuk categorically.

"This tape is for you," I replied.

"Did she tell anyone that she had been raped?" he asked.

"No she didn't."

"Here's the problem. I know she was drugged, but it won't be easy to prove without tracing her whereabouts that evening and then, of course, I'd have to prove an assault. There is no victim to testify. No witnesses. Actually there is no complaint. Professor we have no case. No Crown prosecutor would take this case."

I knew he was right but I went on, "I hear what you are saying, I'm a former state prosecutor myself, but what if Ingrid was to testify about the rape five years before?"

"The one that was never reported to the police? Didn't you say that the university encouraged her to drop the allegations and she did? Good defence counsel would tear her apart on the stand." The detective was right again.

I shifted tactic. "I want to show you something else." I fast forwarded to Associate Professor William Burnside's arrival and I introduced him to the detective.

"You say that the two of them knew each other?"

"Yes."

"Certainly is suspicious. But you know these prowlers, perpetrators, have a keen sense for each other. I've seen it before." He paused, "here is what I will do. I will do a check on Associate Professor William Burnside in our Winnipeg police system. This is not for public consumption, but we do keep a record of suspicious individuals—found-ins so to speak. I will let Ricky know. I can't provide that information to civilians."

"I understand detective. Any help is appreciated."

"It's frustrating isn't it? You know someone has committed a crime, but you can't prove it. Those cases, and I've got a few of them, eat me up." He was being sympathetic, but at the same time was telling us that we may never be able to prove anything.

I took out the USB and turned off the laptop. I gave him the USB. "You know he's coming back next year. He's already booked the same two rooms."

"Now that's worth knowing. What dates?" Detective Semchuk perked up.

"August 13 and 14 of next year."

He fingered the USB and said, "I'm going to think about things. It is still a long shot, but we might be able to do something. I'm going to think long and hard." He looked at both Julie and me and there was determination in his eyes. I would not want Detective Semchuk investigating me.

Too late for Allison Klassen I thought.

We said our goodbyes and he jogged across the open playing field heading home.

We returned to the hotel and toured the downtown. The city is an interesting mix. In its heyday it was Canada's Chicago of the North. But time had passed much of the city by. The 1920 & 1930 buildings were tired. Many were empty or housed pawn shops and second hand stores. There was a surprising number of homeless people. I shivered thinking how they could survive the cold Winnipeg winter. On the south side of Portage Avenue a renaissance was happening with new buildings, a new arena and a new convention centre. We made our way to Portage and Main, which supposedly was the windiest street corner in Canada. It was disappointing. First we could not find it. We got lost in a maze of tunnels under the street. After escaping the underground we found that the street was closed to pedestrians. Cars won over people. We found our way to the forks of the Assiniboine and Red Rivers. In many respects this was the heart of the original city. An abandoned railroad yard had been resurrected as an historic, upscale shopping area. The Canadian Museum of Human Rights looked over the scene. I was unsure what to make of the museum building; it was unique. From the locals we detected mixed reviews. Some gushed over it, others complained of the cost, and many had not yet been.

We found an Italian restaurant for supper and then returned to the hotel. After 8:00 p.m. we went down to talk to the staff. At reception was a good looking, dark haired young man; Don was his name. We introduced ourselves.

"Yes, Mr. Pangatan gave me a heads up that you'd like to talk to me. How can I help?"

It turned out that Don was in first year law at the University of Manitoba, just started law the month before, and worked the weekend shift at the hotel. He loved it. The nights were quiet and this allowed him to get caught up with the week's reading. I told him that I was a law professor and I gave him some advice on surviving law school.

I showed him the photographs of Allison and of Fraser. "This young woman and man stayed here on August 14 and 15 of this year. I understand that you were working that night. Do you remember seeing them?"

Don looked at the photographs. "She looks familiar," he smiled, "I'd notice her. But to be honest I don't remember them. We have a lot of guests coming through." We tried. As we were leaving, I asked him: "By the way back in August did you see Professor Burnside come to the hotel? He's a law professor here."

"Matter of fact I did."

My heart beat faster, "Do you recall anything about that?"

"He was visiting a guest, someone from another law school. He didn't know the room number. I had to check the name and ring up the room. The guest confirmed Professor Burnside and I released the elevator so that it could go to the guest's floor. Professor Burnside then went up. Of course, this was all before law school started and I didn't know Professor Burnside then."

I knew the time Burnside arrived, so I asked him, "Do you recall when Professor Burnside left?"

He thought for a moment, "I'd say it was about 2 to 3 in the morning. It was the middle of the night."

"Do you now have Professor Burnside as a teacher?"

"No, he teaches another section."

"Do you think he recognized you from the hotel?"

"I doubt it. As I said this was all before law school even started. We started law school first week of September and this was two weeks before."

"What time did your shift end Sunday morning?"

"8:00 a.m."

"Did you see the girl, Allison, Sunday morning before you left?"

"No, but if she had a car she may well have taken the elevator to the basement and left without going past reception or left later."

We wished him the best of luck. Don had confirmed that Burnside visited and stayed with Fraser from 10:41 to the early morning hours. Interesting.

We then spoke with the two cafe workers, Melissa and Bill, who worked the weekend. They were considerate, but had no recollection of seeing Allison or Fraser either that evening or the next day. Can't blame them, unless the customers are regulars, or exceptional, their faces would blur one into another and be forgotten.

Chapter 23

The next day Julie and I decided to drive back to Flemington using a different route. To the east of the Red River Valley, Highway 59 would take us to the Minnesota border and from there a series of back roads would take us home. The new route was about the same distance, maybe shorter than the freeway route, but we thought it might be more scenic and an adventure to boot. We fortified ourselves with coffee and gigantic cinnamon buns from the cafe before starting our return trip.

We were impressed with Winnipeg and were more impressed with the people whom we met along the way. The Manitoba licence plate says, "Friendly Manitoba", a most accurate moniker.

The day was bright and beautiful. Our mission in Winnipeg was accomplished. We were in good spirits, actually looking forward to the drive south.

Highway 59 was a good road and in just a little over an hour we were at the border. No wait. We had nothing to declare and received but a cursory look by the border customs people.

Once in Minnesota we started our back road travel to Flemington. I asked Julie to turn on my cell phone. We had turned our cell phones to airplane mode while in Canada, as our phone plan did not extend into Canada and the roaming charges were outrageous. As soon as my phone was activated it chirped with activity. There was a series of text messages from Wilbur and Mark:

Mark: Friday at 4:00 pm: Spoke with doctor. I think found the trigger.

Wilbur: Saturday at 6:25 pm: Need to talk. Uncovered important information.

Mark: Saturday at 7:03 pm: Suggest we meet 3:00 pm on Monday (I know it's a holiday) my office. Sorry rest of week in trial.

Wilbur: Saturday at 7:37 pm: OK with me.

Angela: Saturday at 10:16 pm: Holiday? What holiday? Fine with me.

I had Julie reply for me:

Andrew: Sunday at 9:53 am: Interesting news from Winnipeg. Meeting works for me.

It seemed to me that our investigation was reaching a climax. Yet, I had a nagging feeling that we still did not have enough evidence. If I were prosecuting this case, would I proceed? Truthfully I doubted it. Fraser would fight the allegations and have the faculty association's backing. Any litigation would be a battle and a very costly one at that. Perhaps Mark and Wilbur had uncovered key evidence; I hoped so.

The rolling hills, forests and wood lots of Northern Minnesota provided welcome relief from the flatness of the Red River Valley. Our trip was much slower, but more soothing for the soul. It was not until nearly 3:00 p.m. that we saw the outskirts of Flemington.

Home is always a welcome sight no matter the time away. I drove around the back of the house to the back lane leading to our garage, opened the garage door with the remote and drove in. Julie and I both noticed the open side door of the garage at the same time; the sun shone through the opening. The side door was locked when we left and Mrs. Hilderman didn't have a key. Our hearts sank. Had there been a break-in?

"Julie, stay in the car. Get your cell phone out. I'll take a look around." She nodded.

I got out of the car and went to look at the door. The door was still locked, but the door frame was broken at the lock and no longer caught the door lock. Probably a crowbar was used. Easy to do. We had no security system or alarm; after all we had Bruce the watch dog. Once in the garage the burglar could just walk into the house as we didn't lock the door from the garage to the house. That was my doing. I reasoned that if a burglar broke into the garage he would certainly proceed to break through the house door. Therefore, according to my reasoning, save the damage and just let the burglar in.

I went to the sports locker in the garage and picked up a baseball bat. "Door's been busted. I'll check the house."

"And I'm supposed to stay here?" Julie said sarcastically. She opened her door, "not a chance. Do you think it a wise thing possibly to confront a burglar, who may well still be in the house? Look at you; you have a baseball bat in your hand."

I hate it when Julie is right.

She ordered, "You go around the front and watch the front door and I'll phone the police right now." She dialed emergency and explained the situation. The dispatcher said that a police cruiser was in the vicinity and would be there in less than five minutes. We waited.

The police, young male and female officers, arrived within minutes. We gave them a quick summary and the two officers, guns drawn, entered our home. They emerged a few minutes later weapons holstered. No burglar was found. They examined the broken door and asked us to check the house for any lost items.

"Start with the master bedroom," said the female officer "thieves always head there first." Julie and I searched the room. I had over $100 stashed in my sock drawer. It was still there. Some of Julie's jewelry, which was kept in a small box on her dresser, was still there. We went through the other two bedrooms. Nothing was taken. We were relieved that the burglar or burglars had not vandalized the house.

"Check the bathrooms for any medication missing; addicts often break-in looking for prescription medication," offered the male officer, "or liquor. Check for missing liquor."

I felt somewhat ashamed, had a burglar broken into our house and deemed nothing worthy of stealing? Or, perhaps, the thief was scared off before finding anything.

The female officer took photographs of the door and was busy filling in a police report.

The large screen television was still in the living room, as was the stereo system. The den was the last room to check. The small television was on the small side table. But the laptop was missing.

I called out, "The laptop is missing." Julie and the officers arrived.

The female officer asked, "What type? And do you have the serial number?"

"It was a Dell, PC, over four years old. I'll get the serial number." I replied and went to the den closet where I kept the old computer boxes. I showed the officer the serial number on the box and she wrote it down."

She said, "I trust that the computer was password protected." More of a statement then a question.

"Well, yes and no," I sheepishly replied, "it is password protected; however, we rarely use the Dell. You see we bought a new Mac, which we took with us to Canada and, well, I had a post-it on the computer with the password. The computer and post-it are gone."

The female officer cringed a bit and gave me a 'you're an idiot' look. "Better change all of your passwords for your banking and credit cards," she advised. "Anything else missing?"

I carefully examined the rest of the den. I couldn't tell if my filing cabinet had been gone through, but I didn't off hand see any missing files. Behind one of the bookcases there is a secret compartment, where we keep our true valuables and papers–including the documentation given to me by Beth Jones on Ingrid Hedberg's rape case. The bookcase is on rollers. I hesitated to show even the police this compartment. Julie looked at me and I could tell that she too had reservations about revealing this secret.

Julie took the lead, "Come into the kitchen and you can finish the paperwork. I'll make some coffee as well." She led the officers away.

I followed her lead, "I'll continue checking in the den," I said. Once the officers and Julie were gone, I quickly rolled the bookcase to the side. The bookcase was built on roller castors hidden by the bottom frame of the case. It took a good push, but was manageable. I peered into the entrance hole in the false wall, which was two feet wide by five feet high–perfectly hidden by the bookcase. The compartment itself extended along the entire wall of the den. I had simply built the false wall out three feet from the original wall. In this compartment lay hidden rifles. Julie was a farm girl and she often went hunting with her father. When he passed away we inherited the rifles and Julie couldn't part with them. There was a 30-30 Remington deer hunting rifle, a pump action shotgun, a double barrel shotgun for duck hunting, and two single shot .22 calibre rifles for squirrel hunting plus ammunition in a locked box. Julie's good pieces of jewelry were in a separate fire proof box as were our important papers. The keys were on the ledge above the opening. Only Julie and our now grown-up children knew of the hidden compartment. Today it had served its purpose–all was in place; the vault had not been breached. I rolled the bookcase back and joined the officers in the kitchen.

The report was nearly finished. The officers told us that break-ins were increasing in the area. They attributed the rise to gangs and more drug problems flowing from the prevalence of crystal methamphetamine (ice). Before leaving they suggested that we improve our home security: install an alarm system, movement sensitive lights, and better locks. I could see that Bruce's occupation as a guard dog was in jeopardy. I had been to South Africa and saw firsthand how the white population lived in bunker homes surrounded by eight foot high fences, some electrified, all with glass or razor wire on the top to keep intruders out. I wasn't about to create or live in a bunker. I might invest in a fake alarm sticker instead.

We thanked the officers and watched them leave. Once the door was closed I put my arm around Julie. "Are you okay?" I asked.

She pulled back, "Yes, but I'm angry. This was no regular burglar. Nothing of value was taken other than an out of date laptop. Give me a break. The person who broke in was looking for information and not valuables."

Julie has spunk. She also was thinking exactly what I was thinking. Our burglar wasn't interested in money, electronics or alcohol. He wanted information. Who would want information? Who would want to know what I knew? Fraser. I responded, "You think Fraser was the burglar?"

Her reply was swift and firm, "Yes, I most certainly do. I bet that professor in Canada was on the phone back to Fraser as soon as you walked out of his office. You told him that you were there with me. Fraser would then know that we would be away. He'd have to wonder what you knew, why you were in Winnipeg. As you say, you tipped your hand by showing the professor, what's his name?"

"Burnside."

"Yes, Burnside, you showed him Allison's photograph."

Julie was speaking out loud what I thought. Fraser had also been to our house last year when we hosted a BBQ for a visiting professor and all the academic staff were invited. He knew the layout and he knew that we backed on to the river forest. It would be easy at night to enter the yard unseen from the forest and the garage side door was well hidden from view. Our burglar was no ordinary burglar.

"Julie, if you're right, and I think you are this means two things. First, he is worried. Why break in if there was nothing to find? He has just confirmed that he does have something to hide. Second, he's dangerous. For him to commit a break and enter shows both desperation and a will to do anything to stop me."

"What do we do?"

"I don't know. The problem's the same; we've got no proof. Loads of conjecture but no evidence."

"Should you call Detective Maurice? Maybe a forensic team could find some evidence?"

"I will call Richard, but a forensic team would be a waste of time. Fraser is smart. He'd wear gloves. Also, even if hair or his DNA was found he'd be able to explain that away because he was in our house last year."

"God damn it," was Julie's only reply.

"Let's go and get our guard dog. Who, for the record, was not on duty at the time of the burglary."

We went next door and retrieved Bruce, who was very happy to see us. We told Mrs. Hilderman about the break-in and asked whether she had heard anything. She had heard and seen nothing. We downplayed the break-in so as not to alarm her. We needn't have worried. Mrs. Hilderman was not a woman of faint heart. Although she was now alone—no husband, no dog—she was a feisty lady. We thanked her for taking care of Bruce and returned home.

Bruce was now on high alert; except when she was sleeping.

Julie started to put together a quick supper and I headed to the garage to do a quick repair job. Before I could get there, my cell rang; it was Richard Maurice.

"Hi, Richard, news travels fast."

"What do you mean?" he asked quizzically.

"I assume you're phoning about our break-in."

"What break-in?"

"Someone broke into our house when we were away in Winnipeg."

"Oh, no. Never heard about that. What's the damage and what'd they take?"

"The damage: a broken door jamb. They took an out of date Dell laptop."

"That's it?"

"That's it. They left money, alcohol, jewelry and electronics."

"Strange. Was the money and alcohol easy to find?"

"Where you'd expect it. The burglar was not interested in valuables." I paused and decided not to share with Richard my thoughts about Fraser; he'd think I was paranoid. "What were you calling about?"

"Oh, Detective Semchuk sent me a fax today about a William Burnside. Evidently you had given him that name."

I listened intently, "Yes, I had. And, anything interesting?"

"Well seven years ago William Burnside was investigated about a sexual assault. The complainant was an exchange student at the university from Norway. She claimed that she was raped by Burnside after a late night drinking party. Burnside was identified as her attacker. He denied everything. Before the City of Winnipeg Police could investigate further the student returned home. Case closed. No other criminal involvement."

An unproven claim of sexual assault may not be admissible in a court of law, but police use this type of information all the time to point them in the right direction. Professor Burnside may well be another Fraser.

"I understand that you have a video to show me as well. Detective Semchuk said it was very interesting."

"Yes, I have it on a USB for you. When would you like to pick it up?"

"Could I drop by within the half hour? I'm on duty tonight and am in the neighborhood."

"Sure. I'll be at home."

"See you soon."

"Oh, Richard, thank you for the information on Burnside."

"What information?" he laughed and hung up.

Julie and I discussed whether we should share our view that Fraser committed the burglary, but we both decided to keep this to ourselves at this stage. We'd see what the others found out at the meeting tomorrow.

The doorbell rang. Richard dressed in his homicide detective suit was at the door. Julie offered him something to eat, but he declined, "I had a quick bite at the local diner. My partner is still there nursing a coffee and pie. Thank you for the offer Mrs. Sturgis."

"Do you have a few minutes to watch the video?" I asked.

"Yes, if it's not too long."

I directed Richard into the den, connected the USB to the Mac and fast forwarded to 9:47 pm. I set the scene for him and pressed play. After watching Allison and Fraser take their first sips of coffee, I fast forwarded to 10:03 and we watched until Allison was helped out of the cafe.

"Well?" I asked.

"It appears that she was drugged. She was okay when she entered the cafe and then fifteen minutes later could hardly stand up. Professor it is consistent with what happened to that other student. I'll need to think more about what we can do."

"There's more," I said, "bear with me. At 10:39 watch." I played the segment with Burnside arriving at the cafe. "That is Professor William Burnside. What is he doing at that same hotel at that time of night?"

"How do you know it was Burnside?"

"I met with him Friday afternoon when we first arrived in Winnipeg. I also spoke with the Artist Hotel's reception clerk who was on duty the night we think Allison was attacked. It just so happens that the clerk was a law student to be at the University of Manitoba Faculty of Law. At the time he was not yet in law school, he started in September, and recognized Burnside as visiting the hotel that night."

"So you suspect that Burnside and Fraser were in this together?" Homicide Detective Richard Maurice was now questioning me.

"Yes I do."

"When you met Burnside on Friday, what did you tell him?"

"I asked him about the Winnipeg law conference. He coordinates it. And I asked him whether he recalled seeing Allison."

"How did you bring Allison up?" Richard was zeroing in.

"Unfortunately, I showed him a photograph of Allison."

"And?"

"I told him that Allison had died two days after returning from the conference. His response was strange. He never asked how she died."

"Because he already knew," Richard was quick.

"Yes. That was my conclusion as well."

"The surveillance tape confirms that Burnside and Fraser certainly knew each other and their relationship, at a minimum, was one where Burnside would visit Fraser at his hotel late at night." Richard gave me a penetrating look, "You realize that Burnside no doubt informed Fraser of your visit to Winnipeg, which would provide Fraser with a reason and opportunity to break into your home."

Richard was good. No point denying. "Yes, we thought the same, but we can't prove a darn thing."

"Who are the officers, who took the burglary report?" he asked.

I gave him their names. He knew them. "You said a laptop was taken. What was on the laptop? Anything important regarding Allison's death?"

"No. That laptop was used mostly by Julie. It was more of a back-up computer."

"Of course he'd have to have the password for the computer to find out anything, or hire someone to gain access to it."

Humiliation time again, "I hate to tell you this, but I put a post-it on the computer with the password. He'd have the password."

Richard shook his head, "Of course if Professor Fraser could access the computer and did so when he broke in he'd probably think that he had everything he needed and no need to search further. So he left. Because he was looking for information he would have gone to the den first. Professor, the computer may have saved your house being torn apart. It was like a decoy."

Richard was thinking along our same lines. There were too many coincidences pointing towards Allison being attacked. I felt much better that Richard now knew that we suspected Fraser and, I think, accepted our suspicions.

"I have to go," he said. "Meanwhile I will keep communications open with Detective Semchuk. He's a good cop. Also if you find out anything else please let me know."

"I will."

As he was leaving, he turned to me and said, "Professor be careful. If we are right Professor Fraser has a great deal to lose."

Chapter 24

I spent the morning and early afternoon marking papers, which is the worst part of the job for any professor. The papers were generally disappointing, but this was not unexpected. I saw effort; however, I saw very little application of facts to law. They will learn. Each paper took at least twenty minutes to mark, as I provided detailed feedback. The red ink was flowing. I had been told years before that my marking should be in a gentler colour. Green was suggested and I tried it for a semester. Poppycock. The green markings seem to fade into the paper and I want the students to see their mistakes and take in the feedback. I use pencil for the actual grade, because I often make changes after all the papers are marked. Consistency across marking is not easy and I tend to mark the first papers harder than the last bunch; I guess the students wear me down in terms of my standards. Therefore, my practice is to finish marking and return to the first bunch to double check. Students take their marks seriously and I owe it to them to do the same; some professors unfortunately do not.

Just after 2:30 I left for the meeting. The day was blustery and grey. Rain mixed with squalls of sleet. It was a good day to work. I arrived at Mark's office to see Angela walking from her own downtown office. I waited for her.

"Good day for ducks," I said as she approached.

"Even they'd be heading south. Tell me again why we live in this country?"

"Because we're hardy folk."

I rang the buzzer for Mark's office. He acknowledged and said he would be right down. Wilbur appeared from across the street. Mark greeted us and opened the door. We were thankful to get inside and Mark escorted us up to his firm's office. The boardroom was ready; coffee and muffins were waiting.

As we poured our coffee, I asked Mark, "What trial do you have this week?"

"It's a truck and car accident. My client was driving the car and was seriously injured. Our case is that the truck driver fell asleep at the wheel and drove through the stop sign. He's our first witness and I imagine he is rather nervous right now. We have evidence that he drove over his allotted time that day, after being on the job for eight straight days, and a few other things that he will have to explain. We obviously sued the truck company and I don't understand why they don't settle. They'll wish they had." He shot me a confident grin.

We sat around the boardroom table and Mark took charge.

"Thank you all for coming in today. I'll get right to it; I know we are all very busy. I have important information to report and I think both Wilbur and Andy have new information as well. Once we have digested that new information I think we should look to what, if anything, we do next. Is that fine with everyone?"

We all nodded in agreement.

"I'll go first," said Mark, "I met with Dr. Susan Burnett on Friday in her office. She was Allison's doctor. She was very co-operative and I think it fair to say was shaken by Allison's death. First, the basics, Allison was in extremely good health. She had no medical or physical issues that the doctor knew of. She had done Allison's yearly medical in early August, so it was up to date. I asked her about any depression or mental concerns. There was none. Allison was in good spirits and was looking forward to second year law. Therefore, she had a clean bill of health."

He paused, "I asked her about birth control and she laughed and told me that Allison was taking no birth control measures. She wasn't on the pill, a diaphragm or any other protection. She went on to explain that Allison had told her that she was saving herself for marriage. She felt it was God's will and command and she felt it was the right thing to do. She wanted to be a woman of purity for her husband. Dr. Burnett was impressed by both Allison's conviction and her understanding that others may well look at sex as a healthy activity outside of marriage, but that was not her belief. Dr. Burnett explained that she had been Allison's doctor for two years and on each visit she would question Allison about whether she wished to go on the pill. And Allison would always smile and say, 'No thank you'."

We were all silent.

Mark went on, "I did some quick research and it does appear that in the Bible sex out of wedlock is regarded by some as a sin. I'll read to you a short passage from Corinthians I Chapter 7:2, 'Nevertheless, to avoid fornication, let every man have his own wife, and let every woman have her own husband.' Allison abided by God's will. We can debate the rights and wrongs of her view, but that doesn't matter. What matters is that was her deeply held belief."

"This is the trigger for her suicide. Imagine if she was attacked and raped by Professor Fraser and that in her drugged state she realized what was happening to her and who knows what else he did to her. Her quest for purity and abstinence would be destroyed. Even more so than other rape victims she would go on to blame herself. She had let herself down and God down. You know it's quaint to talk about saving yourself for marriage, but Allison believed that deeply. Professor Fraser, I believe, destroyed that dream. This would have been a terrible psychological blow to her; it would have been devastating to her very being."

None of us said a word. Angela, her voice trembling, finally spoke, "That poor, poor girl. He raped her; why else would she kill herself? This wasn't just a grope, a touching, he raped her. He killed her spirit; he killed her purity."

Mark was right; we had found the trigger for her suicide. My head was spinning. I was convinced that Fraser raped Allison, but I was still grappling with why this would cause her to take her life. We now had the answer. Fraser was responsible, but we still needed to prove the rape.

I broke my silence, "Mark, you're right this is the trigger. I'm shocked. It also makes it all that more important that we find the evidence to make our case."

Wilbur got up to pour himself more coffee. I saw that his hand was shaking. Wilbur was a person who believed in the goodness of people. He always saw the positive in all of us. I think for the first time he now realized that Fraser had raped Allison.

Mark concluded quietly, "I have taken a formal statement from Dr. Burnett. I also called Dr. Markes, the medical examiner, and he confirmed that he found no birth control devices in Allison's body and that her blood tests were not consistent with her being on the pill."

Mark turned to Wilbur, and in a gentle voice he said, "Wilbur, I believe that you have some information to share with us."

"Yes, yes I do," Wilbur sat down and gathered himself. "Over the weekend, as you know, I was in D.C. at the law teacher's hiring fair. We have a low level starting position to fill and are recruiting. I took the opportunity to speak with a couple of senior professors from Professor Fraser's former place of employment, Eastern University. I explained to them that he was coming up for tenure and that any information that they might share would be very helpful and that everything was confidential. They spoke freely and were glad to see Fraser leave Eastern. As we know he is not the easiest person to get along with."

He took a sip of coffee and continued, "I raised with them his treatment of women and I could see that I touched a chord. They looked at each other and after a moment's pause one of them said that there had been rumours that he was seeing students. He emphasized that this was but a rumour. He had nothing concrete and his colleague concurred. So not much there, except that they would not want Fraser tenured."

He went on, "I then contacted Professor Gerald Grant, the Founding Dean of the Caribbean University of Law in Georgetown, Cayman Islands. I left a number of messages, and had no response. He was recruiting for a number of positions so I imagined that he was rather busy, but I also got the feeling that he was avoiding me. I eventually decided to go to his table personally. I introduced myself and I would describe his greeting as frosty. That changed immediately when I said to him that I had some questions about Professor Jerome Fraser, who I understood taught at his school some four years before, and who had now applied for tenure at our school. Professor Grant's demeanour changed completely. We agreed to meet in his hotel room over the lunch hour for a quick chat. He told me that he'd have something for me as well."

Wilbur opened a folder that he had in front him. "When I met with Professor Grant he was forthright. He had fired Fraser and he had fired him because he had in his words 'violated one of his students'. Fraser was hired to teach first year Torts at the school. You need to know that the Caribbean School is based on the English model. Students enter law as a first degree, right out of high school, unlike our system, which requires a prior university degree before entering law. The result is that the students in first year are young, very young. The young woman involved had just turned eighteen years of age. Fraser had invited her out for dinner. During happy hour he bought her a number of drinks. She was by her own admission drunk. He took her to his apartment and they had sex. She didn't say it was rape, but she did say that he took advantage of her. This was in mid November. She went home for Christmas and told her mother. Her mother told her father, who is a prominent barrister in the British Virgin Islands. He was not pleased. Neither was Professor Grant, who called Professor Fraser in and asked him about the student's complaint. Fraser evidently was not contrite and told Professor Grant that it was none of his business; that it was not unusual for American professors to date their students. He said it was totally consensual and off campus. Professor Grant was incensed. He told Fraser that she was an eighteen year old and that in the Cayman Islands there are such things as moral and professional behaviour. He fired Fraser on the spot, called security, had him removed from campus and revoked his work visa so that Fraser had to leave the island within 24 hours."

Out of the open folder, Wilbur took out copies of a document and passed it around. "This is the copy of an email that Professor Grant wrote and sent to our Dean Clarke. I'll give you a moment to read it."

gwgrant@caribbeanlaw.ky

Gerald W. Grant Founding Dean of Law

To: jclarke@flemingtonu.mn
7 January 17:52

Dear Sir:

RE: Assistant Professor Jerome Fraser

Allow me to introduce myself; I am the Founding Dean of the Caribbean Law School, Cayman Islands. Assistant Professor Jerome Fraser was hired by me to teach Torts Law to our first year students. It is my understanding that he is a member of your faculty presently on sabbatical.

I can advise that I terminated Professor Fraser's employment with us earlier today. I did so because of his inappropriate and unprofessional conduct involving one of his first year students.

In summary: he dated one of his students, who at the time had just turned 18 years of age; he plied her with drink and then had sex with her. This is not acceptable under our code of conduct for staff. I confronted Professor Fraser and he saw nothing wrong with his actions. I do not see it that way. We do not expect our professors to become involved with their students.

I am bringing this to your attention as his conduct brings disrepute not only to my university, but to yours as well. As he is an employee of your university, I expect that you may well bring disciplinary action against Professor Fraser, and I would be most happy to co-operate.

Should you require any further information do not hesitate to contact me.

Sincere Regards,

Gerald Grant
Founding Dean of Law
Caribbean University
Georgetown, Cayman Islands
Original to follow in post

Angela was the first to comment, "Fraser just can't keep his pants on."

Looking at Wilbur and me, Mark asked, "Do you know of any disciplinary action brought against Professor Fraser?"

"No," I replied, "and I doubt that we would ever hear. The faculty association would put a lid on this and I doubt that Dean Clarke would have done anything. It would be easier for him to ignore the conduct."

Wilbur provided more, "What I can say is that Dean Clarke did receive the email." He took out more copies from the folder and passed them around:

> jclarke@flemingtonu.mn
>
> To: gwgrant@caribbeanlaw.ky
> 10 January   9:02 am
>
> Dear Dean Grant:
> RE: Assistant Professor Jerome Fraser
>
> Thank you for your email dated January 7. I will certainly look into the allegations and deal with them according to our university processes. I will contact you should I require further information.
>
> Regards,
>
> John Clarke
> Dean of Law
> Flemington University

"So Dean Clarke was made aware of a rape allegation against Professor Fraser the year before, which he dismissed. He was then told of another sexual impropriety involving Professor Fraser and a young woman. Yet, as far as we know, he did nothing. He's bloody well shielding a predator. It's like the Catholic Church shielding and moving their pedophile priests." Mark was putting on his litigation hat, "Did Dean Clarke ever contact Professor Grant?"

"No," said Wilbur, "and I can tell you that Professor Grant was livid about that. He didn't want anything to do with Flemington University and that is why he never returned my calls. Once I explained to him that Professor Fraser was up for tenure and I wanted information he was more than willing to talk to me. He'll do anything we request. Professor Grant was personally offended by Professor Fraser's conduct and attitude."

"Could Dean Clarke have terminated Fraser?" asked Mark.

"It is complicated," I said, "Fraser has a tenure track appointment, which means technically the professor is on probation for up to six years. In the fifth or sixth year the professor applies for tenure. The decision on tenure is made by a university committee; however, a negative word from the dean of the professor's faculty would carry much weight. And, of course, should a professor commit acts contrary to the interests of the university then they can be terminated."

"There actually is more," Wilbur added, "after three years the professor on tenure track is reviewed. A negative review can terminate the appointment. I can tell you that I was on our school's tenure committee at the time when Professor Fraser was up for review and Fraser had Dean Clarke's full support."

"So arguably the university is culpable for keeping a potential predator on staff," concluded Mark.

Wilbur agreed, "The problem, of course, is that the information I uncovered goes more to the university's guilt than it does to Fraser's. I'm afraid that it doesn't help us much in proving that he raped Allison."

"Yes, that's the problem," said Mark, "thank you Wilbur. Andy what did you find out in Winnipeg?"

It was my turn. "I'm going to start by introducing this man." I handed out Associate Professor William Burnside's profile taken off the University of Manitoba's website. It included a photograph of him and brief biography, including personal interests. As they looked at the profile I filled them in, "Associate Professor William Burnside co-ordinates the conference that Fraser goes to each year in Winnipeg. I contacted him in advance and arranged to meet with him on Friday afternoon." I went on to describe our meeting and admitted to them my mistake, given my firm belief that he was a friend of Fraser's and had been in contact with him. "This means that Fraser has a whiff that at least I am doing some snooping around about Allison's death. I'll come back to that later."

"Did you tell the professor that you were staying at the Artist Hotel?" asked Mark.

"Noooo," I was thinking, "no, I did say that I was staying downtown, but there are a number of much larger hotels downtown."

I moved on to the Artist Hotel and Mr. Pangatan. I had made copies of photographs that I had taken of Rembrandt room 2 and distributed those. I then introduced the video surveillance. Mark busied himself connecting my Mac to the video projector in the boardroom. Once it was ready I continued, "The surveillance that I am going to show you is split screen. It will show you Allison and Fraser the evening of Saturday, August 15." I started the video.

It was not easy to watch. I noticed that Mark swallowed hard when Allison appeared. She was so happy, full of life. I paused the video at the point where Fraser got the coffee and took them to the mixing table. "In my view this is when he put the drugs into Allison's drink. Watch his right side very carefully." I played the video. Angela asked to play that segment again. There was agreement around the table that he put something into one of the drinks, and that he appears to have blocked what he was doing by turning his back to Allison's view and that of the surveillance camera. I moved the tape through the next few minutes to just before 10:00 p.m. "Watch how Allison appears now." I stopped the tape with Allison being helped out of the cafe.

More silence.

"She was drugged. There is little doubt about that," said Angela, "I can only imagine what he did to her once he got her up to the room. She'd be defenceless."

Mark had regained his composure, but was white with either rage or sadness or both, "This is the most powerful evidence yet that Allison was drugged and, why drug a young woman? You do it to take advantage of her."

I replied by telling him of Detective Semchuk's counter response and I posed this question to Mark, "If you were defending Fraser think of your line of inquiry. Think of what the video doesn't tell us. We don't have a complainant. We can't question her about what she may have eaten that evening, had she been feeling unwell, isn't Fraser's behaviour consistent with him just helping her to get up and leave?"

"I also want to show you another part of the video surveillance," and I fast forwarded to Burnside. I stopped the tape when he was at the counter and there was a good facial view, "Recognize this man?"

"It's Professor Burnside," exclaimed Angela. The others compared the face on screen to the photograph in the profile

"Yes," and I went on to tell them about Don, the first year law student, who confirmed that Burnside was there and remained in the room until 2:00 or 3:00 a.m. I also told them about what Detective Semchuk had found out about Burnside. "If we accept that Allison was raped by Fraser that evening, then Burnside must have been involved as well."

"You're suggesting that two perpetrators were involved, not just Fraser, but isn't that rather improbable?" questioned Wilbur.

"According to Detective Semchuk predators have a knack of finding each other. Also think about this. Fraser always goes to the Winnipeg conference. Burnside co-ordinates that conference. Both have been involved with young female students. We can now place Burnside at the hotel the night we suspect Allison was attacked. And we have evidence Burnside stayed for three to four hours. Coincidence?" I asked.

Angela spoke up, "Andy would you go back to the start of the surveillance tape. Burnside was carrying something wasn't he?" I went to the time when Burnside first appeared. He did have something strapped over his shoulder.

"A man's purse?" Mark suggested.

"A briefcase, perhaps?" Wilbur threw in.

We continued to scrutinize the tape, "No," Angela spoke out, "It's a camera case. Look at Burnside's profile, 'Professor Burnside enjoys a good game of chess and photography.' That bastard was going to take pictures or videotape what was going on!"

Angela was right. The object was too wide to be a briefcase or purse. It sure looked like a camera case.

We were all stunned. I then said to them, "There's more. As I mentioned I'm sure that Burnside would have contacted Fraser about my visit and my questions about Allison. Burnside also knew that Julie was with me." I went on to tell them about the break-in and the stolen laptop and my conclusion that Fraser was the burglar.

I posed the key question, "What do we do now?"

"What about going to the police? This is getting dangerous," Wilbur suggested.

"Both Detectives Maurice and Semchuk don't feel that they have enough to go on. No complainant and only circumstantial conjecture, which can be explained away. They couldn't get a search warrant or arrest warrant. They could question both Fraser and Burnside, but what is that going to get them? Nothing, other than putting them on notice." I went on, "I also forgot to mention, Mr. Pangatan searched the hotel records for Fraser's reservations for the last five years." I distributed copies of the reservation record. "They confirm his staying in the same room and the student occupants of Rembrandt 2. Note he has made a reservation for next year."

"Shit," said Angela under her breath.

"Detective Semchuk thinks that might be the best opportunity to catch them. He doesn't think we have enough now."

Mark stood up and in an exasperated tone, "Come on folks. Around this table are four strong legal minds, there has to be a way."

"What about a wrongful death suit here in Minnesota?" Angela threw out.

"It would be a tough case, even tougher because so much happened in Canada. I'm sure that Fraser would move to strike and, of course, we'd be showing him our hand. Sorry I just don't see it, without solid proof of a rape." Mark responded.

"Could Ingrid Hedberg be convinced to bring an action?" Wilbur tried.

"Ingrid has made it clear that she will not bring an action," said Angela, "she knows that she would be torn apart on the stand. She's willing to come forward in support of any action brought by the Klassens, but not on her own."

"Angela, what is clear is that you need to re-interview Ingrid. We need more detail, more information as to what happened in that hotel room." Mark continued, "We think that Burnside was in the room as well as Fraser. We need confirmation. You'll have to be very careful how you question her. You can't suggest to her another person was present or that photographs or videos were taken."

"Yes, I agree. I'll be careful, and at least I'll be able to give her more about what we have uncovered, without mentioning Burnside." Angela then suggested, "I'd like Andy to be present. Ingrid respects you a great deal, and it would help to convince her to re-live that night if what you've found came from you. She can always ask you to leave if uncomfortable talking about the attack with you present."

Mark added, "It would also be good if Andy were present as he could testify as to any conversation or attest to the information on any affidavit. Better him then you Angela. No offence but it never looks good having a lawyer testify as to what a witness said or providing an affidavit."

"No offence taken, Mark. I agree with you one hundred per cent. I was actually thinking of having one of my paralegals sit in, until Andy came to mind."

"If it will help, I'll make myself available. Any time this week after 4:00 p.m." I said.

Wilbur had been silent, thinking. He now spoke, "What about bringing a wrongful death suit in Canada? That is where the wrong occurred. Furthermore, in Canada there is such a thing as a civil search warrant; it is called an Anton Piller Order, named after a British case. It was a creation of that great English judge, Lord

Denning. It really is not a search warrant; rather it puts pressure on a party to permit a search. I'll be clearer. It orders a party to give permission for the search and if the party refuses they can be found in contempt of the court order. Clever isn't it? Lord Denning accepted that no court in the land had the power to issue a civil search warrant to enter a person's home forcibly. So he created an order permitting the search. The order is done ex parte. The plaintiff files a statement of claim and motion to obtain an Anton Piller order at the same time, without the defendant knowing. There is a powerful element of surprise."

"What's needed to get such an order?" Wilbur had Mark's attention.

Wilbur was a master of remedy law; he had taught the subject for over twenty years. He continued, "There are four elements, if my memory serves me right, 1) the plaintiff has a strong prima facie case, 2) the conduct allegedly committed by the defendant is serious, 3) there is clear and convincing evidence that the defendant has incriminating evidence and 4) it can be shown that there is a real possibility that the defendant may destroy the evidence. The Anton Piller order does not authorize a search of the defendant's premises. Rather, the defendant is ordered to allow the search. You can't break in; the defendant, or a person authorized by the defendant, must allow the entry and search. Now if the defendant or authorized person doesn't comply then they are in contempt and may be locked up. It is a powerful coercive tool. We have something similar in the United States, called impoundment orders, but these usually only apply in copyright cases."

Mark was now fully engaged, "Let's look at the elements. First, do we have a strong prima facie case? We've accumulated a great deal of circumstantial evidence, is it strong enough? It will be if Ingrid recalls hearing or seeing a second person or a camera or recorder."

Angela confirmed, "That is why interviewing Ingrid is so critical. We should hold off doing anything until we've done that."

"Agreed," said Mark. He went on, "Second, is the defendant's conduct serious? Definitely, we are alleging a rape leading to suicide." No one disagreed.

"What was third?" he asked.

"Clear and convincing evidence the defendant has incriminating evidence," replied Wilbur.

"Once again if we have Ingrid remembering a camera and we have the video showing what seems to be a camera case and we have Burnside's interest in photography, I think we have met that element, which just leaves us with the fourth element, a real possibility of destruction. Anyone who has possession of rape tapes will, when facing a law suit, destroy the evidence–that's a given." Mark ended his summary, "Accepting that we can meet the elements, Wilbur please go over the process again."

"We bring a civil action in Winnipeg on behalf of the Klassens claiming damages on behalf of their deceased daughter's estate for sexual assault. I don't know if Canadian courts will allow for such an action; in many instances any action dies with the deceased victim. We might have to claim for wrongful death, which they do recognize. We'll have to research the law."

Wilbur continued, "We name both Fraser and Burnside as defendants. We simultaneously file the statement of claim and motion for an Anton Piller order complete with affidavits in support. We ask for an emergency motion hearing, or whatever they call it in Canada. We may have to provide a deposit as security to the court to cover damages for a wrongful search. I know that is common."

"What kind of deposit are we talking about?" asked Mark.

"Canadian costs are not nearly as high as in the United States. I'd guess between five to ten thousand dollars. Don't know for sure." Wilbur replied and without losing a beat continued outlining the process. "For Anton Piller orders, you also need to have a supervising solicitor, who will oversee the search. Plaintiff's counsel do not do the searches. The supervising solicitor usually hires experienced police officers or private detectives to do the searches and it is recommended that the searches be videotaped. All of this is contained in an affidavit or in the accompanying order."

Mark was excited, "This might be the answer. I appeared in Manitoba on a case a few years back and worked with a Canadian law firm. They are small, but good. I'll contact them to see about a wrongful death action and they can prepare a statement of claim for me. They'll know the Canadian law. They can also arrange for an independent supervising lawyer. I'll need to get a temporary practicing certificate in Manitoba. Andy, you are most familiar with the case, you can provide the affidavit."

I nodded, but then inserted a note of caution, "Just so I understand an Anton Piller Order, what if we knock on Burnside's door, show him the order, and he says no—you can't come in. He can do that, correct?"

"Yes," replied Wilber, "Except I've never read a case where that happened. I assume the defendants realize that it is a court order, subject to a finding of contempt, which means that they can be imprisoned; although, in fairness, I've never read a case where a defendant was in fact imprisoned. They also face an adverse inference from their refusal. My sense is that most defendants simply are overwhelmed by the shock and circumstance of a lawyer arriving with a court order to search accompanied by a team of searchers. I would want a group of big, burly men--bigger the better."

"But Burnside could refuse?" I pressed.

"Yes."

"Keep in mind he is a law professor and would not be easily intimidated. What do we do if he refuses? Our problem remains, adverse inference or not, we need to prove that the rape occurred." I was playing devil's advocate.

Angela joined in, "I doubt that there would be too many cases where the defendant is alleged to have committed a rape or homicide. Burnside would have a real reason to bar the door."

Mark countered, "If he refuses I think we would then call Detective Semchuk. Surely the refusal in the face of a court order would provide sufficient probable cause for the police to obtain a search warrant."

"And in the meantime Burnside has time to destroy the evidence," I said.

"It's a reality that we have to face, but what other choice do we have?" asked Angela, who continued, "we need proof of the rapes, and if we believe that Burnside was involved, why else would he bring a camera to the hotel late in the night? We have to chance it. A question that I have is whether we tell Detective Semchuk?"

"I'd have concerns about doing that," said Mark, "courts do not like civil processes being used to further police prosecutions. In my view, it is better that we stand separate and apart from the police. Now if we find something that is another matter, but we wait until that occurs."

"What if Burnside refuses us entry, do we contact Detective Semchuk then?" I asked.

"Yes, I would think so. It might be too late, as you mentioned before, Burnside could well destroy the evidence, but we call the police and give them the information and they do what they will with it." replied Mark.

"I wonder if Burnside is married." Mused Wilbur, "Mark, you should have your law firm in Winnipeg do a background check on Burnside, where he lives, married, any children. The reason I mention this is that Anton Piller orders do not require the defendant's permission to enter a premises, rather the order can be crafted so that a person 'appearing to be in charge of the premises'–I think that's the wording used–may permit entry and the search. I would think that Burnside's wife, who knows nothing of his wrongdoing, would be more inclined to allow the search to proceed. We may well look to conducting a search when she is home and he is not. And I also suggest that a female investigator be added to the team, who might be better suited to persuade Mrs. Burnside–that is if there is a Mrs. Burnside."

I had to smile, beneath Wilbur's academic facade, he possessed a calculating mind.

Mark was laughing and said, "Wilbur you have a real conniving streak in you." Wilbur said nothing in reply, but his eyes were twinkling.

Mark then took control, "Are we agreed that we look into an Anton Piller order?" All agreed. He then summarized our tasks, "Angela you will contact Ingrid and arrange, with Andy, a second interview. Wilbur will you do further research on Anton Piller orders in Canada, specifically Manitoba? I will contact my Manitoba firm to give them, at this time only a heads up, and do checks on Burnside. We'll wait to hear back about Ingrid's interview. Angela any point talking to the other former student?"

"Jennifer Cunningham," replied Angela, "No, I really don't think she wants to talk unless there is something concrete."

"Finally, we have to report back to the Klassens. I propose we wait until we have Ingrid's interview, and obviously we can't proceed with any action in Canada without their approval. I'd like to have all information before I meet with them again, and Andy, I think it would be important for you to be there as well." I nodded.

It had been an eventful few hours. We were all, I think, both excited by the day's news but apprehensive in that legal war could well break-out shortly.

It was past 5:00 p.m. and time for us all to call it a day. As we were leaving, Mark asked me to stay for a moment. The others left.

"Andy, I'm worried about the break-in," said Mark, "I agree that the finger points to Professor Fraser, and that's my concern. He's dangerous and if he thinks you are on to him he will strike again."

"I doubt that he'd resort to violence," I replied none too convincingly.

"But you don't know. Here is what I was thinking, why not give him false information that you've found nothing and have given up?"

"How do we do this?"

"You prepare a thin file, labelled 'Allison Klassen Suicide'. In it you place a note, attended Allison's funeral and asked by the Klassens to look into whether anything at the law school caused Allison to kill herself. Include some memos about talking to certain students. You know the type of thing. Nothing found. Maybe indicate possible drug concerns. Whatever. Include your trip to Winnipeg. Say it was already pre-arranged. Maybe include staying at a different hotel. Include meeting with Burnside. Put in how impressed you were with him. And, your conclusion, she must have been depressed, nothing at the law school caused her to take her life. Maybe indicate that you will tell the Klassens. Put this file on your desk or wherever you keep ongoing files. Leave your office door open. Do you do that at times?"

"Yes—all the time."

"I am pretty sure that Fraser will want to search your office, having found nothing on your home computer. With the false file, he'll assume you have closed the case."

Mark had thought this through and in short order. "You called Wilbur conniving," I laughed, "but you know, it could work. I do often leave my office open–nothing in it to take–and Fraser is only four doors down the hall."

"There's more," said Mark, "I have a tech wiz, who does covert work for me. Sometimes we have witnesses or parties under surveillance and he is good. He has a miniature camera that records when triggered by motion. You can activate it by your cell phone. You leave your office, activate the camera, and it will then record only if there is motion. The camera can be easily hidden in one of your bookcases. Easy. What do you think?"

I thought for a moment. It was a simple plan with little downside; I'd simply be putting my own office under surveillance and if I were to be totally honest with myself, Fraser did pose a danger to both me and Julie. "Mark it sounds like a plan. I'll do it."

"Thanks. I feel better. I'll have John call you to place the camera. I'll call him right away. The sooner we do this the better. You work on preparing a false file."

I left feeling more secure.

CHAPTER 25

John turned up at my office right at 3:00 p.m. on Tuesday, as arranged. I knew that Fraser would not be around; he had his Advanced Constitutional Law seminar.

John was an interesting character largely because he was so uninteresting. If I had to describe him I would say nondescript. Distinguishing characteristics, he had none. He was so ordinary looking. Average build, average face, average everything; even his hair was a nondescript brown, cut to average length. He would fade into any crowd and that is probably why he would be so adept at doing surveillance.

We introduced ourselves and I closed my door. John had with him a backpack, which made him look like a student; he opened the pack and took out a box cover for a book and a small camera. "I was told by Mark that you wanted office surveillance and that you had an office full of law books, so I took the liberty of bringing this book along." It was entitled "Convicting the Innocent" by Edwin Borchard. The box for the book was empty. There was a small hole cut in the spine of the box. John took the camera and carefully placed it in the box, fixing it in place with masking tape so that the lens of the camera aligned with the hole. He talked as he worked, "This camera works on a nine volt battery so it will have life for a long time. I'll program the camera to your cell phone. When you leave your office you can turn the camera on. It will start recording based on motion, slight motion will turn it on, after thirty seconds of inactivity it will automatically turn off. That way you won't have hours of wasted recording. The camera records only activity. When you come back you can turn it off."

Brilliant, yet scary at the same time, where has our privacy gone? "How will I know that it has recorded anything?" I asked.

"Your cell phone will receive a message giving you the time. You'll then have to take the camera down, and press play. If it shows you something interesting keep it. If not, delete it. I'll show you."

John finished putting the camera into the box. He then asked me for my cell phone and downloaded an app called "I spy". He was ready to show me.

"Keep in mind that I'm a bit of a dinosaur when it comes to cell phones."

"It's simple," he replied.

I've heard that one before. I swear that techies should test their equipment on idiots like me rather than on themselves. What is easy to a techie is a total mystery to most regular folk. He showed me the app and how to access it. I wrote that all down, step by step. The camera box was placed to the right of my desk and provided a clear view of the door to its right, the desk to its left and bookcase across. The window behind my desk would not shine light directly on to the camera. John explained that it was better to have a camera placed to the side of direct vision when people entered a room. If the camera were placed directly behind me there would be more chance for a person to see the lens. He knew what he was doing. We tested it. Both he and I moved out of the camera's field of vision. I accessed the app and turned the camera on. We waited for a minute. I then walked in front of the camera to my desk and moved back outside of the camera's field. We waited another minute. I turned the app off and immediately received a message the camera had been activated at 3:22 pm. I went to the box, carefully opened it and pressed play. There I was going to my desk. The recording was quite good. I played it and the camera turned off after thirty seconds. I deleted the recording and put the camera box back in place. We tested it again to see if I had put it back correctly. It worked perfectly a second time.

I thanked John and he replied with, "Good hunting", and left as slyly as he had come. I had prepared a false file labelled "Allison Klassen", using an older somewhat worn folder, and was quite proud of its authenticity. I included a website for the Holiday Inn Hotel in Winnipeg, downtown, a note with a reservation number and cost for a room for two nights. I had prepared consecutively dated memos using different pens and paper. The first memo outlined that the Klassens had asked me at the funeral to see if their daughter had had any trouble at the law school and I undertook to ask around. The file was opened. Then there were memos to self about conversations with Maria Dempster, other second year students (taken from the memorial service), and a memo describing my meeting with Professor Burnside in which I described how impressed I was with him and that all was normal. I ended with a conclusion that I would meet with the Klassens when next in Flemington to tell them that I had found nothing. I left the folder on my desk nearby my active file holder. The bait was set. In my view the best days to leave my door open would be on Mondays and Wednesdays, when I did most of my teaching. Fraser was usually in both days in the afternoons.

Later in the afternoon Maria dropped by for our weekly meeting. I asked her whether there was any movement by the law students' executive in response to Fraser's application for tenure and promotion. She told me that the law exec had decided to submit a letter stating their "serious concern" regarding Professor Fraser.

"That's the best I could get them to do," lamented Maria.

I consoled her, "Frankly it is more than I expected, at least it raises student concern."

"I wanted it stronger," said Maria, "I wanted the law exec to say that he ought not to be granted tenure period, but he has his groupies. I know he'll get them to write letters in support. That's why I and about a half dozen other students have written individual negative letters."

"Maria, you've done all you can and in years to come, if he gets tenure, you can still say you tried."

Maria was not pacified, "I don't like to lose."

She was going to be a tough lawyer I thought.

"Got to go we've got our first intramural volleyball game at five." She got up and in sad voice said, "It won't be the same without Allison. She was our best player..."

I had to get to class. The mid-term papers and results were to be returned to the students at the end of class. I had earlier posted online a student's paper, anonymously and with the student's permission. The paper was very well done and showed how the student had applied the facts to the law in a well organized and concise manner. The other students would see what was expected of them and also see that one of their fellow students was capable of such work. An added benefit was that it quelled quibbling from the students over marks; after seeing a polished product they'd be happy with the mediocre grades received. They'd take a passing grade with relief. When I left for class I left my door open, and turned the camera on.

The class turned out to be a real dud. The students were anxious to get their papers returned and their minds were not on the class readings. The class could not end soon enough. In the last ten minutes, I chatted with them about the papers, highlighting common mistakes, missed issues, and wrong arguments. I tried to be gentle but tough at the same time. I encouraged all of them to read the feedback provided very carefully and to learn from it. For some I had written on their papers that they were to come and see me; these were the struggling students. The students took their papers in hand and quickly exited the room to lick their academic wounds.

I returned to my office. Before entering I turned the camera off. It had not been activated. There was a voice message from Angela,

"Interview arranged for Thursday 5:00 p.m. with Ingrid at my office. Please confirm."

I did.

CHAPTER 26

On Thursday we had a brown bag lunch for our adjunct instructors. These downtown lawyers teach over 40% of our courses and we could not provide our program without the adjuncts. The Teaching and Learning Committee puts on two lunches a year for them. Gwen, Wilbur and I attend, representing the Committee, and we invite all members of the faculty as well. Usually four or five attend. Not surprisingly, the faculty who do turn up are the committed teachers, who are in no need of advice or guidance on teaching; those faculty members in need of remedial assistance are nowhere to be seen. It is ever thus. There is no agenda and we spend the lunch hour talking about teaching. We exchange ideas on what works, and what doesn't work. The adjuncts are hungry to learn. In turn, I find the lunches reinvigorating. One cannot help but be refreshed by the enthusiasm and dedication of these young bright lawyers, who are essentially donating their time to educate our students.

The lunch ended and I returned to my office. I had left my door open and had activated the camera. As I approached, I turned the camera off. Immediately I received two text messages; the camera had been turned on at 12:16-12:21 and then again at 12:33-12:34. My heart pounded. Had Fraser taken the bait? I closed my door, retrieved the camera, and played the recorded segments.

At 12:16 Fraser entered my office. Caught! He closed the door, looked around and sat in my chair at my desk. He started to finger through my active files on the desk. As planned, he found the

Allison Klassen folder. He opened it, took a quick look, and got up with folder in hand. He momentarily paused at the door listening and, when satisfied, gently opened the door. Evidently seeing no one in the hall he left leaving the door open.

At 12:33 he returned. This time he did not close the door. He put Allison's file back on my desk and left. I smiled to myself. Usually Fraser did not come in on Thursdays, but he would have known about the lunch session and that I and a number of other staff members would be there and he seized the opportunity. I felt confident that our trap worked and that now he would be lulled into a false sense of security. Concerns about my snooping would vanish. The folder said it all; I found nothing and knew nothing. No doubt he would be calling Burnside to reassure him. I felt relieved that my foolhardy error in going to Burnside had been corrected.

Later that day I drove downtown for the meeting with Ingrid Hedberg. Angela's law office was a stark contrast to Mark's. Her law office was modern, floor to ceiling windows; there was no pretense of traditional law firm trappings. The waiting area had white leather chairs, a white marble reception desk and a bouquet of fresh flowers provided colour and warmth. The law office definitely had a feminine design touch.

I arrived a few minutes early. Angela came out to greet me and invited me to her office. In this day and age of space management, which dictated small work cubicles, Angela's office defied the trend. It was large and tastefully decorated; the white leather furniture complimented the charcoal grey rug. She had a white enamelled wall unit where two framed family photographs were prominently on display along with some character ceramic figurines, a matching round white table was stationed in the middle of a circle of comfortable leather tube chairs. Angela's black enamelled desk was immaculate—no loose files in sight. Her window faced east, so she avoided the late afternoon sun. She told me that she was a morning person and loved the sun streaming into her office in the early hours of the day. Her office, in sum, radiated a warm, calm aura.

Angela directed me to one of the tube chairs. She apologized for missing the brown bag lunch. Angela was a regular, no apologies were needed. We quickly planned our approach to Ingrid. Angela would do the introductions then ask me to brief Ingrid on what we had found, keeping key pieces unsaid, then Angela would ask if Ingrid would mind going over the day of her attack in Winnipeg again. Ingrid would be asked if she minded having me present. The decision would be hers. Angela's phone rang. Ingrid had arrived. Angela left to get her. We were ready.

Ingrid had not changed much in the five years. She was still blonde, wearing her long hair stylishly to the side. She was no longer a student; she was a young professional smartly dressed in a blue tweed dress suit, poised and confident. She still had a beautiful and easy smile, which showed off her dimples. Her greyish blue eyes shone when she smiled. She was athletic and strong; it was obvious that she worked out.

I got up took her hand and said, "Ingrid it is good to see you again."

"Professor Sturgis, it is nice to see you as well. I remember your evidence class as if it was yesterday."

Angela directed us to our seats. We took a few minutes to catch up and talk about the whereabouts of some of her classmates.

Angela then turned to the subject at hand, "Ingrid, as I told you over the phone, we'd like to talk about what happened to you in Winnipeg. I know that you are reluctant to talk about it. The memories must be raw. But, I think you know, we wouldn't be asking this of you if it were not important. You should know that both Professor Sturgis and I are working with Mark Labros, who is acting for the Klassen family. I'm going to ask Professor Sturgis to outline to you some of the things that we have found thus far about Allison Klassen's death. If you don't mind?"

"That would be fine. As I told you, I am willing to help to support, if necessary, any action brought by the Klassens."

"Thank you for that," said Angela.

I began, "Ingrid, before I begin I want to be honest with you; I can't tell you everything in fear that that may taint your evidence. I will try and be as candid as I can." She nodded.

"Here is what we know. First, Allison Klassen was in good health. We have spoken to her doctor. Allison had a physical examination approximately two weeks before her death. There were no physical or mental health issues. She seemed to be in good spirits and was looking forward to second year law. Second, we have evidence that Fraser inflated Allison's grades and, in fact, the grades of his research assistant the previous year. It is our view that these grades were inflated as part of a grooming of these young women to be his research assistants."

"Do you think he did that with me as well?" Ingrid asked.

"Yes I do. Your grade in Torts with Fraser was unusually high, as were the grades of the other research assistant three years ago. We could not confirm that he fudged your grades because the examinations have been destroyed. They are only kept for two years. It is also the case that all of Fraser's research assistants were young, attractive, blonde women."

"So much for being hired on merit," Ingrid said in a sad mocking tone.

I continued, "Third, Fraser attended the Winnipeg conference starting with you. He always took his research assistants along. He stayed at the Artist Hotel in Rembrandt Room 1; the students stayed in an adjoining room Rembrandt 2, which is the room with the painting, The Man with the Golden Helmet."

"You've been to the room?" Ingrid seemed surprised and impressed by our thoroughness.

"Yes, I was there just last week. Ingrid, in your statement to the university you mentioned that you had coffee in a cafe at the hotel."

"You have my statement?" she spoke out.

"Yes, I can't reveal anything more than that. But I will say this, having read the statement and a summary of the meeting with the

Dean; I was angered at how you were treated. They forced you to withdraw your complaint. It was all wrong."

Ingrid sat back in her chair, "I can tell you it took a long while to get over how I was treated. I thought they knew best. I trusted the Dean. It has left a real sour taste in my mouth ever since for Flemington University and the law school." She looked at me, "Certain professors excepted."

"I can't blame you. What I can tell you is that on the Saturday night after the conference ended we have video surveillance that shows Allison in the coffee shop of the Artist Hotel. She looked perfectly fine when she arrived with Fraser. He then ordered drinks, got the order and went to the cream and sugar stand. There, in our view, he put something into her drink and mixed it. After drinking her coffee she looked unsteady, had difficulty walking. We last see her being helped out of the coffee shop by Fraser."

"Which is exactly what Fraser did to me!"

"Yes. We do not know what happened later that evening. Allison never complained to anyone about being raped. However, we do know that Allison did not return to her home town, as was planned after the conference. Instead she returned to her apartment in Flemington. We also know that she never contacted anyone, which was out of character for her. She committed suicide on the Monday."

"That poor, poor girl," Ingrid held her head in her hands.

"We have spoken to the medical examiner. He found no alcohol in her system, which is not surprising because Allison did not drink."

"Did he find drugs?" Ingrid immediately asked.

"No, he advised us that if a date rape drug were used it would have dissipated. Such drugs unfortunately disappear very quickly." I paused before continuing, "However, he did find traces of a lubricant commonly found on condoms. This is important because our information, from Allison's doctor, is that Allison did not want or need any birth control because she believed in abstinence. I didn't mention this before, but Allison was very religious. It is our view that this indicates forced intercourse and her attacker used a condom."

I let this information sink in. Ingrid had her eyes closed and was shaking her head.

"That is what we have."

"Professor, you've done far more than I thought--that poor girl." Ingrid looked at both Angela and me, she took a deep breath, sat up and said, "What do you need from me to put that son-of-a-bitch away?" There was strength and determination in her voice.

Angela took over, "Ingrid, we hate to do this, but we need you to go over what happened that night in Winnipeg. Details are important. Professor Sturgis well understands if you feel uncomfortable speaking in front of him and he is more than willing to leave the room."

"No, no, he has done so much. I may have to repeat this in a courtroom, no please stay Professor. You know the case, and may pick up on the information I provide." She turned to Angela, "I'm ready."

Angela smiled encouragingly, patted her on the hand, and poured a glass of water for her, "You're strong. I'd like you to tell us in your own words what happened that Saturday evening. Do you mind if I record your statement? It will save me having to write things down."

"Not at all, go ahead."

"I'm going to ask you to close your eyes. Try and remember everything you can. Take your time. We won't interrupt. We'll let you tell what happened in your words. Is that fine?"

"Fine."

Angela then introduced the tape: "Time: 5:16 p.m. October 13; place Flemington, Minnesota, in the law office of Angela Crindle; present Professor Andrew Sturgis, Angela Crindle, and Ingrid Hedberg—H-E-D-B-E-R-G. This is the statement of Ingrid Hedberg. Ms Hedberg I ask that you tell us what happened to you when attending a conference in Winnipeg, Manitoba Canada. Please take your time."

Ingrid had closed her eyes, bowed her head and spoke in a soft but clear voice: "I was attending a law conference in Winnipeg, Canada with Professor Jerome Fraser. I was his research assistant. The conference ended on the Saturday. There was a conference dinner that night. I sat at the table with Professor Fraser and other conference participants. I don't know their names. We had wine on the table. Professor Fraser poured me a number of glasses. I also had a drink before dinner. By the end of the dinner I admit I was feeling the effect of the alcohol. The dinner ended, I don't know, maybe about 7:30–fairly early. Professor Fraser invited me to join him and others in the hospitality suite, which had a bar. Professor Fraser bought me another drink, maybe two, I really don't recall exactly. I know I had a drink in hand throughout the time I was in the suite. At about 9:00 p.m. most people were leaving and Professor Fraser suggested that we return to our hotel. We weren't staying at the conference hotel. We were staying downtown. Professor Fraser had taken his car to the conference and we drove back. I don't think he had been drinking much. We got to the hotel and parked in the underground parking. Professor Fraser suggested that we get a coffee in the hotel coffee shop. I had been drinking and it was early so it sounded like a good idea. We went into the coffee shop. He took my order and insisted on paying. He went to the counter and put in the order. When it was ready he went up and got it. The coffee came in the typical waxed paper cups. He went over and put some sugar and cream I guess in his. I take my coffee black. We drank our coffees. After finishing my coffee I felt dizzy. It was as though the room was fading in and out. I had a difficult time speaking. I tried to speak but found it hard. I remember I could hardly walk. I felt like I was going to be sick. Professor Fraser helped me up. We went to the elevator and I remember he held me up against the wall. He walked me to my room. I fumbled for my key card. He got it for me and opened the door to my room. I remember he dropped me on my back onto the bed. I lay there looking up at the ceiling. It was spinning. I closed my eyes. I then heard Professor Fraser. He was still in the room. I felt him taking my boots off. Pulling them. Then he rolled me over on to my stomach. Why I thought? Then I heard and felt the zipper of my dress being pulled down. I tried to get up. I couldn't. I don't remember my dress coming all the way off. Next I felt him trying to take my bra off. He pulled at the back, but the bra–funny how you remember this–the bra opened at the front. He found the clasp and took my bra off. I thought what's he doing? What's happening? I tried to speak, but couldn't. I tried to struggle but couldn't. I closed my eyes. I don't know if I fell asleep."

Ingrid opened her eyes and stopped to take a drink. She kept the glass in her hand and closed her eyes again. "I felt his hands on my breasts. They were cold. He moved his hands down. He began rubbing me. I felt his finger go inside. He kept rubbing. I recall him saying things like, "You'll enjoy this. Just relax...enjoy." I couldn't do anything. I then felt him go inside me. Please stop. Please stop. He didn't. I felt his body slamming into me. He was rough. Then it stopped. I don't know for how long. I never opened my eyes. I couldn't move. Then he was inside me again. I think I fell asleep. I don't know. I heard, "Roll her over." I was rolled over. I felt rubbing more and wetness around my behind. I thought he's going to rape me from the rear. I felt the pushing on my bottom, more rubbing. I tried to move my body. I couldn't. I heard, "Too tight." It went on. I was put on my back. He was having intercourse with me again. When it was over I lay there resting, my eyes closed. I tried to speak, but couldn't. I heard laughter. There was a light shining. "Spread her legs..." My legs were pulled apart. I was told to open my eyes. Smile. I couldn't move. The light shone in my eyes. I couldn't see. He moved to my side. I remember the taste of rubber going into my mouth. I couldn't do anything. I started gagging. Then it stopped. I don't know for how long. Then he came on top of me. He was rubbing himself between my breasts. Rubbing, and rubbing. Something was in me below; moving in and out at the same time. There was laughter. Then it stopped. I lay there. Feeling dirty."

She took a sip of water. The room was completely quiet. She continued, "I don't know how long I lay there. I felt water on my body. I was being washed. A towel dried me. My pyjamas were put on me. A pillow was put under my head and covers pulled up. I lay still. Then nothing. Silence. I think he left. I fell asleep. Next thing I remember I woke up at 6:30. It was still dark. I needed to go to the toilet. I could move. I sat up. The room was only slightly spinning. I carefully stood and walked to the bathroom. I threw up in the toilet. I turned the shower on and showered for a long time. I tried to remember, but couldn't. My legs hurt. My pelvic area hurt. I was sure I had been sexually assaulted. But things weren't clear. I made coffee in the room. I drank it. That helped. I saw my dress folded on the chair and my boots by the door. I needed to leave. I needed to get away. I packed, dressed and left. My mind was foggy. I had difficulty focusing. I stopped by the cafe and ordered a bagel and yogurt. Funny how I remember that. The food gave me strength. I checked out, got my car and drove home."

She stopped. We all took a moment to collect ourselves.

Angela gently spoke, "Ingrid, I have to ask a few follow-up questions."

Ingrid nodded.

"You had your eyes closed for much of the time. Did you actually see your attacker?"

"Yes, it was Fraser. At times I opened my eyes. I saw him. I saw his face. I heard his voice."

"Ingrid, in recounting what happened on a number of occasions you said things like, "Spread her legs and roll her over." Ingrid, was there someone else in the room other than Fraser? Please think hard. Close your eyes."

Ingrid closed her eyes. She was forcing her mind to remember. Then like a light switch going on she cried out, "There must have been. There must have been. The time Fraser was on me rubbing himself between my breasts, someone else was having intercourse with me. There must have been two. There were two! They talked. They laughed. Oh, my God there were two."

"Do you remember what the second person looked like?"

"No, no, I don't think I saw a face–just a voice."

I brought out a photograph of Burnside and showed her, "Do you recognize this man?"

Ingrid looked intensely at the photograph, "He was at the conference; I remember that. Do you think he was the second man?"

"He might be," was all that I could say.

"Ingrid," Angela probed further, "At one point you said a light was shining. This was when you were asked to spread your legs. Ingrid, do you remember seeing a camera?"

Ingrid now looked horrified, "They told me to smile. A picture was being taken. I heard clicking. They photographed me. They photographed me." Her voice was breaking. She buried her head in her hands.

Angela looked at me. We nodded to each other. We had confirmation. We had our proof. Angela terminated the recording at 5:34.

Angela put her arms around Ingrid, who was quietly crying. I felt totally hopeless. What to do? I went to Angela's desk, retrieved a box of tissues, and offered them to Ingrid. She took two and dabbed her eyes. She then sat up and composed herself.

"That was hard. But I feel so much better and I feel so angry–so violated. I want to get Fraser. How can I help?"

I replied, "You have helped a great deal." Before going on I looked at Angela and through her eyes she gave me permission to continue, "We have evidence that the man I showed you, Associate Professor William Burnside, visited the Artist Hotel the night Allison was attacked. His hobby is photography and we have him on surveillance carrying what appears to be a camera case. You just confirmed that a second person was present and that photographs were being taken. That, Ingrid, is very, very important."

Ingrid listened intently. She knew the importance of her evidence. She asked, "What are you going to do next?"

I answered, "We're going to talk things over with Mark. Frankly, I'm not sure the police can do anything, even with your new details, but we are exploring an action in Canada to expose Fraser and Burnside."

"I'll testify," said Ingrid, "we've got to stop him."

I never told Ingrid about Fraser's hotel booking for next year.

"At this stage we probably don't need you to testify, but it certainly could happen down the road. I promise you this, we're going to do all we can to put Fraser away."

Ingrid was composed now. She stood up, "Angela, you know where to find me. Please keep me in the loop. I won't tell anyone, but Professor, from what you have already uncovered I know you are determined. Get the son-of-a-bitch."

I smiled. She then came over and gave me a hug. She whispered in my ear, "Thank you for caring." She hugged Angela and Angela showed her out, coming back moments later.

We high-fived, "I'll get this statement transcribed ASAP," she told me.

"I'll call Mark tonight. I think we need to meet with the Klassens," I said, "I'm going to go home and have a stiff drink. Angela, you were masterful; having her close her eyes and talk allowed Ingrid to re-live that night."

"Well, I've had a bit of practice," she replied, "I think most lawyers ask too many questions. My technique is to listen first and probe later. There is a saying that my Grandmother taught me. It goes like this: There was an old owl, who lived in a tree; the more he saw, the less he spoke: the less he spoke, the more he heard. Why can't we be like that wise old bird?"

Angela showed me to the elevator. I knew she had hours more work to do.

I drove home not minding the rush hour traffic at all. I finally had a feeling that we were close to having the proof we needed. Close, but was it enough? Or am I being too cautious?

When I got home, I gave Julie a big kiss. She knew the news was good. "I think we've got him," I told her and rushed to the den to call Mark.

He was still at the office. I simply told him two things: she remembered a second person and she remembered a camera.

Mark yelled "YES" at the news, "I'll call the Klassens and arrange for them to come in and see me this weekend. Are you around? It would be important for you to attend."

"I'm around."

"I'll get back to you."

After hanging up, I poured myself a tall rum and coke.

CHAPTER 27

Mark called me Friday morning. He had contacted his Canadian law firm and he relayed to me their information. In a nutshell, you can bring actions on behalf of a deceased person, who was the victim of a civil wrong when alive; however, the actions are carefully circumscribed by statute. The bottom line is that an estate action doesn't provide for large awards. For example, under the Manitoba Fatal Accidents Act there is a $30,000 limit. Canadian awards are not nearly as high as in the United States.

With that news, Mark had arranged a meeting with the Klassens for 10:30 Saturday morning. That was going to be a tough meeting. How do you tell parents that you have reason to believe that their beautiful, innocent daughter was gang raped by two professors? How would they react? I know I would be so angry I'd want revenge, but would the Klassens feel the same? Where would their faith direct them?

I arrived at Mark's office early. A number of the lawyers were in. Such is the reality of private practice. Mark had booked the board room. He was serious, introspective. I knew it was not going to be easy for him to tell the Klassens our findings. This was going to be hard.

The Klassens, Doreen, Fred and Megan, arrived as a group right on time and Mark escorted them into the board room. I greeted them all in turn. They were somber. I think they had an inkling that our news was not going to be good. Actually, this meeting was always going to bring them bad news. If we had found nothing then the mystery as to why Allison took her life would continue to haunt them and if we found out the reason she killed herself that too was going to haunt them. There was no way that this meeting was going to be a positive one. Nothing could bring Allison back.

Mark took charge. He got them comfortable. None wanted coffee. He began, "Mrs. Klassen, before we begin, would you offer us a prayer? This will be a difficult meeting and I think it would help us all to get through it."

It was the right way to start. Doreen asked us to hold hands, "Dear Lord, I know You are watching over our Allie. Please also watch over and comfort us today. We thank Mark and Professor Sturgis for their assistance and friendship. We ask for Your guidance and wisdom. Amen." She opened her eyes and gave a painful smile to Mark. It was so thoughtful of him to begin with a prayer.

Mark took a deep breath, "A few weeks ago you gave me and Professor Sturgis permission to do further investigation into Allie's death. We have a great deal of information to share with you. I can tell you that it is our conclusion that Allie took her life because of what happened to her in Winnipeg."

I watched their reaction. They listened quietly, but their eyes showed a bolt of shock.

Mark continued, "I am going to go through our information step by step and in the end I am going to outline our options." Mark then started to walk them through the evidence we had uncovered:

- Allie was physically healthy;
- Mentally she was in good spirits looking forward to second year law;
- When she returned from Winnipeg she went to her apartment in Flemington. She didn't return, as planned, to the farm;
- She made no contact with friends or family upon her return;
- We looked into whether anything had happened to her in Winnipeg;

- Professor Sturgis journeyed to Winnipeg and stayed in the same hotel as Allie and Professor Fraser;
- He obtained access to surveillance camera footage taken on the Saturday night.

He stopped. "I'm going to show you this footage. It will be disturbing. Please let me know if you'd like a break." They nodded, but said nothing.

Mark started the video. Doreen gasped as she saw her daughter appear in the coffee shop. They watched as she was served her drink by Professor Fraser. Then they watched as Allie slowly lost co-ordination. Fred's knuckles went white as he gripped the edge of the table. Megan was crying. Mark stopped the tape.

Gently he spoke, "It is our opinion that Professor Fraser drugged Allie. We think this occurred when he went to the serving table. Allie was then drugged and taken to her room. This is hard, but we believe that Allie was sexually assaulted in her room by Professor Fraser."

Doreen, who remained stoic throughout, bit her lip. She held Megan's hand. "We have found some disturbing things about Professor Fraser." Mark then started to outline the evidence surrounding Professor Fraser:

- The rape complaint made by Ingrid Hedberg, where she reported being drugged and then attacked in the same room, at the same hotel, five years before;
- The complaint brought against him by the Dean in the Cayman Islands;
- The interviews with the two other students, who also attended the Winnipeg conference and their reactions;
- The evidence that Professor Fraser was grooming these young women;
- The pathology report that showed no alcohol in Allie's system;

- The evidence that a date rape drug would quickly dissipate in the body.

Mark then paused to talk about the presence of PDMS: "The Medical Examiner did find the presence of PDMS, which is a lubricant commonly found with condoms. This would be evidence of sexual activity and would be consistent with her attacker using a condom." I watched Doreen and Megan's reaction. Their eyes went wide.

Mark continued, "In speaking with Dr. Burnett I was told that Allie used no birth control, because she believed in abstinence before marriage. Did you know that?"

Megan broke the silence, "Allie had told me. She wasn't pressing me to do the same, but I felt proud of her."

Mrs. Klassen quietly spoke, "I knew. It was her will. She believed that it was God's will. I had told her that it was not necessarily a tenet of our belief; it was her decision."

Mr. Klassen never knew. This was a conversation amongst the women of the family.

Mark continued, "If Allie was viciously raped, her purity was destroyed. We think that this would have devastated her."

"Would she have known if she were drugged?" asked Megan.

Mark answered, "Most date rape drugs immobilize the victim and do cause blackouts or amnesia; however, much depends on the amount and strength of the drug administered and the health and condition of the victim. Allie we know did not drink and was very healthy. We also believe that all the students who attended the conference with Professor Fraser know, to some degree, that they were sexually attacked. They know. The victims know. Ingrid Hedberg knew."

Mark then asked them to watch the surveillance tape again. He introduced them to Professor Burnside. They were told that he was at the hotel that night until the early hours of the morning. Mark went back to focus on what he was carrying and explained that Burnside had an interest in photography. "It's our view that Professor Burnside was involved in the attack and he may well have photographed or videotaped the attack. There is no other reason for him to come to the hotel that night, carrying what we believe is a camera case." He then told them that Ingrid did recall a camera or video, and did recall a second attacker.

Mrs. Klassen wrapped her arms around herself rocking back and forth. Megan cried. Mr. Klassen bowed his head.

Mr. Klassen broke the silence and asked whether the police had been notified?

Mark looked to me and I answered, "I have been in contact with Detective Maurice here in Flemington and with a Detective Semchuk in Winnipeg. Unfortunately, both are of the view that they do not have enough evidence to charge or to obtain a search warrant. They are frustrated. Their hands are tied. The problem is that Allison died in Minnesota, but the attack occurred in Canada. The border makes it difficult."

Mark seized the opening, "This is why I would like you to consider bringing a civil action in Canada against Professors Fraser and Burnside." He went on to outline in simple terms what such an action involved. He explained an Anton Piller order to them and freely admitted that the Canadian action was but an excuse to get the order. He then explained to them that if further evidence was found then they should look at an action in Minnesota against Fraser and Flemington University.

"The university shouldn't be responsible for Professor Fraser's actions should it?" asked Mr. Klassen.

Mark went on to outline how the Dean of Law knew about the complaint brought against Professor Fraser five years ago and reminded them of what Fraser had done in the Cayman Islands, "Yet, the Dean let Fraser continue to go to the Winnipeg conference with young female students. Would you have done that if you knew of a complaint of rape and other sexual impropriety with young female students?"

"What happened to the earlier complaint of rape?" asked Megan. Mark explained that the university convinced the young woman to withdraw the complaint.

The Klassens were saying little. They were scared. A law suit, which was so familiar for Mark and me, was foreign to them. I could feel their discomfort. Mark could as well and he suggested that they take a break, "We've provided you with a great deal of information. We are looking for your guidance. As I promised, we will not do anything without your approval. Let's take a break. I'd like you to talk things over amongst yourselves, Professor Sturgis and I will come back in a few minutes to answer any questions you might have. There is coffee on and drinks in the refrigerator." We left.

As we sat down, I asked Mark, "What do you think they'll do?"

"I really don't know. They may not decide anything today. They believe in the healing power of God and that forgiveness is better than retribution. However, that may not apply to a person who has never been caught, who never admits his sins. I don't know."

We returned to the board room about twenty minutes later. Doreen and Megan's eyes were both red.

As we sat down, Mrs. Klassen asked us, "What will happen to Professor Fraser if we do not bring an action in Canada?"

I replied, "Professor Fraser has applied for tenure and promotion. The Dean supports his appointment. If appointed he will be a professor at Flemington for the next twenty to twenty-five years. I must also tell you this, I asked the hotel manager to check Fraser's reservations at the hotel. Fraser has booked the same rooms, two rooms, for next year. Mr. and Mrs. Klassen, Megan, if we don't do something he will continue to prey on young women. We have to stop him."

"What if we don't find anything in Canada?" Mr. Klassen asked.

Mark replied, "The statement of claim will have been filed. Professors Fraser and Burnside will be on notice. But unless we push the action forward it can die. For example, we may feel that we don't have a strong enough case to proceed and not even serve Professor Fraser with the statement of claim."

"Wouldn't he sue us for defamation?" Mr. Klassen responded.

Mark laughed and replied, "He'd be a fool to do so. All the evidence we have would come out and I doubt that a court would find in his favour."

Mr. Klassen continued, "How much is this going to cost? We aren't rich."

"I have spoken to my partners. We all want to support you and we are prepared to take this on a contingency, a low contingency—10%. What this means is that our firm will receive 10% of any award that you recover. You do not pay us anything unless we are successful. I am personally going to cover the initial costs of filing the action and arranging for the Anton Piller Order."

"Mark, we don't want you to do that," said Mr. Klassen, "we will pay our way. How much will it cost?"

He never asked about how much the family might recover; that was of no interest to him. He was seeking justice for his daughter.

Mark had done his homework, "There will be a requirement of security for costs in obtaining the Anton Piller Order and we anticipate that $10,000 will need to be left with the court. If we find something in the search that money would certainly be returned to us. An additional $10,000 will cover our Canadian counsel costs at least initially. So we are looking at $20,000, but as I said, my firm will cover that initial outlay. It is not unusual for law firms to do so. Please let me do this for you?"

Mrs. Klassen spoke up, "You've done enough for us, Mark; you both have."

There was silence. I spoke up, "I know this must be so difficult for you, but we have to stop him. He will do it again. He won't stop, unless we stop him."

Mrs. Klassen took over. She looked at her husband and at Megan. Through their eyes they had come to an agreement. "Mark you have our permission to commence a law suit in Canada and if evidence is found we agree to sue Professor Fraser and Flemington University here in Minnesota."

Mark got up and hugged her. He hugged Mr. Klassen and Megan. Tears were flowing freely. I too got up and hugged them all. A decision had been made. The Klassens placed their faith in Mark. He quickly prepared a contingency agreement and had the Klassens sign.

Afterwards, Mark insisted that we all have lunch at a local Italian restaurant. We did not speak again about law suits or about Allison. We needed to forget for a time.

We said our goodbyes and Mark asked me to come back with him to his office. We discussed strategy. He told me that the small Canadian firm he had worked with before was on notice. They awaited his word to proceed with drafting the pleading. What he wanted from me was the affidavit to support the Anton Piller Order. Affidavits in Manitoba can be based on 'information and belief'; in other words the person making the affidavit need not personally have seen the information contained in the affidavit, but can advise that he was 'informed and verily does believe' whatever. I had been involved in the case from the start and one affidavit would be the simplest.

"I also want you to come to the Anton Piller hearing. The Canadian law firm told me that having the maker of the affidavit present will give our motion more credence." I agreed. We then worked on dates and circled Wednesday, ten days hence. This would give Mark time to have everything arranged and the materials to be properly prepared. In the interim I would start drafting an affidavit and Mark and the Canadian lawyers would assist.

The date was set. The plan was made.

Chapter 28

The week went quickly. I rescheduled my classes for the Wednesday and Thursday that I was going to be away. I hate cancelling classes. Students may not mind occasionally, but I feel that it is shortchanging students on what they have paid for and are entitled to receive. They paid for a full course of hours and I'm obliged to provide the class hours; call me naïve.

I worked throughout the week drafting the affidavit in support of our Anton Piller Order. It was not an easy task. I began chronologically. The reader understands a story much better when events follow chronologically. Jumping from topic to topic often only confuses the reader. The affidavit also had to be both persuasive and fair. We were bringing a motion ex parte, which meant that the other side would not be represented and the judge was only going to hear one side of the story. Nothing would annoy judges more than if they sensed we weren't being scrupulously fair in outlining all pertinent facts. For example, I included Ingrid Hedberg's complaint of rape, but at the same time I had to tell the judge that she did recant that complaint; of course, I would also tell the judge about the pressure brought to bear by the university to do so. It was a tricky balance between persuasiveness and fairness.

I forwarded my drafts to Mark and he, in turn, ran them by his Canadian counterpart. The red ink flowed. The affidavit went through six or seven drafts before it was finally pronounced satisfactory.

On Monday we received an official email announcement from Dean Clarke. Jerome Fraser had been appointed to Associate Professor and granted tenure. Dean Clarke praised Associate Professor Fraser as a "valued member of the faculty" and that his work as both a teacher and researcher was "exemplary". Dean Clarke asked us all to join in congratulating Associate Professor Fraser. Accolades in the form of a trail of "all staff" emails soon followed from Clarke's sycophant cohort, beginning with Associate Dean Gloria Wesley: "Congrats Jerome. Well done and well deserved!!!!" I hate it when people use excessive exclamation points!!

I was not surprised; disappointed yes; bitter yes. A wry smile came to my lips. Wait a short while. If we find what we think we may find then Associate Professor Fraser's tenure could well be short lived and what a gold mine in any litigation against the university. They granted tenure to a rapist of students!

On Tuesday I headed home right after class. I had already packed. Mark was going to drive us to Winnipeg. His car pulled in front of my house just after 4:00. He left the family van for his wife. Julie packed us a hefty bag of snacks, sandwiches, fruit, vegetables, drinks and cookies. We would not starve.

When I took my seat, Mark said to me, "I heard that Fraser got tenure."

"Yup."

Mark shook his head, "You've got one twisted law school."

"I do not disagree," I said.

We were off. Over the four and half hours we had a pleasant drive and I had a real chance to get to know Mark. He was a proud husband and father. He gushed over his wife Jane and daughter Amy. It was fun to listen to his infatuation with both. About a half hour from the border, Mark turned serious, "Andy I'm scared. This case means so much to me. The Klassens are like family and Allie was like a sister. I'm scared I'm going to let them down."

This is the fear that takes hold of many trial lawyers. It is better not to care, be objective and be aloof from the case. When cases don't matter personally that much, such as when you are defending an accused who has admitted his guilt to you then the fear is low; however, when you really care, when you have a just cause, and people relying on you to succeed this is when fear really reaches out to seize you. Many lawyers who care too much for a client or cause lose focus, and with it, lose their effectiveness.

I reassured him, "Mark, it is always good to be scared. It means that you care. You are also a damn good lawyer and you are well prepared. You will do just fine and in my view, your passion is a positive. The Klassens could not have a better lawyer. Besides, remember, if you're having trouble I'll be there to kick your butt."

"Thanks for the support. But it's foreign territory. I've only had one trial in Manitoba and that was a three day hit and run."

"Yes, but you are not going to have to argue against another lawyer. You'll only have to persuade the judge."

"Believe me the judge scares the day lights out of me."

We rode on in silence. The border crossing lights soon were visible in the distance through the crisp, clear night. Going through customs was uneventful. Winnipeg was only an hour away. Once in the city I guided Mark to the Artist Hotel. We had booked rooms there in part to support Mr. Pangatan, in part because it was convenient to the courts, and in part so that Mark could see the scene of the crime. We arrived at the hotel a little before 9:00 p.m. Serge was on duty and immediately recognized me. We were put into the Da Vinci rooms; the Rembrandt rooms were taken. We had a busy day ahead of us and headed to our rooms. I am certain that Mark spent hours working on his submission.

The next day was clear and cold. A north wind was blowing bringing with it an Arctic taste of the winter to come. We had coats, but hadn't brought gloves. We shifted hands holding our brief cases warming the free hand in our pockets. It was a bloody cold ten minute walk to the law offices of Johns and Mitchell.

The law firm was located on tree lined Broadway Avenue just down from the law courts. This day the trees provided little shelter from the wind; their branches were bare. Johns and Mitchell shared the fourth floor of an eight storey high rise, which was functional but had no creative flourishes. We got to the office at about 8:30 there to be greeted by Michael Johns, Mark's Canadian contact.

Mark and Michael greeted each other warmly and I was introduced. Michael was tall and slim. His face was thin set, but warm. He had no pretenses about him and I had a sense of calmness in his character. I doubted much would ever upset him.

His office had that same calm, comfortable air. There were no expensive pretenses here. This was a plaintiff's law office, a working law office. It was a bit tired looking. The wood panelling could use a good polish and touch up painting. But I think Michael's clients would feel that this firm, these lawyers, would roll up their sleeves and work for them.

"Professor Sturgis, it is good to put a face to a name; we've communicated so much this past week in drafting the affidavit." Michael took my coat and put it into a wall closet.

I responded, "Michael, I now know how my students feel in getting their work marked by me."

"We weren't too hard on you were we?" he smiled, "I did have to correct your American spelling though."

He turned to Mark, "And for God's sake Mark, don't call the judge 'Your Honour'. Remember here in Manitoba we still have Ladies and Lords -- it's 'M'Lord'."

"I'm working on it. Christ I hope we don't have a female judge. I'll be calling her M'Lord."

"Good and bad news," said Michael, "The judge is male, Mr. Justice Chris Stargel. He's the sitting motion judge this week. The good news is that before being appointed he was a federal prosecutor and handled a number of testy pedophile cases. The bad news is that he is extremely smart and can be tough on counsel who are not prepared. He definitely will not be a silent judge."

Michael directed us to the firm's boardroom, "This is headquarters," he said, "Coffee is on, and from the looks of you both you need something warm." He had the coffee pot in hand ready to pour.

A young articling student was introduced, Aaron Levene. He was helping Michael on the file. Michael had some documents for Mark to sign and I chatted with Aaron.

"Where did you graduate from?" I asked.

"Manitoba, this past May," he replied.

"So did you have Professor Burnside as a teacher?"

"Yes, he taught me Administrative Law. He was not a good instructor. Only had him for the one course. That was enough."

"How long do you have to article for?"

"A year. We also have some training and courses to complete from the Law Society and exams to write."

"I often think that is a route that we ought to go in the United States. Our students write the bar exams and become associates."

"Articling is both good and bad. I'm lucky Johns and Mitchell is a small, friendly firm, where I'm given a lot of responsibility and support. Some of my classmates, I can tell you, don't have good articles."

Mark and Michael finished the signing. "Your turn," said Michael looking at me. I signed the affidavit and Michael witnessed my signature.

"There, ready for filing," said Michael, "Justice Stargel likes to have any motion material filed before 10 a.m. the day of the hearing. Aaron usually does this, but I'm going personally to take the documents over for filing and to see that the file is sealed pending the hearing."

At that moment the boardroom phone rang. Michael took it. The independent solicitors had arrived. Michael went out to get them. He came back leading a tall distinguished, gray haired man, in his early sixties I would guess. He introduced himself as James Taylor. His voice was soft, elegant. He oozed integrity and courtesy. Mark had told me that he was a Q.C., Queen's Counsel, past president of the Law Society, and was a senior partner in one of the larger

Winnipeg firms. Michael had worked with him on other files and spoke most highly of him. He was exactly the type of independent counsel that a judge would feel comfortable in overseeing the search–if granted.

"Very pleased to meet you Professor Sturgis," he said. In shaking my hand his grip was firm, but not overpowering. He also looked directly at you when he spoke. His light green eyes were intense, but not threatening, "I have read your affidavit and you are to be commended for all the work you have done for the Klassen family. It is good that you are here for the hearing. That will mean much to the judge."

He turned, and introduced his associate, "Assisting me is Mary Weber. She is the true expert on Anton Piller Orders."

Mary stepped forward, "Professor Sturgis." Mary took care in her apparel. Everything was co-ordinated and tailored. Nothing was overdone or flash. She presented a conservative aura in her wool tweed dress suit. But she wasn't stuffy. She had real warmth. She had Slavic features, a somewhat sharp nose and prominent cheek bones.

With the greetings over, Michael took a moment to fill us all in, "I will be filing the statement of claim and motion for the order shortly. I will ask that it be sealed pending the hearing. The hearing will be before Justice Stargel at 2:00 p.m. The motion's court is usually in courtroom 310. Mark, you will present the argument. I think it will have more meaning coming from you, a lawyer from the home town of the victim. I will sit at the counsel table with you. Professor Sturgis you should be present and the judge may wish to question you. Justice Stargel can be a bit unpredictable. James and Mary will also be present at the counsel table; once again, should there be any questions. James, perhaps you could outline quickly what you have arranged."

James nodded and began, "We have done about a half dozen Anton Piller Orders. What is important is to show that we have covered all contingencies and are prepared to protect the interests of the defendant as well as the plaintiff. I have arranged for two retired police officers, former narcotic detectives, who will be responsible for carrying out the search. A locksmith has been retained and will be on site. We also have a technician from a computer forensics firm and finally a cameraman will be videotaping the search."

He paused and continued, "If we are granted the order we are looking to execute it tomorrow morning. Mary, Mark, Professor Sturgis, and I will approach the Burnside home. We will do so at 9:00 a.m. We know that the Burnside's daughter will be picked up for her kindergarten class at 8:45. We also know, courtesy of Mr. Levene and his contacts at the law school, that Professor Burnside will be teaching from 9:00 to 11:00 Thursday morning. We will serve the court order on Mrs. Burnside, who has authority over the home, and we hope that she will allow us to search."

"James in the other orders that you have been involved in, has anyone refused to allow the search?" Mark asked the same question I was thinking,

James smiled, "Never. Mary is very convincing."

"I'll leave you with Mark to go over more details," said Michael, "I've got to file the claim. Professor Sturgis you are welcome to join me. Aaron has some court duties to do as well. We can walk over together."

"I'd love to see your court house," I said with much enthusiasm. I truly loved snooping around court houses. They each had their own feel and had so many stories to tell. Mark didn't need me around.

We put our coats on and braced ourselves for the outside blast of cold. The court house was about five minutes walk away. There was a new court building adjoined to the old. We entered via the new building. At security Michael had me come with him and Aaron through the lawyer entrance. The security people knew them both by name. Once inside, the main foyer buzzed with the day's legal happenings. Cases were being readied for trial, accused persons were making their appearances, documents were being filed, friends and relatives were arriving to provide litigants with support, jurors were being called, and lawyers ran around in controlled frenzy.

Michael went to file the claim and left me with Aaron as a guide. Aaron showed me the court schedule board and suggested that I should drop in to watch a murder trial in Courtroom 1, which was the main jury courtroom in the old building. I thanked him and told him that I'd find my way around. We were all to meet back at the law firm for lunch at noon.

I wandered into the old building. Footsteps on the white marble floors echoed off the sandstone walls. The wooden oak benches were well aged and suitably uncomfortable. I went into a washroom and was struck by their aged elegance. The fixtures were all old, but impeccably maintained. Marble was everywhere including partitions between the toilet stalls.

Just before 10:00 I went to Courtroom 1. What a courtroom. The ceiling was at least twenty to thirty feet high, arching to a dome. The prisoner's dock was marble, the judge's bench was marble, polished brass railings separated the jury from the well of the courtroom. The counsel tables were gigantic thick slabs of oak. The viewing gallery had seating for at least 150 viewers. It was an impressive room. I took my seat to watch.

The lawyers were gowned. They had black robes that covered black waistcoats, white wing tipped shirts, and tabs, which are shortened v-shaped white ties. At least they didn't wear wigs. I suddenly thought, would Mark need to be gowned? I'd ask at lunch. The presiding judge entered. The bailiff called for everyone to stand. The judge, a slightly overweight older man, was dressed in black, with a waistcoat and tab and a red sash. The jury was summoned.

The prosecutor called a youngish man in his twenties to the stand. The prosecutor walked him through his evidence. There had been a brawl at a local nightclub and the witness had seen the accused stab a man to death. He was certain that the accused was the stabber.

A judge had once said, "Beware the dead sure witness." Well, this witness was dead sure of what he saw. The prosecutor ended his direct examination. Defence counsel went to the podium. At this moment Aaron sat down beside me. We watched.

The defence counsel was good, very good. He dissected the witness's evidence and cut it to shreds. There were hundreds of people at the night club that night. They were dancing, moving about. The lights were dimmed and a strobe light shone off and on. The witness had been drinking. No—he denied that. What? Other witnesses had testified to his drinking. In his group there was a designated driver--not him. He said he saw three or four stabs. The victim was only stabbed once. So much for the dead sure witness.

I whispered to Aaron, "Who is this counsel?"

"That's Darcy Fitzpatrick. He's a top criminal lawyer."

"He's very good."

There was an adjournment and we got up. "What do you think about the barrister having to gown Aaron?"

"I don't mind. It hides the sweat. But I could do without the waistcoat, shirt and tabs. The gown I'd keep."

"At least you don't have to wear wigs. Do you know if Mark needs to be gowned for his motion?" I asked.

"No, don't think you do in motions court. Michael would know for sure."

We walked out of the courtroom. Aaron had some things to do and I decided to do more snooping. I went up to courtroom 310, where our motion was to be heard. The door was open; the courtroom was empty. Room 310 was much smaller than Courtroom 1. It was wood panelled throughout--no marble. The viewing area would only hold about twenty people and there was no jury box.

I ran my hand over the wood railings. There was power in these walls and surroundings. The wood was dark oak, solid, strong. It was strange to be a litigant. I was used to reading and studying other's legal stories. Now I was part of the story. How would it end?

I left the room and made my way back to the offices of Johns and Mitchell.

CHAPTER 29

Michael had ordered in some delicious deli sandwiches, salads and fruits. We relaxed in the tense atmosphere. Mark was nervous, but tried to make light of things. He fidgeted and could not sit still. He had gone over the essentials on Anton Piller Orders with James and Mary; the questions to expect and proper responses.

As we were standing over the luncheon platter, Mary whispered in my ear, "He's ready." I nodded in agreement. I was certain that Mark would do the Klassen's proud. Soon it was time to make our way to the court house.

Michael confirmed room 310 and was told by the judge's clerk that Justice Stargel had spent the morning reviewing our material. The courtroom was empty except for our entourage and court staff. At exactly 2:00 p.m. the bailiff called for us to rise and Mr. Justice Chris Stargel took his place on the bench. He was not robed, but dressed in a smart blue suit. He looked out at us before being seated and did a head bow, we returned the bow. He sat down and told us to be seated. His Lordship was younger than I had expected, about mid-forties. His hair was rusty coloured and his complexion was freckled. He had a mischievously intelligent look about him. After he had arranged his papers he looked to the counsel table. "Mr. Labros, would you please enter your name for the record and introduce the other persons present."

"Yes, Your Honour – sorry M'Lord," Mark gave a sheepish smile and Michael shook his head in good natured pity.

Justice Stargel smiled, "I have been called many things in my time Mr. Labros, between you and me I wish that we would be addressed as Your Honour as well." The ice was broken.

Mark appreciated the gesture, "Mark Labros that is L-A-B-R-O-S for the record of the law firm Theopold, Stenson and Labros in Flemington, Minnesota, I have a temporary practicing certificate granted by the Law Society of Manitoba, M'Lord." He paused deliberately, to emphasize the proper address for the judge. Mark then went on to introduce all the other counsel and I was especially impressed how he remembered Aaron's name and introduced him as a student-at-law. He ended by introducing me, "Also present is Professor Andrew Sturgis of the Flemington University School of Law, who provided the affidavit in support of our motion this afternoon." Justice Stargel gave me a long look, a penetrating look. I was not sure whether it was friendly or unfriendly.

Mark continued, "We have requested that the file at this time be sealed, and that this emergency motion be heard in camera."

"So granted," said Justice Stargel without hesitation.

Mark was now prepared to speak to the merits of our motion. "M'Lord, as our material reveals, we are seeking an Anton Piller Order against one of the named defendants, William Burnside..."

Justice Stargel cut him off; he had just started. I was worried, "You realize Mr. Labros that an Anton Piller Order is an exceptional remedy. I have heard it referred to as a nuclear bomb in the civil litigation arsenal. It is an order not lightly granted."

Was Justice Stargel forewarning us? Mark didn't seem fazed at all. He responded strongly and clearly. "Yes, M'Lord we well realize that; however, this is an exceptional case. Without an Anton Piller Order the evidence we seek, the critical evidence we seek, will no doubt be destroyed as soon as the defendant is informed of this lawsuit. The purpose of the Anton Piller Order is to further the ends of justice by preserving evidence and that is exactly what we seek. The requirements in place before an Anton Piller Order is granted are stringent and are met in this case."

A small smile brushed across Justice Stargel's lips and I think he enjoyed challenging counsel who fought back and were prepared to engage. "Of the four elements Mr. Labros, I'd like you to address the first; you need to present a strong prima facie case. If I am not mistaken you allege that Mr. Burnside was party to a rape of Miss Klassen, but nowhere in your materials did I see a statement by her claiming rape by Mr. Burnside or anyone else. You have a rape case with no complainant. That, Mr. Labros, is a tough case to present."

Justice Stargel had zeroed in on our key weakness. Mark replied, "Allison Klassen never claimed rape because she killed herself two days after being attacked. Correct, there was no rape claim by her, but given Allison's background that is not surprising. As we pointed out in our materials, Allison was very religious. She believed in abstinence. That was destroyed that Saturday night. Rape victims often do not cry out and in Allison's case it is most understandable. What was done to her was shocking; it destroyed her world, her values. Miss Hedberg, the other student mentioned in the affidavit, who alleged that she was raped five years before in similar circumstances, did not report her attack until some two weeks later."

"Miss Hedberg recanted her accusation. What should I make of her evidence?"

"Yes, she did. In blunt terms the university browbeat her into withdrawing the complaint. The important thing is that she is now prepared to come forward to testify and her credibility will be a matter for trial. My understanding is that in Manitoba, as in Minnesota, at this stage the evidence contained in an affidavit is accepted as true."

"That is correct Mr. Labros, but I do think the weight that I attach to Miss Hedberg's claims is still a matter within my domain. I would have given more credence to her evidence had she provided her own separate affidavit."

Damn it. We could have, but we opted for my all encompassing affidavit. Mark was not shaken, "M'Lord, that is my oversight.

There is the reality here that we are dealing cross border, cross country, and we have Professor Sturgis present for examination if need be. What we can say is that the circumstantial case that we have presented points in only one direction–Allison Klassen was raped that Saturday night."

"What evidence do you rely upon?" Justice Stargel was not writing anything down; he was absorbed in Mark's argument.

"M'Lord, we have a young, healthy woman, who when she returned from attending the Winnipeg conference with Professor Fraser, closed herself off; no emails, no texts, no calls to anyone. We have her vow of abstinence. We have the PDMS lubricant, which in all likelihood came from condoms used by her attackers. We have evidence that she was drugged. We have past evidence of drugging. We have evidence that she was groomed–for lack of a better word– by Professor Fraser. And we have evidence that Professor Burnside turned up at the hotel that night and stayed for three or four hours. Why? This wasn't an orgy. This was a gang rape."

"Why do you say she didn't consent, that this wasn't consensual?" Justice Stargel shot back.

In a quiet tone Mark said, "Because the surveillance tape says so. It shows a young woman, who would not have been able to consent. M'Lord, I invite you to view the videotape. It says things so much more powerfully than words."

This was Mark's gamble; I knew he wanted Justice Stargel to view the tape. Justice Stargel, drummed his fingers, moved his head back and forth thinking. "Very well, Mr. Labros, you will need to introduce the videotape through a witness."

Mark then called me to the stand. I admit I was nervous. I was sworn in and Mark walked me quickly through how I had come to obtain the videotape. He then showed me one of my USB's that had been purchased in Winnipeg. I identified it and it was entered as an exhibit. Mark then asked, "M'Lord I would ask that we play the applicable portions of the surveillance tape."

"Very well," replied Justice Stargel.

Michael assisted Mark and the court clerk in setting up the computer to show the videotape. Fortunately Mark had discussed doing so with the clerk in advance of the hearing. I don't think he wanted to make this too obvious to Justice Stargel, but this was planned.

Mark introduced the tape and it was played. Mark stopped it to have me identify the people on the tape. We watched again as Allison descended into a state of helplessness. Mark then asked whether there was more on the tape and I directed him to when Professor Burnside arrived at the Cafe. We watched this segment again.

"And Professor, what did you find out about Professor Burnside?"

"He was an avid photographer, and if you might return to the videotape, you will see that he was carrying with him a camera bag." The tape was played back. I had them stop the tape to highlight the camera case. "It is also my information, given to me by the night clerk in the hotel, who incidentally was entering law school in September so he came to know Professor Burnside, that Professor Burnside remained at the hotel until two or three in the morning."

I could see that Justice Stargel was moved by what he had seen. It was the seriousness in his face. He saw what we saw–a drugged, helpless young woman.

I was excused from the witness stand. Mark continued, "M'Lord, Allison Klassen was in no condition to consent to anything that night. It was a gang rape. And our position is that Professor Burnside photographed or videotaped the attack. Why else arrive at the hotel with a camera bag?"

"What appears to be a camera bag," chided Justice Stargel.

"Yes, we don't know for sure, but that is why it is so important to obtain the Anton Piller Order; then we will know for sure. The defendant will surely destroy that evidence if we are required to proceed with normal discovery."

There was silence. Then Justice Stargel asked, "When do you intend to execute the order?"

Had we passed the hurdle? I wondered. Mark answered the question, "Tomorrow morning at 9:00 a.m." Mark continued; he knew that he had momentum, "Mr. James Taylor, Q.C., experienced in these orders will be the independent supervising solicitor and he has put together a professional team to carry out the order. We have carefully outlined the evidence that we seek. We have provided the specific dates and months that may provide relevant photographs or videotapes. This is a surgical search not a fishing expedition. We will video the search and we are prepared to post a $10,000 bond should we be required to compensate Mr. Burnside. We have incorporated these details into the draft order."

Mark then continued in a subdued but passionate voice, "The Klassen's seek to know why their beloved daughter killed herself. Any parent would want to know. There is a real possibility that the defendant Burnside has the final proof. We ask to search for that proof. The search will be of short duration. It may absolve Mr. Burnside; it may not. We ask for a chance to find out. It is our only chance. The fact that Canadian courts recognize such orders, where the courts in my country do not, speaks to the desire in your courts to see justice done; to see the truth come out. We ask for this opportunity."

Justice Stargel looked intently at Mark, not saying a word. Finally he spoke, "Mr. Labros, I thank you for your submissions and the care and attention that you and your team have taken in preparing the materials. I am prepared to grant the order."

YES! I thought to myself. Justice Stargel, now put on record his reasons: "The misconduct alleged against the defendant Burnside is grievous. His presence at the hotel the night of the alleged attack, carrying what appears to be a camera case, raises a strong inference that incriminating photographs or videotapes were taken and I am convinced beyond any doubt that should that be the case Mr. Burnside would destroy the evidence if put on notice. The law is clear that the plaintiffs seeking such an order have a weighty threshold of proof to pass. They have, in my view, complied with the four elements in place before such an order is granted. I have reviewed the draft order and it carefully protects the rights of the defendant Burnside, including the deposit of $10,000 with the Court should damages or costs be ordered against the plaintiff. However, the reputation and privacy of the defendant Burnside is a matter of concern. Therefore, I grant the order to be carried out as outlined tomorrow during the specified hours. I also make the order returnable for Friday at 2:00 p.m. in this Court. I am seized of the matter and at that time I would like an interim report from the independent supervising solicitor, Mr. James Taylor, Q.C. The claim will remain sealed pending that hearing. Mr. Labros is that satisfactory to you?"

Mark turned to James, who nodded his head, "M'Lord we appreciate the short time line; it is in the interests of all concerned."

"Very well, so ordered, this Court stands adjourned until Friday at 2:00 p.m."

We had succeeded! We all rose as Justice Stargel left the courtroom and when he was gone we erupted in celebration. Congratulations were offered all around. I could see that Mark's eyes looked teary. Mary came up to me with a big smile on her face, "I told you so. He was great."

"Yes, yes he was."

We adjourned to Johns and Mitchell's boardroom. Mark proposed a toast, "To my Canadian friends, to justice, to the law and, most of all, to Allison." We lifted our glasses.

It was arranged that we would meet tomorrow morning in the boardroom at 8:00 a.m. and then we would drive out to the Burnside residence for 8:45. One of James' retired police officers would put the house under surveillance beginning at 7:00 a.m.

That night Mark, Michael and I had a celebratory dinner at a downtown restaurant. We all were in fine spirits and the company was good. Stories flowed--all embellished I am sure. Michael had a fascinating practice filled with unique cases and characters. It is truly amazing the predicaments that people get themselves into and then expect their lawyers to get them out of.

Over after dinner liqueurs the conversation returned to the case at hand. Michael swished his Amaretto in his glass and asked Mark, "What if we don't find anything tomorrow? What happens then?"

Mark took a moment, "Well then the case is dead. It would take too much trial time to prove a wrongful death and it just would not be worth it under your awards. We'd have to abandon the case. Burnside would probably take a few thousand and that would be it."

"Do you think Fraser would bring a defamation action?" I asked.

"No I don't think so," Mark replied, "We do have a fairly strong circumstantial case. He'd be a fool to bring out all the sordid facts."

"He's no fool, but he is extremely revengeful and driven. He'd want his revenge against you, me and the Klassens."

Mark nodded, "I've discussed it with my partners and we are prepared to defend any defamation action brought–pro bono. I know the risks and I'd never leave the Klassens or you exposed to such an action, whether frivolous or not."

"Let's hope we find something," Michael spoke for us all.

"We will," I said, "we will."

"Why are you so sure of that?" Michael asked.

I took a sip of my Bailey's, "Because I have never known a photographer who threw out pictures. Photographers treasure their works, and are pack rats. They'll keep them all. If he took photos, and I think he did, they're there."

"We'll soon know," said Michael, "busy day tomorrow. I'm heading home. Can I give you a ride?"

"No the fresh air will do us good," replied Mark. I belatedly agreed. It wasn't just fresh it was bloody freezing.

CHAPTER 30

We arrived at the offices of Johns and Mitchell at 8:00 a.m. Michael was there to greet us. James and Mary arrived a few minutes later.

James had his game face on; this was his show. "Mark and Professor you come with us. My team is already in the neighbourhood, I think having coffee at a local Tim Horton's restaurant. One of the police officers has the Burnside house under surveillance. Do you have any questions?"

"What happens if the house is empty or no answer?" asked Mark.

"Then we're stymied," said James, "our court order does not permit a forced entry. We must be allowed in. However, if our information is correct, Mrs. Burnside–Margaret is her name–should be there. Fingers crossed."

"Any background on Margaret?" I inquired.

"Not much. She has an education degree and does some substitute teaching. That's about all we know," replied James, "Are we ready? It'll take us about twenty-five minutes to get there. The Winnipeg traffic is horrendous at this time of day."

James drove a black Chrysler 300; a formidable hunk of a car with tinted windows and all. He went over the game plan. "At 9:00 a.m. the four of us will go the residence. Remember the search is to be carried out by the independent supervising solicitor–me. You both are not to get involved. We will only ask you to confirm certain photographs if need be. You are purely observers. When we first encounter Mrs. Burnside, Mary and I will do the talking.

The rest of my team will pull up on the street in front of the house. I will only call them in once we have permission to search."

"What if she won't give permission?" Mark asked.

"Never had that happen before, but I've never executed an Anton Piller Order on a private residence. I'm going to leave Mary to talk to her. The most she can do is stall for two hours in order to contact counsel. I'm hopeful we can convince her to let us carry out the search."

We arrived on Northfield Drive at about 8:40. James parked his car and pointed down the street. "See the beige house with the porch and red car parked out front about seven houses down?" We all looked. "That's the Burnside house." The houses on the street were newer, probably five or so years old. The street was lined with semi-mature trees and the houses all had well cared for lawns. The houses were regulation brown or beige; they were not small, but not large either. This was a starter area for young families.

Mary phoned the team having coffee. All were present and accounted for. She then phoned the police officer on surveillance putting the phone on speaker, "Hi Bill, we've arrived and are parked down the street to the west."

"Yeah, I saw you park."

"Anything happening?"

"Burnside left at 8:32. Nothing else."

"Good, Mrs. Burnside should be coming out any time with her daughter to catch the bus."

We waited. Every minute was like an hour.

Then we saw a woman and a child come out of the house. The little girl skipped to the road side, dressed in a pink poncho, sweat pants, and carrying a little plastic backpack. Mrs. Burnside stood by the road watching her daughter. A woman and boy from across the street came down to the road. The girl and boy played. They picked up acorns on the lawn and threw them into the street. Children can play with anything. The mothers talked. Within a minute or so a small yellow school bus stopped to pick up the children.

They bounded onto the bus, which was no doubt the highlight of their day. No hugs for the mothers; these were independent little kindergarten tykes. The bus left and the mothers took a moment to chat standing by the roadside.

"Don't invite her in for tea," whispered James.

"And don't go to the neighbour's for tea," muttered Mark.

The conversation ended and Mrs. Burnside returned to her house. It was 8:51. We breathed a sigh of relief. We waited some more. James drove closer to the house. We were now only three houses down. Mary phoned for the team to arrive and park down the street. They pulled up a minute later.

It was 8:55. I wondered what James would do if Mrs. Burnside came out and headed for the red car to leave. Would he drive up and block the driveway? I didn't want to ask.

It was 8:58. I knew that James would not execute the order until precisely 9:00.

It was 9:00. James drove the car right in front of the Burnside house. Mary phoned for the rest of the team to park in front as well and to wait. We got out of the car. I wonder what Mrs. Burnside would be thinking, or the neighbours, seeing four 'suits' walking to the front door having gotten out of a black ominous looking car.

James and Mary led the way. James rang the door bell. Mrs. Burnside opened the door. She did not, however, open the screen door.

"Mrs. Margaret Burnside?"

"Yes."

"My name is James Taylor. I am a solicitor and barrister and I am here pursuant to a court order issued by Mr. Justice Stargel of the Manitoba Court of Queen's Bench. With me is Mrs. Mary Weber, a lawyer assisting me, Mr. Mark Labros an attorney acting for the plaintiff in an action brought against your husband and Professor Andrew Sturgis, who is assisting Mr. Labros. I have identification to show and the court order. Do you mind if we come in, I think it would cause less gossip on the street." James smiled.

Mrs. Burnside was wide eyed, but calm. She was slim, average height with pleasant features, mid-thirties; her brown hair was tied back in a ponytail and she wore comfortable at home clothes. She did not immediately open the door, but looked at the four of us. She must have decided that we were safe enough and that this was not a home invasion. She opened the door without saying a word. We entered into the small front hall.

James showed her his Law Society of Manitoba card, "I have formal documents to show to you and I want to inform you as to what this is all about. Do you mind if we sit around the dining room or kitchen table."

"Yes, of course, this way. I'd like to know what this is all about." She said in a matter of fact tone, with no hint of intimidation.

Once at the round red oak dining room table, James sat on one side of her, Mary on the other. We took up chairs across and remained mute. James continued, "The first document I am going to show you is a statement of claim, which was filed in the Court yesterday. You are welcome to read it, but it is quite lengthy. I can tell you that the claim is for assault against your husband and another professor who visited Winnipeg this past August. The assault was against a young woman, who studied at Professor Sturgis' university."

Mrs. Burnside, did not look at James. She leafed through the statement of claim, which was some ten pages in length. I noted that she paused on page four, where the date for the assault was outlined.

She then spoke, "Shouldn't you be taking this up with my husband? Shouldn't you be serving this claim on him at the university?" Her voice had an edge and was more forceful.

James calmly replied, "We normally serve these at the home residence. The second document is an order of Justice Stargel's signed yesterday." He handed her the order, which itself was six pages in length outlining the parameters of our search.

"Mrs. Burnside, this is a court order to search this house for specified information. As co-owner of this house you are bound by it and it orders you to allow us to search for the information outlined on page three. Please turn to page three." She did. "We are authorized to look for photographs, video recordings of any kind, data storage that may contain images on the dates and involving the persons listed. We are also authorized to seize any computer or data storage device and to be provided with any necessary passwords. The order is quite specific. We have a team of retired police officers, and support personnel waiting outside to conduct the search."

Mrs. Burnside was taking this in with her lips pressed in a tight vice. "I think you should talk to my husband. This all relates to him."

James ignored her request and went on, "I am the independent supervising solicitor entrusted by the Court to carry out this search in a proper manner and according to the order. You are welcome to consult with a lawyer, should you wish. However, as I said, I am independent. Under the order you may have up to two hours to seek advice, but we do need to safeguard any information. We would not conduct any search while you seek advice. I must tell you that if you refuse to allow us to search that this is punishable by a finding of contempt of court. You could be imprisoned for failing to allow the search."

"I could go to jail?"

"Yes, but that is a last resort."

"I don't know; I just don't know. Give me a moment." She looked back at the statement of claim. No one rushed her.

"It says that my husband and the other man raped the young woman. That is what it says. William would never do that, never."

Mary now spoke, "Mrs. Burnside that is the allegation. A statement of claim, is just what the plaintiff says happened. At this stage it is just an allegation."

"How could people say that, how? William would never."

Mary responded, "And he will have his chance to defend himself and deny the allegations. Today is the first opportunity for him to do so. The plaintiff has this order from the court seeking photographs or video recordings. If we find none, this will help your husband. If we are not allowed to search then the court will make an adverse inference; the inference being that you may have had something to hide. And that would hurt your husband's case."

"When did this supposedly happen?" Mrs. Burnside looked across the table to Mark and me. We didn't answer. Mary did, "On a Saturday night, August 15, of this year, which was the final day of a law conference."

Mrs. Burnside didn't say anything, but you could see her thinking back to that date. What would her mind tell her? I could see recognition in her eyes.

Mary said to her softly, "Mrs. Burnside, I know this must be a shock for you, but all that the Court wants is to uncover the truth. We're here to carry out that task. I'm married with two girls, ten and twelve, if I were served this order I'd want to know the truth for me and for them. This is your decision to make, not your husband's; you as co-owner of this property have the authority to allow whomsoever you want onto the property."

Mrs. Burnside closed her eyes a moment, "Will you destroy my house in the search?"

James responded, "Certainly not. That is why Mary and I are here and we have a camera person, who will videotape everything to see that it is done properly."

Mrs. Burnside then looked directly at Mark and me and asked, "How old was she?"

Mary nodded to us to answer. Mark replied, "She was just twenty-three years old."

She then turned to James, "My husband keeps all of his photography equipment, everything, in a dark room in the basement, but it is locked and I don't have a key."

"That's not a problem; I have a locksmith with me, who can open the door without damage," said James.

Mrs. Burnside took a further moment and then said, "Very well. You may search. My daughter comes back from pre-school at 11:15. Can you be done by then?"

"We will try Mrs. Burnside. We will try," promised James. He nodded to Mary to call in the team. We had permission. "I have called my team in, which includes two retired police officers, a computer technician, locksmith and camera man. If you show us where the photography room is we can begin there. Do you wish to observe us search or not? I promise you we will not damage anything."

"I'll show you the room, and allow you to search." is all she said.

The team entered the house and all of us were led down to the basement. The basement was half finished; storage was kept in the unfinished half. There was a carpeted play room, half bathroom, and the locked dark room. The locksmith checked the lock, went to his tool bag, found the right tool and in ten seconds the door was open.

The police officers began to search. Mrs. Burnside remained in the background. The dark room was elongated, I would estimate eight feet by twelve. The room was meticulous, just as Burnside's office had been. The far wall had the photo processing pans, chemicals and what I assumed was an enlarger all arranged on a metal desk. Everything had its place. On the side walls were shelves and cabinets containing indexed photographs and video recordings. On the entry wall was a smaller desk with a computer and printer.

The computer technician indicated to James that the computer was password protected. James asked Mrs. Burnside, "Do you know the password?"

"No, it is his computer."

James then said, "We'll need to take it with us and get the password from your husband." Mrs. Burnside nodded.

The police officers began to go through the files. Each one turned out to be as categorized: family holidays, trips abroad, special events. The search was bringing up nothing. I watched Mrs.

Burnside. She sat in the corner looking into space. My sense was that she knew, in her heart, that there was something to be found. Or, at least, she feared that to be.

There were thousands of photographs. Nothing. This was Burnside's den; this was his sanctuary. If he was going to hide something it would be in this room. It had to be. The officers were thorough and careful. It took them time to go through the files. There were video recordings on disc that the computer technician scanned using his own computer. Nothing. I was starting to have doubts.

The officers began tapping on the walls, searching for hollow spaces. Nothing. There was a large clear plastic bin on one of the shelves. The bin was labelled ink and photography supplies. It was located on the third shelf at eye level. The officer lifted the bin off of the shelf. Behind it was a wall panel. The officer started tapping. There was a solid tap. The officer took a closer look. He then pushed the panel and the wooden panel clicked open. It was held in place by a push release. Behind the door was a grey metal electrical box, which was locked. The officer showed James, who, in turn, called on the locksmith to open the box. It was opened within a minute.

I held my breath. I was sure that this was it. In the box there were a number of video tape discs all indexed and there was a small photograph album. When the officer opened the album his face told us that we had found what we were seeking. He handed the photo album over to James. James fingered through it. His face turned white. He turned to Mark and I. "Do you identify any of these women?"

The photo album had nude pictures of women: some fully nude, others semi-nude, some in bondage. There was a photograph of Allison on the bed in the Artist Hotel, she was handcuffed to the bedposts, she was nude and the Man in the Golden Helmet was looking down. The women were named, with dates provided. There were photographs of Ingrid, Victoria and Jennifer. In total there were eleven women and girls, at least two, perhaps three of the photographs were of young girls. I identified the photographs of Allison, Ingrid, Victoria, and Jennifer.

On the one shelf, beside the photo album there were a number of video recorded discs. All were indexed. For each woman there were two discs. We had found Professor Burnside's stash of depravity. On a second shelf there were a number of other discs. James took possession of everything. He had the computer technician quickly play one of the discs. The technician merely nodded his head in agreement. Burnside was being skewered by his own need for order.

James asked the technician to document and catalogue everything taken out of the hidden box. Mrs. Burnside said nothing. There was nothing to be said. She knew that we had found something significant.

The police officers told James that the most common area where items are hidden is in the master bedroom and asked whether he wished for them to search that room. James consulted with Mary and the technician. We weren't privy to that conversation, but the decision was made. There was no need. The evidence sought had been found.

It was 10:35. James terminated the videotaping. He informed Mrs. Burnside that the search was over and that he would be reporting to the Court. He left with her the notice of the hearing to be held at 2:00 p.m. the next day; her husband could appear at that time and seek return of the items seized. He then thanked Mrs. Burnside for allowing them to conduct the search. She said nothing. Her world was now in turmoil. I think she had an inkling. I had to wonder if her daughter Tessa was on any of those discs. I hoped not. We left.

On the drive back to the office James told us that he, Mary and the technician would review the discs taken and provide a report to the court for tomorrow's hearing and provide a report to us on the specific information that we had sought.

We were dropped off. When we got to the Johns and Mitchell office, Michael could tell that we had found what we wanted. We were in a jovial mood and Michael suggested an early lunch at the local deli where we could fill him in on the morning's events.

CHAPTER 31

Reuben's Deli was busy even at 11:20 in the morning, but not 'crazy' is how Michael described it at noon hour. We ordered the house specialty, which was corned beef on rye with pickles and coleslaw on the side. Michael found us a window seat. As we walked to our table Michael had to pause to talk to every second person; he knew everybody and everybody knew him.

Once seated, Mark recounted the events at the Burnside house. Michael was most interested in Mrs. Burnside and her reactions. I shared with him my thoughts that she had an inkling that her husband was up to something and how she had concentrated on the date of Allison's attack. That date resonated with her. She knew he was out that evening and I think she had suspicions.

Michael shook his head, "I feel sorry for her. From what you've said she's a nice person, intelligent and yet felt compelled to do the right thing. I can only imagine what is now going to happen. Her peaceful suburban life is over." He took a big bite of his over-sized sandwich, washed it down with water and said to Mark, "Tomorrow at the hearing Justice Stargel will lift the sealing order. We don't like secret filings in Canada. So the word will get out about Professor Burnside."

"I'd prefer that the sealing order remain in place until we at least get back to Flemington." said Mark.

Michael shrugged, "Simply ask for the sealing order not to be lifted until after the close of business. The order won't be made public until Monday morning." Michael continued, "You will next need to ask that the evidence found by the independent supervising solicitor as per the order be released to you, and I assume that request will be granted. What will you then do now that you have the evidence?"

Mark took a moment, "I think we'll look at bringing an action in Minnesota against Fraser and the University of Flemington. The action we brought here really will not provide much of an award in damages."

Michael looked startled. I thought he was going to choke on his sandwich, "But you can't! You can't use the evidence in another action whether in Canada or in the United States." He blurted out.

Mark and I were now the startled ones. Mark asked, "What do you mean we can't use the evidence?"

Michael wiped his mouth, "There is an implied undertaking rule in our courts that applies to evidence obtained in the course of discovery of one action, which prevents that evidence from being used to support another action."

Both Mark and I listened in stunned silence.

Michael continued, "You obtained the videotapes through a court order that applied to the estate action brought by the Klassens here in Manitoba. You were allowed to obtain evidence and force the defendant to turn over evidence related to that estate action and only that action. You can't, for example, now use that evidence to support actions brought by the other victims. If you did use the evidence to support other actions the other side would seek its exclusion and Justice Stargel would be very upset. He'd probably report you to the Law Society, hell he might even find you in contempt of court."

"But this would be an action in Minnesota, another country, Justice Stargel doesn't have jurisdiction," Mark argued.

"No not for you, but what about me and my law firm? We may not be sanctioned, but I can tell you that our reputation would be seriously sullied. Reputation means everything in a small legal community—you know that. Mark, you can't." Michael was pleading.

Mark was silent. I knew his sense of action was swaying him to run with the evidence back to the United States, but at the same time his sense of justice and respect for the law was holding him back.

Michael continued pleading his case, "Mark you used the law to see that justice was done for the Klassens. With this lawsuit Fraser and Burnside are exposed. You've won. Respect the law."

I played mediator, "Michael are there any exceptions to the implied undertaking rule?"

Michael thought, "I'm no expert on this area. It has never come up in my practice. I know that there are common law decisions and a Manitoba Queen's Bench Rule that applies. I think there are exceptions, but can't tell you offhand."

"Can we research them in time for the hearing tomorrow?" I asked.

"Yes, yes, you can use the boardroom and our internet, which will give you access to our research databases. Aaron might be able to help as well. Unfortunately, I have a motion this afternoon at 2:00."

Mark now spoke, "Michael, I don't want to bring trouble to you or to your firm. You have been too good to us. We need to explore any and all options." He looked at me, "Professor we have some researching to do. I take it that we could raise this with Justice Stargel tomorrow and see if he will release us from the undertaking?"

Michael, looking relieved, nodded yes.

"Well, let's get to it," I said, "We'll need to go back to the hotel get our computers and head back to your boardroom. We've got time."

With that we headed off. We had purpose in our step and little time to waste.

Arriving back at Johns and Mitchell we set up in the board-room. Aaron helped us get our computers online. We decided to divide the research. Mark would concentrate on Manitoba cases involving implied undertakings and cases that applied the Manitoba statute. Aaron readily found the statute for us. I concentrated on the Supreme Court of Canada. Coffee was put on and we got to work.

After a couple of hours we compared notes. We certainly had identified the leading cases and principles of law. Mark began, "Looking at the statute, Rule 30.1 may not apply. That is the statute on implied undertakings and it specifically says that the rule only applies to evidence obtained under Rules 30, 31, 32, 33 and 35--none of which apply to an Anton Piller Order. In fact Rule 30.1(2) says that the implied undertaking rule does not apply unless based on the listed Rules. So we have an argument that the implied undertaking rule has no application to us."

"Yes, but where does that get us?" I commented, "If the statute doesn't apply then the common law does and that was made clear in a number of the Supreme Court of Canada cases. And my under-standing is that the statute rules are based on the common law. So I don't see how it helps us; we are still bound by the common law rule." I continued, "How have the Manitoba Courts interpreted the statute–liberally or restrictively?"

"I think the best word would be to say that they are careful. The fundamental concern is that parties who surrender evidence should not be prejudiced or find themselves subjected to an additional court action, especially one that incriminates them."

"Okay, if that is the principle, what if Burnside is not involved in any subsequent court action? Were you looking to sue him in Minnesota?" I asked.

"No, I really don't care about Burnside. In fact, including him as a party would merely complicate things. I was looking to sue Fraser and the university, as employer of Fraser."

"Well if that is the case, where is there any prejudice to Burnside?" I mused, "Fraser is prejudiced; however, his house was not searched. His privacy was not invaded. He really has no standing to challenge the evidence found at Burnside's residence."

Mark listened intently and responded, "There was a Manitoba case where a former employee had his residence searched for stolen copyright material. Evidence was found. The plaintiff then sought to use the incriminating evidence against the new employer, who used the stolen material to duplicate the plaintiff's invention. The new employer raised the implied undertaking rule and the Manitoba Court of Appeal found that there was no prejudice to the former employee and accordingly the new employer could not take advantage of the rule."

"Say you return to Minnesota with the evidence and the other women, Ingrid, Jennifer and Victoria want to sue Burnside as well. Wouldn't that be in breach of the rule?"

"That may be, and should that be the case I'd have to tell them that we'd have to get permission to use the evidence from the Manitoba court. For the time being my clients are the Klassens and only the Klassens," Mark answered.

"Alright let us put together our 'no prejudice' argument and identify our key cases."

For the next hour we honed the outline of argument. Mark would have to fine tune it in the evening. Such is the life of a litigator.

Michael arrived back from his court motion. "How did it go?" I asked.

"We won. Wasn't much of a win. The other side had no case to present. It was a motion brought by greedy relatives to have the estate, for whom we act, pay their legal fees so that they could contest the will. Imagine, they wanted the estate to fund their action against the estate. Absurd." Michael was fuming, "We asked for increased costs after winning the motion and got those costs. That might scare them off–greedy vultures."

Michael calmed down, "How are you two doing?"

Mark smiled and said, "We have our argument and I think it is a winning one." Mark then outlined the argument.

"So you are not going to sue Burnside in Minnesota?" asked Michael.

"Nope," said Mark, "there is no point. You did a check on him and the only thing he owns is his house and it is mortgaged to the hilt. There is nothing to be gained except unnecessary headaches for us to sue him in Minnesota. Our focus is on Fraser and Flemington University and with them there is no prejudice. They were not the subject of the Anton Piller search. We can rely on a number of supporting cases."

Michael looked relieved, "I knew you'd find and follow the law. Let me check my email to see if James has anything for me." He left the boardroom coming back a few minutes later. He had a copy of an email in hand, and he distributed copies to us.

James had completed an interim report on the information sought through the Anton Piller search. It indicated that for the women listed and dates provided each was found in the photo album, which we already knew, and for each there were two video discs. One was approximately fifteen minutes in length and James listed this video as "Edited video of events night of ….showing sexual assault upon named person." The second disc for each varied in length from 2 hours and 13 minutes to 3 hours and 22 minutes, which James listed as, "Unedited video of events night of …showing sexual assault upon named person."

The email also stated, "As Independent Supervising Solicitor, I will be making submissions to the Court for the release of seized material in the public interest and specifically under authority of section 18 of the Manitoba Child and Family Services Act."

I asked Michael what the last line in the email meant. He replied, "We are obliged to report child pornography where found. James wants to report his findings to the police."

Michael went on, "What is clear from James' email is that you have the material that you sought. You have the evidence.

Tomorrow at the hearing James reports on what he seized. You will need to convince Justice Stargel to release the listed videotapes or copies thereof to you and you will then ask the Court to unseal the claim and make it public. Following that you will ask Justice Stargel to waive the implied undertaking rule so that you can use the evidence against Fraser and Flemington University in Minnesota." Michael smiled, "It will be an interesting hearing. What you certainly have going for you is that Justice Stargel in his former life prosecuted a number of child pornography cases. He well knows the harm that predators inflict on society. He'll be sympathetic to your cause, but, having said that, he will follow the law."

It was now late in the day. Michael got up and said, "It has been a very busy day. I'm tired and I'm going home. No doubt you need a rest as well. The boardroom is yours tomorrow morning."

We gathered up our materials and computers and headed back to the hotel. We didn't sleep. How could we? We had one last battle to prepare for. We worked through the evening on Mark's submission to waive the implied undertaking rule. We ordered a pizza and ate in. Finally at 10:30 I signed off on his argument. It was good. Mark was prepared.

We sat back savoring the moment. Mark laughed, "Burnside must have phoned Fraser by now. Can you imagine that conversation?" He mimicked Burnside, "Uh Jerome, I have some bad news. We are being sued by the parents of the girl who died and they have the videotapes we took of us raping her, uh, and of the other students you brought up here. It's not good Jerome." He changed his voice, "You got that right Professor Burnside. You and Professor Fraser are toast."

"Do you think Burnside will show up at tomorrow's hearing in person or through counsel?"

"Not in person for sure," said Mark, "he'd be a fool to attend tomorrow's hearing in person. He might want to blow some smoke our way through having counsel present, but I doubt it. The gig is up for him; he must realize that."

I nodded in agreement and got up to leave. Looking over at the Mona Lisa I said to Mark, "She's smiling for us."

"Yes she is," replied Mark and his parting words to me were, "You know Fraser will be livid with you."

I had a tinge of apprehension about that. Fraser was not a person to fool with.

CHAPTER 32

Once again the hearing was in courtroom 310 and Michael, Aaron, Mark and I arrived ten minutes early. James and Mary were already there and gave us a nod; across from them at the other counsel table was an overweight, verging on obese, mid-forties, balding man, who could best be described as frumpy. As soon as he saw Michael, he got up from his seat and confronted Michael in a loud, hostile voice, "What gives you the right to conduct a raid on my client's house? I want everything you took given back."

Michael calmly looked at him and replied, "Good afternoon Darryl, I take it you are acting for Mr. Burnside?"

"You got that right," Darryl huffed, "where do you get off busting into a man's home?"

Darryl was an intimidator. I had seen many such lawyers when I was a prosecutor. A few were cagey smart–very few–most were mediocre and some were downright incompetent. Facts mean little to such lawyers and the law even less. They huff and puff and posture usually at the expense of their clients, who have no idea that their lawyer is woefully inept; they make noise to cover up their inadequacies.

Michael replied in a soft, but firm tone, "First, Darryl there was no raid, no busting in, Mr. Taylor acted on order from Mr. Justice Stargel and was allowed to search the house by Mrs. Burnside, co-owner of the house."

"Well I want everything back," said Darryl.

"You'll have to ask Mr. Taylor, because he has all the evidence seized. We have none. This hearing is about us getting access to the evidence, which incidentally I am certain that your client would have destroyed." Michael stared Darryl down. He had dealt with him before I am sure.

Darryl went over to Mr. Taylor. I could see that James could barely be civil. I heard him say, "Read my report. We listed what we seized. And, I'll say this again, I want the password to the computer seized. Your client by order is to provide that password. I told you that this morning and I told you I wanted that password before this hearing started. If not I'll advise Mr. Justice Stargel and seek sanctions against your client." Darryl waddled back to his counsel table.

Michael whispered to me, "Darryl Quinze is a criminal lawyer. I don't think he has ever done a civil case. He was a classmate of Burnside's, poor choice of counsel."

At precisely 2:00 p.m. Mr. Justice Stargel entered the courtroom. We rose, bowed and took our seats. Mr. Justice Stargel was dressed in a different suit today, black. He took a quick look around the court and his eyes fixed on Darryl Quinze. Appearances were taken.

Darryl Quinze, after introducing himself and stating that he was acting for Professor Burnside went on, "I am here today to see to the return of all materials seized at Professor Burnside's home flowing from this illegal raid." Quinze doesn't give up, but it was the wrong thing to say to Mr. Justice Stargel.

"Mr. Quinze, the search was conducted pursuant to an order that I granted on Wednesday of this week. It was not an illegal raid; it was a search allowed under an Anton Piller Order. Mr. Taylor, was the search allowed by a person appearing to be in control of the premises as required by the order?"

James rose, "Yes, M'Lord, the search was authorized by Mrs. Margaret Burnside, who is co-owner of the house and she was fully informed of her rights under your Lordship's order and she remained throughout to observe the search being carried out."

"Thank you Mr. Taylor," Justice Stargel then turned back to Mr. Quinze, "There was no illegality Mr. Quinze and the purpose of the hearing today is to determine what is to be done with any relevant information seized. Please sit down." It was not a request but a politely framed command. "Before we begin, is this hearing to remain in camera and the court file to remain sealed?" Mark and James confirmed that was the case. "Mr. Quinze I assume that is the wish of your client as well?"

"It is," said Quinze.

"Mr. Taylor, as independent supervising solicitor, I ask that you report on the executed order."

James took to the podium. "Justice Stargel, pursuant to your order, I and the named persons in the order, attended to the Burnside residence at 87 Northfield Drive in Winnipeg at 9:00 a.m. Mrs. Burnside was at home. I explained to her the statement of claim and the Anton Piller Order. She was given time to consider her options and she allowed us to search. We were directed by her to the basement where Mr. Burnside had a locked darkroom and photography work room. Mrs. Burnside did not have a key. Our locksmith opened the door to the room, without causing any damage. In the course of the search a hidden locked metal box was found inside one of the walls. The locksmith opened this box. Inside was the material that we seized and outlined in my report. Specifically we seized from the box a photograph album of eleven named females, with photographs of each. The females named in the album were indexed to twenty-two video discs two for each female. I am using the term 'female' because some of the named females appear to be underage girls. In addition fourteen other discs were seized from the hidden box. All together there was a total of 51 hours and 25 minutes of video recording seized. Your Lordship can appreciate that in the intervening time we have only skimmed the content. I can say this that in having scanned the fourteen videotapes they can best be described as being violent and pornographic. Of the twenty-two indexed video discs all show females being sexually assaulted in situations where the females are either in bondage or obviously are in no physical condition to resist or to consent. I have provided a list in my report, which your Lordship has, but I would ask that the report in its entirety be made an exhibit." The report was filed. Copies were provided to all counsel.

James paused, "I spoke with Mr. Quinze this morning when he advised me that he was acting for Mr. Burnside. At that time I provided him with an interim report listing what we seized and I specifically asked him to speak with his client and get the password for the computer seized in Mr. Burnside's darkroom. Mrs. Burnside did not have the password. The computer is listed in our report as item 1. I spoke with Mr. Quinze immediately before court and requested the password again. It is my respectful view that should that password not be provided that sanctions should be brought against Mr. Burnside."

Justice Stargel turned quickly to Mr. Quinze, "Do you have that password?"

Darryl Quinze rose, with considerable difficulty, "No M'Lord, I advised my client to await the outcome of this meeting. It is quite unusual for a defendant to assist the other side."

Justice Stargel's eyes were piercing; his voice was sharp as a knife, "Mr. Quinze that is not how it works, maybe in a criminal court but this is a civil case. I ordered that passwords be provided so that Mr. Taylor would be in a position to report back to me as to what he found on any data storage device. You have until 5:00 p.m. today to provide that password to Mr. Taylor. If your client does not, he will face sanctions. Do you understand?" Mr. Justice Stargel emphasized the last three words, speaking them slowly and distinctly.

Darryl Quinze nodded and took his seat.

Mr. Taylor continued, "The plaintiffs were very specific in what they were looking for. They had provided the names of four persons: Ingrid Hedberg, Jennifer Cunningham, Victoria Palmer and Allison Klassen. Those individuals were named in the photo album and I confirmed with the plaintiff that the photographs in the album matched these women. The discs associated with these individuals are: 3,4,9,10,13,14, and 21,22. I have placed an asterisk beside each number to identify these video discs. Given the allegations in the statement of claim it is my view that all of that evidence is highly relevant. In particular, there are the video discs pertaining to Allison Klassen. That is my report."

Mr. Justice Stargel then turned to Mark, "Mr. Labros do you have any submissions to make."

"Yes, M'Lord, the plaintiff requests that copies of the video discs identified by asterisk by Mr. Taylor be released to us, the originals to remain with Mr. Taylor or be deposited with the Court. The evidence identified is critical evidence for our case. My understanding is that the discs show the actual attacks upon Allison Klassen. The discs also show sexual assaults on the other named students from Flemington University and, in our respectful view, are admissible as similar fact evidence. It is my understanding that relevant evidence so found by way of an Anton Piller Order is generally released to the search party. After all that is the purpose of such an Order. Accordingly, we formally request that copies of the relevant seized video discs and the indexed photo album be released to us."

"Mr. Quinze, any response?" asked Justice Stargel.

Darryl Quinze rose slowly, "I fail to see why the plaintiff should receive this evidence. It can be held by Mr. Taylor, or by the Court for that matter, and released as the action proceeds to trial. There is no reason to rush this evidence into the plaintiff's hands. I also have concerns about editing, modification of the evidence. Those are my submissions."

"Mr. Labros any rebuttal?"

"Having the originals kept by Mr. Taylor or with the Court is a safeguard against any tampering, by both sides. We seek only copies. With respect to timing, this evidence is highly relevant and it would greatly speed up the process saving all concerned expense and court time. Otherwise we are required to turn a blind eye to evidence we now know exists. Subject to any questions Your Lordship may have, those are my submissions."

Justice Stargel was a decisive man, "Thank you counsel, after hearing representations from the Independent Supervising Solicitor, and counsel for the plaintiff and defendant Burnside, I order copies of the identified video disc evidence be released to the plaintiff as soon as practicable, and that the originals of all evidence be retained by the Independent Supervising Solicitor, Mr. Taylor. Furthermore, should Mr. Taylor discover other relevant evidence as described by the plaintiff and contained in the Anton Piller Order, copies of such are to be released to the plaintiff. Are there any other matters to be dealt with?"

Mr. Taylor rose to his feet and took to the podium: "M'Lord, it is usual for the independent supervising solicitor to retain all the evidence seized or deposit same with the Court pending release to the plaintiff, as per your order just now. And all evidence found traditionally is kept confidential between the litigants. However, given the evidence that we have uncovered, I ask the Court to allow me to inform the proper authorities of its existence. I am not seeking actually to release this evidence to the authorities, but at least to make its existence known and allow them to obtain the evidence through their own search powers. This morning I contacted the Law Society of Manitoba and sought their advice. I have a copy of their letter in response and I file it now as part of this hearing. I have made copies for plaintiff and defendant counsel."

Justice Stargel accepted the letter as an exhibit. James gave him time to read it. "As Your Lordship can see, three very well respected Benchers, all Past Presidents of the Law Society of Manitoba, concluded that I do not have grounds to disclose the evidence obtained under our Code of Professional Conduct, which makes disclosure of information mandatory "if the lawyer has reasonable grounds for believing that an identifiable person or group is in imminent danger of death or serious bodily harm and believes disclosure is necessary to prevent the death or harm". The panel did not find that such imminent harm existed; however, the panel went on to advise that I was required to disclose to the authorities that I now have in my possession video discs that appear to contain child pornography under section 18 of the Manitoba Child and Family Services Act. I draw this finding of the Law Society to Your Lordship, not that it is binding, but that it supports my request to disclose the existence of the apparent child pornography. As I mentioned earlier, the video discs show violent sexual acts being perpetrated on young females, who appear to be under age. I appreciate that such a step is not to be taken lightly. Solicitor confidentiality is a sacred trust, but it is not an absolute trust. The law recognizes exceptions and the scourge of child pornography is such that the public interest in protecting children prevails over any requirement of confidentiality. I respectfully request an order to advise the police authorities of the existence of this evidence. Those are my submissions at this time, M'Lord."

Mr. Justice Stargel took a deep breath, "Can you identify the discs that contain the apparent child pornography Mr. Taylor."

"Yes, the discs at issue are: 1,2,15,16,23,27,31 and 35. I have prepared a list." The list was handed to the clerk.

Justice Stargel continued, "Mr. Taylor thank you for your submissions and for obtaining the opinion of the Law Society of Manitoba panel. I am in agreement with their conclusion. The Child and Family Services Act is clear, all professionals, including lawyers, are required to disclose the existence of apparent child pornography. The only exception under the act is for solicitor-client communications, but that has no application here. Mr. Taylor I authorize you to disclose to proper authorities the existence of the listed video discs 1,2,15,16,23,27,31 and 35 and any other evidence uncovered pursuant to the Anton Piller Order that contains apparent child pornography."

"Thank you M'Lord."

Mark stood up, "There is one other matter. I ask for permission to use the evidence released to me today by Mr. Taylor in separate legal proceedings in Minnesota. I will be more exact. It is the intention of the Klassens to bring an action for assault and wrongful death against Professor Jerome Fraser and the same against Professor Fraser's employer, Flemington University. They seek to use the evidence contained on the discs and seized from Mr. Burnside's home in these separate, but related actions."

Justice Stargel was watching Mark intensely. Mark continued, "I am well aware of the implied undertaking rule, which, as a general proposition, means that evidence disclosed in an action is only used in that action and is not to be used in other actions. Simply put evidence exchanged on discovery between litigants in an action remains with that action. However, just as Mr. Taylor spoke earlier, this rule is not absolute. The evidence may be used in other actions where the interests of justice outweigh any prejudice to the affected party. We say that is the case here."

Mark had a rhythm, "Here the interests of justice point to the victimization of four students from Flemington University by one of their professors. The evidence found in this action confirms these attacks. It is critical evidence—not merely supporting evidence."

Justice Stargel asked, "Would this action in Minnesota include the other students as plaintiffs?"

"Yes, they would be invited to join the action. Whether they do, will be up to them; regardless the Klassens will bring an action."

"Do you have case support for waiving the rule to allow other litigants to bring a law suit?"

"Yes, the leading case in Manitoba is Parsons and United Furnace, and it is on point. I have a copy of that case for Your Lordship." Mark handed a copy of the case to Justice Stargel and gave him a moment to examine the case. He then continued, "Parsons suspected that one of their employees had stolen copyrighted information and was selling that information to competitors. Parsons got an Anton Piller Order to search the employee's home, which uncovered evidence that the employee had sold the stolen information to three other competitors. Parsons was then allowed to sue the three other competitors using the evidence found in the employee's home. The principle applied was that the other competitors were not parties to the original seizure of the evidence and the employee suffered no prejudice."

"Do you have a copy for Mr. Quinze?"

"Actually I do; however, I do not believe that Mr. Quinze acting for Mr. Burnside has any interest in this motion."

This caught Justice Stargel's attention, "And why is that?"

"We have no intention of suing Mr. Burnside in Minnesota. You have my undertaking on that. There is no purpose in suing Mr. Burnside. Our action will be brought against Flemington University and its employee, Professor Fraser. Therefore, Mr. Burnside is not prejudiced by our action in the United States. Similarly, Flemington University and Professor Fraser were not the parties searched. They, in turn, do not have standing to address the evidence found from the search of Mr. Burnside's home."

Mr. Quinze stood up, "An undertaking by a foreign lawyer is not worth anything in this country. Once the evidence is released it will be used as Mr. Labros wants."

Justice Stargel was not pleased, "Mr. Quinze when a member of the Manitoba Bar, whether resident or not, makes an undertaking in my courtroom I have every confidence and expectation that that promise will indeed be kept. Mr. Labros in the dealings thus far in this Court has been completely professional. The fact that he is asking for permission to use the evidence seized in the United States speaks volumes. That is the proper way to proceed. He could have taken the evidence and run; he didn't."

He nodded to Mark to continue, "We recognize that the implied undertaking rule is not to be waived unless we can provide special reasons. In this case, what is interesting is that Mr. Burnside never voluntarily turned over this crucial evidence; it had to be seized pursuant to an Anton Piller Order. It should be noted that the Manitoba statute on implied undertakings, Rule 30.1 of the Queen's Bench Rules, does not apply, because it deals with discovery where the parties are compelled to exchange evidence. Here it is safe to say that Mr. Burnside would never have turned over the damning videotapes. That is an important factor in weighing interests. It is one thing voluntarily to provide evidence in confidence that it will only be used in the action before the court; that is the quid pro quo. Evidence is voluntarily exchanged with the understanding that it will only be used in that action. However, Mr. Burnside never turned anything over of his own free will in expectation that it would only be used in the current action. The evidence at bar was seized from him precisely because he would never have turned it over. He was not part of any bargain deserving of protection; there was no quid pro quo."

"Is your position that the statute overrides the common law on implied undertakings?" asked Justice Stargel.

"The statute to the extent that it occupies the field would apply if, for example, Mr. Burnside turned over the tapes as part of discovery. Then the common law would not apply. Here, our position is that the statute does not apply, but that does not mean that there is no applicable law. The statute complements the common law; the common law on implied undertakings applies."

Mark continued, "Of most importance is that this evidence shows attacks upon the young female law students from Flemington University. It is vital evidence of despicable acts that we want to see redressed in Minnesota. These women and their families want and deserve justice. On the other hand, there is no prejudice against Mr. Burnside. Concerns about Mr. Burnside incriminating himself are not on the table in the United States. He is facing no criminal charges in the United States, and, as I have undertaken we will not proceed with any civil action against Mr. Burnside in the United States."

"You indicated that the action may involve the other students in addition to Miss Klassen's estate. What if the other students want to sue Mr. Burnside?"

"Part of any agreement for me to act for them would be respecting the undertaking that I have made here today. Today we are asking that the evidence be released to me on behalf of the Klassen's. I would not be free to use the evidence against Mr. Burnside unless I returned to this Court to ask for a further waiver, which frankly may not be granted."

Mr. Justice Stargel was silent; he nodded to Mark, "Thank you Mr. Labros. Mr. Quinze do you have anything to add?"

Darryl Quinze rose. I am not certain he had a firm grasp of the implied undertaking rule, but he would feel compelled to say something. "M'Lord, the implied undertaking rule is in place to encourage the free exchange of information between litigants. By allowing a litigant to use the evidence in other actions will have a real chilling effect on litigants, who won't want to reveal anything for fear that it might come back to bite them in another court case. What Mr. Labros wants is to bring a lucrative court case in the United States using what was obtained here in Canada. He can't get a high enough award in Canada. So he'll take the evidence to the States to reap big money. He speaks of the public interest; he's not seeking to further the public interest, he's seeking to further his own interest and that is not a valid reason to waive the implied undertaking rule. Mark my words my client will be facing a legal action in the United States." Darryl Quinze turned to Mark, "Undertaking or no undertaking. Those are my submissions."

Mr. Justice Stargel called a short adjournment to consider the matter.

I congratulated Mark on his arguments. I also went over to Mary and I provided her with Detective Semchuk's contact details, "Detective Semchuk is familiar with the case. He would be a proper authority to contact and be more than happy to receive the tip."

Mary smiled and thanked me, "I'll give him a call as soon as we get out of court. I think you're going to get the order. Justice Stargel has been quite impressed by your Mr. Labros and the thoroughness of all the materials provided. Justice Stargel has a real appreciation for good lawyering." I hoped Mary was right.

Mr. Justice Stargel returned to the court some twenty minutes later. He began: "I am prepared to rule on the request brought by Mr. Labros on behalf of the plaintiffs to waive the implied undertaking rule. It is important to note that the evidence released to the plaintiff in this action under the Anton Piller Order is powerful evidence of attacks upon Miss Klassen and other young female students from Flemington University in Flemington, Minnesota. This evidence was not voluntarily turned over to the plaintiff by the defendant, Burnside. It was seized under the Anton Piller Order. The implied undertaking order is not absolute. It will not stand should the public interest demand that it be used in other actions. In this case the public interest is high, if not overwhelming. Does it outweigh prejudice to the defendant Burnside? The plaintiff has undertaken not to bring a civil action in the United States against Mr. Burnside. Nor would Mr. Burnside be facing any criminal action in the United States. The prejudice to Mr. Burnside is low. Prejudice to the University of Flemington or to the defendant Fraser is of no moment; they were not the subject of the search that uncovered the evidence. Mr. Burnside's privacy interest was intruded upon not theirs. In light of the undertaking by the plaintiff and in the final balancing of the public interest versus potential prejudice to Mr. Burnside I find in favour of the public interest. Therefore, the implied undertaking rule is waived with respect to the evidence released to the plaintiff under the Anton Piller Order in this action. This waiver applies to any action brought by the plaintiff and others against the University of Flemington and Professor Jerome Fraser."

Justice Stargel looked up, "Counsel that is my decision."

Mark rose, "Thank you M'Lord. There are just a couple of housekeeping matters. First, the plaintiff deposited with the court the sum of $10,000 as a bond against damages or costs imposed flowing from executing the Anton Piller Order. Given the evidence located and seized, we would request that this bond be returned to the plaintiff."

"Mr. Taylor, Mr. Quinze, any submissions on this point." Both said no. "The deposit of $10,000 is to be returned to the plaintiff." Mark continued, "We would request that the file now be unsealed, perhaps not until the close of court today. It is my understanding that Canadian courts do not look favourably upon closed hearings and filing."

"You are quite correct Mr. Labros," Justice Stargel smiled, "Mr. Taylor, Mr. Quinze?"

Darryl Quinze stood up, "We ask that the sealing order remain in place. The allegations brought against Professor Burnside are scurrilous and great harm will come to his reputation and position if the statement of claim and Anton Piller Order filings are made public and available to the media."

"Mr. Quinze, the fact that the allegations are serious is reason why the open court principle applies. Loss of reputation or position is no reason to keep the matter closed. The file is to be unsealed after close of Court today. Anything else?"

"No M'Lord that deals with all our matters," replied Mark.

"Mr. Labros, I wish you a safe journey home. It has been a pleasure having you appear in my Court. Court is adjourned." With that Mr. Justice Stargel rose and left the courtroom.

We had won.

Congratulations were shared all around. Mary handed Mark a small package that contained copies of the video discs, she had made two copies of each in advance of the hearing. In handing them to Mark she said, "They are disgusting. Those poor women. Get him and get that University."

We did not have time to savour our victory. We returned to the offices of Johns and Mitchell to retrieve our computers and work materials. We had packed our bags that morning and they were already in the car parked in the lot below. It was our intent to head back to Flemington immediately.

We had a change of clothes. Off went the suits, on went the jeans and comfortable shirts. Michael, like a doting mother made sure we had a few drinks and deli sandwiches to take with us on the road.

Mark discussed with Michael about any media inquiries once Monday morning came around. The court filings would be sealed until then, which is exactly what Mark wanted. I could see how proud Michael was to have been part of this successful and unique litigation experience. He told us as we were leaving, "My friends you have given me a wonderful new story to brag about."

Mark gave him a pat on the shoulder, "We couldn't have done it without you. We'll be in touch."

We said our goodbyes. We had much to do.

CHAPTER 33

Mark drove. I navigated. It was around 4:30 p.m. when we left the offices of Johns and Mitchell and we were caught in the end of day rush hour. It wasn't until almost an hour later that we emerged from the city and were on the highway heading south. As we drove we talked about what we'd do now.

Mark had a plan, a brilliant plan. He proposed meeting with Flemington University and getting a settlement before the allegations were reported in the media. He would encourage the university to be proactive and support the victims, rather than defending an unwinnable case. Timing was everything. The action in Winnipeg was under wraps until Monday morning. We had no idea how vigilant the Winnipeg news outlets would be or how porous was the court's internal gossip line. We assumed that we had until Tuesday before the story would explode and we had to act before then. We needed to lead the news and not react to it.

There was much to do and I took over the driving; giving Mark time to work. First things first, he had to review the video discs. It was a terrible task that had to be done. Mark needed to know what had happened to the women. "Mark you have to review the discs and the fewer people to see them the better." He gave me a sad nod of his head and took out his laptop, plugged in his earplugs and loaded Allison Klassen's disc. I concentrated on my driving.

The sun was setting and there is nothing more spectacular than a prairie sunset. With little obstructing this flat landscape and big blue sky we had a panoramic view. Over a palette of blue, pale yellow and orange-pink, fluffy white clouds wandered silently on their way. It was Mother Nature's last hurrah of the day.

After about fifteen minutes Mark removed the disc; he said nothing. He had only jotted a few notes on a notepad. He looked away from me out of the window. Then he put his face in his hands and wept. His sobs were deep, painful, from his heart. I put my hand on his shoulder in a weak gesture of support and understanding.

"Andy it was terrible. They defiled her. They laughed. They played with Allie. Her eyes were open. She knew what they were doing to her. Those goddamn sons of bitches." He cried some more.

"We're going to get them," I said.

"I know we are," he replied in a quiet voice.

It took a few minutes for him to emerge from his despair and he took out a second disc; this was Ingrid Hedberg's. We rode on in silence. Mark watched the disc. We were nearing the border. Mark removed the disc and put it back into the package, which was addressed to him. The last thing we wanted was for the discs to be confiscated. We figured that if anyone wanted to look in the package Mark could claim solicitor privilege—good luck.

The U.S. Border Security Officer was a young man. I wondered if he even shaved. We told him that we were in Winnipeg appearing in a court case. He didn't care. We hardly posed a security risk and were waved through. Once in North Dakota, Mark began contacting people putting the plan into action.

The first persons he contacted were the Klassens. All that he told them was that the action in Winnipeg had gone very well and that he had to talk to them. It was urgent. He suggested Saturday 11:00 a.m. at his office. They'd be there. The Klassens were always obliging; they didn't want to inconvenience Mark. What nice people.

He called his associate, William, and asked him to do a damage award assessment for rape complainants. Mark apologized for dumping on him over the weekend, but it was an emergency. Mark outlined a few key facts enough to do an adequate database search.

The assessment was needed for Sunday morning. The message was clear, drop everything, all hands on deck. William agreed. What else could the associate say?

He phoned a second associate, Elizabeth, and asked her to come in tomorrow to work on a statement of claim. She too said yes and he gave her some precedent files to look up.

He phoned Angela putting the call on speaker. "Angela? Mark here. Sorry to bother you. Angela, Andy is with me. We are driving back from Winnipeg and you know what? We have with us video discs of attacks on all of the Flemington students."

"You're kidding! All of them."

"Yes, our Professor Burnside was a very meticulous recorder," I chirped.

Mark went on, "Angela, we need a favour. Could you contact Ingrid Hedberg and Jennifer Cunningham and arrange for them to come and see me tomorrow afternoon? Ingrid first and Jennifer second. Angela, time really is of the essence; it is imperative that I talk to them tomorrow."

"I'll get on it," Angela replied, "they'll be there even if I have to handcuff them and drag them in. Any times in particular?"

"No, I'll leave that to you. I'll need an hour with each—so long as they both don't come at the same time. Angela it would be good if you came as well."

"Sure, not a problem. What do you have in mind, Mark?" Angela asked.

"I'll tell you tomorrow. I'll be in the office all day. Come in about a half hour before the first interview and I'll fill you in. Thanks Angela. You're an angel."

We phoned Maria Dempster. I had her cell number on my phone and we put the call through. I did the talking. I asked her whether she had Victoria Palmer's phone number. I mentioned that I was driving back to Flemington from Winnipeg with Mark and that it was urgent that we speak with Victoria. Maria provided Victoria's number, and I simply said to her, "Stay tuned." Mark would contact Victoria directly to arrange an appointment.

We phoned Wilbur, who would meet with Mark and me on Sunday at noon.

A text came through on my phone. It was from Detective Semchuk. All that it said was, "Thanks!"

Mark had a text message from Mary:

> Burnside won't turn over password. Claims self-incrimination.
> Probably right. Tell Professor S. that Detective Semchuk
> is very interested. Expect search warrant over weekend.
> Safe trip. Mary

Finally we called our wives and gave them an estimated time of arrival.

Mark turned back to the video discs. I listened to a night time sports talk show. The pundits had written off the Vikings and we weren't even at the halfway point in the season.

We drove without stopping and without much conversation. Michael's supplies of drinks and sandwiches sustained us. About an hour and a half out of Flemington, Mark had finished with the video discs. He took the wheel once more.

We discussed strategy. Mark began by asking me about the three young women raped by Fraser and Burnside, "Do you think that they will all join the lawsuit?"

I thought for a moment, "I think that Ingrid will want to sue the university and Fraser, after all she brought a complaint five years ago. She wanted to do something then, but was stonewalled by the Dean and the university. Her concern has always been proving the complaint. She recognized that her case was a weak one. We are now giving her the ammunition necessary to move forward. She'll come on board. You wanted to interview her first and that is a good idea. Getting her onside will encourage the others to follow suit."

Mark nodded in agreement.

I continued, "You will need to be more careful with both Jennifer and Victoria. Remember they initially did not want to get involved. We also don't know what they remember of the attack. They may recall it vividly, but not want to relive it; they may not recall it at all, which means that your telling them of the videotapes will be a real shock or, more likely, they recall parts, bits of what occurred, but may want to forget or are confused as to what actually happened. And, if they recall the attacks, they may well be blaming themselves. There are a lot of ifs. Tread carefully. I suggest that you start from the proposition that they don't remember; they were drugged and couldn't be expected to remember anything. That is your safest approach. From there raise with them Ingrid's desire to seek justice and the Klassens as well."

Mark replied, "You've confirmed exactly what I was thinking."

"Mark, there is one other thing; the existence of the videotapes will be a surprise for each of the women. I would stress that your plan is a means to keep the tapes confidential and out of open court. I would think keeping the videotapes private will be a real concern for them."

"Good point and I am going to keep the viewing of the tapes to as few people as possible."

Mark changed subjects, "What do you know of the Chancellor of the University, Jorgeson?"

"I actually taught Erik Jorgeson about 20 years ago. He came to law school late. His family is wealthy and he was involved in the family business, lumber and home building supplies. He then decided to study law. He was like a sponge soaking up the law. He loved it and proved to be a delight in and out of class. I worked with him as coach of our trial moot team and got to know him well. Erik is smart. He won't say much, but little will get past him. He has a strong sense of fairness and justice. What you must not do is try to flatter him or exaggerate. He is a straight shooter and admires forthright honesty. He will be persuaded by reason, logic and a just cause. He will also look to do what is best for the university. Be diplomatic in your attack on the university, attack people yes, but show him that as an alumnus you too care about Flemington University. You are as hurt by these vicious attacks as he is. If you dump on Flemington U he will become defensive." I continued, "He has no ulterior motives. I'll put it to you this way; Erik and his wife have donated literally millions of dollars to causes throughout Flemington, but he does so anonymously. You won't see his name plastered on buildings all over the city."

"I've never met him," said Mark, "he sounds like an impressive individual."

"Yes," I replied, "I think he's the one who will ultimately make the decisions and not the President."

"What about President Frinkle?" asked Mark.

I laughed, "Howard Frinkle is a light weight. He is obsessed with optics and working the media. He came to the university five years ago from a larger university out West; I forget which one. In my view Frinkle avoids conflict; he doesn't like to make difficult decisions that will make people unhappy. For example, he has negotiated terrible contracts with the faculty association. I think the last contract provided for a 5% increase in salary. 5% in this day and age! Unheard of, but he wanted labour peace."

"How do you think he'll react to our news?"

"I think he'll be terrified. Work on that fear. The media will cry for blood and Frinkle will look for any lifeline to turn this into a positive spin. I don't foresee him as being much of an obstacle. But here is your difficulty, he is like a weathervane and will swing whichever way the last person sways him. You'll need to get his signature on any agreement before he changes his mind; don't give him time to waffle. I also think at times that he's cowered by Sid Ashter. Why I don't know."

Mark was taking everything in, "Who should we invite to the meeting?"

"The Chancellor, the President, the university lawyer, Sid Ashter, will have to be there, and Dean Clarke that's it." I replied.

"Do you really think it wise to have Ashter and Clarke there? They are largely responsible for burying Ingrid's complaint." Mark wondered.

"Exactly. It will be an opportunity for you to dump on them and to show the Chancellor how the university failed to protect Ingrid and all the other women. Ashter is a bully. Let him show his bully side."

"I see your point. What about demanding that they both be fired?" asked Mark.

"I wouldn't go there," I replied, "It is one thing for the university to turn over money; it is quite different for the university to fire anyone at your demand. That would look like you, the plaintiff, dictating policy and staffing within the university. The administration would fight back hard. Why not let them come to that decision? Show them the wisdom of that course of action, but let them pull the trigger. Take the easy way. You might include them as named parties, which would mark them as targets. Same with Fraser, you don't need to demand that he be fired. They'll have to fire him."

Mark smiled, "Wise counsel Professor. You truly are a lawyer at heart. I think I'll call Jeff Couster, who often acts for the university, to set up the meeting, and to be there. I've worked with him before and he's a good, reasonable man. He settles cases that deserve settling and fights those that do not. He understands litigation and is a formidable force, who they will listen to. He'll be a counterweight to Ashter."

The lights of Flemington were now on the horizon. Mark dropped me off at my home. I'd see him on Sunday at noon for our meeting with Wilbur.

The front porch light was on, a sign of welcome. I walked through the door; Julie and Bruce were there to greet me. With a hug and a kiss from Julie and wags and whines from Bruce, it was good to be home. Over coffee I told Julie all that had occurred in Winnipeg. Julie, as always, was a good listener.

CHAPTER 34

Sunday morning and Mark's office was busy; the office was on litigation war footing. The associates were in drafting and preparing documents. The place was abuzz with litigation excitement. I had arrived early and was a fly on the wall. Mark was in his element. He had briefed the team and they were energized by the cause. On the white board in the boardroom someone had written– 'FOR ALLISON'. Wilbur joined me a few minutes later and we stood together and watched. The day before I had given Wilber the blow by blow details of what had happened in Winnipeg. He was very proud of our Anton Piller success, which was his doing.

"Ah to be twenty-five again," said Wilbur.

"Yes, to be twenty-five again in so many ways," I laughed, "but we aren't my friend."

"Speak for yourself; I at least feel twenty-five," replied Wilbur.

Mark saw us and motioned us into his office. "Pizza in the boardroom if you're hungry." We declined. Mark filled us in on the weekend's developments. "The Klassens are on board, Ingrid is on board, Jennifer and Victoria--everyone."

"How did they react to your news?" I asked.

"The Klassens took it stoically. Megan was with Fred and Doreen. They held hands. No tears. They were quiet. When I explained the proposed action and settlement they baulked and told me that it was not about the money. I knew that. I finally convinced them that the damages were a way to partly right a wrong."

"Did they ask about the videotape?" asked Wilbur.

"Yes, I told them that I was the only one to have watched the one disc and that I didn't want them to see it. I explained that Allie was defiled and the image would scar them for the rest of their days. They didn't pursue it."

"Ingrid? How did it go with her?"

"As you expected Andy, Ingrid wants her revenge. She is a fighter. I'd love to have her at our firm. She volunteered to help in any way and signed up right away. The videotape was no surprise to her. She was concerned about who would see it and I assured her that I would do my best to limit the viewers."

"And Jennifer?" I asked.

"She was the toughest. I'm glad Angela was there to support her. I think she was in denial. She had wanted mentally to block out what happened that night. It was her way of coping with the nightmare. When I told her about the videotape she broke down and I had to tell her that I had viewed the tape. She was very emotional. We took a break and Angela comforted her. I gave them time. When I came back to the room, Jennifer was composed. Angela turned her pain into anger. Angela was a real strength for her. She asked me what I wanted to do and I told her about the lawsuit against the university and Fraser. I told her about the Klassens and their pain. She was heartened by Ingrid already signing on. It was her decision. She looked at Angela, then turned to me and said, 'Where do I sign?' I was so relieved. Angela took her home. Three down one to go."

"And what about Victoria?"

"I met her this morning. Elizabeth, one of my associates, sat in. Victoria said that she honestly could not remember a thing about that evening. I told her that we had conclusive evidence that she was drugged and raped by Professors Fraser and Burnside. She didn't believe it and I then told her about the videotapes. She was shocked and she was angry. Her biggest concern was keeping the videotapes private. She became our fourth plaintiff. I told her that she could take some time, but she was adamant. She's a strong willed young woman."

Mark continued, "After getting Victoria on board I called Jeff Couster to set up the meeting with the university for Monday. I danced around the specifics for a time, but Jeff said to me–quite rightly–that I couldn't get a meeting with the Chancellor and the President because it was 'important'. He needed to know what it was about. I got his attention when I told him, 'I represent four young female Flemington students raped by a professor and one of those students is dead as a result.' Hearing that he promised to set up the meeting. I gave him our list of invitees. He proposed noon and wanted more specifics. I refused. I told him, he'd find out tomorrow. He hasn't got back to me yet."

"What I need from both of you is information about the tenure and hiring process at the law school. I'm still baffled by the fact Fraser wasn't fired."

Wilbur answered first, "Let's start with the basics. Fraser was hired on a tenure track position at the rank of assistant professor, which is the lowest rank. The tenure process essentially is a probationary period of up to six years."

"Could Fraser have been fired at anytime during this probationary period?" asked Mark.

"The simple answer is yes," answered Wilbur, "but firing anyone, even on probation is not easy. There is a tenure review conducted at the end of the assistant professor's third year."

"Who conducts that review?"

"The law school has an internal tenure and promotion committee. I actually sat on Fraser's tenure review." Wilbur replied.

"You did?" Mark said with interest.

"Don't get too excited, I am bound to respect the confidences of the committee. I can say this, because the Dean provided this to the whole faculty at the time. He said Fraser was doing stellar research and was doing an excellent job in the classroom. I can find that email for you."

"Please do," said Mark, "Do you recall whether the Dean provided any recommendation."

"The Dean had to. In fact there are annual reports prepared on each faculty member. Without divulging their content I'll simply say this, they were all very positive."

"So down the line, if this ever went to trial, I'd have to seek discovery of those reviews?"

"Definitely," said Wilbur, "I don't know if the reviews would be privileged. Andy, you're the evidence professor."

"I doubt that they would be privileged," I said, "These are annual work reviews and are not confidential reference letters. And the issue at trial would focus on why the university did not act to protect the students. In my view they'd have to be made available to Mark on discovery."

"What I don't understand is that knowing about the complaints that were brought to the Dean's attention, why do you think he was so positive about Fraser? Why not get rid of him?" Mark asked quizzically.

I answered, "Mark, you have to realize that to write a negative assessment invites a grievance from the faculty association. The path of least resistance is not to rock the boat and just fudge him through."

"Is it fair to say that had the Dean provided a negative review then Fraser could have been fired three years ago?" pressed Mark.

"The Dean could have fired him at any time with grounds and, in my view, had he seriously investigated Ingrid's allegations and that combined with the Caribbean complaint the Dean could have pushed for termination," I replied, "but it would have been messy."

"Don't forget, Dean Clarke hired Fraser, and I don't think he wanted to fire a person whom he hired," added Wilbur.

"This can't be happening," Mark shook his head, "what an unreal world."

He went on, "Fraser just got tenure. How important would the Dean's recommendation have been?"

"Very important," Wilbur and I both agreed.

"So it is safe to say that the Dean was still in Fraser's camp?"

"Yes," Wilbur added, "and the Dean's congratulatory email announcing Fraser's tenure and appointment speaks to that."

"What role would Sid Ashter be playing in all of this?" Mark asked.

"We know that Ashter was instrumental in Ingrid's recantation, and I think it very likely that the Dean would have contacted him about the Caribbean University complaint." But I had to concede, "Don't know for sure."

"Would the President or Chancellor have been informed?"

I answered, "I doubt it; the Dean in particular would not want this to find its way to the President. The Chancellor would not have been consulted. You see all administrators want to handle their little domains themselves. If the Dean could see that the problem wasn't going to go away that's different. Then you call for reinforcements. In both cases the problems could be buried. Ingrid recanted so close the file; the Caribbean student won't complain so ignore the complaint. It is administrative wilful blindness. The Dean really did not want to know the truth because, if he pursued the matter and found wrongdoing by Fraser, he might then really have to do something. Better to remain ignorant and when the time comes plead ignorance."

Wilbur added, "Cover-up is the ethos of administrators–do nothing and cover-up."

Mark shook his head but seemed satisfied, "Just so you know, I have arranged a news conference for noon on Tuesday that way it will make the six o'clock news on all the media outlets. I'd appreciate it if you could both attend."

Wilbur and I looked at each other. We both smiled, "So you want two senior professors from the law school to attend a news conference that announces a lawsuit against the university? You are inviting early retirement for us both." I laughed.

"I don't know," said Mark, "seems to me that it underscores your commitment to justice for your students."

"Yes it does," said Wilbur, "I'd be honoured to be there. I am very proud of what we all have done--Andy, in particular."

"Mark, of course I will attend." I answered.

"Good," Mark replied, "Andy, you and I have already talked about the meeting tomorrow, and our strategy."

"Yes, assuming that the meeting goes," I said.

"Oh, it will," Mark was certain.

I received a call from Mark that evening; the meeting was on. I also got a text from Mary:

> Advised by Detective Semchuk that a search warrant will be executed at 9:00 a.m. Monday at our offices. We are co-operating. Originals of all video evidence, computer, and photographs to be seized. We have made copies.

There was a text from Richard Maurice, which was short and terse:

Call me.

I did. I told Richard that evidence was found that Professor Fraser and Professor William Burnside raped Allison Klassen and other Flemington University students and I told him that he should liaise with Detective Semchuk, who would be accessing that evidence. I ended the call by saying, "Remember the Stephenson Case."

Richard replied, "I do."

After I hung up I wondered what Fraser was doing now.

CHAPTER 35

Fortunately, I had my Criminal Law class to occupy my morning. Prior to class I had checked on Fraser's whereabouts. He was nowhere to be seen and there was a notice posted informing the students that his classes were cancelled for the day. I wasn't surprised. He would have been told by Burnside about the tapes being seized. I wouldn't be surprised that he was now on the run. Finding him wasn't my concern; leave that for the police.

My class went slowly, or at least it seemed that way to me. Finally the class ended and I went back to my office. Mark was going to meet me there at 11:15.

Mark knocked on my door. He was dressed in his power suit prepared to do battle. He ran by me a few quick scenarios and I checked that he had everything with him. We were ready. The excitement and tension permeated us. For some this breeds panic; nerves for us were good. We'd do well. Whether we succeeded in convincing the powers that be was out of our hands. Over the centuries of man's existence many times people, even well meaning people, do not take the right or reasonable path.

We got up and walked to the 'tower'. Every university has one; the bunker where administrators hole up and hold court. It is where they separate themselves from the student and academic masses. Flemington University's tower was the "Gordon P. Hammond Administration Building". Gordon P. Hammond was Flemington's first President. The building was eight stories high and was cold concrete; it was a beautiful example of brutalism--truly a bunker. The President's office was on the top floor.

We were deposited on the eighth floor by the cold stainless steel elevator. The elevator opened to a large foyer with double doors leading into the President's inner sanctum. A young, attractive receptionist, flawlessly dressed greeted us and took our names; she offered us a seat and made a call to the guardian of the sanctum, Mrs. Judith Frederickson. Judith had been the executive assistant to at least four Presidents. She came with the job. Judith always was impeccably dressed. Always had a fake smile; there was nothing warm about her. She wore her hair in a tight bun and she was a formidable force. I had many dealings with her over the years, especially when I was the Chair of the University Senate Appeal Committee. We got along like two weary polecats marking their territory.

A few minutes later Mrs. Judith Frederickson came out to reception, fake smile plastered on her face. "Nice to see you again Professor Sturgis," she was lying. She turned to Mark, "You must be Mr. Labros." We both got up from our seats and nodded greetings in response.

She continued giving me the eye, "We hadn't expected to see you Professor Sturgis. Do you intend to go into the meeting?"

"I do, yes," I didn't say anything further, which I knew irritated her.

"Do you mind me asking, in what capacity?"

"No, you can ask," I said. I was having too much fun not answering her–rustling her feathers.

She gave me a withering look, "Please come this way, we are in the conference room." She turned and walked to a large oak door and opened it. We followed her.

The conference room was a large classroom size room. Windows dominated the south wall. The other walls were wood panelled oak. There was a small table in the corner with coffee, drinks, and water. The centre piece of the room was a gigantic horseshoe table, with a small rectangular table in its opening. It was like the congressional hearing rooms that you see on television. For me it always brought thoughts of the English Star Chamber or the Spanish Inquisition. Men with little heads hiding behind the horseshoe of desks would determine life or death. I had given Mark a heads up about the Star Chamber; I didn't want him to be thrown off. It was meant to be an intimidating room. Judith motioned for Mark to sit at the rectangular table. There was only one chair. Judith didn't know what to do with me; she showed me a side chair along the wall.

Mark broke the silence, "I'd like Professor Sturgis to sit with me at the table, if we could have a chair please."

The President was seated beside the Chancellor at the head of the horseshoe. The President spoke, "Professor Sturgis, we are surprised to see you, you were not expected." I had already moved to the wall and pushed one of the roller chairs to the table.

Once seated Mark and I could take a good look at the university entourage; in all there were fourteen people seated in the horseshoe. Jeff Couster was there with two of his firm's lawyers, Sid Ashter was there with his deputy, Dean Clarke was there with the Associate Dean Gloria Wesley, there was the University Provost, the Dean of Students, the Chief Financial Officer, the Director of Public Relations, a secretary presumably to take notes and, of course, the President and Chancellor.

Mark took his time bringing out his papers and files from his briefcase, and his computer. I watched the inquisitors. The President waited. Judith put a second glass on our table, a small glass water jug already sat on the table perspiring from the chilled water. Mark took time to pour some water into his glass. He was now ready.

The President opened the meeting, "Mr. Labros I would like to begin by introducing the people around the table. To my..."

Mark interrupted, "I'm sorry President Frinkle, but that is not necessary." President Frinkle looked up in surprise. He was not used to interruptions; administrative minions do not interrupt the President. For lawyers it is second nature.

"It's not necessary, because most of these people can't stay." Mark was calm and spoke slowly, "I am sure that Mr. Couster told you who I represent. The information that I am going to share with you is both personal and extremely sensitive. I have no intention of telling it to a room full of people. It is also obvious that a lawsuit may result. One of the purposes of this meeting will be to ward that off and settle the matter. Mr. Couster can explain to you that settlement discussions are regarded as privileged communications covered by litigation privilege. But that privilege must be carefully guarded. Having a room of fourteen people is not guarding the confidentiality of the communications."

Mark continued, "When I contacted Mr. Couster we requested you, the Chancellor, your University Counsel, Mr. Ashter, the Dean of Law and Mr. Couster. That's it. Everyone else should leave." Mark then looked at Mr. Couster and smiled, "Jeff you hardly need two associates from your firm here, you know the law too well." Jeff gave Mark a small smile in return.

Mark waited--tension was building. I could see the President waffling. Sid Ashter broke the silence, "Mr. President you have the right to decide who should be here." As he was speaking, Jeff Couster whispered to his two associates. They began collecting their things and got up to leave. Good on him. Jeff wasn't going to have the meeting scuttled by this posturing. This gave the President his cue, "Very well Mr. Labros, I appreciate your point. Would all persons not named by Mr. Labros please leave." They left.

The first skirmish was over. We had anticipated that the President would do this; I've seen him do it before. He likes intimidation through numbers. We waited for the room to clear.

Mark, in a gesture of good faith, said, "Thank you President Frinkle and I also want to thank the Chancellor for being here this afternoon. Just to be clear I want to confirm that these discussions today are for the purpose of settlement and are indeed privileged communications."

Sid Ashter interrupted, "Hold it. Is there any reason Professor Sturgis is still here?"

Mark replied, "My clients insist. Professor Sturgis has been instrumental in the investigation and has detailed knowledge of the entire case."

Sid Ashter, perhaps miffed at being upstaged by Jeff Couster, after all he was supposedly the university's legal expert, or more probably it was simply his style to be obstructionist, continued, "Professor Sturgis is an employee of this university and any outside work is unauthorized. His working for you is not allowed under his terms of employment. And the fact that he is an employee of the university and of you raises a serious conflict of interest."

We were ready for this gambit. I responded in a soft, professorial voice, "I can assure you that my work for Mr. Labros violated no terms of my employment. The collective agreement only refers to needing authorization from one's Dean to engage in "paid" outside activity. I am working for Mr. Labros pro bono and I receive no payment. Moreover, there is no conflict, because it is my duty as a professor to protect my students and that is the university's duty as well. We are on the same side."

President Frinkle had heard enough, "I think Professor Sturgis should remain and anything said is privileged. Now Mr. Labros in speaking to Mr. Couster, I am very concerned about the allegations that you are making."

Mark had his opening, "First, President Frinkle these are not allegations. We have conclusive evidence that four Flemington University School of Law students were gang raped by Professor Jerome Fraser and a Canadian Professor, William Burnside. One of these young women, Allison Klassen, as a result of being brutally raped killed herself. She killed herself a little over two months ago."

Mark got up from the table. Litigators, like teachers, do not like to sit. Orators stand. He opened a file and took out an enlarged photograph of Allison. "This is a photograph of Allison Klassen." He went and handed the photographs directly to each. He let it sink in. "She was beautiful, witty, happy, healthy and very much looking forward to going into her second year in law."

"Allison worked as a research assistant with Assistant Professor Jerome Fraser. He took her to a law conference in Winnipeg, Canada, which would be a great honour for a first year law student. It was there that Professor Fraser and Professor Burnside, who incidentally organized the Winnipeg conference, gang raped Allison in her hotel room. The rape occurred on Saturday, August 15 of this year. Allison killed herself two days later. She jumped off the balcony of her apartment in Flemington."

"Allow me to show you some more photographs; these are of Ingrid Hedberg, Jennifer Cunningham and Victoria Palmer. They all were law students at Flemington's School of Law." Mark, once again, went around to hand each the photographs.

"Ingrid Hedberg was a student five years ago. She too was Professor Fraser's summer research assistant. She too went to Winnipeg for the legal conference. She too was raped by Professors Fraser and Burnside." I watched Dean Clarke's and Sid Ashter's reactions. They both went white.

"Jennifer Cunningham was a student three years ago. She too was Professor Fraser's summer research assistant. She too went to the Winnipeg conference and she too was gang raped by Professors Fraser and Burnside."

"Victoria Palmer is still a student at the Law School in her third year. She was Professor Fraser's summer research assistant two summers ago. She went to Winnipeg for the conference and she was gang raped as well. In fact, all the women were raped in the same hotel room, which was an adjoining room to Professor Fraser's. The hotel room was in the Artist Hotel on Portage Avenue in Winnipeg, and Fraser and his students always stayed in a secluded wing called the Rembrandt rooms. The women were attacked in the same room, in the same bed, which had a replica of Rembrandt's painting of "The Man with the Golden Helmet" hung over the bed." Mark was using the power of specific facts to show the other side that we had detailed knowledge. There is power through the command of facts.

Mark took a sip of water, keeping eye contact at all times, as he would with a jury, on the five men listening. "Professor Sturgis is responsible for uncovering these vile attacks. He was troubled by Allison's death. He had taught her and went to her funeral in the small town of Stanthorpe about an hour and fifteen minute drive to the west. He heard and felt the love that so many people in that town had for Allison. It troubled him that Allison would take her life. Why? It made no sense."

The room was completely silent. The men were captivated by Allison's story. "Professor Sturgis' own summer student, Maria Dempster, who was a close friend of Allison, came to him troubled by Allison's suicide. Maria was convinced that something had happened in Winnipeg because when Allison returned from the conference she spoke to no one. No communication. No texts. Nothing. Allison shut herself off from her friends and family. She was supposed to return to Stanthorpe to be with her family before the start of term. She didn't go home. She returned to her apartment in Flemington."

"Professor Sturgis started to investigate. He wondered why Allison was picked as Fraser's research assistant, although she was a good student she wasn't one of the top in her class. He checked her grades, just to make sure, and he found that she had gotten an "A" in Torts – Professor Fraser's course. It was her only "A". He had her examination papers, both the January and April examinations re-marked by Professor Flood, who also teaches Torts. Professor Flood concluded that the "A" grade was inflated. Professor Sturgis suspected that Fraser was seducing Allison by wooing her with good grades. The better term would be grooming, like a paedophile grooming a victim."

"He then looked to Victoria Palmer. She was just like Allison a good student, but not great. She too had an uncharacteristically high grade in Fraser's Torts class. Her examinations were still available and they were re-read by Professor Flood. His conclusion, once again, the grade of "A" was inflated. She too was being groomed."

"It was then that Professors Sturgis and Flood had Professor Angela Crindle, an adjunct instructor, speak to Fraser's other summer students Ingrid Hedberg and Jennifer Cunningham, who were now practicing law in Flemington. Ingrid Hedberg told Angela Crindle that she had been raped–not seduced, but raped."

"And she recanted that story," snapped Sid Ashter.

Mark looked at Ashter and slowly, deliberately said, "Yes, we'll get to that."

He continued, "We spoke to Jennifer and Victoria, neither said much. We weren't sure why. But Ingrid thought that she was drugged. We spoke with the Medical Examiner and he provided us with new interesting information. First Allison had no alcohol in her system; alcohol can still be detected days post mortem. So she was not intoxicated. In fact, Allison did not drink. Nor were there drugs in her system, which was troubling, until the medical examiner explained that date rape drugs dissipate in the body very quickly and would not be found two days after being administered. The medical examiner also told us that traces of a lubricant PDMS was found in Allison's body. PDMS is commonly used as a lubricant for condoms. Her attackers wore condoms."

Mark took another sip of water; pausing for effect. "Professor Sturgis then travelled to Winnipeg to the Artist Hotel. He actually met with Professor Burnside, who told Professor Sturgis that Allison had been drinking, which was troubling. We know that was a lie. The toxicology report told us that. Professor Sturgis next met with the Hotel manager and was allowed to review the security tape for the night of August 15. The hotel surveillance tapes had already been destroyed, but the camera footage from the hotel coffee shop was still available. I'd like to show you what we found on the surveillance tape."

President Frinkle nodded. They all wanted to hear more of the story.

Mark got his computer, "Perhaps your assistant could help with connecting the room's audiovisual equipment?"

President Frinkle rang for Mrs. Frederickson, who arrived and diligently set up the computer to the audiovisual projector. The Chancellor, Jeff Couster and I went to get some coffee.

The Chancellor quietly said to me, "Professor it is nice to see you again, although I wish it were not in this situation."

"Chancellor, it is good to see you as well. Thank you for coming." We got our coffees and returned to our seats.

Mark played the video. He introduced Allison and Fraser. He stopped the tape when Fraser went to the condiment table. "That is when we think Fraser put the date rape drug into Allison's drink. Please watch her reaction over the next few minutes." We watched as Allison slipped into unco-ordinated helplessness.

There was absolute silence as Allison was carried, helped out of the coffee shop by Fraser. "There is little doubt that she was drugged. But there is more. Let me fast forward some thirty-five minutes to 10:39." Mark fast forwarded to William Burnside, "Gentlemen this is Professor William Burnside, he arrived at 10:39. Note what he is carrying; in our opinion it is a camera case. Professor Burnside is an avid photographer. It just so happens that the night clerk at the hotel was entering the Manitoba Law School, where Burnside teaches. He recognized Professor Burnside and confirmed that he was there until the early hours of the morning."

Mark was now aiming the knockout blow, "With this information the Klassens filed a civil suit for assault and wrongful death in Winnipeg against Professor Fraser and Professor Burnside. I emphasize that Flemington University was not named as a party. That suit was filed Wednesday of last week. It was sealed by the Court of Queen's Bench, but will be open to the public at 9:00 a.m. today."

"Professor Sturgis and I went to Winnipeg. Besides filing the claim in the court, we also sought what is called an Anton Piller

Order. It amounts to a civil search warrant and is available in Canada where there is a real risk that evidence may be destroyed. Mr. Justice Stargel of the Manitoba Court of Queen's Bench granted us the order on Wednesday last week. Under the order an independent lawyer conducts the search on behalf of the Court. Mr. Burnside's house was searched last Thursday. The search focussed on Burnside's locked photography and darkroom in the basement. In a hidden, locked compartment videotapes and a photo album were found. The photo album contained nude photos of eleven women or children. They were named, with dates. The four Flemington law students were in that album. The album was a memory aid and index for the videotapes kept in the hidden compartment. We then went back to Court this past Friday to obtain access to the photographs and videodiscs. You see items seized under an Anton Piller Order are kept by the independent supervising solicitor and we as plaintiffs needed the Court's permission to access the tapes. We obtained that permission and copies of the specific tapes were turned over to us. I also received permission from Mr. Justice Stargel to use this evidence in a civil action against Flemington University and Professor Fraser to be brought here in Minnesota."

Mark let this sink in. "Gentlemen, all the gang rapes of the Flemington law students were videotaped and we have those tapes. They are absolutely disgusting."

Sid Ashter interrupted, as he was want to do, intent upon showing his alleged legal knowledge: "The tapes may show that Professor Fraser is guilty of rape, but we can't be held responsible. He did these things off the university campus. The university isn't liable for anything. And you're going to have one hell of a time proving that any rape caused the one student to kill herself. Students commit suicide for all sorts of reasons."

Thanks to Ashter's outburst Mark had his openings, "I'd like to address both of those points. First, why do we connect the rape to the suicide of Allison Klassen? Timing, of course, is one thing; it was only two days after the rape, and there is her withdrawal after returning from Winnipeg. But there is much more. We spoke to Allison's doctor, Dr. Burnett, who told us that in Allison's last physical examination conducted in early August Allison was physically and mentally healthy. She also told us something surprising; Allison believed in abstinence. Allison was a religious woman and she believed that it was God's will that people not engage in sex outside of wedlock. Therefore, although the good doctor suggested that Allison have some form of birth control, Allison refused; it wasn't necessary for her. We spoke with Megan Klassen, Allison's sister, and she confirmed Allison's decision to abstain from sex until married. Don't take this lightly gentlemen; Allison was committed to her beliefs."

"Now just imagine what being gang raped would do to your psyche, your faith and belief in God to have your purity and virginity ripped from you in such a terrible way. I don't think any jury in the land would have little doubt connecting the rapes with her death—no difficulty whatsoever. I've seen the tape. Her eyes were open. She was drugged, could not move, but she knew what they were doing to her."

"Second, why is Flemington University at fault? To a large extent the university is innocent and a victim as much as the young women, but certain administrators are not innocent and they allowed this to happen. They failed to protect the students. And their failure is the university's failure."

"Dean Clarke and Sid Ashter, four years ago Ingrid Hedberg complained to you of being raped by Professor Fraser when at the Winnipeg conference. Instead of supporting her you attacked her. You never investigated her complaint in any way. Professor Fraser called in his faculty association lawyer and you both caved. You believed him and not her."

"She recanted her complaint for Christ sake," yelled Sid Ashter.

"Yes she did, because you both browbeat her into the recantation. You Mr. Ashter told her that under the sexual assault policy she could not discuss the complaint with anyone. She would have to stand alone. You threatened her with the suggestion of defamation. And Dean Clarke you did nothing." Mark returned to his desk and picked up a file. "Here is a memo written by the Dean concerning this complaint; and it includes a detailed outline of a meeting that the Dean and Sid Ashter had with Ingrid Hedberg. It is shocking to read. It is intimidation at its worst; it is an attack on rape victims." Mark distributed a copy of the memorandum.

"How did you get this? It's confidential," shouted Ashter.

Mark turned to him and said simply, "It doesn't matter how we got it, we have it and it's not confidential any more. President Frinkle and Chancellor Jorgeson I invite you to read that memo and read it in light of the university's purported zero tolerance policy and encouragement for sexual assault victims to come forward. I'm assuming that neither Dean Clarke nor Mr. Ashter told you of the rape complaint." Neither answered; they didn't have to it was obvious they had no knowledge.

Mark gave them time to read and digest the memo; it made for sordid reading.

Mark then continued, "So four years ago Dean Clarke was on notice as to a rape complaint made by a female student against Professor Fraser. Three years ago Professor Fraser went on sabbatical to the Cayman Islands to teach at the Caribbean University of Law. Dean Clarke, you received a damning email from Professor Gilbert Grant the Founding Dean of Law at Caribbean University of Law. I have a copy of that email to show you." Mark handed out a copy of the email to each.

"As you can see, Dean Grant was upset because Professor Fraser took advantage of a young eighteen year old student who was intoxicated at the time. Surely this would or should have raised alarm bells Dean Clarke? Professor Fraser was doing it again! What did you do in reply?"

"I, I, ah, I don't recall receiving this email," stammered Dean Clarke. A forgotten memory is the refuge of the scoundrel.

"You don't recall?" said Mark, "well I have your reply." Mark handed it around. "You didn't do anything did you? And was that on Sid Ashter's advice?"

"He told me that it was outside our jurisdiction. There was nothing for us to do." Dean Clarke whined like a sick dog.

Mark shook his head, "You did nothing. And during this time Professor Fraser was on probation, subject to annual reviews and you provided an annual report on him. Those reports were always glowing weren't they? Never once did you take him to task. So three years ago in his review you provided a positive recommendation, and his appointment was renewed, and just two weeks ago you provided another positive recommendation and, as a result, Assistant Professor Fraser was promoted to Associate Professor and granted tenure."

Mark gave Dean Clarke a scathing glance, "You promoted a rapist." Mark then turned back to President Frinkle and Chancellor Jorgeson, "The university is responsible because nothing was done to investigate or stop Professor Fraser. Dean Clarke and Sid Ashter failed to protect the law students. A jury will not be pleased to see how Professor Fraser was protected at the expense of students. So Professor Fraser continued to rape; no one was going to stop him. Dean Clarke continued to authorize the Winnipeg trips and do you know what? Professor Fraser has already booked rooms at the Artist Hotel for next year; he was going to do it again. We have the booking."

Mark paused for emphasis. He continued, "Flemington University will be jointly and severally responsible not only for Professor's Fraser's crimes against his students, but also for the failures to act by his supervisors. There is no doubt about this."

Mark went back to his table and picked up more material, "This is the claim that we are prepared to file tomorrow in court. It names Flemington University, Professor Fraser, Dean Clarke and Sid Ashter as defendants. The story that I told you this past hour is contained in the claim."

"I am also prepared now to show Mr. Couster, and only Mr. Couster, the videotapes of the attacks so that he can verify what I have just told you. It will be my intent, should this matter proceed to court, that viewing of the tapes will be restricted only to the senior counsel involved. The fewer people exposed to these monstrous tapes the better. I also ask that Dean Clarke and Sid Ashter leave the room. They are named parties in any potential action and may need independent counsel. I would like to speak with you, President Frinkle and Chancellor Jorgeson, privately once Mr. Couster has viewed the tapes."

Sid Ashter was fuming, but said nothing. President Frinkle looked to Chancellor Jorgeson, who nodded his head. "Very well," President Frinkle replied, "John, Sid please leave." They got up and left. Dean Clarke looked dazed; Sid Ashter looked like a defeated fighter, who still claimed he won the fight, and he stomped out.

With Ashter and Dean Clarke out of the room, Mark gave copies of the claim to President Frinkle, the Chancellor and to Jeff Couster. Mark deliberately wasn't going to give it to Ashter and Clarke. As President Frinkle fingered the claim, he said, "I'll ring Judith to find you a room." He spoke on the phone and Judith knocked and entered moments later. She brought with her a small plate of sandwiches, dainties and fresh coffee and chilled drinks. Judith was ever efficient and had anticipated the President's whims.

Mark and Jeff adjourned to another room. I was left with President Frinkle and Chancellor Jorgeson, which was our plan.

Chapter 36

We gathered around the serving table getting refreshments. The tension in the room had vanished with Sid Ashter. Chancellor Jorgeson, who was probably in his mid-sixties, had aged well. His white hair was still thick. He was tanned, thin framed, agile, and had an aristocratic face, a chiselled square jaw, but at the same time was warm and compassionate. President Frinkle had not aged well. He was overweight, like a Buddha, he had small hands and quick eyes that flittered. He never seemed to be calm or relaxed; rather he was anxious, almost like a little dog eager to please jumping all over the place. He was now immersed in his cell phone.

Chancellor Jorgeson chatted. I asked him if he kept contact with his class. He did and soon we were exchanging news on their whereabouts.

"You were like a big brother to so many of your classmates," I observed.

"You mean an older brother," he replied. Erik was always self-deprecating.

We sat down in comfortable lounge chairs that were in an alcove near the window. Erik turned the conversation back to the purpose of our meeting, "Andy tell me about Allison Klassen."

"She was special and I'm not just saying that. She was genuinely a nice person, hard working in class, as Mark said not a stellar student but diligent and solid. She had many friends. There was a memorial ceremony put on by her class. They told stories of her being the designated driver and acting as nurse maid for her companions."

"When you say the memorial was put on by her class, not by the law school?"

"No, evidently the university did not want to associate itself with her suicide. The students did it; actually it was done on the quiet in my class in the main lecture hall. It was very moving."

"What is her family like?" Erik was probing; he sincerely wanted to know more about these people.

"They farm near Stanthorpe and are good people. I think Mr. Klassen's father homesteaded there. Doreen the mother is the organized one. Fred is a quiet farmer. He says little and thinks carefully before speaking. They have one other child, Megan, who actually is studying sociology at Flemington. They are a religious family, but not pushy. They're comfortable with their religion. They were very proud of Allison, who had gone west to study and get her first degree." I paused, "You will not find nicer people."

"How have they handled Allison's death?"

"Stoically, they pray for understanding, but they are hurting, hurting very much especially now that they have found out why their beloved daughter died. I can't imagine their pain, if one of my daughters was raped that way I just don't know how I would cope. You know, you have two daughters don't you?"

"Yes, and three granddaughters," Erik looked away and in a sad voice, "a father's love." After a moment he asked, "How did you and Mr. Labros get together on this?"

"Mark gave the eulogy at Allison's funeral. He did a superb job. Mark and his family live next door to the Klassens. Allison was like a little sister to him. He actually persuaded her to go to law school. Mark was a student of mine; he's proud to be a graduate of this university and that is one reason we are here today. After I found evidence pointing at Fraser, it was natural to contact Mark, who is a very good lawyer."

"So he has a personal stake in this matter?"

"Yes, it certainly is not about money."

"What about the other young women: Ingrid, Jennifer and Victoria?"

I was impressed that he had remembered their names. They were people to him, not nameless victims or 'students'. "They were solid good students. I taught two of them. Ingrid is the strongest and it troubled her as to how she was treated. She now feels vindicated. The other two I think want to forget, but they remember. They are scarred. All are nice young women, who were terribly violated. It is hard to fathom what must have been going through their minds when they were helpless, lying there, and repeatedly being raped and they could do nothing to stop it."

"What about Professor Fraser, what is he like?"

I took some time putting together my answer, "I never liked him. I found him to be egotistical and arrogant. Everything was about him. He is clever and mean, which is not a good combination. He is quick to anger and takes all slights or perceived slights personally. I also hate how he treats our staff. I don't like people who, when they reach a certain position, pick on those who cannot fight back."

"How is he in the classroom? Do the students like him?"

"No, he is not well liked. The test lies in his electives; they are never filled and this year I noticed that few women take his classes. My wife maintains that women have a sixth sense about men and I think she's right. I am sure that if you look at his teaching evaluations you'll find that they are not that good. It is troubling that Dean Clarke supported him."

"What about Dean Clarke?"

"Well he's no Dean Alcock, who cared, really cared about the law school. You know that. Dean Clarke is an administrator, who is passing through. He'll move on and what is important for him is not to rock the boat. He wants to sail out of here on calm seas to another deanship or administrative post."

"How do the students regard him?"

"He's never around. He rarely leaves the office. I doubt that he knows many of the students by name. Dean Alcock taught at least one class and that kept him grounded. He knew all the students by name. Dean Clarke has never taught a course." I thought for a moment, "I suppose a good way of describing things is that the law school is being maintained, but that is all. It lacks heart and vision."

We sipped our coffees in silence, both deep in thought.

Erik then said to me, "Andy, I respect you, what would you do with Ashter and Dean Clarke?"

Without hesitation I replied, "I'd fire them. Flemington University has to disassociate itself from what these two did and condemn their actions. You can't have it both ways. You can't keep them in their positions, but at the same time say that they did wrong. You can't say that you are serious about protecting students, when these two did nothing to protect students. As a professor of mine once said, 'you can't suck and blow at the same time.' But that is your call."

Mark and Jeff returned to the room. Jeff's face was grim. He came over to the Chancellor, who stood up, excused himself, and they moved to a corner of the room where they had a quiet conversation. President Frinkle arrived and the three huddled. I did hear the Chancellor say, "We need to see those annual reviews."

Mark showed me a text that he had received from Michael, who had been directed to send him an update at 2:00. The text read:

> Meeting with reporter from Winnipeg Free Press at 4:00 pm. Will try to stall him. Please advise when we can make a formal statement.

The meeting reconvened.

Mark began anew, "We've shown you what we have and we've done so not to shake you down or threaten, rather we would like to work with you. Time is pressing. It is important that we stay ahead of events. I will share with you a text that I just received from our Canadian lawyer in Winnipeg. He read the text. The point is we simply do not have much time. I have arranged for a news conference to be held tomorrow noon at my firm's office. There, if we have to, we will announce that we have filed a suit against Flemington University for the rapes. Ingrid, Jennifer, Victoria and Megan representing the Klassen family have all agreed to be present. What I would like is to have you there as well, to stand with them and support them."

"We've shown our hand, because we have a compelling case. If you fight it you will lose and you will lose big time. As soon as the jury sees those tapes I would say that you could see awards in the ten million dollar range--minimum. Jeff knows the ball park. And there is the negative publicity. Think about it, you would be perceived as fighting rape victims, fighting your own students. Instead of protecting students, you will be seen as the university that promotes rapists. The damage to your reputation will be immense. I plead with you not to fight an indefensible case."

"We all know that Professor Fraser and Professor Burnside are the real wrongdoers, the criminals. To a certain extent Flemington University is also a victim, and we are asking that you stand by the real victims. If you do so, you prove that there is zero tolerance and that you truly protect your students."

"It is important then that at the first opportunity you show your support. Will this absolve you of blame or ridicule, no. But it will put you on the right side. You can turn this terrible situation into a positive. The decision is yours."

"You have our prepared claim. I have also prepared a settlement agreement, which incidentally I have already signed on behalf of my clients. They are all fully behind what I am doing here today. And I do want to make it clear; the terms of this agreement I am presenting are non-negotiable. We are presenting a generous, rea-sonable way forward for the university. If not agreed to the claim is filed. Here is a copy of that agreement."

Mark gave them each a copy. It was a short two page document and he gave them time to read it. "Let me briefly go through this agreement with you. First, we are looking for two million dollars to be put into a fund in Allison Klassen's name aimed at supporting law students. The fund will be operated by the university philanthropy department; however, funding decisions will be made by named persons approved of by the Klassens."

"Second, the Klassens will receive the sum of one million dollars for the death of their daughter. I want to emphasize; the Klassens are not in this for the money and I had to pressure them to accept anything. They may well put that award into the support fund. The point is that they lost the support and guidance of their eldest daughter for decades to come and that must be compensated."

"Third, for each of the Flemington law students: Ingrid Hedberg, Jennifer Cunningham, and Victoria Palmer, they are to receive a lump sum of $400,000."

Mark paused momentarily. He knew that the figures involved amounted to millions of dollars. "I am providing you with a damage award assessment, which shows awards in similar cases. No doubt Jeff will have his staff do the same. We have not found a case right on point, but what you will see is that the figures I have set out are in the mid to lower range. Why? Because my clients want this resolved. They want you on their side."

"Fourth, most importantly, besides the money, my clients want an apology from Flemington University–a public apology."

"Fifth, there are the legal fees. My firm is charging the lowest contingency fee I have ever seen, 10%. That amounts to $420,000, inclusive of all disbursements. I can tell you that I will be donating my share of this fee to the Allison Klassen Support Fund. I cannot speak for my partners."

"In total the settlement involves Flemington University agreeing to pay $4,620,000. It is a large amount of money, but is commensurate with the wrongdoing. President Frinkle and Chancellor Jorgeson, you are authorized under the University Charter to make payments up to five million dollars in exceptional circumstances. The university is self-insured up to five million dollars so there is no insurance company to deal with. The decision is yours to make."

"Sixth, we agree to keep the settlement figures confidential, with the exception of the Law Student Support Fund; we assume the university would like to inform the public of that donation."

"All monies are to be transferred into my firm's trust account within thirty days and this agreement is open until midnight tonight."

Chancellor Jorgeson had a question, "Your claim includes Professor Fraser, Sid Ashter and Dean Clarke. Won't they have to agree?"

"No," replied Mark, "It is not uncommon for one defendant to settle leaving the others to contest the claim. However, in this case, once we receive full compensation from Flemington University we have no intention of proceeding against the other defendants. You see that in the agreement, the second last paragraph, where we agree not to proceed with any civil actions against Flemington University and its employees. In so doing, it does leave you without a means to have them pay their share of damages. But here is the reality. We've looked into Fraser's finances and there isn't much there and to go after Ashter and Dean Clarke would be a long litigation road, perhaps leading to a trial, for little purpose. We want this matter closed for you and for us. We leave it to you, what you do with these named parties. Of course, you realize that the university is jointly and severally liable for all damages caused by the co-defendants."

Jeff spoke, "Your time line is tight. The agreement expires at midnight tonight. We've got a great deal to consider and to check; after all there is a lot of money to be considered."

"Jeff, I appreciate that, but we're both under the same time constraints." Mark replied, "I actually expect criminal charges to be laid shortly. The City of Winnipeg Police executed a search warrant to seize the video evidence taken from Burnside's home. They are probably reviewing it as we speak and the tapes are self-explanatory.

My own experience with the police in these circumstances is that if they have a solid case they charge and arrest and add additional charges as they proceed with their investigation. I expect Burnside to be charged with child pornography offences as well. We also know that the City of Winnipeg Police are in contact with the Flemington Police and Fraser may well be arrested. If we delay, if we do not stay in front of this case, we will lose control and the media frenzy will take over without us being in a position to do what is right. If the frenzy starts, and let's face it, this is a salacious story, anything you do will be seen as a belated, forced apology. If we lead the news, you will come out as one of the victims, doing the right thing."

"That is all I have to say. I do hope that we can stand together tomorrow. Thank you for your time." Mark sat down.

We collected our papers and prepared to leave. Chancellor Jorgeson was the first to get up. He came over and thanked us both. We then shook hands with President Frinkle and Jeff Couster.

We went back to the law school, where Wilbur was waiting. Drinks were soon in our hands and we had to tell Wilbur all the details. After hearing all Wilbur concluded, "They'll agree. They have no choice. You did well in getting 'Stonewall Ashter' out of the picture."

I wasn't so sure. I've seen too many sure settlements rejected by pique or sheer stupidity.

After an anxious evening, at 11:00 p.m. I received a call from Mark.

"They've agreed!" He shouted into the phone when I answered, "They only want to change the press conference to the School of Law main lecture hall at noon. Chancellor Jorgeson and President Frinkle also want to meet the young women a half hour before. They speak first and we will follow. Andy it's over!"

I was speechless and tears came to my eyes. After I hung up, Julie could see the result in my face; I was beaming. She came over, put her arm around me and whispered, "You've done good."

Chapter 37

When I arrived at my office the next morning the law school was electric. A notice was posted and an email sent out to all students and staff that the President of the University was going to deliver an important announcement at noon in the main lecture hall. The email came from Associate Dean Gloria Wesley.

Professor Fraser's office door was closed. He was not around.

Maria came to my door. "Is it true the Dean and Professor Fraser were fired?" The rumour mill was cooking.

I asked Maria to close the door. "Maria, this is between you and me. You will find out shortly, Allison was raped by Fraser in Winnipeg. I'm certain that he will be charged in Canada; it's only a matter of hours."

"Wow, wow, how awful," Maria was stunned, "how terrible for Allison. I knew it; I knew that Fraser had done something."

"Yes, and it was your coming to me with your suspicions that got me investigating. We'll have to sit down and I'll tell you the whole story, but not today. Say nothing. Wait until noon."

She left smiling, "I can hardly wait."

I received a call from Richard Maurice. I had texted him late the night before advising him that there would be an announcement today at noon at the law school.

"Professor Sturgis, Ricky Maurice."

"Hi Richard, you got my text about the noon announcement?"

"Yes, and I wanted to share some news that I just received from the City of Winnipeg Police Service. You might need a pen."

"Got one–go on," I replied.

"Professor William Burnside has been charged and arrested for multiple counts of forcible confinement, sexual assault, aggravated sexual assault, administering a noxious substance and multiple counts of making and possessing child pornography. Professor Fraser has been charged with four counts of sexual assault, aggravated sexual assault, forcible confinement, and administering a noxious substance and an arrest warrant has been issued. I was advised by Detective Semchuk that they will be looking to extradite Fraser to Canada to face the charges."

"Thanks for this Richard, may I tell Mark Labros, who will be speaking at the announcement?"

"Yes, that's not a problem."

"What about you, are you looking to charge Fraser with manslaughter here in Minnesota?"

"Let me put it this way, the death of Allison Klassen has been re-opened and we're investigating."

"Thanks Richard, you have been very helpful."

"I'm only sorry I couldn't have done more; it is you that deserves thanks; you got the tapes."

"Any word on where Fraser is?" I asked.

"No, I had some uniforms visually check his house and all was quiet. His name has been put on a watch list at the border and at airports. As soon as we get the extradition request we'll act."

"Thanks Richard got to go to class."

"See you at the announcement."

My evidence class at 10:00 was a shambles. As soon as I started class a student's hand went up, "Yes Fred."

"Is it true Professor Sturgis that the Dean and Professor Fraser have been given the sack?"

"Well, Fred, thank you for your question, which has nothing to do with evidence and the topic of today's class, which is hearsay.

So what I suggest to you and the other members of class is have patience. You will know in two hours time."

A second hand went up, "Yes Yolanda?"

"I take it then by your response that first of all you know the answer to Fred's question and second, you are not denying the rumour?" A number of students laughed.

"Ah Yolanda, you will make a good trial lawyer, if we can get you through evidence. Evidence, let's start with the definition of hearsay."

I tried. Everyone's mind was elsewhere. At 11:30 I called it quits. "See you in the main lecture hall. Class adjourned."

It was arranged that the 'plaintiff's group' would meet in an ante room off of the lecture hall. When I got there at 11:45 Wilbur was present along with Angela. The true plaintiffs were absent. Mark arrived at 11:50. He looked refreshed and relieved. I took him aside and gave him a note outlining the charges brought in Winnipeg against Burnside and Fraser. He smiled. He had a busy day ahead of him; a tele-conference call with the Winnipeg media was scheduled for 2:00 p.m. and there was an interview at 3:00 p.m. with the Flemington ABC local news anchor to be aired on the 6:00 p.m. news. The story was now out there. We were just in time.

Just before noon Ingrid, Jennifer, Victoria and Megan arrived. It was obvious that they had been crying and were solemn. They had met privately with President Frinkle and Chancellor Jorgeson. They told us that both men were sincere and gracious. They all felt comforted by the gesture. Evidently Chancellor Jorgeson shed tears. He told them that they reminded him of his own daughters. He had special words for Megan and gave her a note to give to her parents. Saying sorry, apologizing is a powerful healer.

It was time; we were told to take seats to the left of the podium. As we took to the stage, the room was packed to overflowing. The press were seated in the front row to the side. Cameramen and photographers were stationed along the wall.

Associate Dean Wesley was at the podium. President Frinkle, Chancellor Jorgeson and the administrative entourage were seated to her right.

"Students, faculty, President Frinkle has an important announcement for you. President Frinkle."

President Frinkle moved to the podium, adjusted the microphone. He was getting better at public speaking, but still needed to follow a written script, which was already placed on the podium for him. He began, "Chancellor Jorgeson, students, faculty, members of the press, I do have an important announcement that directly affects the School of Law and that is why I wanted to deliver it here to you the students and staff first."

His voice was somewhat shaky. He took a deep breath and spoke more naturally, "Yesterday Chancellor Jorgeson and I were presented with conclusive evidence showing that Assistant Professor Jerome Fraser of the School of Law had over the course of five years viciously raped four Flemington Law School students. Three of these former and current students are here on stage for this announcement. They have chosen not to keep their identities private. They want you to know who they are, as a message to all victims of sexual assault to come forward, make your voices heard as a way to stop this violence. Ms Ingrid Hedberg, Ms Jennifer Cunningham, and Ms Victoria Power were all sexually assaulted by Assistant Professor Fraser. And it grieves me deeply to say..." His voice was cracking, "that his last victim, Allison Klassen, was sexually assaulted this past summer, and took her life two days after the attack."

There were a few gasps in the audience then silence. "All of the attacks took place in Winnipeg, Canada, where the women were isolated and vulnerable. They were attending a law conference in Winnipeg at the time and were there at Professor Fraser's invitation. We have information that a Canadian Professor, William Burnside, was involved in each attack."

He took a moment before going on. "Professor Fraser has been summarily fired and we anticipate criminal charges will be laid against him. However, we too must take responsibility for what occurred. We did not do enough to protect these victims. Ingrid Hedberg made a complaint against Professor Fraser four years ago. Regretfully that complaint was not investigated as it should have been, and Ingrid was not provided with support as she should have been. Those responsible have been held accountable. This morning I asked for and received the resignation of John Clarke, Dean of this Law School, and I asked for and received the resignation of Sid Ashter, the University's Chief Legal Officer."

He paused and turned to look our way, "To Ingrid, Jennifer and Victoria please accept my personal apology made on behalf of Flemington University and Chancellor Erik Jorgeson. We are truly sorry. To Megan Klassen, Allison's sister, who is here representing the Klassen family, I am so sorry for what happened to Allison." President Frinkle needed to collect himself.

"I am pleased to inform people present that a new scholarship and support fund will be established in Allison Klassen's name and we have agreed to provide an initial contribution of two million dollars."

"That concludes my prepared remarks. I will be available to answer questions from the press in room 210 immediately following Mr. Labros's words. Mr. Labros." President Frinkle took his seat.

Mark replaced him at the podium, "Thank you President Frinkle and Chancellor Jorgeson. My name is Mark Labros and I am a partner at the firm of Theopold, Stenson and Labros here in Flemington. We act for Ingrid, Jennifer, Victoria and the Klassen family."

"I will not mince words; Professor Fraser viciously and violently violated each of these young women. He worked with an accomplice, a Professor from the University of Manitoba–William Burnside. The attacks were carefully planned. The unsuspecting victims were drugged, rendered helpless and then raped repeatedly;

the actions of Professors Fraser and Burnside were cruel and criminal. Indeed I have been advised that the City of Winnipeg Police Service today charged both Professor Burnside and Professor Fraser with numerous criminal offences."

He looked out over the lecture hall. "I am a graduate of this law school. I remember taking classes in this very room. Professor Fraser's actions have stained this school's reputation for us all, but I want to say to you that today is the school's finest hour."

He paused, "You see Professor Fraser's crimes would never have come to light without the devotion and perseverance of three members of this law school's faculty. Professor Andrew Sturgis was troubled by Allison's death. He started investigating. The more he dug the more he found. Professor Wilbur Flood and Professor Angela Crindle joined him in the investigating. The three of them were tenacious. This case is their case and they handed it to me. Please join me in thanking these three professors who did so much to protect you."

The room erupted in applause, whistles and calls and the students rose en masse. Wilbur, Angela and I were embarrassed. Mark beckoned us to stand and we did so reluctantly. The applause continued unabated. I saw that Maria was cheering, clapping, and at the same time was crying.

We sat down and the applause finally ended. Mark continued, "Yesterday we presented to the President and Chancellor the evidence of Professor Fraser's criminal acts. You should be proud of their reaction. They recognized the university's responsibility to protect students from predators like Professor Fraser. And they chose to stand with Ingrid, Jennifer, Victoria and Allison to support them. To President Frinkle and Chancellor Jorgeson this is a difficult time for you, but I congratulate you for having the courage to do the right thing. It is also a difficult time for Ingrid, Jennifer and Victoria. They are very brave to come forward." He looked at the press, "I ask the press to respect their privacy. They will not be taking any questions at this time."

"Unfortunately we cannot bring Allison Klassen back to us, her death is a real tragedy, but those of us who knew her, know what a special person she was. Remember her."

"Thank you for listening."

The room erupted again in applause, this time more restrained and respectful. Chancellor Jorgeson immediately got up and walked over to Mark to shake his hand. Pandemonium reigned. Students descended on us offering congratulations. It was as though Fraser's veil of evil was lifted and that the sun again shone through the halls of the law school.

Mark and I eventually made our way to the press room. Mark fielded the questions directly and deftly; he knew where to draw the line in order to protect the agreement and the privacy of his clients. I managed to sneak out and found my way to Wilbur's office. Angela was there, shoes off, feet up, chatting with him. I joined them; it was a refuge from the drama of the day. We relaxed and patted each other on the back.

It was time for me to go; I had to teach. As I left I said to my colleagues, "I'm afraid with this case solved, the Dean gone and Fraser gone, it will be rather boring around here."

Wilbur replied, "Boring is just fine."

CHAPTER 38

Not surprisingly my afternoon class was another washout. The students were in a tizzy about the Dean and Fraser and they wanted me to tell them the story. I took fifteen minutes at the start of class to give them a condensed, much edited, carefully circumscribed telling of what happened.

After class I wanted to get away from the law school, colleagues were as curious as the students. Just after 4:00 p.m., when I knew that classes would be in, I slipped out heading for the refuge of home.

When I got home, I decided that it would be nice to have dinner out, just Julie and me. I left a note on the kitchen table:

Let's go out for supper to celebrate. Taking Bruce for a walk.

I changed into my dog walking attire: sweat pants, sweat top, poncho, boots, and my favourite Pittsburgh Pirates baseball cap. I grabbed a cigar and cut it. I was ready.

Bruce was too. When I went into the back yard, Bruce was ecstatic to see me; true, that was Bruce's nature, nevertheless it felt good to be adored and slobbered over. She saw the leash in hand and knew that a walk was in the offing. I lit my cigar in the lea of the house. The wind was up, blowing from the west. The light cumulus clouds breezed by quickly. The sun strained to break through. We had had two days of cloud and rain, so the glimpse of sun was welcome.

At the gate I put Bruce's leash on, as she braced in expectation of bounding out of the back yard. Once we were near the river forest I let Bruce off the leash. Off she went to mark her territory, sniff at everything, and track imaginary critters always keeping an eye on my whereabouts. I took in the fresh, brisk air. Along the river where the frost hit first and hardest the trees were bare. The dead leaves crackled and scrunched underfoot as I walked. The trees were ready to hibernate--that is my term and is probably not biologically correct.

Bruce meanwhile was not interested at all in the cycle of the seasons; she had spotted a flock of geese resting in an oxbow lake cut off from the river. She's a retriever and geese are retrieved; it is in her blood. I was too slow to call her and she was off heading for the lake and the geese. The geese were in no danger; they saw her coming, but it annoyed them to have their afternoon slumber interrupted by a silly dog. Bruce ran and dived right into the water in pursuit of a decoy goose, whose task it was to preoccupy this canine beast and guide her away from the flock. Bruce was easily decoyed. I watched the show for about ten minutes until a frustrated, but happy, Bruce gave up the chase and waded through the mud to come back to her master for a congratulatory pat. Of course, she was going to shake as soon as she got near spraying water, mud and algae in all directions. I tried to flee the scene and escaped the brunt of the spray.

There Bruce stood panting, head slightly down but so pleased with herself. How could I berate her? She was doing what retrievers do. I didn't pat her, but I did tell her that it was time to go home.

We made our way back to the yard. Bruce was a sad mess. There was no way I was going to let her into the house. I got the hose and put water into a bucket. After filling it up I put each of Bruce's legs into the bucket. Although she wasn't pleased, she did stand still. I washed her legs. Then it was her underbelly. She took objection to being put on her back so that I could spray water on her stomach. Washing a dog is never fun. With the bulk of the mud off I gave her a final hosing, chasing her in the yard as she tried to avoid the spray. It was okay for her to spray me, but not for me to spray her. With the washing done, Bruce stalked me intent upon shaking. Eventually she did a half shake and sprayed me partially. Then she rolled in the grass and finally found a spot in the sun where she was content to lick herself; dogs need to clean themselves after being washed.

I left her and headed into the back door mud room. Julie would be home now and we could decide on where we wanted to eat. It was a Tuesday night so no need for reservations. I opened the door, closed it and bent over to take off my boots; I had pulled off my second boot when I was struck on the side of the head.

The blow was sharp; I felt an intense flash of pain; needles of sharp pain pounded through my head. I had been pistol whipped. The pain was brutal. I could feel the moistness in my hair as the blood flowed—my blood. I fell to the ground. My hands instinctively went up to hold my head. Then I heard the voice, "You fucking asshole. You nosy fucking asshole."

I was kicked in the stomach; kicked again. All the while the voice kept swearing. I curled up in a fetal position to no avail. The kicks kept coming. My attacker was in a rage. My attacker was Jerome Fraser. Through my pain I thought of Julie. Had he hurt Julie? Not Julie.

I lay still, the kicks stopped. He put his knee in my back. I felt the barrel of a gun held against my neck. "Put your hands behind your back, now." He pressed his knee down into the small of my back. I moved my left arm to my back. I then felt the metal of a handcuff being closed tight over my left wrist. Mark had told me that Fraser had used handcuffs on all of his victims.

"The other arm. Now," he ordered. I started to move my right arm. He grabbed it and twisted it around to my back. He didn't care if he broke my arm. I then felt the handcuff close around my right wrist. I was helpless. Was Julie okay? Where was Julie? He removed the gun from my neck and pulled me up. He patted me down and seized my cell phone and put it on the kitchen table.

"Get up," he said gruffly, angrily.

"You better not have hurt Julie." I gasped, my weak voice lacking any sort of conviction or authority.

"She's just fine; we've been waiting for you." Fraser sneered. "Move to the den."

I focused. Fraser was dressed in black pants and a grey jacket. He wore a baseball type cap, with no insignia. I noticed that he kept his boots on and wore black tight fitting gloves. He didn't want to leave any trace evidence. On the way to the den I saw that the front door was locked. Where was Julie?

I decided to stall. What else could I do? "The police will know it's you. They know you broke in here a few weeks ago."

"Is that so," Fraser said sarcastically and with poison, "well funny that they haven't arrested me isn't it. I'm not one of your stupid students. They have nothing to connect me with the break-in."

I stopped, "What did you do with my computer?"

"That piece of crap; it was almost as ancient as you. Now get going." He gave me a push.

I moved to the den door, which was locked. Fraser pushed me aside, took the key from the ledge and opened the door. How did he know about the key? Julie must have told him. I had a chance to look at his face. He was flushed, angry and his eyes were slits, pupils dilated. Drugs I thought. I should have known he would want revenge. I should have known, but I got caught up in our success. Some success I thought; he's going to kill us. He pushed me through the door and shoved me into the reading chair. Julie was seated behind the desk. When we came in Julie showed initial alarm at seeing me, but otherwise looked calm, composed; it was surreal. How could she be so calm and collected when facing a maniac with a gun? "Are you okay, you're bleeding?" she asked.

"I'm fine, I'm fine. Has he hurt you?"

"Shut up both of you." Fraser ordered.

He stood behind me just inside the den door. There was nothing I could do. I was in the chair, handcuffed, and for me to get up and out of the chair I'd need to twist around and use my knees to hoist me up. I was helpless. I could see that the phone line was cut. There was no computer. The windows in the den were high ceiling louver windows, good for allowing light into the room, but useless for escape.

I kept talking, "Leave Julie alone. She didn't do anything to you. It's me. I'm the one."

"Yes, it was you, but there is always collateral damage. Isn't there?" Fraser laughed.

He liked being in control. He liked dominating people. And he liked hurting people.

"You'll never get away with it. Arrest warrants have already been issued in Canada." I was stalling again.

"Yes, and thanks to you I had a heads up. That stupid Burnside phoned me on Thursday and I've been planning. Thank you for giving me time to prepare my escape."

"Escape, you'll never escape." I challenged him. I wanted to keep him talking. I knew he'd want to brag about how smart he was.

"Oh, I'll escape alright. I have false ID, money, a car registered in my mother's maiden name. I'll disappear easily enough and when the time is right I'll be in Mexico. But before that I've got some unfinished business here."

So typical of Fraser, instead of fleeing he wanted to exact his revenge on me first. "Why did you do it to those girls? You don't need to drug women do you?"

"It wasn't the sex, although that was fun, it was the hunt and capture. The planning was done to perfection. I did it because I could and get away with it."

"So what went wrong?" I asked.

"That Klassen bitch killed herself and that caused you to start snooping around. What a weakling she was and Burnside that idiot. I told him to destroy the tapes. I told him."

"Tell me how did you meet him?"

Fraser laughed, "The internet. What else? We started chatting on an underground site. Soon we realized that we were both law professors and were interested in the same things. The Winnipeg conference was perfect. Things went from there."

"Who got the date rape drugs?"

"That was Burnside. He had a bit of experience with using it. He'd give it to me at the conference and I'd take care of it. Everything worked perfectly." Fraser loved to brag.

Julie sat still very calm. Her eyes communicated to me. I saw her move her eyes towards the bookcase. I took a hidden glance that way. The bookcase had been moved, there was an inch gap exposing the hidden compartment!

"What's your plan with us?" I wanted to keep him talking.

"Oh, I think a murder suicide is in the works. This revolver can't be traced to me or to anyone. Why a husband kills his wife and then himself is common enough. Who knows the stories that will come out about the good professor?"

"So you don't want to take credit for killing us?" Julie piped in.

"Oh there will be suspicions, but how will they be able to prove anything. Proof--right Andy, you're the evidence Prof, they will have no proof. My car is parked on the next street over and I'll slip out the back door as soon as it is dark."

"You'll have to deal with our dog in the back." I said.

He laughed, "That watch dog. I'll pet her on the way out." His voice then changed, became cruel, distant, "But I think I might have a little fun before I bid you both adieu, something for both of you to remember me by, a last memory so to speak."

He moved out from behind me towards Julie. He had to walk along the wall to get around the desk. As he did so, in a flurry Julie pushed her chair back from the desk and swivelled. Her right hand was handcuffed to the chair. Her left arm was free. She held the double barrel shotgun taken from the hidden compartment. She had been holding it hidden beneath the desk top. Her handcuffed hand was at the trigger and the left arm aimed it. The shots boomed, almost simultaneously both barrels were fired. Fraser was dead before he hit the ground. Both shells found their target dead centre in his chest. His eyes were wide open in shocked disbelief.

The smell of gunpowder and slight haze of smoke filled the room. There was silence. Time was suspended. Fraser was dead lying at the side of the desk. Eyes open.

It was over. I was so relieved. Julie was calm, then she said, "And that's for all the people you've hurt. You bastard." Her voice was soft, but clear and strong. There was no shakiness.

"Julie are you okay?"

"Yes, yes, he didn't hurt me."

My shock was over. Remorse I had none. Regret I had none. Jerome Fraser deserved to die. My mind clicked into action, "Julie I'm going to get my cell phone and bring it to you. We need to call the police right now. Stay where you are and I will get it. We shouldn't touch anything. Put the shotgun down, but don't do anything with it. Don't unload it. Just put it down. Are you okay with that?"

"Yes, I had to kill him. We know that. He was going to kill us both."

I nodded and got up from the chair and walked to the kitchen where Fraser had put my cell phone. I manoeuvred myself backwards, leaned on to the table and grasped the cell phone. I returned to the den. Julie had put the shotgun onto the desk. I dropped the phone onto the desk and Julie picked it up in her free hand.

"Call 911," I said.

She did, putting the phone on speaker. "Hello Flemington Emergency Dispatch. What is your emergency?"

"We had an armed intruder break into our home. We had to shoot him. He is dead. Please send the police." My voice was excited, loud.

"What is your address?"

"22 Morningvale Lane."

"Who am I speaking to?"

"My name is Andrew Sturgis and my wife Julie Sturgis is with me. We live here. We are handcuffed."

"I have sent out the emergency. The police have been dispatched. Are there any other armed intruders?"

"No. The house is secure. Please advise the police the house is secure."

"I will do so. Is either of you hurt?"

"No we are both unharmed."

"The police are on their way."

I then said, "I am going to hang up now. I have other calls to make."

"Please stay on ..."

We hung up.

Julie asked, "Should we call Mark? Shouldn't we call a lawyer?"

"No," I replied, "suspicion always flows when you call your lawyer. Julie, we've done nothing wrong. We tell the truth and all is fine. I do want to call Richard Maurice. You'll see his number in my list of contacts."

Julie scrolled through the contacts and we called Richard. The call was directed to his voicemail. "Richard, Professor Sturgis. Jerome Fraser broke into our home to kill us. Julie had to shoot him. The police have been called. You might want to attend. The officers will need background."

The calls were made. "How did Fraser get in?" I asked.

"It was my fault. I'm too trusting. I had just arrived home, saw your note, and the doorbell rang. I went to the door and saw a man holding a package. He said 'FedEx parcel for Professor Sturgis' and I opened the door. It was Fraser. He pushed himself inside and had a gun hidden by the parcel."

"Did he say anything?"

"He was looking for you and was surprised that you weren't home. He said that he had seen you come home. He had followed you from the university. I told him that you were out walking the dog. He then told me to get into the den, told me to sit in the desk chair and handcuffed me. He cut the phone line, checked for any computer and checked that I didn't have a cell phone. I tried to reason with him. He told me to shut up. He said we'd wait for you. You were taking your time. I could see that he was getting more agitated. He'd constantly move back and forth from the kitchen to the den. He was watching for you. I then told him about the den door that it locked from the outside and the key was on the ledge. I suggested that he didn't need to handcuff me, just lock the door. He laughed and said, "You think I'm stupid." He locked the door, and kept me handcuffed. That was exactly what I wanted. I waited, hoping he wouldn't come back. I then heard the water and knew you were back. Good thing you took your time before coming in. It gave me time. I rolled the desk chair to the bookcase and as quietly as I could I pushed it open. I had my left arm free, fortunately I'm left handed. I then got the keys for the guns and the ammunition. I unlocked the double barrel shotgun, breached it and unlocked the ammunition. I put two shells into the shotgun, and put two more in my pocket. It wasn't easy and I was so afraid that he'd return. I closed the shotgun, put it down and pushed the bookcase back as best I could. I heard more water. Whatever you were doing occupied Fraser. I then rolled the chair back to the desk and rested the shotgun, cocked both hammers and hid it under the desk. You know this was my hunting shotgun when I was a girl. I only hoped that the shells were still good. I then sat with it resting on the arms of the chair underneath the desk top. I practiced a couple times pushing back and aiming the rifle. I was ready. When you came in I was tempted to fire then, but you would've been in the line of fire. I had to wait until he moved away from you. When he did, I had my shot."

Her voice was matter of fact. There was no sorrow. "You had no choice," I reassured her.

"I know that. I don't feel anything. I'm not sorry for killing him. Should I be?"

"No, no not at all. He was going to kill us." Approaching sirens could be heard in the distance.

"He was an evil person," she said quietly.

Epilogue

The fall term was over. The snow had arrived with winter. The new term is set to begin in a few days. The university cycle continues unperturbed by the events of the past term. As I walked on the trampled path along the Kocheta River, I reflected on the term that was and the lives that were changed forever.

Professor Wilbur Flood is the new interim Dean of Law. He is a good pick, loved by students, respected by colleagues and committed to the law school. He is still going to teach Torts Law; in fact he is going to teach both sections given that Fraser is no longer with us. We also continue to have our weekly Friday seminars in his office. I'm confident that the title of 'Dean' will not change Wilbur.

Mark Labros received wide publicity and evidently his practice is flourishing. He hired Ingrid Hedberg to join his team.

The Klassens are coping. Nothing could bring back their beloved daughter. Megan continues her studies and told me that she's intending to go to law school to follow in her older sister's footsteps. I was asked by the Klassen family to chair the Allison Klassen Support Fund Committee, which of course I accepted.

President Frinkle became a bit of a celebrity for his handling of the scandal. Unbeknownst to all, Mark had guided the good President to the right path. I am certain that President Frinkle will be moving on to a bigger university, which will be no loss for Flemington.

Dean Clarke is still looking for a position.

Sid Ashter has joined a large corporate law firm in the city, which is a perfect fit for his obstructionist tactics.

Professor William Burnside pleaded guilty to eleven counts of aggravated sexual assault, three counts of producing child pornography and four counts of possession of child pornography, and was sentenced to fourteen years in prison. He'll be eligible for parole in seven years.

Margaret Burnside has filed for divorce and she hired the firm of Johns and Mitchell to act as her legal counsel.

Julie is just fine. The shooting was accepted as justified self-defence. Julie returned to work the next week. She is one strong person.

As for me, life is experience and I have learned much:

I have new respect for intuition,

I acknowledge the power of happenstance, and

I now recognize more than ever that good people need to be vigilant to see that evil does not prevail.

Oh – and Bruce continues to enjoy doing what dogs do.

Life is good.

ABOUT THE AUTHOR

Lee Stuesser was born on the prairies and is a prairie boy. He is a teacher turned law professor and has taught law for over 30 years in Canada and in Australia. He has authored two texts on advocacy, one in Canada, *An Advocacy Primer*, and one in Australia, *An Introduction to Advocacy*. He has also co-authored, with Mr. Justice David Paciocco, a text on Evidence. This is his first novel.

Lightning Source UK Ltd.
Milton Keynes UK
UKHW01f2210040918
328335UK00001B/196/P